WILD BERRIES

Poetry by Yevgeny Yevtushenko
Also Available from Henry Holt

Almost at the End

WILD BERRIES

A NOVEL

YEVGENY YEVTUSHENKO

Translated by Antonina W. Bouis

An Owl Book

Henry Holt and Company / New York

Published by Henry Holt and Company, Inc.,
115 West 18th Street, New York, New York 10011.
Published in Canada by Fitzhenry & Whiteside Limited,
195 Allstate Parkway, Markham, Ontario L3R 4T8.

Library of Congress Cataloging-in-Publication Data
Yevtushenko, Yevgeny Aleksandrovich, 1933–
[IAgodnye mesta. English]
Wild berries / Yevgeny Yevtushenko ; translated by Antonina W.
Bouis. — (1st Owl book ed.)
p.   cm.
Translation of: IAgodnye mesta.
"An Owl Book."
ISBN 0-8050-1178-1 (pbk.)
I. Title.
PG3476.E96I2513   1989
891.73′44—dc20   89-7501
CIP

Henry Holt books are available at special discounts for bulk
purchases for sales promotions, premiums, fund-raising, or
educational use. Special editions or book excerpts can also be
created to specification.

For details contact:

Special Sales Director
Henry Holt and Company, Inc.
115 West 18th Street
New York, New York 10011

Originally published in 1981 in the U.S.S.R. in *Moskva*.
First published in the United States in hardcover by William
Morrow and Company, Inc., in 1984.

First Owl Book Edition—1989
Printed in the United States of America
1 3 5 7 9 10 8 6 4 2

WILD BERRIES

E P I L O G U E

"Along the midnight sky an angel flew. . . ."*

The cosmonaut recalled the poem and smiled sadly. "Some angel I make!" His face, reflected in the porthole of the capsule, was tired, no longer young, yet animated with childlike curiosity. He had never been beyond his country's borders before. And suddenly there were no borders; the striped barriers, no-man's-lands, border guards, German shepherds, and customs points all had disappeared. Now they seemed unnatural, ridiculous. Other things were difficult even to imagine: for instance, the idea of mandatory residency registration.

Below, the lights of Paris glittered, a handful of gold dust scattered across black velvet. The cosmonaut shifted his gaze a bit to the left and found himself in London, his peripheral vision catching a glowing piece of Copenhagen. Gagarin had probably been scared. It was a bit scary now, too, but not as much as it had been then. And yet Gagarin had said in such a simple way, in such a Russian way, "Let's go!," turning the cosmos into something immediately familiar, homey. What a face Gagarin had . . . That was one reason they'd chosen him, of course, but you couldn't design a face like that with any top-secret blueprint. It seemed to have been assembled by Mother Earth herself, combining all the smiles that had miraculously survived among the smirks and sneers. And afterward how gracefully he let himself be dragged all over the world and triumphantly covered with mountains of flowers and medals. Still, his smile outshone the smiles of prime ministers, presidents, kings, and queens.

The cosmonaut had seen Gagarin unhappy, too.

"I'm tired," Gagarin used to say. "But I want to fly. . . ."

His face reveals a touch of sadness in the late photographs. You

*From the poem "Angel" by Mikhail Lermontov.

9

can see the scar which gave rise to so many rumors. By then his face was so famous even the man on the street considered it his personal property. Contrary to Gagarin's own wishes, it became a barrier, separating him from ordinary life. Once he told his fellow cosmonauts about a trip to Latin America. He suddenly grew sad, and if he smiled, it was only a reflex at a defenseless moment.

"And next to the official platform on which I sat roasting in the sun for three hours stood a mulatto girl with a cart. She was selling lemonade. Made from real lemons. She was extraordinarily beautiful; her black eyes filled almost half her face. But the most amazing thing was that she was wearing a wedding dress. Made out of lace, like a cloud. Expensive, probably. But it didn't seem new to me for some reason. It was clean but yellowed. Maybe it was her grandmother's— taken out of a trunk for a special occasion? The girl's eyes and mine immediately met. She looked down at her lemonade with big black eyes—come on, have some. . . . But how could I get down from the dais? . . . It wouldn't be polite. . . . They wouldn't understand. . . . But the girl had a sense of humor. She poured some lemonade in a glass, put in a straw, and, laughing, brought it up to her breast. I didn't understand at first, but then I looked closer: She was wearing a button with my face on her wedding dress. And she gave some lemonade to the button instead of me."

Gagarin never hurt people on purpose, and if he unintentionally did, he always tried to make up for it. Once at a conference of young writers he gave a speech chastising a certain famous poet for bragging in his autobiography that he didn't understand where electricity came from. Later a senior physicist, who was at the conference, took Gagarin aside and looked slyly into his eyes.

"Yuri Alekseyevich, dear fellow, I wish you would share your discovery about the origin of electricity with the rest of us. I've been struggling with the problem for fifty years and still haven't gotten anywhere. And if I'm confused about this problem, what do you expect from a poet? Even Pushkin said that poetry had to be, God forgive me, stupid. . . . By the way, you chose the worst possible time to pick on that poet." He was in disfavor just then, having completed a new poem whose fate had not been decided.

Gagarin called up the poet himself and asked him not to be angry, inviting him to read at a festival to be held at Zvezdnyi, the space center. Gagarin was trying to help; the ceremony was to be televised nationwide. The great day arrived, and as the program began, Gagarin sat next to one of the officials, at the end of the first row. From there they could see backstage, where the disheveled poet was pacing back and forth, crumpling typed pages in his hands, and muttering something under his breath.

"What's he doing here?" the official suddenly asked tensely.

"We invited him to read," Gagarin replied.

"And who gave permission?" the official hissed.

"I did," Gagarin replied.

"You may be in charge in space," his furious neighbor said, "but not on the ground."

The official went backstage and flashed his red party badge at the MC, a man famous for thunderously recounting heroics over the radio during World War II. He yielded immediately and babbled inarticulately to the poet that his performance was canceled. The poet turned white with hurt and humiliation, grabbed his raincoat and cap, and rushed out into the driving rain. Then he got into his Moskvich and zoomed off, unable to distinguish between the rain and the tears in his eyes. He drove blindly—the wipers couldn't work fast enough to clear the windshield.

Gagarin ran after him, but it was too late. "Find him. Wherever he is. He can't be left alone," he ordered. They raced after him in the car of a composer who had already appeared onstage. The poet was found at the bar of the Writers' Union, gulping down glasses of vodka. His shaking hands still gripped the unread pages, and he was weeping inconsolably, like a child. But that was a long time ago. . . .

The cosmonaut, Gagarin's student and friend, had waited a long time for his turn in space. Others at Zvezdnyi had hustled and plotted. But he waited, aging, his hair thinning noticeably, like the poet's— they had become friends after that aborted performance. He read a lot, discovering Dostoyevsky, a writer whom he had previously regarded as confused and unpleasant. He thought: *Well, why should literature be pleasant? What is it—a diversion?* When they told him once again,

"Well, you're next . . ." he didn't quite believe it, because he'd been a stand-by many times. But, as usual, he prepared himself seriously and calmly. When he finally peered through the porthole at a tiny earth, he thought: *It's a good thing I didn't fly earlier; this is the right time for me.*

The cosmonaut's reflection in the little mirror on the wall caught his eye, and involuntarily, he began examining his face, as though it belonged to someone else. His cheekbones were prominent, like those of many of his fellow Siberians. The teeth were white and strong, probably thanks to "sulfur"—a Siberian chewing gum made from leaf resin. As a going-away present, his uncle in Zima Junction had sent him a cellophane-wrapped bar. Now he chewed it happily, feeling he had accomplished a tiny sedition since sulfur had been strictly banned at school when he was a child and, before the flight, the physicians had had long discussions about the consequences of excessive salivation. Zima Junction was now an invisible dot on the tiny sphere of the earth, but it was precisely there that the world began for him, that humanity began.

He didn't remember his father, who had been killed right before the end of the war somewhere near Berlin. He was only five at the time but already gathering wheat from the prickly threshing-room floor and putting it into canvas bags. After the children were through, the birds didn't bother to alight there since not a grain was left. From walking barefoot in the morning dew, his feet were covered with festering boils. Even now his shins bore the scars of those boils just above the ankles—round spots, as shiny as copper coins: the children's war medals. His mother worked as a film operator in the Zima railroad workers' club. Now his only mementos of her were the frames she had cut out of the constantly breaking films of Lubov Orlova, Marina Ladynina, Boris Babochkin, Nikolai Kruchkov, and a foreign actress who played Lady Hamilton. . . . The cosmonaut's mother gave blood for the wounded too often and she grew very weak. They began giving her transfusions, but it was too late.

The boy was taken in by his uncle, a war veteran himself. He treated him like his own son, and even though he sometimes struck his three daughters in the heat of anger, he never touched the boy. He worked as a truck driver. Oil was scarce then, but the uncle's truck had a wood-burning engine. The boy could often be found pulling with all his childish might on one end of a two-man saw, after which he helped stoke up the chocks. His uncle explained everything about the truck, pointing at the engine's insides with his greasy finger. He even let the boy drive over the taiga roads. Once Uncle drank too much at a hospitable farm and started to nod off at the wheel. So he pulled the truck over to one side of the road for a nap. When he woke up, he discovered that the truck was expertly parked by the gates of his house, and at the wheel was his twelve-year-old nephew or, as he called him, "son." Uncle kept a pigeon coop filled with cooing, fluttering doves, not to mention the smell of droppings. He and his nephew drove the birds into the air by waving poles on the roof and whistling like Nightingale the Robber. Watching a warm, trembling ball of feathers abruptly take off into the sky made the boy want to fly up after it. One day his uncle caught him, head thrown back, transported with giddy delight, as he followed the doves' free tumble among the clouds. Flashing his eagle eye, Uncle slapped the boy's shoulder with his clumsy but gentle hand.

"You'll be a pilot, I think, son. . . ."

How could he have known that his "son" would become not only a pilot but a cosmonaut? The word hadn't been coined yet.

Uncle was not only an incorrigible pigeon fancier but also an incorrigible woman fancier. To hear him tell it, he almost paid with his life for it once. Just before the end of the war Uncle found himself billeted at the house of a blond German widow whose charms were not beneath his notice. The widow's husband had been killed near Stalingrad, and her inconsolable grief for him took the form of a particular mania: Every evening she begged Uncle to wear her precious Paul's noncom uniform at supper. Uncle, an actor at heart, consented to this sentimental charade and laughingly got into the uniform. Once, however, his superiors needed him on urgent business (Uncle drove the staff jeep), and they barged in without knocking. To their astonishment they found an Aryan family idyll: the kirsch-pinkened widow and a German noncom in full uniform, sitting down to supper. Pistols were drawn. It would have been curtains for Uncle had it not been for his encyclopedic knowledge of specialized Russian expressions that no German soldier could possibly have known.

Returning from the war and merrily repenting to his wife, who did not accept said repentance quite so merrily, Uncle paid his dues, briefly, to the quiet family life. He was a tender father to his three daughters, and he loved his wife, in his own fashion. But, he felt that fidelity for a man was a sign of giving up, and he would never stoop to giving up himself. One of the objects of his inexhaustible prowess was the new bookkeeper at the regional credit union. She had piqued Uncle's interest because she seemed so inaccessible behind her glasses, which formed an integral part of her young but stony face. Later Uncle would flash his eagle eye and say, "A woman with glasses is really two women." "Credit Union" fell to his frontal attack. And at this point Uncle developed a weak spot: He grew attached to her. Uncle's wife had resigned herself to his passing sins. But this sin (in Uncle's words, "with two women at once") turned out to be extended. In a tiny town illicit love is impossible to hide. Uncle's wife was exhausted by the sympathy of the neighbors. "Credit Union" was given the nickname Snake-in-the-Glasses. But Uncle had descended from a long line of explorers and liked paddling against the current. He built a house for his lover, and it stood as his monument to freedom of the spirit. To tell the truth, he was rather bored by "Credit Union," but he never ceased to be touched by the way her face changed when she removed her glasses. As far as anyone could tell, his wife resigned herself to the situation in order to keep her family together. Uncle had solemnly promised not to leave, provided there was no interference with his freedom.

But Uncle forgot one thing: the fatal age difference. When he turned sixty, "Credit Union" was just barely in her fortyish prime, and she brazenly informed him that he was too old for her now. Uncle couldn't bear the insult. In the middle of the day, as sober as a judge, he drove up to the log house he'd built, poured two canisters of benzene over it, and set fire to it, seriously burning his face in the process. Uncle was expelled from the party, fired from his job as head of the garage, and sentenced to a year in jail for malicious hooliganism. However, he was granted probation in view of his wartime and labor record. He was transferred to work as a driver for a bread factory, where he traded in the steering wheel for reins, so to speak. That one spark cost him eight thousand, and he had to telegram his cosmonaut nephew asking for money for the first and only time in his life: "IN CONNECTION ARSON SEND ALL YOU CAN." However, Uncle did not give up. He completely subjugated the director of the bread factory, and became, in effect, director himself. He invented a new method of baking, and through some deal no one could figure out, he traded the sad, mangy mare for a snazzy dapple-gray trotter. Soon the bread factory's wagon could be seen, parked as ostentatiously as possible, by the new house of the same old "Credit Union," who had evidently decided it was a bad idea to press any opinion about Uncle's age.

. . . The cosmonaut munched on the sulfur and smiled. He pictured his uncle docking the bread wagon next to the capsule. Floating up, Uncle clumsily waved his arms, his untamable roving eye gleaming and looking around: Were there any women in glasses up here? Uncle settled down by the porthole, and on his arm with the pale green tattoo, "Love to the grave" (even though it didn't specify for whom), fluttered a Zima Junction mail pigeon, with white spurs on its feet. Uncle shouted with delight, "Australia, son!," pointing the pigeon at the porthole, and the cosmonaut envisioned the day when an ordinary Siberian truck driver or lumberjack would wake up late on his first day of vacation and, stretching luxuriously, mutter to his wife, who was radiating heat like a big white stove, "Well, Mashka, it's vacation. Let's hop down to Miami Beach? Or the Easter Islands? They say it's not bad in Hawaii either—you can breathe. . . . Then there's the Galápagos. . . ." And Mashka will answer, "We ain't even been to Greece, you jerk. . . . It's the cradle of culture, nothing to sneeze at. . . . And I'm interested in the Baalbek temple, Vanya. And I'm drawn to Tibet. . . ." And Vanya will yawn at this cultural overreaching and suggest a compromise: "Maybe, Mashka, we should just go to the beach at Sochi? It's closer, and the nightclubs are better than in any old Miami. . . ." "All you want is nightclubs," his wife grumbles. "Weren't Crazy Horse and the Lido enough for you last summer in Paris? I'll never set foot in Paris again, Vanya. Those French literally hounded me to death with their demands. Either it's perfume from Kostroma I have to bring them or sweaters from Lipetsk. Another one wanted pantyhose from Mytishchi. . . . Those Americans are nuts, too. Like the ones who were practically ripping Melitopol jeans off the legs of our tourist group. No national pride at all! No, Vanya, it's either Tibet or Africa—for a safari. . . ."

The metal four-poster on which the imaginary pair was planning their vacation swayed melodiously inside the spaceship. A white goose feather poked through the lace pillowcase and slowly floated down onto the logbook.

The cosmonaut's reflection in the mirror revealed the scar on his forehead, the souvenir of a schoolboy fight in an alley near the school in Zima Junction. They fought with briefcases, and one blow landed right on his brow with the clasp. The girl they were fighting over was the daughter of the director of the hydrolysis plant, which produced the local rotgut. She stood nearby and watched the combat with fear and pride, nudging transparent pieces of ice into the roiling spring stream with her rubber boot. She was so upset that she gulped down Mishka candies, hard to come by in Zima Junction, and the tiny reproductions of Shishkin on the wrappers fell into the stream, unexpectedly launched into uncharted waters.

The cosmonaut liked fighting in general. Actually it wasn't that he liked to fight—he had to. Whenever he saw a troublemaker, he wanted to smash his ugly face. He tried to stop himself, practiced self-control, but it didn't help. After all, he was of Siberian stock. Once, in summer school, he was offended by the nasty jokes of a pimply student, and he hit him so hard that his cheekbone was twisted to one side. He was almost expelled. Another time, when he was already in the space program, he was riding on a late commuter train. A young girl was dozing on the seat, instinctively hugging her net shopping bag, which held a bottle of kefir and orange wafers. Two drunks started winking cynically at him and discussing the girl. One of them deftly fished out a package of wafers through the netting of her sack and began munching on them. The other tickled her with the antenna of his transistor radio. The cosmonaut couldn't control himself. As a result of the "bodily harm" he inflicted on the men, he found himself at the police station. A report was sent to his superior, who chewed him out severely: Cosmonauts were not supposed to end up in jail. It may have explained why he was removed from his first scheduled flight. But the girl from the train became his wife. So fists sometimes do help.

He hadn't gotten a good look at her in the train, but only later at the police station. She'd come voluntarily as a witness, which doesn't happen often. The most extraordinary thing about her were her tiny black eyes, which glittered when she concentrated—like moist watermelon seeds.

"So it's like this, Comrade Colonel," she said, promoting the duty officer by two ranks. He looked at the floor with embarrassment, confronted by the sparkle of her small, ruthless eyes. "So this means . . . defending a woman from hooligans is hooliganism? I'm glad I'm not dating you. . . ." Suddenly she turned to the cosmonaut and, rising on tiptoe, kissed his cheek with her small and cool lips.

"Comrades, please, this is a police station after all," the duty officer mumbled ineffectually.

"Now that's what I call a woman," one of the drunks drawled with delight. Forgetting his black eye, he nudged the cosmonaut in the ribs amiably, to express solidarity with him against the implacability of protocol.

The girl from the train worked as a makeup artist at a film studio. Her world was made up of tiny spy mustaches, Musketeer goatees, bushy Old Believer beards, glue-on eyebrows, and wigs for empresses and mermaids. At a screening she suddenly started crying at the happiest part. "His left eyebrow is unglued. . . ." More than anything else she loved nature, perhaps because nature didn't need any makeup.

Once he called her and she practically screamed into the phone, "It's you! I burned an actress's cheek with a curling iron today because I was thinking of you. I have half a day today. Listen, what are you doing? Nothing? Great! Let's go to the woods?"

He picked her up in his new Zhiguli. She was waiting for him at the back door of the studio, and when he arrived, she delightedly clapped her hands, which smelled of polish and acetone.

"Oh, wonderful, you have a car! What were you doing riding around on the train?"

"I work as a private vigilante," he joked, but he was thinking warily: *Is she another one of those who are only interested in cosmonauts and cars?* But she didn't seem like a groupie. Her watermelon-seed eyes sparkled, and in her hands were more orange wafers, which she adored.

"These wafers brought us together," she said. "Help yourself."

"Where to?" the cosmonaut asked.

"Somewhere far away. You're a terrific fighter. I like that. Sometimes I feel like punching people, too. . . . You know, I'm rich today. I got a bonus the size of my monthly salary. Eighty rubles! Let's buy some champagne! Do you like champagne?"

At the grocery store she firmly pushed away his hand when he tried to pay.

"No, no, no . . . You're paying for gas; I'm paying for champagne."

As soon as they got back in the car, she had another idea: "Do you like watermelons? They say there are melons at the market. Have you had any this year? Then you can make a wish. . . ."

At the market she spent a long time thumping the melons' striped sides, bringing them to her ear, squeezing them, driving the woman crazy, but at last she made her choice.

"This one . . . It has such a cute bald spot. And a piggy tail."

She paid once more. Then she exclaimed, "And what will we cut the watermelon with? Do you have a knife? You do? Wonderful! And what will we drink champagne out of? Let's go to housewares. . . ."

From the depths of the dark housewares store, stinking of rusty nails, came a hostile voice, hoarse with alcohol. "No glasses."

But her eyes persisted in roaming the shelves.

"Hmm . . . do you have a pair of vases?"

The owner of the boozy voice showed his equally boozy face, and from somewhere out of that red-veined road map emitted a rasp that signaled confidentiality. "I have one vase. Czech crystal. The last one. I was saving it for myself. Two hundred rubles. Just for you, young lady."

Her tiny eyes leaped under their brows. "No, no, why deprive yourself! Your wife will scold you. You see, we just need something to drink champagne out of."

From the darkness of the housewares store suddenly emerged suggestions from various people, who apparently were groping about with specific and unspecific purposes:

"You need champagne glasses for champagne."

"Come on, you bumpkin . . . there's even a special name for them —tulip glasses!"

"Yeah, you can't sip champagne from the bottle. The bubbles hit you in the nose."

"A regular glass is the best thing. You can drink anything at all from it. . . . That's why you can't get any."

But her sharp eyes had fallen upon two small vessels, dark blue with metal caps and painted with white flowers.

"What are these?"

"Those, young lady, are for storing tea leaves," the boozy voice responded with unexpected dignity, and the owner's face huffily disappeared into the semidarkness.

"Don't be ashamed to show them to me." And her small fingers busily unscrewed the caps. "These are marvelous champagne glasses! The caps will keep the champagne from going flat! How much are they?"

"Two fifty each." The boozy voice sighed. "You must be joking, young lady."

"Hey there, give me a dozen!" A sudden, businesslike voice came from behind, where a stout woman in a white coat splattered with innocent calf blood rummaged in her stocking top. She extracted a wad of money tied with a shoelace. "This young lady obviously knows what's fashionable. My daughter's wedding is just around the corner. . . ."

When a scrawny black cat ran in front of the Zhiguli, the cosmonaut joked as he braked. "We have to wait for another car . . . or we won't have a good trip."

The girl gave a sly look and said, "And what if your path had been crossed by a black cat carrying full buckets?"*

---

*This refers to the Russian superstition that passing someone carrying empty buckets presages a bad journey.

He couldn't think of anything to say and laughed.

He remembered that day always, as his Zhiguli squeezed through a pack of cars to get to the country. It was so hot that all the tank trucks dispensing kvass were mobbed by clusters of women holding empty jugs, and sopping wet drivers pulled over to ask for a glass out of turn and without correct change. After greedily drinking to the accompaniment of angry grumbling from the women, they would throw themselves into the sticky seats of their stuffy cars, exulting in the sensation of the half-evaporated reddish drops sprinkling off their chins onto their shirts. The soda machines went crazy, spitting out bubbles, which danced for a split second like tiny swans in the heavy, chipped glasses, and if the machines swallowed coins only to sneeze impotently, sweaty fists hammered on their red sides. Ice cream which had just been removed from the smoking light blue portable freezers would start to soften and melt rapidly in your fingers, turning back into milk, leaking beneath wedding rings and watchbands, dripping onto cotton-blend dresses and jeans. The fire-breathing asphalt felt soft under your feet, pulling anything to itself with voluptuous indifference; whether it be sandals with a piece of cotton stuffed under the strap or soldiers' boots, marching to the steam bath, they seemed to be woven out of black, crinkly cobbler's wax ready to melt at any second. The cupolas of the churches glinted painfully, swaying in the shimmering heat, and it seemed that the molten gilt was about to start dripping right onto the white polka-dotted scarves of the old women who were rapidly making tiny signs of the cross. You turn on the tap, waiting in vain for the water to get colder, and when you finally put your mouth under the stream, it's still too warm, so you open the refrigerator and curse because you forgot to fill the plastic ice-cube tray, and you're reduced to taking a knife or spoon and scraping shaggy snow from the sides of the freezer, and you dump the needly mush into a glass of water, and the water is still warm, warm, warm. On days like that your whole body, even your thoughts are crushed by the heat, which weighs on you like a tombstone, and you spread out, collapse, and irrationally hate your family and boss as though they spitefully caused this suffocating drought, just to punish you for something or other, and you think you'll go crazy if you don't escape from the monotonous click of the accounting abacus, the humming electronic monsters, the howling lathes, the blueprints dissolving before your eyes, the papers awaiting your signature, the hysterically pealing telephones—just to run away, tear off your sticky clothes, and immerse yourself chin-deep in the Moscow River, and sit there all day without coming out. But the Moscow River is also warm, warm, warm, like the kvass in the hot tanks. . . . On days like that there's only one salvation: the forest, which mightily guards its lifesaving shade and where, despite the heat, the mushrooms silently grow, following their own mysterious law, belatedly giving thanks for the day-before-yesterday's rain.

A half-empty bottle of champagne cooled in the forest brook where it was buried in the silt, and silvery minnows collided with its dark green sides. It was weird but fun drinking out of the blue and white flowered containers with the metal caps. A watermelon, broken in half, emitted red sparks, creating the peculiar sensation of a light frost, even though it was almost hot. Its black moist seeds exchanged familiar glances with the girl's eyes. They had parked the Zhiguli in a place where its roof was gently caressed by hazelnut tree branches barely stirring in an invisible breeze. They spread his jacket on the grass nearby and, lying side by side, looked not at each other but at the clouds floating above them. It was impossible for them to tell each other what they were thinking about. But this inarticulateness bound them together more effectively than any words.

Suddenly, close by, from beyond the trees came businesslike voices.

"Vitya, why aren't you looking under your feet? There it is, a birch mushroom. . . . No worms, clean."

"I'm sick of mushrooms. My back's killing me," Vitya complained. "I should have gone to the soccer game."

"You can go to soccer any day. When we get home, I'll fry up these mushrooms. With sour cream and onions. I set aside a bottle just for a special occasion like this. Not just anything—embassy vodka."

The cosmonaut and the girl laughed with their eyes.

"I feel sorry for them, the mushroom fanatics," the girl said. "They see all of nature as something to fry or pickle. I like being in the woods just like this." She jumped up, brushed off her skirt, which was stained green from the grass, and headed for the Zhiguli barefoot, carrying her white sandals in her hands. Blades of grass and bluebells shot up between her tiny toes. Suddenly she froze. "Look at this giant!"

Right by her foot stood a solid white mushroom; it looked like a statue carved in marble.

"Give me your penknife. There. Here I was, laughing at mushroom hunters, and . . ."

She cut the mushroom off neatly, leaving the root in the ground. Bringing it to her face, she inhaled with pleasure. Then, shoving her sandals into the cosmonaut's hands, she ran over to a birch tree, where she stood on tiptoe, to break up the mushroom and stick the pieces onto the branches.

"Why are you doing that?" the cosmonaut asked.

"For the squirrels," she replied simply, surprised that he hadn't understood that right away.

"Will you marry me?" he asked quickly, wiping his penknife, which was redolent of mushroom.

"Yes," she replied without hesitation. "You know, you're the only man I wanted to marry from the very first moment I saw you —back in the train, when I woke up and saw you fighting."

"What about the actors you work with?" he asked. "You never wanted to marry one of them?"

She laughed. "Actors? They're children!"

"What do you mean, children?"

"Just that . . . They play, just like children."

"Do you know they might not let me go into space? Because of the fight."

"So what? You won't be any the worse for it. If they hadn't published Pushkin, I'd still love him."

Once the cosmonaut came to visit her on location in Kaluga, where they were making a film about the Tatar invasion. Instead of flowers, he brought smoked sausage in reference to a local joke: What's long, green, and smells of sausage? Answer: The Moscow–Kaluga train.

Next to a highway where trucks rumbled, carrying bricks and

pipes, Kaluga policemen costumed as the Tatar conquerors pranced in a meadow. They dashingly adjusted and tugged at their chain mail, through which one expected to see badges proclaiming, "Ready for Work and Defense." The girl used her soft brush to paint bloody wounds on the foreheads of the barefoot Russian prisoners, one of whom was smoking Marlboros, now produced under American licensing in Moscow. The cosmonaut tried to get near her, shyly hiding his sausage in a clear plastic shopping bag, but suddenly someone grasped him firmly by the shoulders with two fat hands.

"What a Russian face! Into makeup immediately," the owner of the hands said without asking for any consent.

The cosmonaut was immediately grabbed by other hands and relentlessly put into a scratchy sackcloth shirt and pants, a gray wig, a wooden yoke, and shackles, with a rope tying his hands to those of the other prisoners. The makeup brush with the movie blood touched his face several times, but the girl didn't even recognize him, she had had so much bloody work to do that day. The director roared, "Camera! Action!" and a crowd of prisoners dragged the cosmonaut along behind them. His hands, tied with rope, really began to hurt, and so did his feet, fettered by shackles, and his back because it was struck full force by the knotted Tatar whip of a Kaluga policeman who was really living his part. Something bizarre occurred: Forgetting that it was only a movie, he felt he had been born in another time, was walking on blood-soaked Russian soil. Everything great still lay ahead: Kulikovo Field, Peter the Great, Pushkin, Tsiolkovsky, Gagarin. . . . The girl recognized him only when she was removing the wounds and scars from his face with acetone and taking off his wig. His face, which she already loved, seemed to be created anew by her.

"You?" she whispered in amazement.

"Me," the cosmonaut replied with embarrassment. "I brought you some sausage."

Then they drove to the Optina Desert, where Dostoyevsky wrote *The Brothers Karamazov,* and amid the ruins and neglect they found the grave of Father Zossima. Its location could be determined only by the glass pickle jars and kefir bottles containing flowers, brought by unknown admirers. The grave marker, as a local little old man told them, had been removed and was languishing in some storeroom. The cosmonaut thought bitterly: *If you turn history into a storeroom, what will the future grow on?* And he suddenly wanted children, the children of this small Russian girl, pressed against him under the trees that once had given shade to Dostoyevsky.

He brought her to Siberia, for his uncle to meet. Uncle evaluated her with his eagle eye, even though she didn't wear glasses, and taught her to send pigeons into the clouds and to dance the Gypsy. He also menacingly demanded children: "Give me three explorers off the bat!"

He personally spread his bear-fur coat for them in the haystack and conjured pregnancy with vagabond's gibberish. He gave them a magic cedar cone to use whenever they started arguing—each had to eat a seed, and the argument would cease immediately. He unexpectedly burst into tears and said he had been a scoundrel to his own wife, and that if his nephew followed his example, he would beat him in front of all decent folk. He swore to forget "Credit Union." . . .

Uncle . . . Zima Junction . . .

And suddenly—space . . . It was incomprehensible. And once upon a time it had been truly incomprehensible. He had brought with him only one book: a thin, yellowing brochure by Tsiolkovsky, *Sorrow and Genius,* published in Kaluga in 1916 at the author's expense. It certainly had every right to end up in space. The cosmonaut opened to a page at random. "It is obviously not easy to find a genius, and there is nothing amazing about the fact that we don't see them even when they do exist. You will say that the genius must make himself manifest, step out into the light, show himself to the people with great deeds. True, it is sometimes possible, but not always. History teaches us how many geniuses weren't appreciated, were nipped in the bud by the limited intelligence of those around them. . . ."

An awkward bearded man in a black cape with lion-head buckles, Tsiolkovsky, splashed through the Kaluga puddles, in which drowned the seemingly inaccessible stars. Eccentrics, the ones considered crazy, had been right so many times.

Tsiolkovsky put things wonderfully: "All our knowledge—past, present, and future—is nothing compared to what we will never know." It wasn't sad. It was marvelous. When there is an infinity of the unknown, then knowledge itself has the hope of infinity. And man also has that hope because man himself is knowledge, learning about himself. The highest intelligence of the universe is not something separate from man. Man is part of it. Perhaps even the greater part. The cosmonaut thought: *Maybe I am the solitary angel that flies in the midnight sky. That's terrifying. . . . That means that if we grow dumber, then the higher intelligence grows dumber, too. . . . But knowledge by itself can be heartless. There is something higher than the infinity of knowledge —the infinity of the heart. . . .*

. . . A black cat with full buckets purred and swam weightlessly toward the cosmonaut, rubbing up against his sleeve. His wife floated up, holding the hands of their two children, who were as sturdy as white mushrooms. "And where's the other one?" his uncle from Zima said, eagle eye blazing, unhappy that his nephew had produced only two descendants.

The cosmonaut was sleepy. But according to the schedule, he was supposed to eat dinner—liver pâté, strong tea, and strawberry paste, from a tube, on bread. It tasted good, but how could you compare it to the wild berries in Siberia . . . ?

CHAPTER · 1

The berry commissioner was a man made up of miscellaneous parts: His tiny head was set with sly, oily (but self-important) eyes and crowned with a silver-black skullcap. It seemed to protrude by accident on a long, thin neck from his stout, doughlike body, which was somehow squeezed into a soiled, singed sailcloth jacket, its pockets billowing with invoices. To his belly were incongruously attached short, sturdy legs swathed in policeman's jodhpurs. Instead of being tucked into his boots, these merrily flapped their tied laces over his beige sandals. The sum of all these parts together was berry commissioner of the Zima Regional Consumer Union, Tikhon Tikhonovich Tugikh. Tikhon Tikhonovich bustled around an old, beat-up truck, its sides flung open, his precious advice impeding the truckers who were piling the back with empty wooden tubs awaiting freshly picked berries, sacks of sugar, and new zinc pails that still had their labels.

"What's taking so long?" Tikhon Tikhonovich shouted. "Let's get going!"

Grisha, the driver, supervised the loading process with aristocratic aloofness, puffing on a Belomor and also chatting with the plump but comely storekeeper. She was obviously interested in him, and kept trying to let him accidentally catch a glimpse of the sparkling pull-on boots beneath her gray work overalls.

"I stuck some beer under your seat, Grisha," she said quickly. "But be sure to let it cool off in the river—it'll taste better." Grisha shook his pitch pompadour indifferently.

"And I baked you some buns; they're wrapped up with it."

"Now, that wasn't necessary." Grisha frowned. "We're going into the taiga after all. It's not the desert, but *wild berry country.*"

At these words, he suddenly smiled with charming baseness at some secret thought, which, however, wasn't too hard for the store-keeper to guess.

"You miserable stud." She sighed. "I know your berries. . . ." Just then the commissioner approached and gave the storekeeper a stern, inquisitive look, whose meaning was known only to the two of them.

"OK, OK, Tikhon Tikhonovich. I got it ready yesterday. Just a minute." The storekeeper rushed off guiltily.

She disappeared into the semidarkness of the storeroom and soon returned, hugging a full pint bottle to her chest.

"Essence," Tikhon Tikhonovich explained laconically, in response to the unhealthy animation the bottle had inspired in the eyes of the loaders. Handing the invoice back to the storekeeper, he said, "Are you crazy? You marked it 1873. Wrong by a hundred years. Here now, fix it in your own handwriting." The pint was then carefully swaddled in an old sheepskin jacket and placed in the back.

With a sigh, Tikhon Tikhonovich looked over the two men who had asked to hitch a ride with them: a dried-up old mushroom hunter with several baskets, one nesting inside the other, and a rather thin young geologist, carrying a flimsy Aeroflot bag.

"It's not allowed, but all right . . . get in."

"Tikhon Tikhonovich, would you prefer to ride in the cab or the fresh air?" the driver asked considerately.

The berry commissioner squinted at the bottle sticking out from his jacket in the back.

"I like the fresh air."

"Then you can sit in front, grandpa," the driver said to the old mushroomer.

"I'll sit in back, too, son, so I can swallow some taiga breezes." The old man declined gently.

"So will I," said the geologist.

The storekeeper suddenly perked up.

"In that case, Tikhon Tikhonovich, with your permission, I'll accompany you in the cab as far as Old Zima. I have some business there," she babbled to the berry commissioner, all the while looking at Grisha with imploring eyes.

"Well, if it's business," Tikhon Tikhonovich said grudgingly.

"I won't be in your way, Grisha?" asked the storekeeper, her sparkling pull-on boot already on the cab step.

"My pleasure," the driver said morosely, spitting out the cigarette which had stuck to his lip. He lived for that blissful moment when he got behind the wheel, turned on the ignition, stepped on the gas, and roared off into the taiga; it was a moment of escape into the relative unknown from what you might call everyday life. But everyday life sometimes clung to you, especially in the form of a woman.

The old man and the geologist were already in the back. The loaders helped up Tikhon Tikhonovich, who toppled safely over the side. Settling down with his back to the cab, the berry commissioner hugged the mysterious essence between his police jodhpurs for extra insurance.

"Big berries to you, Tikhon Tikhonovich," said the senior loader as he noisily slammed the loading sides, and he glanced with mock sadness one last time at the bottle heading off into the great expanse of the taiga.

Tikhon Tikhonovich grunted as he squirmed into a more comfortable position, and the truck started off, raising dust in the streets of Zima and scattering the lazily waddling ducks.

"You didn't lock the storeroom!" one of the loaders shouted to the storekeeper, but it was too late.

"Look what love does to these females," the second loader said, with surprise but not envy, and he scratched the back of his head.

"Well, we'll have to keep an eye on the storeroom now," the third loader said, winking merrily. "And at the same time we can take inventory; maybe we'll find some more of that—what do you call it? —essence."

Laughing, they headed for the storeroom.

Grisha drove the truck with grim concentration, pretending to be busy with important chauffeuring duties for the benefit of the storekeeper sitting next to him. *I'm too easy on these women,* Grisha thought. *Their hopes get raised. And then what am I supposed to do with their hopes?*

Hope, in fact, was patent in the storekeeper's behavior at that very moment as she removed her colorful kerchief and began wiping the windshield in a helpful and proprietary way. Then she adjusted the rearview mirror in order to check the curls at her temples.

As soon as you let a woman in the cab, you can count on the mirror getting crooked, Grisha thought unhappily, noticing with his right eye that the storekeeper's left thigh seemed to be edging closer to him with every jolt of the truck. But he was protected by the gearshift.

"I'll miss you, Grish, I will. How about you?" She began feeling out the climate for reciprocity.

"Uh-huh," Grisha muttered. *You have to be tougher with them, harder,* he thought. *Most important, not a hint of marriage. Otherwise, they'll be on your back forever.*

But the storekeeper went on. "Who'll wash your shirts and socks in the village, my messy slob?"

"I'll find some old woman," Grisha said dismissively.

"I know your old women. . . . Just don't let them iron that foreign shirt I gave you. If they burn it, it'll melt. They're bumpkins, villagers, and they don't understand," the storekeeper said, proudly displaying her pull-on boot, as if it set her apart from those village girls.

"That depends," Grisha said mysteriously, reminding the storekeeper yet again that he was a free man, just in case.

"I'm not being jealous, Grisha. It's just that those village girls have all kinds of infections. They're a motley bunch there; just think of the ones sent on expeditions. Don't pick up any diseases."

"Scare tales," Grisha said, grinning. "Won't work on me."

The storekeeper realized she was pushing it and changed tactics. "Grisha, why haven't you ever been married? Don't consider anyone worthy of you or what?"

Here goes, Grisha thought, gritting his teeth. *That beer is going to cost me dearly.*

"I love freedom," he said. "Understand, freedom . . . as the poet said: There is no unhappiness in the world, but only space and freedom."

Whenever Grisha quoted these lines, which a regional journalist had read to him, he changed the word *peace* to *space.* Peace was something he couldn't understand, something fuzzy. But space—that he understood and loved.

"Did Yesenin write that?" the storekeeper asked, simultaneously inclining to a lyrical mood and trying to show her education. Still, she was wary of finding a dirty trick in the lines.

"Who else?"

"Well, I'm free, but I'm still not happy. I'd rather not be free, but happy," the storekeeper said sadly, touching Grisha's hand, which jiggled on the black plastic knob of the gearshift. All the while she was thinking: *I'm in your power anyway, you miserable stud. Why don't you make it legal once and for all and let me have some self-respect?* Grisha gently but firmly removed her hand.

"A man is tied down enough without letting himself get caught in family life. A man's got enough to put up with as it is—work, bosses, the regional committee. At least you don't have to have a boss at home."

Grisha purposely hit a pothole in the road, just to give his uninvited passenger a good jolt. But the storekeeper was not deterred.

"How can there be a boss at home if it's mutual?"

"One of the two is always the boss. And most often it's the woman," the driver barked.

"Come on, Grisha, you'll never let anyone boss you around." The woman flattered him, while secretly hoping just the opposite, of course. "My, what a touchy fellow I have."

Feeling the mounting danger in such phrases as "I have," Grisha thought: *Now I have to keep my eyes open with her. Once she steps on you casually with her sparkling pull-on boots, you'd stick to her heel forever.*

"Well, here's Old Zima," said Grisha, with more than a little relief. "Where do you want to go?"

The storekeeper sadly detected the note of joy in his voice. *I'm not subtle. I don't know how to hide my feelings, and so he takes advantage of me. He's afraid of ending up under a woman's heel, but he regularly squashes women with his cheap leather boots. He's picked all my berries, and now he's looking for new berry patches. And like a fool, I ran to the express courier's for beer and baked him buns. Who knows who he'll drink the beer and eat the buns with? I hope all his shirts burn to cinders under those village irons!*

"Grisha, that's the doctor on the road!" she said and grabbed his sleeve. A man in a white coat was on the roadside, his arm raised. The storekeeper was so happy you would have thought the doctor was there to operate on the driver's alienated feelings.

"Need a lift, Doctor?" Grisha asked quickly, hoping for a reprieve. "I always respect medicine."

"It's not me," said the young doctor, pushing up his glasses. "It's a delicate situation, you might say. Are you headed for Shelaputinki?"

"It's on the way, doc," said Grisha, still hoping.

Just then the berry commissioner's bass voice issued from the flatbed. "Comrade Doctor, are you getting in or not? With all respect, we're already behind."

Realizing the bass voice belonged to the man in charge, the doctor approached the flatbed. Tikhon Tikhonovich was crouching, the bottle still clamped between his jodhpurs.

Sensing that Tikhon Tikhonovich did not intend to get down, the doctor spoke again, spreading his hands in a helpless gesture. "It's a delicate situation, you might say."

Tikhon Tikhonovich was wary of delicate situations but at the same time he liked them. When he was in charge, they frightened him. But they also gave him the chance to raise himself in his own esteem. They demonstrated that society placed its confidence in him. Therefore, he leaned toward the doctor, creating a certain intimacy, even though they were on different levels.

"A woman and child," said the doctor simply but with significance.

"We'll deliver them," Tikhon Tikhonovich said, somewhat disappointed.

"Do you know Ivan Kuzmich Belomestnykh in Shelaputinki?" the doctor asked.

"Of course, who doesn't?" Tikhon Tikhonovich spoke in a calm basso, but already catching the dangerous whiff of a delicate situation. "He doesn't live in Shelaputinki, though, but on Belaya Zaimka."

"It's his daughter, Ksiuta," the doctor spoke quickly. "Ivan Kuzmich threw her out when she got pregnant. She gave birth here. The child is adorable, weighs three hundred eighty grams. We pleaded with her: 'Stay in the hospital and work as a nurse's aide, we'll put the child in the nursery,' but she was stubborn—no way. 'I'll go to my father,' she said, 'and kneel at his feet.' "

"Who's the father then?" Tikhon Tikhonovich frowned, relaxing his calves around the essence but knitting his brow.

"Ivan Kuzmich Belomestnykh, I told you," the doctor said desperately.

"Not her father, Comrade Doctor, I understood that part. Who's the father of her child?" Tikhon Tikhonovich said angrily, making mental calculations, the meaning of which was clear only to himself.

"Some berry commissioner."

"What?" roared Tikhon Tikhonovich, turning purple and looking around at the mushroomer and the geologist. The storekeeper and the driver got out of the cab. "That's me—the berry commissioner. I'm a friend of Ivan Kuzmich's, you might say. I stayed in their house last summer, and I know Ksiuta. But I'm old enough to be her father, her grandfather. I'm no stick-in-the-mud, you know, but I have high moral standards and do not permit myself diversions from my family life. This is an insult!"

"Perhaps it's some other berry commissioner," the doctor said, meekly retreating from this attack.

"There are no other berry commissioners in our region," Tikhon Tikhonovich said curtly.

"Excuse me, but what's your surname?"

"My surname is Tugikh, and Tikhon Tikhonovich Tugikh is my full name."

The doctor studied the enraged, indignant berry commissioner, and shaking his head, he said with controlled, sorrowful anger, "As far as I know, that is the exact name of the child's father."

Tikhon Tikhonovich let go of the essence between his police jodhpurs and, puffing, climbed over the side of the truck.

"Where is she?" He shook his head, which made his skullcap slip over one ear.

"I must ask you not to upset the mother. It affects the milk," the doctor muttered, leading Tikhon Tikhonovich to the hospital.

"That old goat," the storekeeper exclaimed indignantly, clapping her hands.

"I know Ksiuta—she's nuts," Grisha noted dispiritedly, but the storekeeper stopped him with a surge of female solidarity.

"You're all like that, all of you. . . . First you seduce a girl, and then having the baby is none of your business. You just run for all you're worth. And you call us nuts."

"But how did he manage it?" Grisha mused. "We were both in that house, and I didn't notice anything like that going on. He did drop in to the village store a couple of times, but as for Ksiuta—nothing. Of course, once . . ."

"What do you mean, 'once'?"

"He said very sternly to me, 'Don't you touch the girl, Grisha —she's too young.' "

"What did you do?"

"What? I had enough to do without her."

"I know what you do. . . . So you think Tikhon Tikhonovich was saving her for himself?"

"I didn't say that. But it looks like it now."

"It doesn't look like it to me," the storekeeper said, looking at him closely. "Tikhon Tikhonovich is a respectable man, reasonable. Maybe you're the father?"

"I'm the father? Of course I am!" Grisha exploded. "There, see that blond kid sucking his thumb by the fence—he's mine. And the dark-haired one on the bike—mine, too. All the maternity homes, all the nurseries, kindergartens, and orphanages of the great Soviet Union are stuffed with my productions. You're nuts yourself. You have a sick mind, that's what you have. You should go to the hospital for treatment."

"That's just what I'll do, go to the hospital," the storekeeper said quickly. "I'll go find out the truth." And with a determined step she set out after Tikhon Tikhonovich and the doctor.

"We'll be experiencing a short delay," Grisha addressed the men seated in the flatbed. "An unexpected pothole in the road of life, you might say."

The old mushroomer declined participation in the general discussion. "My business is agarics."

The geologist pulled out a book by Saint Exupéry from his Aeroflot bag and lost himself in it.

"What's it about?" Grisha asked.

"Pilots."

"We drivers are the pilots of the earth," Grisha joked, and slapped his truck. "And this is my little jet. . . ."

CHAPTER · 2

When the storekeeper entered the intern's room, the atmosphere was charged with confusion. A full-breasted village girl with tearstained yellow-flecked eyes sat in a chair, awkwardly holding a bundle from which poked an infant's wrinkled face.

Tikhon Tikhonovich was hysterical and kept grabbing the doctor's white sleeve, as though trying to get his support.

"What the devil are you doing here?" he hollered at the storekeeper. "Well, maybe it's a good thing. You'll be a witness."

"Don't shout, for God's sake," the doctor said, trying to soothe him. "The child is here."

"The child isn't guilty," Tikhon Tikhonovich agreed, and raising his finger, he continued the interrogation in a hoarse whisper. "So tell me, Ksiuta, who's the father?"

Ksiuta shook her head. "I can't, Tikhon Tikhonovich, don't ask."

"But I'm not the father, am I?" Tikhon Tikhonovich asked, repeating the question apparently for the benefit of the storekeeper and the doctor.

"No, you're not, Tikhon Tikhonovich."

"How about the driver Grigori?" the storekeeper interrupted, turning pale with fear but trying to maintain her dignity.

"He's not."

The storekeeper breathed a sigh of relief and wholeheartedly went over to Ksiuta's side.

"What are you tormenting this woman for, Tikhon Tikhonovich! She clearly admitted that you are not the father. . . ."

"She told *me* that," the berry commissioner answered angrily, but without raising his voice. "But she told her father, Ivan Kuzmich, that I was. And she doesn't say why such confusion overcame her."

Ksiuta dropped her head on her chest and barely forced out the words: "I was ashamed."

Tikhon Tikhonovich broke out in a sweat, he was so angry.

"How interesting. You're ashamed to say who the father is, but you're not ashamed to lie about me, to slander me despite my age. Who's the father? What's his surname?"

"I don't know his surname," Ksiuta replied sadly. "Or his name. I don't know anything."

The berry commissioner gazed at the witnesses with somber eyes and said, "You go out for a bit, comrades. Ksiuta and I will figure things out for ourselves."

The doctor and the storekeeper left, the former apparently with relief, the latter obviously with reluctance.

"So what was it, rape?" the berry commissioner asked very softly, his anger changing to pity.

"No. I did it of my own free will. It's not his fault."

"He, eh . . . who is he? Some heavenly angel or a charming devil?"* The berry commissioner fumed again.

"Don't ask me, Tikhon Tikhonovich," Ksiuta muttered, staring dully into space.

The infant squealed.

"Turn around, Tikhon Tikhonovich. I have to feed him."

Tikhon Tikhonovich, muttering something, walked over to the window, where he began chipping off the plaster. The sounds of the child's smacking came from behind his back.

"Now, Ksiuta, just tell me the honest truth, since you've elected me to fatherhood," he said, without turning around.

"You won't tell Ivan Kuzmich?" Ksiuta's eyelashes flew up in fear.

"I'll be the judge of that." The berry commissioner's back shuddered.

"No, first, promise."

*Ivan Kuzmich is misquoting a famous line from Pushkin's *Eugene Onegin*.

"I won't promise a thing. I'll do whatever's best."

"Best for who?" Ksiuta lowered her eyes hopelessly.

"For the child, you fool." The berry commissioner said over his shoulder, "I'm a man with high moral standards, but I'm human, too. . . . It can happen to anyone . . . we're not heartless brutes, are we?"

CHAPTER · 3

The previous summer had been unbearably hot in the wild berry country of Siberia.

For long periods it seemed as if the sun had eaten the wind. Familiar sounds—the drone of the taiga's tree trunks, the restless stirring of branches, the light whispering of the treetops—disappeared completely. But it was so still that even the distances traveled by sound were swallowed up. So when the dogs barked in Shelaputinki, Charlie, Ivan Kuzmich Belomestnykh's wolfhound, would rouse himself from heat exhaustion and start lazily talking back to them from Belaya Zaimka, five versts away.

"Long time we haven't had heat like this," Ivan Kuzmich, an old man composed of solid Siberian bone with young Gypsy eyes, would say. Then he'd send his daughter, Ksiuta, the only other living creature around besides Charlie, down to the cellar for red bilberry juice.

Ksiuta would take the jug, lift the trapdoor by its iron ring, which her grandfather had put in, and descend into the sweet-smelling darkness. She didn't need to see because she knew everything by touch: where the sacks of potatoes were, the pickles and sauerkraut, the vat with salt *khairuz,** the blueberry and blackberry preserves, the cans with evening milk and those with morning milk.

When she came up, Ksiuta would set the jug on the long table, which had been intended for a large family; it was never covered but always scraped clean with a knife. Then she'd pour out the dark red, foamy juice with bilberries and pieces of cinnamon floating in it. Her father drank from a beer mug he'd brought back from Germany, with a metal cover that may even have been real silver; Ksiuta herself used

Khairuz is a Siberian river fish of the salmon family.

her mother's porcelain cup, harmlessly cracked long ago across its painted rose, which was blue for some reason.

Her mother looked down from a purplish photograph on the wall. Still young, she wore a dress with a high lace collar and snuggled against the shoulder of a soldier with a forelock and a bravura mustache, who wore a St. George's Cross. Burdened by a hard life of almost eighty years, Ivan Kuzmich now little resembled that young fellow, except for his Gypsy eyes. Ksiuta's mother, on the other hand, of whom there were no later photographs, had the gift of eternal youth in a purplish haze. But looking down from the wall, she didn't seem to notice Ivan Kuzmich's age, and apparently she was pleased that her husband and daughter lived together so happily and peacefully in this clean house, as well tended as it had been in her day.

Ksiuta and her father never sat next to each other at the table, but at opposite ends, separated by the clean-scraped, undulating wooden space. Ksiuta happily got up to pour some more juice respectfully for her father from the jug standing in the middle of the table, and her father even more happily followed her considerate, graceful movements, as though he were seeing his wife, unclaimed by death.

Ksiuta was born to Ivan Kuzmich late in life, after the war.

Three sons had served in the Siberian Division and were killed in '41 near Moscow. Ivan Kuzmich had been spared by the Second World War, as well as the First, even though he undertook it without the exuberance of youth. He returned in '45, having added a dozen medals to his St. George, including one "For Taking Berlin," when he was already over fifty. While he was in the army, Ivan Kuzmich had stayed away from women, so that first evening home, after a four-year separation from his wife, he regarded the creamy, fluffed-up pillows with a certain embarrassment. His wife was also embarrassed, and when she awkwardly blew out the kerosene lamp and lay down next to him, he felt confused. He was used to sleeping only next to soldiers, like himself. Ivan Kuzmich thought sadly he had lost his male powers and that he had returned home an old man. But his wife pressed against him with her whole body. She was no longer young, but still redolent of hay and milk, and she whispered hotly, "Give me one more son, Vanya, just one . . ." and Ivan Kuzmich realized he wasn't an old man yet.

But they didn't have a son; they had a daughter. His wife passed away soon after this late birth, and Ivan Kuzmich was left alone with the infant. She was constantly ill at first. He named her Ksiuta in honor of her mother and treated her with taiga herbs, conifer infusions, and goat's milk.

The Shelaputinki widows often flirted with Ivan Kuzmich, dropping by Zaimka, swinging their uncaressed hips. But they had no success; he behaved properly with them, respecting their female loneliness but unwilling to share it. He simply took care of Ksiuta, worked in the kolkhoz, fished, hunted, and ran the house in such a way that no unexpected guest ever noticed the absence of a wife. And she wasn't absent but always looking down from the wall in a way that made any other female presence in the house unthinkable. It made him feel pleasant yet sad to walk barefoot on the wet floor which gave off an odor that reminded him of his wife's housekeeping. He didn't sell the cow but milked it himself. And then Ksiuta grew up, and her girlish fingers made the taut white streams sound completely different against the bottom of the pail. She was a perfect replica of her mother, and this filled Ivan Kuzmich with a special sadness and joy. Marriage for him was now totally impossible, for every day the lithe, living shadow of his young wife ran before him. Ivan Kuzmich did not move away from Belaya Zaimka, even though there were many good houses standing with boarded-up windows in Shelaputinki. People were leaving the village, and you could buy any house there for a bottle, almost. But to leave Belaya Zaimka would have been a betrayal of his grandfather, who had built the house before Shelaputinki existed; and of his father, who had himself carved the ornamental window carvings; and of his wife, who had given birth to three sons there; and of the sons themselves, who had taken their first steps on the same floorboards that now sang under Ksiuta's feet.

Ksiuta had to run five versts to school every day, but she was light on her feet; the path led through the taiga, but it didn't frighten her in the least. When she graduated from the seven-year village school, Ivan Kuzmich decided to end her education. He knew that education, by itself, could not make a person either good or happy. Some educated people he had met in life were not the least bit happy, and some of them were downright bad. Ivan Kuzmich tried to inculcate his own taiga learning in Ksiuta. He taught her how to do a peasant's work, how to set seines, and how to hunt on skis. To keep the skis from slipping on the mountain or rustling in the snow, he sewed hides onto them. He taught her to find medicinal herbs and to forecast changes in weather by signs that were scarcely perceptible. He tried to reveal all the beauty of taiga life to Ksiuta, not only to keep her at his side but also because he had been other places and hadn't found a better life.

"They always exiled the best people to Siberia," Ivan Kuzmich told Ksiuta. "That's why you can recognize a Siberian a verst away, because our land absorbed the spirit of those people. And no land is held together by those who pass through, saying 'hello—good-bye,' but by the people rooted there. Now you and I are indigenous Siberian people, daughter. We're not even villagers but farmers. And all of Siberia began with *zaimkas*."*

Ivan Kuzmich would take a branch of taiga strawberry in his hand and thoughtfully inhale its aroma.

"There's nothing like our Siberian berries anywhere. Each one has a devilish little kick in it. You can dump a whole pile of coal on one berry like this, and the smell will still come through."

But as Ksiuta grew prettier, Ivan Kuzmich grew more grim, fearful that life would take her away from him forever. He saw that in Shelaputinki the children applied either to an institute or a construction project as soon as they grew up, and their mothers and fathers grew old alone. Ivan Kuzmich would not imagine himself in the same predicament.

When a movie came to the village, he did not allow his daughter to go to the village hall alone. He would sit next to her, jealously squinting at her face, which was upturned in rapt attention to the screen life so foreign to her. When Ksiuta tacked up over her bed a color picture of the smiling film actor Vyacheslav Tikhonov, Ivan Kuzmich's eyes searched first the poster's face, then his daughter's for an explanation: What did she see in him; why was she so attracted to this man so far removed from the taiga?

Zaimkas are separate allotment farms in Siberia.

Ivan Kuzmich liked the village boys no better; there weren't many of them, and as a rule, they didn't stay very long, and if they did, they drank and swore. Ivan Kuzmich drank, but rarely, and he never permitted himself to swear—that wasn't in the old Siberian ways. A man could curse out of exhaustion—he was unloading his soul —but cursing to show off was shameful, revealing spiritual emptiness. He grumbled about the village lads, "You want to know what kind of people they are, go find out! In the old days we were afraid to say an extra word around our fathers and mothers, but now they bark out anything. They love to sit around rinsing their teeth, but as for work —that's what mothers, and fathers, and grandmothers are for." Ivan Kuzmich didn't want to give up his daughter to either a distant postcard actor or a local foulmouthed lout. To tell the truth, he'd never met a single person to whom he'd give his daughter in marriage.

Ivan Kuzmich went so far as to accompany Ksiuta to the village dances. This practice elicited furtive smirks from the other girls and fear from the boys. The old women repeated an ancient rumor— perhaps made up, perhaps true—that once upon a time before the war a man was found on the threshing-room floor, murdered with a wooden beam, and that man had flirted with the other Ksiuta—the wife of Ivan Kuzmich. So an invisible wall of fear protected Ksiuta from passes, but not infrequently she perceived it as a prison wall. Sometimes Ivan Kuzmich sadly accused himself of being like an old miser, hiding his daughter at the *zaimka*. But as soon as one of their rare guests looked at her unambiguously, Ivan Kuzmich was beside himself. When the driver Grisha stayed at their house, along with the berry commissioner, he merely looked Ksiuta over, and old man Belomestnykh called him out back. With his crazy Gypsy eyes glinting under their gray brows, he warned, "Grisha, I killed my first bear with a knife back before the First War. But even now my hand is steady. . . ."

Grisha didn't even try to make light of the incident. He abandoned his regional pride and immediately redirected his attentions from Ksiuta to Klava, the kolkhoz stable girl, making sure he was seen with her by Ivan Kuzmich as often as possible.

Yet Ivan Kuzmich felt in his gut that he wouldn't be able to hold on to his daughter. How could he keep her back when the buttons literally flew off her blouse, straining to contain her breasts, which were rising like bread dough, while her yellow-flecked eyes were more and more frequently clouded by vagueness?

Ivan Kuzmich suddenly turned religious, and on those scorching evenings when he and Ksiuta sat together, washing down cheese buns with red bilberry juice, he took his grandfather's Bible with the mouse-gnawed leather cover down from the closet. Perching glasses held together with fishing line on his large, straight nose, he read excerpts aloud to Ksiuta. Like many indigenous Siberians, Ivan Kuzmich did not think about God much, but he still feared Him. In the same way he feared an invisible grizzly bear. Ksiuta enjoyed listening to the Bible; it was the most beautiful book she knew, even though it was rather foggy in spots. Ivan Kuzmich not only read the Bible but expounded on it, talking about temptation and sin with particular frequency. However, he repeated the word *sin* so often and so vaguely and with such a nuance of unconvincing doom that Ksiuta's curiosity was aroused. She had trouble falling asleep in her luxurious bed, and she would push her small knees, which surged full of unspent power, into the cool oilcloth with swans painted on it that hung over the bed. The hazy word *sin* began enveloping her like a white cloud, intoxicatingly perfumed with taiga berries. It started to coalesce into a blurred face with the eyes of the film actor Vyacheslav Tikhonov. Ksiuta was already twenty-seven, and the girls hissed behind her back, "Old maid . . ." She had no one. Once, however, she asked Grisha, as a man of the world, "Grisha, what's a sin?"

Grisha looked around with fright and responded curtly, trying not to get involved, "I'm no priest. . . . They're the specialists in these things. . . ."

"But yesterday you came back from Klava's all covered with straw. Is that a sin or what?"

"That's no sin, that's love." Grisha laughed.

"You mean, love isn't a sin?"

"That's what I mean. But don't you go telling your father about our little exchange of opinions here. He doesn't make a distinction between love and sin."

"And you do, Grisha?"

Grisha was stunned. No one had ever asked him that question. And now it came from the lips of this hopelessly ignorant old maid from a farm, who was standing before him with shamelessly full breasts.

"Listen, leave me alone, or I can't promise to control myself. Don't get in my way, especially when I've been drinking. Or I'll lose control and sin," he warned her angrily.

"Grisha, but you said yourself that you love Klava."

"I did, I did. . . . My tongue won't fall off. And what if I do love her? I could fall in love with you, too. I have a big heart."

"But I don't love you, Grisha. What kind of love would that be?"

Grisha was furious. He had never heard such words from a member of the opposite sex.

"Are you crazy? Your father is crazy, and so are you. . . . Who needs you?"

Another time she caught the berry commissioner by the sleeve as he was heading to see his lady friend, the clerk at the village store.

"Tikhon Tikhonovich, I was asking Grisha about this, but he didn't answer me right. How do you tell love from sin?"

Tikhon Tikhonovich looked at Ksiuta closely and shook his head with pity. Obviously Ivan Kuzmich had driven her crazy with life on the *zaimka* and his mouse-eaten Bible. But Tikhon Tikhonovich was sentimental, and something of a philosopher as well. Something in her pure, childlike, inquisitive eyes touched him, forcing him to mock and pity himself rather than her.

"Love, Ksiuta, is if it comes from the heart. If that happens, nothing is a sin," Tikhon Tikhonovich said. "And a sin is if it comes from those . . . dark insticks. Understand, silly?"

"I understand," Ksiuta replied, wondering what "dark insticks" could be but sensing they were bad.

And the berry commissioner went off to visit his lady clerk down the path of dark instincts, calling himself an insatiable old devil and feeling in his jacket pocket, not without a little pleasure, the half liter bottle of essence. This all happened that summer when the heat intensified, increasing Ksiuta's desire for something that would release her soul and body. Like the parched earth, she was exhausted by an inner fire.

One morning, when her father had gone off on a fishing trip with the berry commissioner and Grisha, Ksiuta went to finish the mowing in the meadow on the riverbank.

It was a baking, dewless morning, and the grass wilted from the heat. Charlie, the wolfhound, tongue hanging out and panting hard, watched his mistress from the shade. Ksiuta's scythe did not travel across the grass with its usual merry zip but joylessly rustled along, getting stuck in the wilting stalks as they drooped on the ground. Even the taiga strawberries, mixed in with the grass, had no time to ripen to a full-bodied blush, and they already tasted dried up; only in the depths of the taiga did they manage to survive, but in the open meadow they couldn't bear the heat and surrendered their juice to the thirsty air. The birch, aspen, and alder leaves and even the larch pine needles looked sick and yellow. The clouds of gnats that usually buzzed overhead disappeared somewhere, hiding from the terrible heat as they did from the cold. All that was left was an occasional bee. *In the spring the bee takes even from the pussywillow,* thought Ksiuta. *The best pollen is from clover, though. But can you even call this grass? It's just weeds. All dried up and fading. Even the bees want to get into the shade.* . . . As the taiga grew quieter, the murmur of the river beyond the trees grew more distinct, turning into a beckoning roar.

Ksiuta gave up trying to mow the fallen grass below the root and clumsily jabbed the scythe into the ground. Stepping softly in the leather moccasins her father had sewn for her, she followed the voice of the river, and soon that voice was joined by an iridescent sparkle beyond the trees. As she walked, Ksiuta untied her white scarf with its black polka dots and released her hair so that it swept across her shoulders in a flaxen wave. She panted as she began tossing off her clothes. The scarf landed on the flowers of the marsh tea bush, the unbuttoned blouse on a willow bush, the tight black bra on the exposed roots of an old larch. Her only thought was to immerse her overheated body in the water's fresh breath.

Right by the river, on a narrow strip of pebbles, Ksiuta took off her moccasins, skirt, and blue panties with three elastic bands. She didn't fear a stranger's eyes—this was a lonely spot. Freed of everything, she felt as light as a feather, as if a gust of wind would snatch her up and fly her off to distant lands. But there was no wind, and in another minute she started to get hot again, even though she was naked.

Ksiuta felt the water with her bare foot and shrieked as it burned her with its cold, which had coursed over the rapids from the Sayan Mountains. Charlie plunged in and instantly plunged out, shaking himself noisily.

Ksiuta chose a different spot, one between two sandbars, where the water was quiet and had warmed up some. She went in gradually. With an "ooh," she crouched chest-deep, relishing the tickling touch of a school of minnows scattering against her legs, and then she swam out with strong, rapid strokes.

The calm water ended quickly, and Ksiuta again felt the burning, dragging force of the stream. She started playing with the river, diving into the powerful, surging iciness of the swift current and then squirming out of its grasping clutches by slashing her arms, struggling until she found herself once more in the warm, gently rocking backwater. It was extremely difficult to stay in place in the fast current, but through experience, Ksiuta knew how to pick out a snag onshore and stay directly opposite it by using all her strength, so that the current wouldn't sweep her away. Then she would double the frequency of her strokes to conquer tiny pieces of water, and seeming to remain in place, she would actually crawl slowly forward, ending up downstream of her landmark snag, almost exhausted, blissfully floating on her back, arms flung out, in the quiet water. The weight of her flaxen mane dragged down her head, so that only her eyes and bilberry nipples stuck up above the surface of the water she had tamed. It had resembled a desperate struggle between two bodies—Ksiuta's and the river's, but they were old friends and posed no danger to each other. However, this battle made Charlie uneasy. The whole time he remained at his post by the clothing, squealing and whimpering, even though he didn't dare join this risky game.

But suddenly Charlie's sharp, angry bark replaced his whimper. Ksiuta lifted her head out of the water and saw on the pebble strip next to her clothes a black-bearded man who didn't look like a villager.

Dressed in a checked shirt with rolled-up sleeves, he was using a geologist's hammer to fend off the angry Charlie, who leaped at his feet.

Ksiuta knew Charlie was basically good-natured, but he was still a farm hound and might not spare a stranger, especially one who got too close to his mistress's clothing. Two feelings fought each other inside Ksiuta: shame, because she was naked, and fear that Charlie might tear this man apart.

"Down, Charlie!" she shouted, chin-deep in water.

Either because of the roar of the river or because he was caught up in a frenzy, the dog didn't hear his mistress or pretended not to. Forgetting her embarrassment, Ksiuta ran from the water and grabbed Charlie's collar with one hand and tossed her hair over her breasts with the other. She crouched, hoping that her hair would shield as much of her body as possible from the stranger.

"Turn around! What're you staring at!" Ksiuta shouted right into the face of the black-bearded man, who was stunned by the sight of her white body, sparkling with water drops and half-enveloped in wild, tangled hair. Black Beard did not turn away immediately; his eyes grabbed all of her—her wet, angry, enormous eyes, the almost crude brick-colored tan on her face and forearms, changing suddenly to a soft but blinding white, sprinkled with dark, berrylike birthmarks. And one of her red bilberry nipples defiantly jutted through the hair that was trying to cover her breast.

"What a beauty you are . . ." the stranger said slowly, holding his breath. Then he turned sharply, and in a different voice, a sensible one, said, "Forgive me."

"Stay!" Ksiuta shouted to the wolfhound, who obeyed unwillingly, and she began dressing while keeping a wary eye on the stranger's back. She couldn't find her bra and blouse and remembered she had dropped them on the way.

"Don't turn around!" Ksiuta ordered the stranger, clambering up the slope. Putting on her bra and blouse and tying her scarf, Ksiuta tried not to think about the way she had appeared before the stranger, but his gasping, slow words—"What a beauty you are . . ."—echoed inside her. Her father had used those same words, but in a completely different voice, and when he realized what he said, he angrily changed the subject.

Oh, God, is Charlie staying put? Ksiuta thought with growing fear for the stranger, and she scrambled down the slope barefoot but fully dressed.

He was in the same position she had left him—with his back to her moccasins, near which Charlie was growling. Listening to the growling behind his back, he clutched his geological hammer as a precaution.

Ksiuta's laugh rang out; this tall, black-bearded stranger suddenly seemed so helpless.

"What's the matter, have you turned into a pillar of salt?"

The stranger turned but looked first at Charlie, not at Ksiuta.

"Don't you like dogs?" Ksiuta asked.

"Why not? Of course . . ." Relaxing, the stranger smiled. He had a nice smile. There were gray hairs in his beard, but he was hardly old.

"Dogs only bite people who are afraid of them," Ksiuta said, sitting down on the pebbles and ruffling Charlie's neck. "Right, Charlie?"

"You know, your dog is just too big," the stranger said, still smiling. "I have a dog. A setter."

"Where is it?"

"At home, in Moscow," he said, sitting down next to her but not too close.

"You mean you're from *Moscow*?" Ksiuta's eyes opened wide in amazement. She had never met anyone from Moscow before. "And what are you doing here?" For her the distance between the words *Moscow* and *here* was mind-boggling.

"Looking for rocks." The stranger smiled again and extended his hand to pat Charlie. But Charlie growled, and he drew back his hand.

"Your hound has a strong personality," he said with cautious respect, and squinting slightly in the sun, he studied Ksiuta. Despite her clothes, he continued to see her as she had emerged from the river. Ksiuta sensed this and ran her fingers over the buttons of her blouse, checking them.

"Where do you live—in Shelaputinki?" the stranger asked.

"No, in Belaya Zaimka."

"Aha, you're a farm girl."

"A *zaimka* girl," Ksiuta insisted, even though she sensed that the words were similar.

"Have you been to Moscow?"

"No . . ." Ksiuta sighed inadvertently but immediately added with pride, "It's good enough for me here."

"Have you ever been to the city?"

"To Zima," Ksiuta replied. "But I didn't like it there; it's crowded, people pressing against each other. Of course, I did like the trains."

She recalled that during her only trip to Zima her father took her to the railroad station, and on the platform he bought her ice cream, which she'd never tasted before. Holding the dried stick of the "eskimo," she stared at the white plaques on the car for a long time: "Vladivostok–Moscow," "Moscow–Vladivostock," and many others. There wasn't a single "Moscow–Zima" plaque because passengers usually just jumped out onto the platform there, to buy the hard, venomously gold meat pies and local citrus soda with flaky sediment or simply to stretch their legs. Zima—the largest city in Ksiuta's life—was merely a ten-minute stopover for them.

Boys and girls in dark green matching jackets, bearing the incomprehensible initials MEI, MATI, and MVTU,* strolled about with their arms around each other, which wasn't done in Shelaputinki, or stood in a circle and sang to guitar accompaniment. Ksiuta would like to have written down, the words to some of the songs, which didn't sound like folk songs, but the trains zoomed off, taking away with them the half-remembered lyrics: "The girl weeps, but the balloon flies off. . . ." "The flowers are unusually beautiful in the neutral zone. . . ." Ksiuta particularly remembered one passenger: He was short, and his slanted eyes and yellowish face made him resemble a Buryat, except his features were finer. Draped with cameras, he hopped around Ksiuta and Ivan Kuzmich, babbling in Russian and in sign language for permission to photograph them. Ivan Kuzmich whispered to

*Initials of Moscow schools.

Ksiuta, "He's Japanese." Then he tugged at his jacket, straightened his beard, and nodded in agreement.

Receiving permission, the Japanese man fell to one knee on the platform, which was strewn with shells from sunflower seeds, and unconcerned about his blindingly cream-colored trousers, he clicked several times, twisting this way and that, each time with a different camera. Then, revealing his widely spaced but firm teeth and bowing gratefully, he pulled out a black wallet, opened it, and showed them behind a cellophane window a color photograph of a woman; she was slant-eyed like him and holding the hand of a slant-eyed little girl. He handed Ivan Kuzmich a hard white strip of cardboard and hopped into an open car with special curtains as the train lurched and started. The Japanese man waved to them, his hand as narrow as a child's, carrying away the sunflower seeds on his cream-colored trousers.

Bewildered, Ivan Kuzmich was turning the calling card when he was approached by a neatly groomed station policeman.

"Allow me to take a look," said the policeman, who took the card and began studying it attentively. "This isn't our language. Aha, hieroglyphs . . ." Then he turned it over. "This is ours." And he read aloud: "Sotokiti Kusaka, professor of Waseda University, member of the Japan-USSR Society."

The policeman returned the card to Ivan Kuzmich, having copied down the Japanese man's name into his notebook, just in case, and saluted.

"Everything's in order. Détente, basically." But at the same time he inquired, "What did he ask?"

"Nothing," Ivan Kuzmich replied angrily, leading Ksiuta from the platform. Ksiuta later put the card into her grandmother's iron box where her father's medals were kept. And that ended her contact with the foreign world, the one even more far away than Moscow or Vladivostok.

"I have a Japanese acquaintance," Ksiuta told the black-bearded stranger, her bare foot playing with the hot pebbles. "Have you ever been to Japan?"

"No, I haven't. But I've been to France, in a tour group," the stranger replied.

"And what, did you like it?"

The stranger suddenly sounded as if he were speaking to himself, almost forgetting Ksiuta. "I liked Paris. Every stone there reeks of history. You walk along, and you think: *Where does history go? It goes into the stones.*"

Some secret memory made him smile in a peculiar way, and then he frowned. "But the Parisians disappointed me."

"Why is that?" Ksiuta was amazed. There was beauty in the very word *Parisians* as far as she was concerned.

She's just a child, he thought, and unwittingly switched to the familiar "you" form with her. "How can I put it?" He poked at the gravel with his hammer. "Have you read *The Three Musketeers?*"

"I saw it in the movies."

The stranger smiled, recalling what a Moscow friend of his had said: "All humanity is divided into three categories: Those who have read *The Brothers Karamazov,* those who haven't read it yet, and those who will never read it." *There's another category,* he thought. *Those who saw* The Brothers Karamazov *in the movies. But what a wonderful girl she is anyway. A child of the taiga . . .*

"Do you remember the names of the musketeers?" he asked.

"I forget," Ksiuta replied, unhappy in the face of this interrogation.

"D'Artagnan, Athos, Porthos, and Aramis. Remember now?"

"Now I do. It was a long time ago."

The stranger continued, striking the gravel with his hammer, as though hammering his words into Ksiuta. "Strong personalities. That's what I admire most in people. And even in dogs," he said, nodding at Charlie. "Well, before my trip I always imagined Parisians were like D'Artagnan, Athos, Porthos, and Aramis. Maybe it was just my bad luck, but I didn't find any musketeers in Paris." He stopped, suddenly remembering who his companion was. *Why am I telling her all this? How can this be of any help to her? Paris is as far away for her as Mars.* But anyone who's been in the taiga knows how its green limitless expanse leads you to reveal yourself to strangers, which it thrusts at you and then sucks up again, as though they'd never existed.

"Do you have a strong personality?" Ksiuta asked.

"It's not for me to judge. But I hope I'm not a weak one," the stranger replied, half-joking, half-serious.

"But Charlie scared you." Ksiuta laughed, and her white teeth sparkled against the golden bloom of her cheeks.

The stranger once more helplessly marveled at her beauty.

"I think I'll go for a swim," he said. He quickly unlaced his heavy hiking boots, tossed off his worn, faded jeans and shirt, and stood up, wearing only tight red and white striped swimming trunks. Despite the gray hairs in his beard, his body was quite young and tanned, and the muscles bulged in his arms. He undressed so quickly that Ksiuta didn't even have time to look away, but he wasn't embarrassed.

"Don't swim out into the swift current," Ksiuta advised, but he had already run into the water and was swimming in a way Ksiuta had never seen—sometimes lowering his head into the water, sometimes rising above the waves and throwing both arms in front of him. It was a pleasing and astonishing sight. He struggled expertly with the river, as though he had been born in the taiga and spent his whole life here.

No, he's strong, thought Ksiuta, and she grew a little sad because she hadn't understood everything he'd said about the French.

The stranger got out of the river, snorting, and lay down next to her, offering his body to the sun. Ksiuta noticed a deep scar on his side.

"Where did you get that?" Ksiuta asked.

"The war," the stranger replied.

"What? You were in the war?"

"How old do you think I am?" The stranger turned to her, putting his black beard with its prickly gray wires on his cast-iron fist, which bore the traces of a tattoo that had been removed.

Ksiuta was confused and said nothing.

"I'm a whole fifty-two," the stranger said, stressing each word. "And you?"

Ksiuta didn't reply, even more confused.

"Around twenty," he replied for her. "That means I could be your father."

Ksiuta shook her head. "No, I'll be thirty soon. . . . But you're still very young. And handsome," she added softly, as a way of thanking him for being the first outsider to tell her she was beautiful.

How frank she is, the stranger thought. *Is she really almost thirty?*

"Are you married?" he asked with apparent indifference.

"No, of course not!"

"Well, do you have a betrothed?"

"No."

"Why not?"

"I'm not in love with anyone," Ksiuta replied simply, lowering her gaze, and the simplicity and defenselessness of her reply pierced through him.

"It'll come," he said. "Love is like death or prison—don't think you can avoid it. Besides, no one really knows what love is."

"How can that be?" Ksiuta was shocked.

"It's true. Love has no laws. It's a law unto itself, and it's different in every case. It sounds so boring—'making it legal.' "

"Are you married?"

"Yes! That's why I know what I'm talking about."

"Do you love your wife?"

"Probably. But not the way I used to—more the way you love a family member, I guess. Family life kills love. Love is astonishment, and as soon as it turns into habit, it's over. Therefore, if you do fall in love, don't think about marriage. I'm telling you unorthodox things, but what won't a person say out here, in the wilds of the taiga? . . . Are you afraid of me?"

"I'm not," Ksiuta said, even though it wasn't completely true. "Go on, keep talking. . . . No one's ever talked to me like this before."

"It's a good thing you're not afraid." The stranger scrutinized her with such profundity that she looked away. "Don't be afraid of chance. Do you believe in God?"

"N-no . . . I love the Bible. . . ."

"Neither do I. My god is chance. In the hands of chance everyone is a chess piece, and it throws them off the board when it wants to, or it moves them together, the way it did us on the bank of this river. Chance rules everything—war and love. Do you understand everything I'm saying?"

"Yes," Ksiuta replied, a bit subdued by his words. But she asked unexpectedly, "How do you distinguish love from sin?"

"Sin?" The stranger laughed, feeling benignly superior, and suddenly he spoke harshly, abruptly. "What is sin? I don't know what that thing is. They say killing is the biggest sin. But I was at the front and I killed, understand? With these very hands I killed fascists, and I didn't feel as if I'd committed any sin because they were the enemy and if I hadn't killed them, they would have killed me. And if bloodshed isn't a sin, then how can it be a sin when a man and a woman come together of their own free will? Who judges what's a sin or what isn't? God? If He exists, then His hands are bloodstained to the elbow, and He's not fit to judge matters like love. There is no such thing as good or bad, only good and bad memories."

His naked, angry words were killing something in Ksiuta, while simultaneously overpowering her. But for some reason she didn't resist and surrendered to the force of the stranger's words with fear and pleasure.

"In our tour group in Paris there was an artist," the stranger went on. "A peach of a young woman." He smiled slightly. "Almost every year she managed to go on tour to some African nation—Africa was her passion. And everywhere she went, she drew. Trips like that cost a lot of money; we geologists can't afford to travel very year. So I thought this artist was very rich. When she invited me to visit her in Moscow, I expected to see a luxurious apartment. But she had only simple office chairs, a table, an iron bed. Yet on all the walls hung memories—her paintings and souvenirs. We drank, and she said to me, 'The only bank where you can deposit all your savings is your memory. That bank will never go bankrupt.' That artist was right. You can strip a person naked, toss him onto a stone floor in solitary confinement, but no one can take away his memories. I haven't saved up a thing in my nomadic life, but I treasure my memories like King Midas. Who can take away from me the sight of you jumping out of the river or the way we're talking together now? No one. Only I can, if I forget."

"Will you forget?" Ksiuta asked, without looking into his eyes, but feeling them on her face and her whole body.

Why am I babbling on like this? the stranger thought. *She doesn't understand a thing probably.* But he replied, "I won't forget."

Ksiuta said uncertainly, "Well, I have to mow now. . . ." And she stood up to put on her moccasins.

The stranger, enflamed by his own recent monologue, suddenly couldn't tolerate the thought that she would disappear from his life, melting forever into the taiga. He was drawn to her with the thirst characteristic of rootless people.

"Will you teach me how to mow?" he asked jokingly, but still Ksiuta felt in every sinew that he was asking something else.

Struggling with her own confusion, she merrily nodded her head. "All right. I even have a second scythe. Just don't chop off your feet."

"They're made of iron. Any scythe will break on them," the stranger shouted, relaxing, feeling a surge of reckless bravado brought on by his own words and already prepared for what would inexorably happen.

Viktor Petrovich Kolomeitsev, head of a geological expedition group camped about forty versts from Shelaputinki, really was fifty-two years old, he really had fought in the war, and he really had been to Paris once. He rarely saw his family and during his travels believed most of all in his own will and chance. This combination—willpower and chance—armed him with supreme confidence in both his work and his relations with women.

And so when he took a scythe into his hands for the first time in his life, he began mowing next to Ksiuta with such broad, powerful sweeps that one would have thought he'd been mowing since childhood, instead of playing cards with the tough kids from Maryina Roshcha (who, incidentally, gave him the tattoo he had later eradicated).

Kolomeitsev wanted to mow beautifully; that meant the will was there, the scythe glittered in his hands. And Ksiuta was at his side—so chance was there. Everything was in place, and nothing in the world could get in his way.

Ksiuta looked at him with amazement. "You tricked me; this isn't your first time."

"I did trick you!" he shouted across the whole taiga, brazenly winking at her. "Yes, I did!" And he slashed triumphantly through the meadow, feeling himself master of the taiga, of Ksiuta, and even of the wolfhound Charlie, who suspiciously watched him from the shade of the pines. Mowing together reminded Kolomeitsev of dancing somehow—the same abandonment of two bodies to a common rhythm; the same exchange of glances, eyes glistening with excitement; the same music, pulsing inside the brain; the same drunken swaying of a listing world.

"Do you like it?" Ksiuta shouted, trying not to fall behind but strangely pleased that she was a bit behind.

"It's fantastic!" Kolomeitsev shouted, and he really did feel good.

One quality he possessed: He knew how to give himself up to the moment, as though it were the last one in his life. It had been born in the dark alleys of Maryina Roshcha, shining with the glint of switchblades; in the foxholes at the front, slimy with blood and mud; and later at the geology department of Moscow State University, when he loaded coal at night to earn enough money for two tickets to the theater, and in the cliffs of the Khibiny Mountains and the thickets of Altai and Siberia, where his profession took him. He liked the line, written, he thought, by Kipling: "After the endless prairie I drink the royal coffee." His royal coffee after the endless prairie was women.

Sometimes it seemed to him he had lived several lives: the closed lips of his first kiss, from a schoolgirl in fourth grade on the Ferris wheel; the shamelessly businesslike lips of a Maryina Roshcha whore, who tucked his pocket money into her purse; the lips, reeking of alcohol and opening with dreary haste, of the nurses and traffic controllers at the front; the lips of students in the geology department, breathing cider at holiday parties; the lips of city women met by chance, smelling of recently removed lipstick; the chapped, rough lips of village girls; and the lips that unexpectedly pressed his in Paris, belonging to a black-eyed girl in a purple leotard, during Mardi Gras in Montmartre.

Among his friends, Kolomeitsev was not considered a skirt chaser, and he didn't see himself that way either. But he thought his several lives were the inevitable result of a life determined by chance and will. And now, while mowing, he glanced at the moist, half-opened lips of the girl he had just met and felt an irresistible need for them.

He hadn't asked Ksiuta's name and knew nothing about her, but it wasn't necessary. In his opinion, the most wonderful relationships between a man and a woman were those with no strings attached, where will and chance urged them together, with no thought of future consequence.

Growing tired, Kolomeitsev threw away the scythe and picked up as much hay as he could hold, just to look at it. "There are so many different grasses and flowers in here. . . . And it's called by a single word —hay. . . . What's this one?"

"That's a grenade flower," Ksiuta explained. "It's light violet until August, but you see, it's fading already. . . . Its head is like a grenade—like someone whittled it with facets. And there's sort of dimples along the head. It stops you when you mow. . . . It's sturdy. . . ."

"And this?"

"That's Marya Koreshka—a tall one. It has a bouquet of colors. It's raspberry at yuletide. You drink it for cancer. . . ."

"And this herb, what's it for?"

"That's bindweed—it's a busy grass, gets all mixed up. . . . I don't know what it's for. . . . Probably for something. Grasses don't grow for nothing. . . . Don't throw the hay around like that. You have to put it in rows, let it rest from the soil. That's what the rake is for. . . . Like that, like that . . . But in even rows, not any which way. The topping comes later."

"What comes later?" Kolomeitsev didn't understand.

Ksiuta laughed. "Topping is when you whip up a stack and finish off its top. It has to be thoroughly dry, roasted. You have to do it well, so that it doesn't get soaked. Father and I already topped on the next meadow. The rows dried up in two days. But things are worse with this batch. It's awfully hot, and I'm afraid the rain might start. Then they'll rot. Things rot without roots."

"Things rot without roots," repeated Kolomeitsev out loud, and something nudged at him, worried him. But he checked this useless reflection.

The heat was still almost unbearable. But suddenly from some unknown place there stirred a breath of wind, forgotten by the yellowed grass. Leaves and needles joyously began to tremble and flutter around him, and the just-mown hay rustled, flying up under sudden gusts.

Kolomeitsev and Ksiuta threw back their heads and saw that dark clouds, which had previously been hiding somewhere, were rolling over the mountains one after another.

A warning rumble came from far away, and Charlie barked.

"A storm is coming," Ksiuta said. "And a huge one, I think. . . . But it's all right, it usually clears up in the same place the storm clouds came from."

The clouds relentlessly moved across the sun and melded together, covering it. The whole sky, which just a minute ago had been unbearably blue, turned into an enormous, oppressively heavy cloud.

Ksiuta looked at Kolomeitsev, and he at her, with that lightning-fast, almost imperceptible understanding that decides everything. Kolomeitsev had long ago bent chance to his will, and Ksiuta understood instinctively: It would happen as inevitably as the storm. Therefore, when Kolomeitsev asked her, "Where will we go for shelter?" Ksiuta led him to the neighboring meadow, to the haystack she and her father had recently topped. Her legs barely moved, obeying a will of their own.

They quickly dug out a cave of sorts in the fresh, loosely packed hay, and they dived into its green, sweet-smelling darkness just as the lightning ripped open the sky and a roaring wall of rain collapsed onto the earth.

But the darkness resounded with a growl from Charlie, who had jumped into the cave a few seconds before them and now lay between them.

"Oho, your bodyguard is here already," Kolomeitsev joked without any great joy.

And suddenly, surprising herself, Ksiuta said, "Go away, Charlie. . . ." And she pulled him out by his collar into the rain. Charlie resisted, meanly baring his yellow eyeteeth. But giving in to his mistress's will, he crawled toward the exit and the lashing streams of water.

"I'll be only a minute," Ksiuta said, running out after the dog.

She won't come back, Kolomeitsev thought wearily. *Maybe that's for the best. No, she'll be back.*

The storm embraced Ksiuta with its wet, warm arms, showering her with thousands of greedy, rough kisses, blinding her with the white zigzag explosions of uncountable lightning bolts, deafening her with ear-splitting rolls of thunder, while she feverishly dug a separate shelter for Charlie in the haystack and pushed him into it.

Then, already hopelessly soaked, she stood up straight, offering her body to the powerful surge of water. For an instant the thought crossed her mind to run wherever her feet took her, away from the man who was waiting for her in the green cave, but she knew she wouldn't.

She crawled back into the haystack and lay as still as a corpse, her arms stretched along the wet clothing sticking to her body. The reflection of the lightning snatched out of the semidarkness her frightened, immobile face. Her eyes were closed, and for a second Kolomeitsev felt uneasy. *Can she really be almost thirty?* he thought. But another flash of lightning struck with its white light, and on her breasts, which jutted from the bodice of her blouse, the drops of water lit up enticingly with fiery blue sparks. Kolomeitsev gingerly ran his hand along Ksiuta's body, and then more and more insistently.

"You're completely wet. . . . Undress. . . ."

When it hurt Ksiuta, she didn't cry but gritted her teeth.

"Why didn't you tell me you were a virgin?" Kolomeitsev muttered. *She wanted this herself,* he thought, trying to suppress his dislike of himself.

"You won't forget me, will you?" she asked, as she had back on the riverbank.

"I won't," he replied, again not quite able to decide whether this was the truth or a lie.

Her chest was rising and falling, and green hayseeds clung to it. He kissed it and suddenly heard her heart beating strongly and unevenly. Then he put his hand on his own chest and couldn't feel the slightest beat.

"Where did my heart go?" he said, trying to smile. "Yours is beating so loudly, and I can't even hear mine."

Ksiuta put her strong but small hand on his chest.

"It hasn't gone anywhere," she said. "It's beating. Right there." And she tried to help him find his own heart, but he still couldn't feel a thing.

"Maybe I'm heartless?" He tried to joke.

"No, you're not heartless," Ksiuta said softly. "You just don't hear it yourself. But I do. I hear it righteously. . . ."

"Righteously—what does that mean?" Kolomeitsev asked anxiously.

"Truly, really," Ksiuta said, and Kolomeitsev thought: *How strange. You can translate from Russian to Russian. No, I must really be losing my heart. I spew nonsense at this poor kid, and what for? A roll in the hay. And she'll grieve over it, probably for a long time. "Chess pieces." "Memory bank"* . . . *Lots of pretty words, but there's something predatory behind it. I hate grabbers, but I'm turning into a spiritual grabber. I grabbed a piece of this girl's pure soul, and now I run off into the bushes. It's been said: "Just don't touch the ones who were never kissed; just don't tempt the ones who were never burned." I can't even hear my own heart. Why make someone else's heart beat so wildly?* Kolomeitsev suddenly felt a distaste for Ksiuta, lying next to him, because she had elicited the pangs of conscience he disliked so much. But he knew how to overlook his conscience; he banned what he called geological expeditions into the mind. *Well, and what if I hadn't done it? Someone else would have, and it might have been much cruder and more cynical. Some tractor driver somewhere at harvest or threshing time, covering her mouth with a hand that reeked of black oil, or one of the recruits brought out here who'd give her the clap. Even if she marries well, she'll give birth to a litter of kids, fatten up on bread and potatoes, and stoop under her workload; her husband will take to drink and beat her. At least this way she'll have something to remember: the storm, the haystack, a stranger from another world, who said most incomprehensible but very unusual things to her. Why indulge in cannibalism, Kolomeitsev? You must be getting old if you choose to complicate things that are really quite simple. Don't be a weakling.*

But it was hard for him not to give in to sentimentality, which he detested but which was now pouring over him. His life was hard and it had made him hard, but not completely.

Ksiuta's hand was still pressed to his heart. His skin felt the rough mounds of calluses on her palms, but the tips of her small, fragile fingers were soft and defenseless. Ksiuta was not crying, but her eyes were filled with a moist flickering, as if a large drop of the storm had lodged in each eye.

What if I chuck everything, take her to Moscow, and live alone with her for the rest of my life? She has a pure soul, like a white sheet of paper. You can write whatever you want on it. This unexpected thought flew through his mind.

There was another clap of thunder in the sky, but it was quieter now, more peaceful, and Kolomeitsev again made love to Ksiuta—this time without the devouring greed, but more tenderly, more kindly. Ksiuta sensed the change in him and she pressed closer, no longer afraid to feel the pain again, only wanting to do whatever would make him feel good. And he felt good, so good that the green cave, illuminated by Ksiuta's eyes, which were open this time and fixed on his face, swayed in the clatter of the downpour and seemed to float off into the unknown.

"Do you love me?" asked Ksiuta, barely audible. At that moment her heart hammered against his chest from beneath, seeking his own heart. Kolomeitsev said nothing and, gently taking her lips into his, made his response no longer important; the kiss had replaced it.

So what if he doesn't love me? I don't care that he doesn't ask my name or say anything. I love him anyway. It may be for only an hour, but it belongs to me.

"Does it hurt anymore?" Kolomeitsev asked, trying to be careful.

"Thank you," she breathed into his chest.

"For what?"

"For asking whether it hurts or not. . . . It doesn't, don't worry. . . . Give me a child, please. . . ."

"A child?" Kolomeitsev was astounded, being used to women who were generally afraid of that. "Why do you want one?"

"So that he'll look like you. You'll leave, but the child will stay. You said yourself, 'Memory is the most important thing.' You spoke the truth. . . . God, how good this is. . . . No, it's not a sin. . . ." The words tumbled from Ksiuta's lips, and she held Kolomeitsev so close, as if to hold him forever.

She felt something akin to pain but completely different, pleasurable, burning, as though a lightning bolt had blazed through her body in slow motion, piercing it in half from bottom to top, and when it disappeared, there remained only tranquillity and gratitude.

The tranquillity gradually turned to overpowering exhaustion, and Ksiuta could not help falling asleep.

Kolomeitsev lay next to her, and inside him was a long-familiar emptiness. His glance fell upon Ksiuta's wet clothing, her pale blue panties, and the thought of taking her to Moscow now seemed ridiculous. She was inseparable from the river out of which she had come to him, from the taiga hay on which she now lay, naked, her knees folded up to her belly, her slightly pouting lips moving gently, childlike in her sleep; Kolomeitsev couldn't imagine her in his Moscow life.

The raging downpour of the storm had changed to the steady patter of a light drizzle, and Ksiuta slept on soundly, shivering once in a while. *I should leave,* Kolomeitsev thought. *It'll be better to go while she's asleep. There might be tears, pointless questions: "When will I see you? Will you write?" The whole thing will be ruined.* But he still felt bad about abandoning her, unprotected, covered only with gooseflesh. Kolomeitsev pulled off his shirt and covered Ksiuta. Then, trying not to wake her, he climbed out of the green cave.

The wet shaggy wolfhound, it turned out, was not in his shelter, but nearby, at the entrance to theirs. He didn't growl at Kolomeitsev but looked away.

A strong personality. Kolomeitsev laughed, and wearing only his undershirt, he strode off, glad his body was exposed to the last, slightly stinging drops. Before stepping into the taiga from the meadow grass, he wanted to look back, but he suppressed the desire. There, in the haystack, covered with his shirt, slept merely one of the many adventures in his long life, and he had the rest of his life before him.

The sun's rays broke through the clouds and penetrated the green cave, waking Ksiuta. She saw the shirt tossed over her body and Charlie's sad face poking into the haystack.

"He's gone . . ." Ksiuta whispered, pressing the sleeve to her lip. It had a strong male odor. "Completely gone. But he covered me with his shirt, he felt sorry for me. . . ."

Of course, she had known that the stranger would leave, but she still didn't want to believe it. She put on the shirt and crawled out. Squinting in the sun, she hung up her wet clothes on some branches and thought: *While the grasses are wet, I have to keep raking, or it'll rot. Rake until it dries.*

And she began raking the hay, which she'd mowed together with the stranger who had disappeared. The shirt felt strange on her shoulders, implanting in Ksiuta a small hope that he would return. But the hay was already raked up, Ksiuta's clothes were dry, the sun was setting, and still the stranger did not appear.

Ksiuta felt no resentment toward him, she had no sense of shame about what had happened, but she was afraid of her father. Ivan Kuzmich loved Ksiuta, and he could forgive her many things. But he would never forgive the fact that her first man was someone whose name she didn't even know. In order to understand her, her father would have to become her, and that was impossible.

Ksiuta dressed and, putting the shirt over her arm, she went down to the riverbank where she had met the stranger. But he wasn't there either, and Ksiuta realized he would never return. At first she wanted to throw the shirt into the river, but then she changed her mind and hid it in the hollow of a larch that stood on the slope. Then she hid her face in Charlie's and whimpered in fright, "What will happen now?"

Returning to Belaya Zaimka, Ksiuta tried to forget the incident, but it came back to haunt her almost every night just before she fell asleep. Her father noticed something was wrong with his daughter. She no longer looked forward to parties or the movies in Shelaputinki but preferred to spend the evening at home and asked him herself to read the Bible. She became excited only once, when some people, carrying the same kind of hammers as the stranger's, came to the farm and asked for milk. But the stranger was not among them.

Yet Ksiuta did see Kolomeitsev again, in late autumn. It happened when she went into Shelaputinki for groceries. Kolomeitsev was sitting near the village store in a jeep, poring over some well-worn maps and waiting for the driver he had sent in for cigarettes. His face was preoccupied, alien. Sensing that he was being watched, Kolomeitsev looked up and saw Ksiuta, clutching a few packages of soap and a bag of nails to her chest in bewilderment. Kolomeitsev immediately recognized her yellow-flecked eyes.

"Ah, it's you," he said, without getting out and noticing with relief that the driver was already coming out of the store with the cigarettes. "Hello."

"Hello," Ksiuta barely managed to get out.

The driver got in the car and, sensing his boss's predicament, immediately switched on the ignition.

"Your shirt . . . you forgot your shirt. . . ." Ksiuta approached the truck.

"Keep it as a memento," Kolomeitsev said with a strained smile. "Well, God willing, we'll see each other again."

The driver, interpreting this as a command, stepped on the gas, and the car sped away. The paper wrapping opened in Ksiuta's hands, and the glistening nails fell into the dust. As she bent over to pick them up, she became nauseated and felt the first jabbing pain in her stomach. She knew instantly it was a child beginning inside her. Ksiuta didn't tell her father about it, and she had no girl friends in the village. She carried the secret inside her, listening to this other life quietly developing. Even her eyes became totally different, as though turned inward.

Once that winter Ksiuta was passing the river on skis and found the larch in which she had hidden the stranger's shirt. She brushed off the snow and pulled it out, ice-covered and faded. It no longer smelled of sweat, which made Ksiuta feel better for some reason.

In the spring she went back and took the shirt out from the hollow once more. It had thawed and was permeated with the aroma of wet wood, apparently having forgotten the smell of its former owner. Ksiuta had almost forgotten about him, too, thinking only of the child stirring within her, and the shirt's very existence disturbed her. She went down to the river, where the last chunks of ice floated, twisting and capsizing. Swinging her arms, she heaved the shirt out. It fell on and almost covered a smallish gray piece of ice, its checked sleeves dangling in the water. Together, they drifted away slowly, almost reluctantly, but soon they were caught up by a swift current, spun, and swirled, and the water-darkened sleeve flew up for a second, as if to say farewell, and then disappeared around the bend.

When Ksiuta fell at Ivan Kuzmich's feet and told him she was pregnant, the old man was astonished: Ksiuta hardly ever went into the village, and she was always under his watchful eye.

"Who?" he rasped, feeling a shame he had never experienced before. "Who?"

Ksiuta was silent. She couldn't tell him that she didn't even know the man's name. That would make her disgrace even greater in her father's eyes. She remained before Ivan Kuzmich on her knees, shielding only her belly with her hands.

"Grishka, the driver?" Ivan Kuzmich shouted fiercely. "That lowlife? I'll kill him."

"Not him . . . not him . . ." Ksiuta wept, grabbing her father by the boots.

"Well, it wasn't Tikhon. . . ." Old man Belomestnykh recalled the berry commissioner and suddenly thought: *But the old goat still sees women.* Ivan Kuzmich grabbed Ksiuta's hair and pulled her toward him, terrifying her with his blood-engorged eyes. "Tikhon?"

And Ksiuta, without realizing what she was doing, trying only to end her father's cruel interrogation in any way she could, whispered, "Yes, him . . ."

Ivan Kuzmich choked with hatred and disgust, imagining his daughter with the potbellied sixty-year-old berry commissioner, stinking of essence. The stable world of Ivan Kuzmich's life with his daughter crumbled and collapsed, leaving only unbearable shame.

He ordered Ksiuta to gather her things, and he took her in the cart to the Old Zima hospital, not uttering a single word along the way. As a farewell he simply said, "Here's your passport. Here's money to start with. Forget the road that leads to me. I am no father to you; you are no daughter to me."

Then Ivan Kuzmich drove to the house of the berry commissioner, tethered his horse to the telegraph pole, and went into the yard with a shotgun. It was twilight. A light burned in the open window;

he could hear voices. Ivan Kuzmich trampled the lovingly planted dahlias as he approached the window with stealthy steps.

The berry commissioner was in his undershirt and underpants; his portly wife in rollers and a half-open robe, revealing her fat yellowish breasts. They were sitting at a table near the samovar, drinking tea with sugar and playing cards. Their faces were covered with beads of perspiration and expressed good-natured slyness.

"And I'll take your club with a trump sixie, Polina Kharitonna." The berry commissioner grinned with an air of triumph.

"But I'll find a sixie of clubs for you, Tikhon Tikhonovich. . . . You'll have to cover that with a trump ace . . ." his wife replied sassily.

The berry commissioner sniffled and scratched his bald pate, and Ivan Kuzmich suddenly saw very clearly: *No, it's not him. . . . Ksiuta deceived me. But who then? It doesn't matter. She'll crawl back with the kid and tell me then. . . .*

And the berry commissioner was never to know how close he had come to this undeserved punishment. Ivan Kuzmich headed back for Belaya Zaimka, racking his brains. *Who? Who?*

Afraid that his disgrace would become public, he told everyone in Shelaputinki that he had sent Ksiuta to enroll in a technical school. But it had been difficult for Ksiuta to hide her condition from the women's eyes, and everyone guessed why she had disappeared. Ivan Kuzmich had no idea that people—especially those widows whose advances he had once spurned—were giggling and gossiping behind his back.

He longed to go to Zima to find out what had happened to Ksiuta, but he waited out the time; he knew she would come back on her own. Charlie often lay by the gate, staring at the road with hopeful eyes.

"Ksiuta will come back. . . . She has nowhere to go . . ." Ivan Kuzmich would say, picking burrs from Charlie's matted fur. And when he sat down to eat, he tried not to look into his wife's eyes, reproaching him from the purplish photograph.

Then, as usual, he read the Bible, aloud out of habit—even though there was no one with him.

CHAPTER · 4

The berry commissioner's calves once again embraced the bottle of essence, and Ksiuta and the child were in the cab. The truck was already traveling through the taiga, which spread to the left and right as far as the eye could see. The berry commissioner thought about the approaching meeting with old Belomestnykh and sighed heavily. *He'll kill me. . . . He thinks I'm the father. The girl got me mixed up in this. . . . I have to help her. But how?*

Aside from everything else, Ksiuta's somewhat confused account of her meeting with the black-bearded stranger set the berry commissioner to musing about life in general and his own in particular. *I'm a fine one to talk,* thought Tikhon Tikhonovich. *Haven't things like that ever happened to me? How many times have I walked all over girls as though they were garbage because I was too busy rushing toward my bright future, so to speak? Who knows, maybe I have children that I don't know about, walking this earth?*

Tikhon Tikhonovich Tugikh did not at all look like a man who secretly suffered from a guilty conscience, but he did occasionally, as does everyone who hasn't lost his conscience completely. There are different kinds of guilt inflicted by conscience: Sometimes it's very tiny, brief, other times it's bigger and longer, but scratch almost any person, and you'll find at least one incident from the distant past that inspires regret. It's not that you constantly think about what you did wrong, but the guilt wanders throughout your whole body like a shard of glass, and it'll stick you—just when you least expect it. For some time now Tikhon Tikhonovich had shielded himself with his dough-like body from the many jabs of the outside world, but in the folds of that flesh lived a painful, special guilt that jabbed him from within.

Many years ago his unit of Komsomol members was sent to the upper reaches of the Lena River to rid the taiga of rich peasants, called kulaks. In those days Tikhon Tikhonovich, whose nickname was then Tisha, worked as a grease monkey at the Zima depot, and he accepted with pride the chance to become a representative of the dictatorship of the proletariat—somehow he forgot he was a peasant rather than a true proletarian. The order came down to find one kulak for every ten peasants and then to exile them, as Tisha was severely instructed by their swollen-eyed leader. Because of the fact that they were already in Siberia, the kulaks could not be exiled very far (after all, they couldn't be exiled to European sections like Ryazan or Smolensk), so they were relocated within Siberia. On the Lena River the kulaks from downriver villages were shipped under guard by barge to some upriver village, and then the same barge with the same guards brought upriver kulaks to a downriver village.

At their new locations the former kulaks had to sign a paper stating that they wouldn't move away, but they worked without trying to get settled or put down roots because they hoped to return. So many from the downriver villages died and were buried in the cemeteries of the upriver villages, and vice versa, and both sets of deceased were put into the earth next to strange grandfathers and great-grandfathers, even though the remains of their own ancestors were a stone's throw away.

Throughout this class struggle a most active role was played by twenty-year-old Siberian proletarian Tisha Tugikh, still with a wasp waist, encircled by a stiff and squeaky gun belt. But Tisha and his comrades, despite their energetic search, just couldn't scrape up the required number of peasants to dekulak. Of course, there were real kulaks—those who kept hired laborers and squeezed them in their fist (*kulak*), which was probably why they were called kulaks. Tisha didn't feel sorry for them and thought that their social punishment was just. But there weren't many of them. In the Lena areas of Tisha's jurisdiction, anyone who was needy could hunt, fish, or prospect, and therefore, there were almost no hired workers and consequently not so many kulaks. Tisha had a particularly difficult time finding any in Teteryovka—a one-street village in the upper reaches of the Lena, where among 120 villagers, as though for spite, there wasn't a single kulak.

The local activist, Spirin, always ready to denounce anyone, hinted that the Zalogins were suitable for dekulakization, but he did it so furiously that Tisha was suspicious.

The Zalogin house stood on the edge of the village. It was an enormous five-walled wooden house, the only one in Teteryovka with an iron roof. Its bizarrely carved window fretwork had shutters painted a vivid light blue, with heart-shaped cutouts. In the six windows that opened on the street stood white-pink geraniums in metal cans which had once held prerevolutionary multicolored fruit drops called montpensiers. In the evenings the shutters were closed with heavy bolts. The solid fence was made of grooved boat planks, and there were wide gates with faceted posts. Everything was solid and dependable, and this, apparently, irked Spirin, whose roof leaked steadily and whose fence listed.

When Tisha came to the Zalogins for the first time, as part of his initial investigation, there was no one in the house except Dasha —the youngest daughter of old man Sevastyan Prokofich. She was rolling dough for *pelmeni* and cutting out circles with a glass. Her arms were covered up to the elbows in flour, and there was a sprinkling of flour in the tan hollow between her breasts, which changed to white behind the low neck of her dress. Her dimpled cheeks glowed through the flour's gentle fuzz. And Dasha's eyes were so green that they resembled two pieces of malachite.

"Help me make the *pelmeni*!" Dasha called provocatively. "Or don't Red commanders know how?"

In Dasha's eyes the man with the gun belt, having arrived from the unknown distant regional center, was naturally an important boss, but she wanted to show him that she wasn't afraid.

"Why wouldn't they know how?" Tisha smiled as he wielded the rolling pin, put the edge of the glass on the dough, and cut out a very neat circle. After putting a bloody pinch of meat filling in the middle, he deftly joined the edges with his fingers and rolled the *pelmen,* trying to do it the way his mother had taught him—so that it looked like a child's translucent ear. Then he showed it to Dasha.

"Like that?"

"Like that, but not quite." Dasha laughed. "The dough's too

thick; it isn't rolled out enough. The filling doesn't shine through."

"But you shine through all over . . ." Tisha said to her. Dasha was standing directly in a golden column of light, filled with swirling flour and dust, and her dress was iridescent, breathing as if it were alive, and under its streaming, scintillating flow the dark outline of her light, lithe body was visible.

Dasha smelled of flour, dough, meat, onion, love. Tisha, not doubting the irresistibility of his gun belt, drew Dasha toward him by the waist, but he immediately received a slap on the cheek—not a hard one, but painful.

"Don't rush, Red Commander," Dasha said with a smile that forgave all.

Boots clattered on the porch, scraping mud from their soles, and voices were heard. Dasha ran up to Tisha, pulled off her scarf, and wiped the traces of her floury hand from his cheek. That quick, stealthy movement immediately created a tiny secret between them.

Old man Zalogin, mother Zalogin, three of their sons and daughters-in-law entered, and a bunch of kids piled in after. The room, which was previously quite spacious, became crowded. Everyone was back from the fields. Dasha began shaking the *pelmeni* off the board into a pot of water, rapidly boiling on the fire.

"I'm here to do a survey." Tisha breathed uneasily under the questioning stares of the Zalogins and pulled out from his jodhpurs a notebook with a pencil in it.

"Why haven't you seated our guest, Darya?" severely demanded Sevastyan Prokofich, who had, of course, already seen Tisha in Teteryovka—you can't miss anyone on a single street!—and knew what he was here for.

"Please accept our hospitality," said old woman Zalogin, but not in a very hospitable voice.

Tisha himself was an indigenous Siberian, and he knew that conversation wouldn't start without a glass of vodka. The steaming *pelmeni* were dumped from the pot into a large, colored bowl in the middle of the table. Dash a poured first-distillation vodka, clean as dew, from a bottle.

"What do you make it from?" Tisha asked despondently.

"From wheat, son," Sevastyan Prokofich replied. "It's good made from wheat."

"That means you have the coil and the rest of the apparatus?" Tisha continued with even greater despondency.

"How else?" Sevastyan Prokofich fingered a *pelmen* with dignity and popped it into his beard.

"You'll have to turn it in," Tisha said, tossing back his glass and feeling the pleasant burning of the first shot.

"We'll turn it in if there's an order to that effect."

"There's been one for a long time now," Tisha said, pouring another.

"Well, they take a long time sailing out here, those orders." Sevastyan Prokofich squinted. "The Lena is a long river. . . . As for turning in the grain—have no worries. Darya, bring the receipts; they're gathering dust behind the icons."

Tisha carefully examined the receipts; there was nothing out of order.

"Turn in your entire still to the village soviet tomorrow and pay the fine," Tisha said.

"Then let all the others turn theirs in," old woman Zalogin countered.

"Who else has one?" Tisha raised his pencil.

"The Zalogins have never been informers," said Sevastyan Prokofich, throwing a violent look at his old woman. "You go peek into other people's sheds by yourself, son. We're not going to help you."

"How many cattle do you have?" Tisha asked.

"Three horses and three cows, through the grace of God."

"How about pigs and sheep?"

"About ten each. And one she-goat, if that counts as cattle."

"How about chickens and geese?"

"Who can count them! We have a big family, we barely fit in this house. When we make soup, with good stock, that's one noisy cock and his mate gone. And the street in the village belongs to everyone. All the chickens and geese are mixed up—sometimes you kill a goose and don't even know if it's yours or a neighbor's. . . ." Sevastyan Prokofich squinted again.

"You live well," Tisha said, scratching behind his ear with the pencil.

"And is it bad for a peasant to live well?" Sevastyan Prokofich answered dryly. "I didn't live like this my whole life, you know. I drove a boat along the Lena and worked as a hired hand. But nobody's ever worked for me! Everything I have, I got with my own two hands. Look at these hands: I can pick up steaming *pelmeni* and not get burned —that's how rough they are from work."

"Which side were you on in the Civil War?" Tisha asked hopefully.

"No one's. I was too old. I was already sixty then, son. . . ."

"What do you mean, no one's?" The old woman forced herself into the conversation again. "Don't you remember how you hid wounded Red soldiers?"

"That was because they were wounded, not because they were Red," Sevastyan said, angrily withdrawing into himself.

When Tisha was leaving, Dasha ran out into the yard after him to hold the dog, which had been let off its chain. Unexpectedly she whispered in his ear, "Come to Crooked Hill tomorrow at noon. . . . I'll be picking bird cherries. . . ."

The bird cherry trees were a marvelous sight on Crooked Hill. The bushes were weighed down by the black fruit, sprinkled with last night's rain. You could pick a big bunch, toss a handful of berries into your mouth, and using your tongue to separate the flesh from the pits, cover your whole palate with a tart, sweet film. Tisha bent the bushes down to make it easier for Dasha to pick, and she squealed like a child when the rain from the branches showered down on her, creeping in under her neckline and trickling down her back. Two baskets were quickly filled.

"Too many leaves!" Dasha sighed. "I'll have to pick over them."

And suddenly she strode over to Tisha, put her hands on his shoulders, and pressed up against him. Her malachite eyes were so close to his that he could see thin veins in them, as if they were real malachite. . . .

They lay next to each other between the two baskets filled with berries. A clumsy movement of Tisha's turned over a basket, and the berries fell on Dasha's naked breasts. Tisha kissed the berries from her.

They met several times in the bird cherry groves or in the hawthorns, leaving separately to hide their love from people.

"You won't do anything bad to our family, will you?" Dasha asked once. "We're no kulaks, Tisha."

And then a nasty thought crept into Tisha's mind: What if Sevastyan Prokofich had sent him his daughter as a bribe? He was a bootlegger, and even though he personally broke up his still and paid the fine, what if he had a second still? And even though he didn't have hired help, Zalogin was rich, compared to the others. Tisha tried to chase away the thought of Dasha's insincerity, but it kept returning; it was a convenient thought.

Tisha was recalled to the regional center and mercilessly worked over by the commissar with swollen eyes for weakening before the kulak element. He banged the burnished handle of his Nagant pistol on a mahogany table, which he'd confiscated somewhere. The surface of the table was covered with dents and scratches—probably from frequent banging by the Nagant.

"We're not asking for anything beyond the call of duty, just what's expected from you. In Sychyovka you found kulaks? You did. In Krutogorye you found them? You did. And in Teteryovka you can't? What does that mean? Does it mean that Teteryovka is a paradise and already has a classless society? Open your eyes. . . . You've been hanging around there a whole month, and apparently you've been corrupted by the local situation."

The commissar, coughing from his endless cigarettes, pulled a pitcher over and was about to pour a glass of water but he stopped: The pitcher was empty, and a fly buzzed in it, noisily striking the glass walls. The commissar grew even angrier with Tisha, who he now regarded as a witness to the impotence caused even by this trifling incident. He asked grimly, "Are you from kulak stock yourself? Watch out, we'll check."

In those days such words were threatening, and Tisha returned to Teteryovka after this brainwashing and held a council with two local activists. The first was Eriugin—a former Red partisan, one of the poorest people in the village because he had one leg and lived alone.

His poverty, however, had never caused him to envy, typically of those who are made poor by inability rather than bad luck. The other was Spirin, who was eaten with the constant envy of the slightly better-off. Spirin was also an invalid from the Civil War—the fingers of his wounded left hand did not bend. According to rumors, Spirin had shot himself. He had fought with the Reds for a short time before being wounded, but when they won, he acted as though he had routed Kolchak single-handedly. Surrounded by children, one younger than the next, and graced with a slovenly wife who was always pregnant, Spirin grew embittered.

Tisha put the list of Teteryovka's inhabitants on the table and sadly but firmly said, "Well, let's look for kulaks."

Eriugin scraped his cane on the floor.

"First tell me, what's a kulak?"

"What's the matter, you were a Red partisan and you don't know?" Tisha tried to avoid the question.

"I know, but I want to hear it from you."

"A kulak is someone, well, who exploits someone else's labor," Tisha said reluctantly, his ears still ringing with "Are you from kulak stock yourself? Watch out, we'll check."

"Well, and where do we have any exploiters in Teteryovka?" Eriugin shook his head. "Nobody's ever had any farmhands here. No wealth here, just people who aren't hungry, is all."

Spirin could not contain himself. Eriugin and his wooden leg annoyed him; this was a real wound, proof positive, and Spirin knew the things people said behind his back about his self-inflicted wound.

"Tell me this, Comrade Eriugin, do you have a horse?"

"No."

"A cow?"

"No."

"So why can't you identify the class of those who have two and even three horses and cows? Isn't that exploitation of animals, Comrade Eriugin?" Spirin was excited.

"You have a horse and a cow. Does that make you an exploiter?" Eriugin asked.

"I have only one horse!" Spirin angrily crooked one finger of his good hand. "And one cow!" He bent another finger and then straightened both. "And with nine mouths to feed that's not exploitation but necessity. But when you have three horses, like the Zalogins..." Spirin triumphantly bent three fingers. "And three cows!" Spirin almost choked, either because he was so angry at the Zalogins or because the fingers of his left hand wouldn't bend, interfering with his counting. "That's your out-and-out exploitation!"

Spirin's use of the name Zalogin, which stuck like a bone in his throat, stunned Tisha. Something was being inexorably set in motion, to drive Dasha away from him. *Does Spirin know or not?* Tisha thought warily.

"Anyway, that's exploitation of animals not of people, Comrade Spirin," Tisha said placatingly. "No one's been dekulaked for that yet. . . ."

"I have two mutts, two, not one, hear that, Spirin!" Eriugin laughed heavily. "If I had one, that would be necessity, and two makes it exploitation? Are you going to dekulak me for an extra dog?"

But Spirin's eyes were staring at Tisha, boring through him like drills.

He knows, Tisha thought.

"The Zalogins exploit people, too," Spirin maintained stubbornly.

"And who is that? They all do all the work themselves. They don't have any hired help." Eriugin shrugged.

"They exploit one another! That's how! Otherwise, how would they end up with three horses and three cows!" Spirin shouted triumphantly.

Those three horses and three cows just won't give you any peace, thought Tisha but said nothing.

"You exploit your wife when she patches your pants," Eriugin said.

"And don't the Zalogins run a still?" Spirin wouldn't give up.

"Then our whole village is filled with kulaks . . ." Eriugin countered.

Spirin lowered his voice and added stealthily, "And besides all that, the Zalogins lend money and then take it back in labor."

"What's that?" Tisha asked, tensing up. This business was smelling of kulak behavior.

"This is how. . . . About three years ago during a fierce winter old man Zalogin loaned me a sack of grain, and then in the summer, when he met me, he stared. In a special way. 'What are you staring at?' I said. 'Reminding me of my debt?' 'Don't worry about it,' he says. 'You and your wife do some mowing for me, and it's all even.'"

"Well, and what did you do?"

"What, me? Naturally, I mowed. . . ."

"And did he forget the loan?"

"He did, but I didn't. . . . Isn't lending money and then getting it back in labor the purest exploitation?" Spirin grabbed the list, pointed at it with his mutilated hand, and bored his eyes into Tisha again.

"And look, there are exactly twelve Zalogins! There's your twelve kulak souls! Exactly!"

"Have some fear of God. Three are just children," Eriugin said.

"Apples don't fall far from the tree. A kulak's kids are tomorrow's kulaks. Except there won't be any tomorrow for them. And you mention God an awful lot, Comrade Eriugin. God, as you know, does not exist, so there's no reason to fear Him. I naturally value your achievements, Comrade Eriugin, but sometimes I'm amazed at how many blemishes you still carry with you. You can't get by on past services. You have to perform new services for the Soviet regime," Spirin said, his voice rising threateningly.

Then Spirin cast a glance at Tisha and added, "And by the way, in a social cause you must override personal considerations, Comrade Tugikh."

And Tisha, despite his inner qualms, gave in. . . .

The muzhik committee went to the Zalogin house and explained things to Sevastyan Prokofich with gloom and guilt: "It's this way, the times are very hard now, and even though we know you're no kulak, somebody has to be the kulak, suffer for society; since you're the richest in the village—and don't judge us too harshly—we've chosen you to be the sacrifice, and then, you'll see, the times will change and you'll be back." Sevastyan Prokofich's elder sons went for their shotguns, but their father stopped them with a movement of his hand: "Bloodshed leads to more bloodshed, and that never did anyone any good." Sevastyan Prokofich ordered his sons to slaughter a calf, and for three days his house was open to any guest. The whole village drank moonshine, sang songs, and wept as they saw the Zalogins off.

Sevastyan Prokofich was an expansive soul, and even when Spirin entered his house, he didn't lift an eyebrow—everyone was honored and had a place—but he did laugh bitterly when Spirin's eyes started darting around the room, running his hands over the honestly hewn walls and the enormous chest of drawers that had been brought in by boat from distant parts. Only two people didn't come: Eriugin, who was dead drunk in his bachelor shanty, and Tisha, who was so ashamed to face Dasha that he went into the taiga to hunt ducks on the lakes. And it was just Tisha's luck that he came back from the taiga not after, but right as, the Zalogins were meeting the barge. So he saw Dasha once again—but only from a distance. The barge had come from downriver, bringing another dekulaked family to be settled in Teteryovka; there were about fifteen of them. The first one off the boat was a tall, erect woman, holding an icon in front of her. After her came young men and women with bundles and sacks, a squealing piglet struggling in one of the sacks, then two boys, dragging a samovar by the handles on each side—it shone gaily amid the general unhappiness. Last off was the old man, the same age as Sevastyan Prokofich, holding a kerosene lamp in one hand, and a collection of family photographs under glass in the other. The old man put down the lamp on the ground, carefully leaned the photographs against his leg, so that their unfamiliar faces looked at the faces of the gathered Teteryovka villagers, and bowed to the people.

"Where did they bring you from?" Sevastyan Prokofich asked the old man.

"From Vostryakovo," he replied without grumbling, as if this was the way it should have been.

"And where are we going?" Sevastyan Prokofich asked the homely and pathetic-looking escort, carrying an equally homely and pathetic-looking rifle.

"The same place, Vostryakovo," the escort said, sniffling.

"Upriver, then downriver—that's our life. Don't be so glum, old man, the people are friendly there."

Sevastyan Prokofich calculated—it wasn't that far, just three hundred versts—and he and the gray-bearded man came to an agreement: His family would live in the Zalogin house, and the Zalogins in theirs. And someday, God willing, everything would return to normal.

The old woman from Vostryakovo came up to Sevastyan Prokofich and handed him her icon. "Take it, dear man. For a century this icon lived in our house. Let it stay there now."

"Then you take ours," said Sevastyan Prokofich. "Let it wait for us, too."

And so they exchanged icons, even though the one from Vostryakovo was probably richer in ornamentation.

Standing on the steep slope in the shade of a larch, a sack slung over his shoulder, full of needlessly killed ducks, Tisha saw Dasha, looking at no one, carrying two fruit drop jars with white-pink geraniums. She looked broken and stood sharply apart from the rest of the family, who maintained a somber dignity. The confiscation, despite Spirin's attempts to give the Zalogins a hard time, was done tenderly, without rancor, and touched only the immovable property and cattle.

When the Zalogins loaded the barge, the disembarkation was repeated, only in reverse: First on board was old woman Zalogin with the icon, followed by the sons and daughters-in-law carrying sacks, one of which also held a squealing piglet, two boys also dragged a samovar, and the head of the family carried a collection of family photographs behind glass. Standing at the barge's prow, Sevastyan Prokofich said, "Don't think badly of us!" and the barge set off. No tears were shed by the well-wishers or the Zalogin family; everything had been wept dry over vodka and the slaughtered calf. Tisha watched the barge from the bank and saw Dasha's scarf fluttering in the wind, and he didn't want to live. Feathers from the Zalogins' pillows bobbed on the water near the shore for some time before they were carried away by the current.

The Vostryakovo family didn't get the Zalogins' house—Spirin grabbed it up for himself and gave them his. The barge came back with a letter from the Zalogins, which made it clear that they had settled in the empty house, the local folk had welcomed them kindly, and there were no problems, even though they were depressed.

Tisha decided to get out of social work and applied for work as a lumberjack in the Sayans, as far away as possible. He tried to forget everything that happened in Teteryovka, but he couldn't get rid of his guilt. In one of the newspapers that infrequently reached the lumber camp, Tisha read a word he had never heard before: *peregib*, which means "excess" but is literally "overbend," and he thought: *What an accurate word that is; nothing that's been overbent can be unbent.* Once, as he jumped from log to log, using a gaff to break up a logjam in the river, Tisha slipped and got badly crushed by the logs. He changed jobs many times after that, for some reason working mostly in state supply offices. Finally, he became the berry commissioner in whom the former Tisha was unrecognizable.

Tikhon Tikhonovich picked a wife from the merchant class—convenient for purposes of family income. They didn't have children, or any great love either, and for some reason all his women friends were involved in commerce and differed little from his wife. Tikhon Tikhonovich drank and played around, and occasionally he recalled the bird cherry grove in Teteryovka as perhaps the best part of his life, which he himself had turned his back on.

Sometimes it gnawed at him: He and Dasha had been inexperienced; they weren't careful; what if there had been a child? But Tikhon Tikhonovich never did learn the subsequent fate of the Zalogins. He could have found out, but he was afraid to. Those words spoken in the regional office—"Are you from kulak stock yourself? Watch out, we'll check"—had broken him. And now it was too late to find out.

Even though Tikhon had done no wrong to Ksiuta, he was afraid of having to talk with old man Belomestnykh, as though he would be held responsible by him for Dasha. The truck carrying the berry commissioner and his jumbled reflections on the past; and the essence hugged between the legs of his police jodhpurs; and Ksiuta and her innocent child; and the mushroom-picking old man, the young geologist, and Grisha, the driver, rumbled toward Belaya Zaimka.

CHAPTER · 5

Threat hard-packed road connecting the villages ended after the fork to Shelaputinki. Here began the real deep woods taiga road, on which two cars or even two carts couldn't pass at the same time. Dark, stagnant water filled the deep ruts formed by tractors, and branches, blown down by the wind, lay across the road. The taiga enveloped the truck, as though trying to swallow it forever into its dark belly. Branches of larch and pine lashed the heads of the passengers who didn't duck in time and forced their way into the driver's cab, then straightened out with a ferocious crackle. The wheels repeatedly stuck in the clay, whistling as they spun and splashing mud. They had to stop and toss small branches under them and sometimes even use a lever. Every time the truck lunged into another puddle, the bottle of "essence" leaped between the legs of the berry commissioner.

The young geologist put aside his Saint Exupéry since reading was impossible—the letters danced before his eyes. Strangely enough Ksiuta's child didn't cry; it seemed he had been born for these roads.

The little old mushroomer tormented Grisha by banging his spindly fist on the roof; this meant he saw some unusual mushroom on the side of the road. If Grisha stopped, the old man would scramble overboard with an agility amazing for his years and then quickly reappear in the back, triumphantly displaying some gigantic mushroom with yellowed pine needles on its cap. Finally, Grisha told him that they couldn't stop for every mushroom—the road was difficult enough as it was—and the mushroomer, peering over the side, merely groaned as marvels of nature sped past his very nose.

"Look at that mushroom coming, what a mushroom!" the little man said, sharply elbowing the geologist. "There she is, Mother Nature. How generous she is! How much kindness she has! People have ruined her with smoky businesses, but she doesn't seem to get mad. But what if she does get mad one day? . . . You're from far away, I see?"

"From Leningrad, grandpa," the geologist replied.

"Haven't been there, only seen pictures," the mushroomer said. "Not enough words for the beauty. But that beauty was built on bones. Even though Tsar Peter was a great man, of course, think how many he killed in those swamps. But nature built this wonderful milk agaric and didn't kill anyone for that beauty." And enjoying its perfection, the mushroomer twirled in his hands an enormous mushroom, smelling of the soil.

"I don't agree with you, grandpa," the geologist said. "What does all of nature stand on, if not bones? The entire surface of the earth is someone's bones. By the way, a few years ago right in these parts they discovered the bones of a mammoth. And not so long ago they came upon mounds of human bones. They thought it was a campsite from Neolithic times. But it turned out that the skull formation was modern. And your mushrooms are growing on all those bones, grandpa."

The little mushroomer mused. "It's true, but it's frightening. You can justify almost anything if you try to make the laws of history fit those of nature. On the other hand, it's not so frightening. Death walks by my side nowadays, but perhaps I'll come up as a milk agaric somewhere. . . ."

"Grandpa, do you believe in the immortality of nature or in God?"

"I believe in milk agarics," the mushroomer replied craftily. "Nobody's ever come back from the other world and told us what it's like, that world. Maybe that's what it was invented for, to make man fear punishment for his deeds in this world. Maybe there's no punishment at all, but the fear itself is a punishment while you're alive. Now that they've flown up into space, photographed the moon and the other planets, and didn't find any other world, there's less fear. And less fear means more sin."

"But how can you build things on fear, grandpa?"

"It depends on the kind of fear. If you're my boss and I'm afraid of you and I do your bidding, but I don't respect you, that's a bad fear, evil. It's bad for you, the boss, because I'll never come to love you, and when you die, I won't lift a finger and won't say a kind word.

And it's bad for carrying out orders because out of fear I'll carry out your orders stupidly; even if your orders are good, I'll spoil everything with my fear. And it's bad for me because out of fear I'll never blossom into a flower or grow up as a milk agaric, but I'll just curl up as a rusty leaf. And it's bad for the people because when they start to fear, it'll pass from one to the other, and soon there'll be a great fear, like an invisible fire. It won't seem as though anything's burning, but everything will end up as ashes.

"But there's another kind of fear, not forced on you but developed by a person himself—the fear of ending up before the final judgment, when you can't hide any of your sins from all-seeing eyes. That fear makes a person a person."

"That means you do believe in God, right, grandpa?"

"In a grandfather with a gray beard sitting in a cloud, no. I'm a grandfather myself, but I haven't become all-seeing, and I haven't met any all-seeing grandfathers either. You young folks, when you think of us grandfathers, either you think we're very stupid or you respect us for being too wise. But we grandfathers are all different, and sometimes stupidity and wisdom are all mixed up inside us, like they are in young people."

"But you spoke of all-seeing eyes on Judgment Day. Does that mean you think someone has eyes like that?"

"If you mean eyes to look around and see everything, well, nobody has that kind of eyes. But eyes to look inside yourself and see everything, that's the kind everyone should have, and everyone should fear the judgment that comes from himself. Our conscience is our God. And as for the other world, well, that's probably just a story, but a helpful story, to scare us. You need that scare, oh, do you need it, so that you'll be afraid of doing bad deeds. Aren't you afraid?"

"I don't know," the young geologist said uncertainly. "I don't do bad things; my father and mother brought me up right, grandpa. But I'm afraid I might not do good deeds."

"But that's a bad thing—not doing good ones. So you're right to be afraid. Now what is the human spirit—according to you, scientifically? Energy?"

"Yes, you could say that it's energy, spiritual energy."

"And does that spiritual energy ever disappear? You're reading a book. Who wrote it?"

"A Frenchman, Saint Exupéry."

"Never heard of him . . . Hugh de Flaubert and Gustave Maupassant I know, but that Zaperi, not yet. Is he alive?"

"No, he was a pilot. He crashed."

"He crashed, but his spiritual energy didn't. Because you, a person from a different country, sitting in the Siberian taiga far from France, are reading his book. Am I right?"

"Right."

"Well, then, think how many people there were, since the beginning, who were good, and even though they died, their spiritual energy lives on with us and acts on us sort of like the sun. I've never been to Leningrad, but I have been to Moscow. Some people come to Moscow with endless lists from all their family and friends and wear out their legs running through the stores, buying up everything from outboard motors to bras, and they never see Moscow. They run around like they've got the plague. Of course, they tried to give me lists, too, but I wouldn't pay any attention. The hell with bras, I thought, I'm too old to unfasten them now; I'd rather go to the museums. First I joined tour groups at the train station, but that was like being in a herd. I began going by myself. Sometimes I'd listen to some guide; other times I'd stand alone and look. Sometimes it's better when no one's explaining anything or forcing you to see things his way. And once I spent a long time looking at a portrait; I was really taken by it. Foreign. Therefore, a lot of people crowded around it. But with good reason. It showed a woman, and she was lost in thought, smiling with the corners of her mouth. How many centuries had she smiled for, damn it! and there I stood, and I felt something through her smile. . . . Energy. That's what that artist did with that smile. And then I thought: All good deeds, they're like a white cloud of spiritual energy over us, and they act on us. It was in that cloud that people began to find God. But there are also bad deeds. There were so many tyrants and petty bloodsuckers throughout history, and they also exuded energy, and it's also floating over our heads like a cloud, but it's a black cloud and it also affects us. We called it the devil in our stories. That's the whole solution. Now as to which cloud we help—the white or the black—that depends on our conscience. And if you don't add anything to the white cloud, you'll go up as empty smoke, and that smoke will join the black cloud anyway."

"You're chewing this fellow's ear off," grumbled Tikhon Tikhonovich, half-asleep. "I listen and listen to you, and there's one thing I don't understand: What if I'm no writer and no artist, then what can I add to that cloud since I don't write books or paint pictures?"

"Well, just smile, Tikhon Tikhonovich, just smile," the little mushroomer replied meckly.

C H A P T E R · 6

As for the little old mushroom man himself, he was known as Nikanor Sergeyevich Barkhotkin, and he was a kind of artist, although he didn't like to talk about it.

Now he was seventy-five, but his talent for drawing had first amazed his teacher back in the church parish school. He would sit in religion class, drawing Siberian houses, old women sitting on *zavalinki,* * peasants at the market, beggars by the church. The beggars came out particularly well: Nikanor's memory was tenacious, and whenever he saw a suffering face, it stuck in his mind until he could release it with pencil onto paper. He painted, too: fiery blue Siberian sunsets and sunrises; a yellow, sickly moon over a bluish fence; unmatched wedding horses with scarlet ribbons braided into their manes, dashing down a snowy street, pulling a painted sleigh, filled to the brim; a brown bear on its hind legs, eating raspberries. Paints were expensive, and Nikanor's father—a tightfisted Old Believer, who kept a shop, which the sign announced as CHANDLERY BARKHOTKIN AND CO., even though there was no Co.—grumbled a lot.

"You're not doing what you should be, son," Barkhotkin senior would say. "You should be learning the trade, not daubing pictures. What profit is there in them!"

Barkhotkin senior was especially irritated by Nikanor's passion for drawing beggars, and he ruthlessly tore up those pictures.

"What interest can you find in these wretches? A rich man would never in his life hang a picture like that in his house—it would remind him of someone else's misery—and as for a poor man, he'll want it

Zavalinki are earthen mounds built around peasants' huts. They help insulate and also serve as benches.

even less—a poor man wants to be a rich one and not think about poverty."

When the First World War started, Barkhotkin senior brought home a popular print, which he had bought at a bazaar. It depicted a hero of the times—the Don Cossack Kuzma Kruchkov—on his dashing steed impaling four Germans with his lance. The Germans' legs dangled in the air, and they looked as if they were roasting on a spit.

"Can you copy this? Only it has to be bigger. I'll give you oil paints and real canvas."

Before then, when Nikanor painted, he had used only water colors and paper; he'd never even dared think about real oil paints and canvas.

"I can," Nikanor said.

"And can you add another German to even it up?"

"I can," said Nikanor.

He huffed and puffed over the canvas for two weeks—and turned out a gigantic painting, just like the little print; only the nostrils of Kruchkov's steed flared even wider, and dangling from the lance there was a fifth German. For greater effect, Nikanor made him look like Kaiser Wilhelm himself.

"Now that's really something!" Barkhotkin senior said. "That's no beggar!"

And he hung the painting right in his store window so that no one would doubt his patriotism.

Once Karyakin, the haberdasher, came by and examined the painting for a long time. Then, smoothing his hair, greased with burdock oil and cut "in parentheses," he asked Barkhotkin senior, "Where'd you buy that?"

"My Nikanor daubed that up," Barkhotkin senior replied, for the first time feeling pride in his son's artistry.

"Will you sell it?"

"I won't sell it," Barkhotkin senior replied. "But if you want, Nikanor will paint you another. How much will you pay?"

The haberdasher offered three rubles. Barkhotkin senior demanded ten, they compromised on five, and Nikanor puffed away again, tongue sticking out, copying this time not from the little print but from his own canvas. The haberdasher was particularly pleased that the kaiser's eyes were popped out, like a lobster's. This was Barkhotkin junior's first painting sold. Next came the local butcher, the baker, and grocer. They all had to keep up with one another and wanted to have the same glorious Kuzma Kruchkov, and each asked that his be a little bigger, and that added to the price. It was boring to copy the same thing over and over, and Nikanor tried to vary the facial expressions of the Germans stuck on the lance, and made Kruchkov's horse variously bay, gray with dapples, and black, but the spirit of the work didn't change. Nikanor began hating the brave Cossack, and on one of his copies it seemed, if one looked closely, that Kruchkov's face was completely heartless, cruel, as though he had picked up Nikanor with his lance as well. And the poor kaiser's face appeared somehow sympathetic in its misery, but that, luckily, wasn't noticed by the buyer.

The district police chief himself paid a visit to the shop and patted Nikanor's locks with a fatherly hand. At that time a delegation was supposed to come to Zima to collect donations for the army in the field. Since it was thought that a general might come as its head, they wanted to welcome the delegation properly: with bread and salt and a portrait of the tsar. But the tsar's portrait at the town hall was exceedingly mediocre: an ordinary lithograph behind glass. The police chief wanted to excel, so he commissioned a portrait from Nikanor. It was a rush job. Nikanor was excused from school because of the importance of his assignment, and he slaved three days and three nights, drawing the tsar's mustache and imperial aiguillettes. When it was finished, the district chief approved, and it was brought out with the bread and salt to meet the train.

There wasn't any general. But Nikanor, specially dressed up for the occasion, was presented to the gallant lieutenant colonel, who had his arm in a black sling. He praised the boy for his diligence and even said, "Russia hasn't lost its talent, it hasn't."

So Nikanor had to paint a portrait of the tsar for the high school, and the railroad station, and even for the police precinct.

During the Civil War eighteen-year-old Nikanor was drafted into the White Army, and he served as a striker to Staff Captain Ochakovsky. The captain had a weakness for vodka, brawling, and pornographic postcards. One day he came across Nikanor sketching with a pencil and so ordered him to copy and enlarge several of the postcards. Nikanor copied everything required, with a grimace brought on by spiritual simplicity and provincial disgust. The staff captain later showed off the pictures to the other officers, remarking, "You see what a perverted striker I have. His face doesn't give anything away. He looks like a hick, but he's a satyr."

Nikanor didn't like the White Army, and after two fellow Zimans were flogged to death with ramrods before his very eyes, because they tried to miss during the shooting execution of some Red partisans, Nikanor switched to the Red Army. There he once again worked with his brush—painting slogans and posters depicting tiny, pathetic White Guards taking to their heels at the bayonet of a mighty Red giant with a star on his cap.

When Nikanor returned to Zima, Soviet power was firmly entrenched. Barkhotkin senior had been shot for collaborating with the Whites. Nikanor's portraits of the tsar and Kuzma Kruchkov had vanished. Under the New Economic Policy, Nikanor tried reopening his father's shop, but his heart wasn't in it. He was too trusting and clumsy in trade, and he barely made ends meet before finally going bankrupt. Nikanor began painting other portraits, and that helped buy food. In the thirties, when times took a turn for the worse, an important visitor suddenly noticed a secret mockery painted in a portrait of Nikanor's that hung at the railroad club. In reality it did not exist, and if there was a little crookedness in the image, it was due to the tiredness of his hand and nothing else. But this aroused interest in the background of the artist, and immediately everything came out: the tsar's portraits, the executed father, service in the White Army, and even Nikanor's unsuccessful NEPmanism.

He served a long sentence in the Far East—working first in a lumber camp, then on the construction of a railroad branch line. What little drawing he did was only for slogans and posters; he refused portraits, pleading lack of talent. Nikanor came across many good people there, and he heard quite a few wise conversations around campfires. Sometimes he didn't understand these conversations, but he was drawn to them, and he eventually noticed that he himself was getting wiser. After the war, when Nikanor was commissioned to design the village club next to the railroad branch line construction, he was given as an assistant a Japanese POW whose name was Kuroda-san. He was also an artist, but Nikanor realized immediately that Kuroda-san was a real artist, standing head and shoulders above him. In his pencil drawings Kuroda-san caught not only a physical likeness but something more important: the character of his subjects. And he did this without even drawing the insignificant details.

The chief of the guards was kindly disposed toward Kuroda for a portrait he had painted for his wife's birthday. He even gave him a large leather folder with sheets of beautiful Whatman paper and gave orders that Kuroda should not be kept from drawing anything he wanted, with the exception of classified sites.

"You good man, boss," Kuroda said.

"Now what kind of good man am I?" The chief guard laughed. "I'm supposed to be strict, not good."

"Is your job, boss, which is strict, not you yourserf, boss. The Lusski is a good man. When I go back Japan, I show my pictures of Lusski people to everyone—see what good faces. In our newspapers they draw Lusskis like animals. Plopaganda is bad, boss. Face is good."

"All right, we'll help you take your pictures back to Japan with you," the chief guard promised, and he subsequently kept that promise.

Kuroda-san and Nikanor became friends, understanding each other perfectly. There was just one thing that Kuroda-san could not understand at all: why such a good man as the boss had to guard such a good man as Nikanor, who was not Japanese and had not fought against Russia.

Kuroda-san was from Hiroshima and knew that the atom bomb had been dropped on his native city. He had a mother, a father, and two younger brothers there, and Kuroda didn't know what had happened to them.

"Maybe I olphan rike you, Nikanol-san," Kuroda would say. "What I do? I know one thing: I dlaw. Dlaw people. Why don't you dlaw people, Nikanol-san?"

Nikanor never replied. Since he had drawn Kuzma Kruchkov, his whole life had gone askew.

Kuroda left with all the other POWs, and soon after, Nikanor went home, too. He got a job as a watchman at a warehouse, lived a quiet bachelor existence, and developed a love of books. Once he ran across the former haberdasher, who had miraculously survived and was now a very old man earning a few extra coins selling odds and ends at the bazaar. The haberdasher, recalling Nikanor's talent for drawing, talked him into undertaking a profitable business—drawing swans on oilcloth. Nikanor left the warehouse and went into business; at first he improvised, but then he figured out how to ply his paints by stencil. What was important was that the swans be bright white with a rosy tinge and gilded beaks; that the cypresses, which Nikanor had never seen in real life, possess an emerald darkness; and that the moon's path on the water be silvery.

With the money he earned, Nikanor Sergeyevich bought himself a small house but didn't marry. He felt it was too late. He didn't think it was too late to read books, though, so he bought an enormous number of them and discovered for himself the authors whose names had been mentioned by the wise men around the campfires in the Far East. And once again Nikanor Sergeyevich felt himself growing wiser, but this belated wisdom existed separately from the swan oilcloths, which he continued to make, hating them almost as much as he had once hated Kuzma Kruchkov on his dashing steed. No one ever wrote him letters—there was no one to write them—but once the head of the post office himself called for Nikanor and personally had him sign for a large, valuable package from Japan.

The package contained a letter and books. The letter was written in Japanese, and naturally he couldn't understand a thing. But when he opened one of the books, he saw Kuroda on the jacket—still wiry but now with graying hair. He wore a jacket and tie and stood in front of some monument. Nikanor Sergeyevich expected to see the old, familiar drawings in the book, but he didn't find them. Instead, there were reproductions of Kuroda's new pictures, depicting people running down streets in the light of bloodred flames, mounds of mutilated bodies, children's eyes open wide in terror. He understood that this was Hiroshima.

Nikanor Sergeyevich managed to find a student in Zima who was spending his summer vacation there from Irkutsk, where he was studying Japanese, and he translated Kuroda's letter. Kuroda wrote that when he returned to Japan, he and the other POWs were held for more than a month by occupation intelligence made up of Japanese men of American origin. They interrogated them, trying to find out if the POWs had become Red spies. They took away all the drawings he had done in the camps, and these disappeared without a trace. Returning to Hiroshima, Kuroda learned that his family had perished on the terrible day the bomb was dropped. Kuroda married, had three children, and hoped one day to show them the railroad branch line on which he had worked with Nikanor.

Nikanor Sergeyevich looked once more at Kuroda's pictures, then at his swans, and he felt bad. He didn't have his own Hiroshima, but he did have something that was known to him alone. And it would die with him, not remaining for other people as a painting or something else.

That's when he decided to go to Moscow, where he saw the Mona Lisa's smile. He vowed not to take up painting oilcloth again and planned to go back to being a watchman. But the swan oilcloths were sticky and wouldn't release him. His only joys were reading and taking trips into the taiga to fish or hunt for mushrooms.

There was no worse moment for him than to come across his swans somewhere in a peasant's hut, where they would proudly bend their necks against the background of cypresses. . . . His flock of swans had flown around the world, and if, as the Russian saying goes, a word is not a sparrow—once it flies off, you can't catch it—then what can you do about the innumerable swans you've painted by stencil?

One thing saved Nikanor Sergeyevich: For all the trials that befell him, he did not become bitter about life, he did not stop loving people, and when he managed to break away from the beaks of his swans, he was an amiable, even a joyful man. He had not forgotten how to be surprised by the variety of things under the sky, even though they did not at all resemble the ones he drew on his oilcloths.

CHAPTER · 7

Ivan Kuzmich Belomestnykh had a premonition that day.

Zorka, his black cow with the white star on her forehead, was always docile when he milked her, but that morning she acted up a bit in her stall and knocked over the milk bucket with her hoof. Charlie followed him around too much, beseechingly rubbing against his boot, peering into his eyes. Ivan Kuzmich thought about how strange the face of a dog was: Even if a dog is happy, his eyes are still sad. He can't smile with his face, but only with his tail and by yelping. And when he really is sad, his eyes look so worried they seem to have sole responsibility for saving the world from some unknown threat. Ivan Kuzmich also thought about why a dog's life is so short. Probably it is because dogs are more sensitive than people—they die early not exactly from excessive emotion but from excessive premonition. Every time his master leaves the house, for even a short time, the dog imagines he's leaving forever. Yet no one knows how to wait like a dog, and there are stories about dogs waiting for dead masters at their gravesides. In his long life Ivan Kuzmich had buried many dogs, but Charlie would probably be the dog that outlived him and would wait for him to return from the dead. Yet sometimes Ivan Kuzmich kicked him in anger. Ivan Kuzmich wasn't cruel, but he frequently acted a bit harshly. Who can tell where harshness ends and cruelty begins? He had been harsh with his mother. Sometimes she would say, "Tell me, son, how are you?" and he would respond sullenly, "There's nothing to tell." He used to be harsh with his wife. She'd say, "Vanya, whisper just one tender word," and he'd mutter something ill-tempered. He loved his wife, but he was never tender with her; he considered tenderness a woman's feeling, not a man's. He brought up his sons strictly, making them kneel on dried peas in a dark corner and using his strap. Now it was too late to be nice to them. He had been harsh with Ksiuta, too, and what had come of that? All the tender things you didn't say can't be said now, and everything hard that you said can't be taken back. Now why had he tormented Ksiuta with questions, forcing her to make the ridiculous confession that the child's father was Tikhon Tikhonovich? Where could he have gotten such an idea, old fool that he was? Maybe because once, after his wife's death, he had gotten drunk and sinned with the daughter of a beekeeper, a young girl of Ksiuta's age. But why attribute your own sins to others? He himself had turned his daughter into an old maid. And sin was everywhere about, waiting in broad daylight, just looking for someone to turn into a sinner. Whatever happened couldn't be undone. But the child was innocent. *Why did you throw out your daughter, Ivan Kuzmich?*

Tormented by such thoughts, old Belomestnykh picked up his ax and started chopping wood, even though his woodshed was piled high. He set sawed logs with the fresher cut up, drove a heavy wedge into them, causing them to crackle and split in half, and then he chopped them into tiny pieces, so small as to be useless—just to make the work last longer. He often felt his age, but not when he undertook some hard labor.

Suddenly Charlie pricked up his ears and then rushed to the gate and began scratching at it. Ivan Kuzmich's ax froze in midair, and he heard the approaching throb of a truck. Cars rarely came to Belaya Zaimka, and Ivan Kuzmich went back to his chopping—who the hell cared who it was!

The truck rumbled nearby and stopped, invisible behind the high wall. The iron ring in the gate turned, and the berry commissioner, who stumbled into the yard, was immediately almost knocked to the ground by the dog.

"Come on, Charlie, boy, come on. Don't you know Tikhon Tikhonovich?" the berry commissioner muttered with nervous playfulness, and suddenly, spying the ax in old man Belomestnykh's hands, he babbled, "Ivan Kuzmich, what's the matter, what's the matter? I'm as pure as the driven snow before you. . . . Why the ax, why?"

"I'm chopping wood," Ivan Kuzmich said reluctantly. "What do you want here?"

"Nothing, Ivan Kuzmich, I don't want a thing," the berry commissioner continued babbling, backing toward the gate. "I brought Ksiuta to you with your grandson."

Ivan Kuzmich, without letting go of the ax, ran to the gate.

One thought flashed through the berry commissioner's mind: *He'll kill Ksiuta!*, and he grabbed the old man. "Ivan Kuzmich, why the ax? I ask you, why the ax?"

The old man finally realized what he meant. Sticking the ax in a nearby log, he charged through the gate, shoving aside the berry commissioner.

But Charlie had beat him to it and was already jumping around the cab, where he could see the white face of Ksiuta, who was clutching the infant to her.

Seeing her, Ivan Kuzmich regained some of his self-control, slowing to a measured tread, as though he had been expecting her that very day, in that very truck, and everything was just as it should be.

"Well, then, mother, let's have my grandson."

Ksiuta, sobbing, passed the bundle with the child's face peeking out to its grandfather.

"Just don't scratch him with your beard. . . ."

Ivan Kuzmich took the child, feeling an unaccustomed shakiness in his hands, exactly as he had he felt long ago, taking his first son from his wife's arms.

There was a lump in the old man's throat, but he controlled the tears welling up in his eyes and did not allow himself to go soft. He merely said, "Look at you—tiny but heavy! Siberian bone, it's heavy. Well, come on, Siberian, into your house."

Ivan Kuzmich stopped at the gate and bowed to his unexpected guests. "You all look tired. Please let me invite you all into the house. Let the mother rest, and I'll play lady of the house, beard and all."

"And I have some essence with me, for this occasion, Ivan Kuzmich," the berry commissioner warbled near him, still not believing that everything had gone so well.

"It fits the occasion," Ivan Kuzmich said. "I'll drink today myself." And then, bending over, he added so that no one else could hear, "Even though you're a bit of a coward . . . papa."

CHAPTER · 8

Everything they could find in the house was on the table: pickled *khairuz,* a Siberian salmon, sauerkraut, marinated bilberries, fried mushrooms, potatoes with oil and shallots. Even canned pineapple from faraway Mexico was opened for the great occasion. Grisha donated his beer, which was set in a pail of well water.

The guest of honor—the new, living little bundle of humanity —slept soundly behind the wall with his mother. Much essence had been drunk already, but the conversation around the table hadn't died down.

"Now, what is a child?" the berry commissioner said. "It is the chalice of nature, and we can fill it with poison or with . . . with . . ." Tikhon Tikhonovich stammered, seeking the right word.

"Or with essence," Grisha prompted jokingly.

"Yes, or with essence," the berry commissioner said, suddenly sad. "And what am I? I am a child, filled with essence."

"Some child." Ivan Kuzmich sniggered without malice.

"But Tikhon Tikhonovich is right," said the mushroomer. "Everything inside us, even now, was put there in our childhood. Now the only way I resemble a child is that I'm just as wrinkled. But if you look closely, the same little Nikanor is in there that my father used to pull by the hair. I don't like children who are ungrateful to their fathers, but to tell the truth, I'm very ungrateful to mine. Ungrateful because he made me afraid of him. He thought fear was the best teacher. True, fear teaches, but what? Subjugation to something you don't agree with. And if you bow before what you hate and despise, you become what you despise. There is no way back out of your fear. There is only one fear that should be instilled in a child—the fear of conscience. That fear is, you might say, a brave fear. And when the child grows up, and life tries to bend him with cowardly fears, they'll come up against the brave fear like a rock and leave him alone."

"You overestimate the power of a family upbringing, Nikanor Sergeyevich," Grisha said. "My father and mother didn't teach me anything bad or instill any fear in me. But when I left my backyard and went out into the streets, then I was afraid. Hoods playing with knives, drunks lying in the gutter, filthy language, our neighbor beating up his wife. I never saw anything like that at home, so I grew afraid I wasn't enough like the streets, but more like an indoor geranium facing barbed nettles. I got beaten up a few times for being a mama's boy. I was ashamed they thought I was weak. So I got myself a knife, hung blat over my boots."

"What's *blat*?" the geologist asked.

"That's when you roll up the cuffs tight and then drape the trouser leg over the boot. . . . Once I came home around dawn. My first vodka had made me throw up on the threshing-room floor. I took off my shirt in the garden and poured a bucket of cold water over myself. My mother came out and asked, 'What's that on your chest, Grishenka?' I looked, and my whole chest was covered with hickies; I couldn't even remember who had done it. I was only seventeen then. My mother picked up the wet shirt and started lashing me across the face—the first time she ever beat me! And I swore at her—a curse I learned on the street. My mother began to cry and asked, "Grish, did your father and I teach you all this?' Of course not, but their influence couldn't compete with my other teachers."

"Why did you pick such bad teachers?" Tikhon Tikhonovich grumbled. "Or don't good teachers walk around the streets?"

"They do," Grisha agreed. "But good teachers are usually boring; they set your teeth on edge. When you do find one who's not boring, you turn him into a god. And then if you find some tiny flaw that doesn't go with his lofty words, your god crumbles like a sand castle. You become afraid of lofty words; they all seem deceptive. Just hypocritical nonsense to hide a person's sins. But bad teachers always seem interesting, unusual; they don't preach. So you start imitating them. That's how I got caught at eighteen, playing around with a knife. Thank God I hadn't killed anyone yet. I might have—out of fear of being a coward."

"Now, Grisha, don't talk so badly of yourself. . . . Chase your essence with some bilberry juice," Tikhon Tikhonovich said. "You served your time for hooliganism, but it turned you into a man, not a killer. Everyone respects you."

"Fear saved me," Grisha said. "In prison I wasn't around a gang of hoods anymore. There were real killers in there. They wanted to be my teachers, too. That's when the fear of becoming a killer struck me. I wouldn't have gotten away with just a wet towel across the face from my mother; she would have cursed my soul."

"Now that's the brave fear I'm talking about, Grisha," Nikanor Sergeyevich said. He gulped down another glass of essence, followed it with a *khairuz,* and said to the geologist, "Now don't think I'm picking on the younger generation. It's better than ours. But how much better? It should be a lot better. Take all our good qualities, but don't take our faults. . . . What's your name?"

"Seryozha Lachugin," the young geologist replied.

"Your surname—let's be frank—isn't from the ranks of the nobility. What does your father do?"

"Professor of glaciology."

"What's that? I understand biology, I understand physiology, psychology, zoology, but I never heard of glaciology."

"It's the study of ice."

Nikanor Sergeyevich thought awhile.

"Everything began with ice, and it all will end with ice. . . . Aha, I see, then you need to study it. . . . Well, and what was your father's father?"

"A worker in the Putilov factory, a Red Army man."

"There you see, and his grandson is a geologist. Would that have been possible before the October Revolution?" the berry commissioner interrupted gleefully.

"Who's arguing?" Nikanor Sergeyevich said. "It would have been impossible. Of course, Lomonosov was the son of a peasant, and he became famous under the tsaritsa."

"He was the illegitimate son of Peter the Great," the berry commissioner stated, satisfied he had showed up Nikanor Sergeyevich with this significant, albeit unproved, bit of information.

"I don't care anything about Peter the Great," Nikanor Sergeyevich said. "As I see it, the founder of the Russian intelligentsia was Pushkin."

"What—do you think everyone understands Pushkin now?" Grisha laughed. "Just because people rush off to buy books like they were oranges doesn't mean anything. Do you know what the storekeeper told me about her new apartment? 'I have a Lola double bed from Egypt, Grisha. I have the Gdansk Polish kitchen, though the accessories have disappeared somewheres. I have Czech bookshelves, too, but as for the books—and I used the tape measure myself!—I need another meter twenty to fill it up!' "

"That happens," Nikanor Sergeyevich agreed. "But a library can be passed down, and maybe your storekeeper's children will read them. The intelligentsia in Pushkin's day was the elite. By the October Revolution, if my memory serves, we were seventy percent illiterate."

"We liquidated illiteracy like we did classes," the berry commissioner said triumphantly, lurching slightly from his new glass of essence.

"But real literacy comes gradually, not in one fell swoop. I've bought a lot of books in my old age. I'm reading all kinds of great works, but it's too late—I won't be an intellectual," Nikanor Sergeyevich continued. "That woman from the foreign portrait—Mona Lisa—smiled at me too late. An intellectual is a real intellectual probably only in the third generation, when he isn't snatching up scraps of culture, but growing up surrounded by it, breathing it like fresh air."

"Wait a minute, Nikanor Sergeyevich," Grisha said. "What about Gorky? He isn't an intellectual according to you?"

"Gorky is the exception that proves the rule."

"Wait, wait." The berry commissioner grew worried. "What are you driving at, Nikanor? That our intelligentsia isn't really an intelligentsia?"

"Not at all, don't get excited, Tikhon Tikhonovich." The mushroomer placated him.

He took a deep bowl of fish chowder in one hand and a painted metal tray with sliced bread in the other.

"The tray is wider, of course, than the bowl. But the bowl is deeper. If you pour chowder into the tray, it'll spread out, but it'll be harder to scoop up with a spoon—you probably won't even get a single spoonful. I'm saying that our Russian intelligentsia has grown wider, covering the surface of our whole country, but it still lacks depth."

Grisha got upset, forgetting his story about the storekeeper. "What about Gagarin? And our nuclear icebreakers? And the Bratsk Station that's right under your nose, Nikanor Sergeyevich? Who's behind it—if not the intelligentsia, together with the working class?"

"We built the Bratsk Hydroelectric Station, all right, but that's technology. We haven't built our own Pushkin yet, Grisha. And no milkmaid on the covers of *Ogoniok* smiles like that woman in the ancient foreign portrait."

"Oh-oh, you better watch that—what do you call it?—that kowtowing to foreign styles," the berry commissioner warned in a deep voice.

"What do you mean—kowtowing?" the mushroomer smiled and asked. "I'm not bowing down to foreign capital or imperialism, but to a smile, created by a working artist, and that makes him no foreigner to me. The reason I ache so badly for our new intelligentsia is that I didn't become an intellectual myself, and I want everything for them that I didn't have. In the breadth of our intelligentsia we got the better, but we don't have depth. And if we go deeper with that breadth, in the third generation of our intelligentsia, then one day we'll awaken as the first nation of intellectuals in human history," the mushroomer said, taking a bellicose drink of essence to this pronouncement. "I was lucky in life; I met many real intellectuals in the Far East and warmed myself at their conversations because a real intellectual doesn't condescend to ordinary people, like me. He speaks as seriously to them as he does to himself because he's part of the people himself."

"And what is the people, according to you?" the geological fellow asked.

"The people are the best people in a nation. And being best doesn't depend on education alone. Pushkin's nanny Arina Rodionovna, may she rest in peace, was one of the people, even though she wasn't educated—and that made Pushkin one of the people."

"I don't understand you again, Nikanor," the berry commissioner said, setting his wrinkles in motion. "First you say education is the most important thing; now you say a kind soul is, even when it has no education."

"A kind soul is the most important thing, but without education it's weak. And an evil soul—the better educated it gets, the more terrible it gets," the mushroomer said, and turned to the host. "Ivan Kuzmich, let's drink to your grandson. We seem to be forgetting him. Actually, we're not. We're really talking about him. May he grow up to have both a kind and an educated soul. I mean, who is that nuzzling his mother's breast behind the wall there? Russia's future . . ."

The berry commissioner shook his head at the word *Russia*, poured himself some more essence, drank, and sang in a voice that was unexpectedly high for a man of his size:

The birds of passage are flying . . .

Grisha, harmonizing, brought out the high notes with his velvety baritone and seemed to relish the beauty of his voice as if it belonged to someone else:

I don't need the Turkish shore
And I don't need Africa.

"I know why the old men aren't singing. This song is too new for them," the berry commissioner said, nodding at the mushroomer and his host and clearly not counting himself among the old men. "But why aren't you singing along, geologist? Is this song too old for you?"

"I don't know the words," the geologist replied. "And I wouldn't mind seeing Turkey and Africa and a few other places."

"Ah, the younger generation," the berry commissioner said, and wagged his finger at him. "What songs do you know? Ditties to twist by."

"Leave the poor kid alone, Tikhon Tikhonovich," the mushroomer said. "I'll start one now, and I'll bet he'll sing along."

Nikanor Sergeyevich—scrawny, pushed around by life—stood

up and wiped his mouth with the back of his hand, as though clearing the way for the song welling up within him. A wave of grandeur swept over his beak-nosed, time-ravaged face and washed away the wrinkles. His thin shoulders straightened, and his sparse beard thrust proudly upward. A song poured forth, mighty and youthful, as though it weren't Nikanor Sergeyevich singing, but someone hidden inside him:

A great sea is the holy Baikal . . .

Grisha rose and sang even more broadly, with bravura:

A great ship is a fish barrel . . .

Tikhon Tikhonovich joined in, waving a *khairuz* tail and weeping tears into his essence:

Hey, wind, move the flow

Ivan Kuzmich, up till now sitting silently, rose, shook his old head and revealed a hollow, heart-rending basso:

He doesn't have far to go!

And the geologist also joined in, though not very beautifully, but with feeling. As it turned out, he did know the words:

I wore heavy chains a long time

"Aha! He does know our Siberian song! And you said he only knew the twist, Tikhon Tikhonovich!" A triumphant look gleamed in Nikanor's eyes. He embraced the geologist with his left arm and, clenching his right hand into a small but sturdy fist, threatened some invisible person:

I spent a long time in the hills of Akatui . . .

Grisha, completely forgetting who was boss, hugged the berry commissioner and, squinting at him slyly, mischievously drawled out:

An old tramp helped me escape . . .

And the berry commissioner sang, sighing as though the words had been written for him personally:

I came to life, sensing freedom . . .

Ksiuta came out from behind the wall, rubbing her sleepy eyes, and gently put her finger to her lips. Out of respect for the infant, they stopped singing.

And then Ivan Kuzmich Belomestnykh said, "People should live together the way they know how to sing together. Everything would be all right then. And, people should start talking and not be afraid of their thoughts. For if you're afraid of your thoughts, you won't have any at all.

"Thank you, dear guests, for coming with this precious present —my grandson. I'm often not kind enough, and there's no point in even talking about education. Forgive me for that. And you forgive me, Ksiuta. People fight against each other, mostly over trifles. If we stop fighting over trifles, then, God willing, there won't be another big war either."

"To peace!" the berry commissioner cried out ecstatically, hugging Belomestnykh. "Hey, Ivan Kuzmich, you and I . . . You and I . . . And all of us . . . I'm staying with you, my native land. Yes, staying! Where else can I go?"

And he offered a large tear in place of the innumerable emotions he couldn't express with words. And then fell asleep in the chair where he sat, his head in the sauerkraut. Grisha and the geologist lay down in the haystack. The night wind, penetrating the cracks, rustled the hay, and it moved, breathing as if alive, trying to share its thoughts with people, but unable. The pole over the well creaked in the wind, its long neck swaying under the tired stars, which continued to shine for all their weariness. And they would have to shine for a long time more, so that people, weighed down by the earth's gravity, could sometimes raise their heads, look at the stars, and think that besides funny things and sad things, besides meanness and kindness, besides life and death on earth there was a universal eternity.

The mushroomer was put in the side room on a creaking iron bed with nickel-plated knobs, and when Ivan Kuzmich lit the way for him with a kerosene lantern, Nikanor Sergeyevich saw, hanging over his bed, an oilcloth with swans. *They even flew this far,* Nikanor Sergeyevich thought, and laughed sadly. But he slept soundly, dreaming that he and Kuroda were in some extraordinary forest, where giant mushrooms grew taller than a man. They were using a saw to cut the stem of an agaric so gigantic that your arms wouldn't fit around it. They would take it in Grisha's truck to Hiroshima and show all mankind, to make them ashamed of that other, terrifying mushroom, invented by man.

And the infant, probably, didn't dream anything, because he still had no past and, therefore, no memories to give birth to dreams.

CHAPTER · 9

Seryozha Lachugin woke up before everyone else. Grisha was snoring lustily next to him, having pulled the sheepskin jacket Ivan Kuzmich gave both of them over to his side. The sky was a piercing blue, smothering the light of the stars, now no longer necessary. A vermilion glow hung over the edge of the taiga, out of which the sun rose, stately and self-important.

Seryozha crawled over the hay, trying not to wake Grisha, then jumped down from the loft to the dew-covered ground. His feet welcomed the sensation that the world was still there. He wrote a note on a piece of paper from his pad—"Thank you for your hospitality. S. Lachugin"—and attached it to a nail by the front door, on which hung an old yoke. Ruffling Charlie's scruff as the dog whirled around him affectionately, he left, trying not to let the iron gate handle creak too loudly.

It was about forty kilometers to his expedition campsite, and he had to make good time to get there before dark. But when you're twenty years old, the earth seems to bounce off each step instead of dragging your feet down. In his Aeroflot bag, besides the Saint Exupéry, Seryozha carried mail for the expedition, which had collected over an entire month at the Zima post office, including one special letter, and a few packages of bullets—although Seryozha had no weapons, unless you count a camper's pocketknife. Being on his own in the taiga filled Seryozha with joyous dignity and masculine strength —the kind that expands inside a man as he walks and thinks.

The village road that Seryozha took led him to Shelaputinki— a one-street village on the banks of the river. Many of the houses, although still sturdy, looked abandoned, their windows crisscrossed by planks. But there were still a few poeple. An old woman, with galoshes over her bare feet and carrying a yoke with buckets, was crossing the street. She stopped abruptly, having noticed Seryozha, and said, "Wait a bit, young fellow, I'm carrying empty buckets, you'll have a bad trip."

Seryozha obeyed her and stopped.

Galoshes flopping in the dust, the old woman went over to a well covered by a sloping roof encrusted with dingy green mold. Rattling the chains twice, she hoisted water out of the dark depths, deftly attached the full pails to the ends of the yoke, and went back across the street, slowing down a little in the middle and smiling at Seryozha. "Now you can go. You'll have a good trip."

Seryozha smiled back at her, and with some sort of secret purpose, he stepped over the drops that had fallen from the pails, transparent beads of water that hadn't been absorbed yet by the dust.

Seryozha knew the old woman, even though she hadn't recognized him; this wasn't surprising, considering how many geologists had been through the village. She was alone; her sons had left her and gone off to large construction projects. But she cheerfully offered hospitality to those passing through, never, God forbid, taking money from them. Once Seryozha slept in her passageway next to a carefully tended young calf, separated from him only by planks. Early the next morning he went out into the yard to do his exercises. Suddenly he spotted the old woman with a rag in her hand, staring at him with horror and crossing herself.

"What's the matter with you, dear boy? Some illness befall you? I know the falling-down disease, but I've never seen the hopping-around one."

"It's exercise, grandmother. Calisthenics," Seryozha said, laughing.

"What this calloussenics for?" the old woman asked, not understanding.

"To develop muscles, grandmother," Seryozha explained.

The old woman came up to him and extended her arm. "Well, then, feel that, son. Don't be afraid, it won't crumple."

Giving her arm a little squeeze above its bent elbow, Seryozha suddenly felt a small but iron-hard pellet of muscle, which seemed totally incongruous with her bony fingers, disfigured by time and labor.

"Seems, son, that I've been doing calloussenics every day in the garden and the field, but my feet still haven't tried hopping."

That's the kind of old woman she was.

Seryozha continued on to the Shelaputinki general store, and there, emerging from its doors, he encountered another yoke, this one spilling dark red drops from its pails. It was carried by a man who staggered wildly, apparently not only from the weight. He was vainly trying to get his cigarette going by noisily sucking the air.

"What's in there?" Seryozha asked with surprise, nodding at the pails.

The man reeled affably in his direction and giggled, making his cigarette fall into the pail.

"This is face-bender. . . . Whoops. It's all right, it'll be stronger with the tobacco," he said, trying to pick out the butt with two fingers.

"What's face-bender?"

"A wine, that's what we call it. They sent us some barrels of it from Moldavia; it must have been good there, but it soured on the way. You can drink and drink it, and you don't feel a thing. You have to drink half a pail, and then it really grabs you. But your head really aches in the morning, and your face is pulled all crooked. That's why we call it face-bender. Want to try some? Don't worry, I have a cup, too."

The man set the pails on the ground, pulled an aluminum mug from his pocket, and wiped it on the hem of his jacket. He dipped the mug into the pail with the cigarette floating in it and then offered it to Seryozha.

"Try it."

Seryozha sipped; it was a crisp, dry wine with a slightly astringent taste.

"This is very good wine," Seryozha said.

"Then why did it sour?" the man demanded suspiciously.

"It's a special wine, without sugar. It's called dry."

"How can it be dry if it's wet? You joking, pal?" the man said, wagging his finger. He put the yoke back on his shoulder and went on his way. "Everybody jokes with us, always joking."

He doesn't believe me, thought Seryozha without condescension. He knew that dry wine almost never reached these backwoods villages, so how could the inhabitants have subtle palates? Here they drank vodka and called it wine, hard liquor they called spirits, and all forms of fortified wines, no matter the color, were called red stuff.

Leaving the outskirts of Shelaputinki, Seryozha turned onto the taiga path. The larch roots bulged under his sneakers as he walked alongside the river, whose fresh, punctuating sounds could be heard beyond the trees. A light breeze from the river fluttered the flowers of the marsh tree and the willow herb. This, with the quiet rocking of the conifers, created the special sound of the taiga; perhaps the taiga thinks of this as its own silence. Other kinds of sound were known to it, too—when lightning struck the trees, splitting them; when terrifying forest fires broke out; when blizzards began to howl like wolves, bending and breaking trees and hurling down so much snow in the villages that it was impossible for the peasants to open their doors in the morning without chopping them down from inside.

People who knew the taiga made up many legends and songs about its cruelty, but they knew its kindness as well, revealed to them in countless ways: in the pinkish green of the paunchy little taiga strawberries, sweetly peeking out; in the dull glimmer of the whortleberry bushes; in the dazzling bloody red thickets of the stone bramble, and the crimson sprays of red bilberry, hardening on dark lacquered leaves; and in the noisy flight of the wood grouse, carrying in its beak the sweet heaviness of berries, the gift of the taiga.

Seryozha came across a winter cabin, its door held shut from the outside by a freshly cut block of wood. By the rules of the taiga, which even he knew by now, something had to be left inside for the next traveler. He opened the door. He found an opened package of salt and several boxes of matches on the table and two dried *khairuzy* attached to the wall by their gills. Seryozha took one fish and left a package of bullets on the table. Then he secured the door once again with the wood block and went on his way. As he walked, he crumbled the fish, and its skin gave off the smoky aroma of some unknown person's hands, warmed by a campfire. Seryozha followed the fish with a handful of whortleberries, which easily came off the bush through his fingers. They immediately turned into a refreshing, slightly sour juice, leaving a narrow little leaf stuck to the roof of his mouth.

Seryozha discovered a lonely grave, marked by a granite boulder. No cross had survived; perhaps there had never been one. Through the moss Seryozha read the crudely carved words: "Timofey Shadrin, Prospector. 1902." Seryozha bent over the boulder, pulling off the moss with his fingers, and more words appeared: "Never did nothing bad." Seryozha stopped awhile by the grave, feeling the cold passing from the tombstone to his fingertips. Many people had perished in these parts; they had come from all over with ragged footwear and pans, seeking the blessed, damned gold. Sometimes they died here alone, and there was no one to scratch their names on the boulders. Seryozha imagined that somewhere among the trees their ghosts still wandered, restless, unable to die. Threads of gold dust, perhaps never found, suddenly stretched toward Seryozha, intertwining with the glistening thread of drops that had fallen from the pail of the old woman who had wished him a good journey.

Never did nothing bad, Seryozha repeated to himself, trying to memorize that artless definition of a human life, and his own life, though just beginning, now seemed inseparable from this unknown prospector's. The taiga seemed to sense the purity filling him and responded to it with a steady hum. It seemed to be the resonance of history—memories that had absorbed so much horror but nevertheless remained pure.

Seryozha suddenly started. Right in front of him a bear cub ran out of the bushes. The cub was still full of an unreasonable joy of living, unblemished by caution, unafraid. Seryozha froze. The cub ran toward him, its damp black nose and curious, childish eyes shining. It began rubbing against his jeans, catching and scratching them with its teeth, which, though playful, still belonged to a bear. Seryozha knew from stories that the mother bear was nearby and that a confrontation with her augured no good. Without moving from the spot, he took out his pocketknife and opened it. The hawthorn bushes moved heavily, and the huge brown carcass of a she-bear emerged, burrs sticking in her fur. She stopped and looked into Seryozha's eyes. Her eyes were questioning; there was no anger in them.

Slowly she ambled around behind his back. His terror intensified when she was behind him, where he could only hear her hoarse breathing and smell her. But Seryozha knew he must not move.

Suddenly the she-bear lunged out and grabbed the cub with her teeth by the scruff of its neck, and jerked it away from Seryozha. Then, gently nudging her disobedient son, she drove him back into the bushes. Seryozha didn't move until the growling and the crackling of twigs behind him ceased. The pocketknife twitched in his hand. Seryozha looked at it and suddenly realized he had opened it to the spoon! At last he laughed, even though just then his knees began shaking. He beat his knees with his fists, but still they wouldn't stop.

He walked on, and in a space between two trees he saw the she-bear, swimming in the river, holding her cub with her teeth by the nape of its neck.

"So long!" hollered Seryozha to them at the top of his lungs, happy to have met them and even happier that he was still alive to tell about it."

"Long-long-long!" answered the taiga.

CHAPTER · 10

When Seryozha's father was still a student at the workers' high school, he wore a peacoat liberally festooned with buttons proclaiming solidarity with aviation, chemistry, and fighters for revolution. The first time he was invited to the house of Professor of Ancient History Zagoryansky, his white sailcloth shoes, which had been polished for the occasion with tooth powder, left telltale white tracks on the parquet floor, and his eyes bulged with astonishment.

There was nothing especially luxurious about this roomy, old Petersburg flat, except one thing, passed from generation to generation: books. Books rose along every wall, lay on chairs, tables, and windowsills. And no one set any teapots on them, as they sometimes did in the workers' high school dormitories.

"I'd like you to meet each other. Volodya, this is my father," said Irina, the professor's daughter, and it was only then that Lachugin noticed him up among the towering bookshelves, which were filled with nobly glowing spines. He was an old man of medium height, possessing a lively face that seemed to give the impression he was winking at someone all the time. Red, disheveled hair whimsically fluttered out from under his black skullcap.

The old man climbed down the library ladder with simian agility, holding an enormous folio in his hands, and the worker-student's hand automatically reached for the book, not the professor's hand.

"Let me excuse myself," Lachugin said.

"Shake hands with the history of Byzantium, go ahead." Zagoryansky laughed. "It's more reliable than many human hands. And you, young man, as I understand it, are Irina's husband? Everything happens so quickly now—in this era of social cataclysms."

Lachugin was stunned.

"Papa," Irina said reproachfully, "Volodya and I are just friends."

"All the more reason—why isn't he your husband if you're friends?" Zagoryansky asked mischievously, peering intently into Lachugin's face. "I like the way you look at books. But forgive my pedantry, it's immodest to excuse yourself. You seem to be forgiving yourself. You must say 'excuse me.'"

Lachugin did become Irina's husband. Old Zagoryansky spent many hours with him, telling him about Byzantine culture, and Sparta, and ancient Rome, while the wisps of red hair under his skullcap waved, like the tongues of a torch, above his youthful eyes, which looked old only when he made sad analogies.

"They are shortening the course of ancient history intolerably now," Zagoryansky said, raising a freckled hand over his head, seeming to seek a Spartan sword in the air. "I understand your slogan 'Let's renounce the old world.' But must you renounce everything that comes from the old world? The old world isn't only slavery and tyranny. It's also culture. Publius Ovidius Naso wrote:

> If from small care you move to matters more important,
> If we continue our path, opening our sails,
> Then try to make your faces more pleasant—
> Meekness becomes humans, anger is for beasts.

"I see too much anger and too little meakness. Renounce Nero, Caligula, but not Ovid. Besides, even to renounce, you must study the object of your renunciation. Historical tragedies creep over from epoch to epoch because they are insufficiently studied. They can repeat themselves as farce, as we were warned by Marx, who knew history very well. Some new Caligula may appear and not in a luxurious toga. He could be wearing the most modest suit and sleep on a hard bed. The study of history is mankind's warning to itself."

When Volodya Lachugin's father, a worker from a family of workers, came to visit Zagoryansky, the intellectual from a long line of intellectuals, they always found a common language, even though they argued a lot over tea and sometimes, to tell the truth, over vodka.

"Did you come to tea in '17?" Zagoryansky once asked slyly. "You were in the Red Army, weren't you?"

"I don't recall," Lachugin senior replied, also slyly. "Why, did you run a Red Army tearoom? I don't seem to remember one."

Seryozha had never seen his grandfathers—they both had died before he was born. They died far away, and who knows, perhaps the old mushroom gatherer had sat around the same campfire with them. But they had lived to pat the head of his older brother, who later died during the blockade. His mother miraculously survived. She taught at the conservatory, and when Seryozha was still little, she took him to the Piskaryov Cemetery, where his brother was buried. Once at the movies, when they were showing a documentary about the tragedy and great victory of Leningrad, his mother suddenly gasped and squeezed Seryozha's hand in the dark, which shimmered with tears falling from so many eyes. "Look . . . that's your brother . . . that's me." On the screen in the snow walked a stooped figure with an emaciated old woman's face, which Seryozha barely recognized as his mother's. Over her quilted jacket she had wrapped an old-fashioned patterned drape with tassels. Her feet barely shuffled in ugly, ragged footwear, and she was pulling an aluminum sled bearing a child's corpse, its face covered with a scarf. From that time Seryozha never failed to see in his mother the woman pulling that sled.

Seryozha's brother hadn't had time to become anyone—he had died at the age of ten. He was known to Seryozha only from the photograph on the wall, in which he was wearing a tasseled Spanish-style cape, unknown to Seryozha's generation, and holding a shiny Pioneer* bugle in his outstretched hand.

Also from the walls of the old Petersburg apartment shone two other faces: a powerful face belonging to a Putilov factory worker who wore a leather jacket with a Red Army armband, and the professor of ancient history's face, which, though soft, betrayed a sly animation of the mind.

During the blockade Leningraders sometimes had to burn pre-

*Pioneers is the Soviet equivalent of the Cub Scouts.

cious books as fuel. Crinkling in the fire of the revived "bourgeois" stoves, they gave up the warmth of their pages to half-frozen people. But Irina Apollinarievna had preserved Professor Zagoryansky's library intact, and Seryozha grew up among books, which he thought of as the kind and wise house spirits of their apartment. The volumes of the *Granat Encyclopedia*, the *Brockhaus* and *Efron Encyclopedia*, books on the history of ancient Babylon, Assyria, Byzantium, Egypt, Greece, and Rome were like living, thinking creatures surrounding him. And there were so many books on the history of Russia. Shcherbatov, Tatishchev, Karamzin, Kostomarov, Soloviev, Klyuchevsky— they all revealed the country that was Seryozha's inheritance in different ways, but one thing was certain: that history was great, resembling no other, and it had to be continued in a great way, in its own way. Of all the Leningrad museums, Seryozha loved Peter the Great's house best.

Seryozha studied at the special English school. Starting at age five. He took lessons in music and figure skating and played tennis.

Vladimir Vikentievich Lachugin had become an important scientist, and it was difficult to recognize in him that workers' high school student in sailcloth shoes polished with tooth powder. Sometimes he worried that his son would be spoiled.

Irina Apollinarievna consoled him. "Seryozha is kind by nature. Even when he was very little, he gave away his toys to the other children who liked them."

"Yes, but he had more toys than the others. Kindness is a child giving away his only toy," Vladimir Vikentievich said with a frown.

"Volodya, are you saying that we should create the same obstacles for our children that we ourselves had to overcome? They'll have their own . . ." Irina Apollinarieva said, squinting at him.

The Lachugins' housekeeper, Auntie Klanya, was born in the Vologda region, and she took care of the house and Seryozha. A middle-aged, lonely woman whose movements were timid and rushed, she was in perpetual fear of displeasing her masters, even though no one ever scolded her for burning the cereal, or scorching the trousers she was ironing, or breaking the dishes. She had no children, and she adored Seryozha, overfeeding him and spoiling him. Actually Irina

Apollinarievna promoted this overfeeding herself; the memory of her first son starving to death never left her. Auntie Klanya squeezed fresh oranges and grapefruit for Seryozha, the way her mistress taught her. The meat patties she made for him contained only fresh meat, never frozen.

Irina Apollinarievna brought home the groceries once a week in a large cardboard box from the store, where they saved things for her because she had "pull." (She and Vladimir Vikentievich detested that expression, but they justified the reality of it with the excuse that they were so busy.)

"Caviar for breakfast again." Seryozha would grimace.

"Eat, Seryozhenka, eat." Auntie Klanya fussed. "It's so expensive."

Auntie Klanya stood next to Seryozha while he ate—God forbid he might not finish anything. Seryozha particularly hated potatoes, and the moment Auntie Klanya turned her back, he would quickly fish them out of his soup and toss them over the cupboard, so that they fell in the crevice behind it. Once, when Auntie Klanya was cleaning up, she discovered the whole trove of desiccated potatoes and burst into tears.

"That's bad, Seryozha, oh, so bad. . . . Every potato was planted by hand in the soil, Seryozha, mounded up by hand, picked out of the soil by hand. And when it rains, the damp earth gnarls your hands. You see my hands, Seryozha, the rheumatism still hurts them, I picked and pulled a lot of potatoes from the ground. And you make pellets out of bread—that's a real sin, Seryozha. Don't play with your bread, or else God will punish you—you won't have bread when you need it."

Seryozha listened. He was ashamed. Auntie Klanya rarely scolded him, and if she wept, well, then it really was bad to play with potatoes and bread.

One of Seryozha's classmates, Kostya Krivtsov, was a loner, surly, tormented by his awkwardness. He was prepared to use his fists on anyone who made fun of him. But Krivtsov's hazel eyes were astonishingly beautiful; beneath long, girlish lashes they trembled like two chocolate butterflies. In class Krivtsov was always scribbling in his thick oilcloth-bound notebook, shielding it with his hand from his deskmate. But everyone knew that Krivtsov was writing poetry. When he was asked to contribute a poem for the May First issue of the school newspaper, Krivtsov answered glumly, "I'm not a specialist in occasional poetry."

"What do you mean, 'occasional'?" repeated pretty Alla, editor of the paper and the daughter of the deputy director of the Orient Restaurant.

"Occasional poetry is poetry written for special occasions," Krivtsov explained with a sneer.

Once Krivtsov came up to Seryozha and, with his usual abruptness, said, "Listen, Lachugin, they say you have a good library. May I have a look? I promise there won't be any expropriations."

In the Lachugin flat Krivtsov was at first as stunned by the kingdom of books as had been the worker-student in sailcloth shoes. But it lasted only an instant. Krivtsov climbed up Professor Zagoryansky's rickety ladder and boldly began pulling out volumes and greedily leafing through them.

"The full set of *Vesy* and *Apollo*—that's a rarity. I knew, of course, these magazines existed, but I've never held one in my hands. I subscribe to *Yunost* and *Novy mir*, but unfortunately there are no subscriptions to the past. Aha, Mandelstam's 'The Rock,' autographed even. Who's it to?"

"My grandfather."

"I stood in line all night at the Writers' Bookstore to buy the one-volume Mandelstam but didn't get it. I found it on Nevsky for fifty, from book scalpers."

"Where did you get money like that, Krivtsov?" Seryozha was amazed.

"I worked at a furniture store; I hauled chairs, tables, and bureaus with another guy. We moved one couch that was so heavy my stomach hurt for a week afterward. But at least I have the Mandelstam now."

"Do you like his poetry?"

"He disappointed me somehow. Not my taste, really, even though his writing is powerful. But you have to know everything, so as not to repeat it."

"Which contemporary poet do you like, Krivtsov?"

"Pushkin."

"No, you didn't understand me, I'm asking about contemporary poets."

"He is the most contemporary."

"No, I mean, contemporary in the sense of being alive."

"He is the most alive."

"What about Voznesensky?"

"His stuff is pleasant. I can't write the way he does. But I don't want to either. He'll have someone beating up a woman in a car and then pile up beautiful images: 'And her legs pounded the ceiling, like white searchlights.' If someone's beating a woman in front of you, you should punch the bastard, not admire her legs."

"What about Yevtushenko?"

"He's also passé. Look at this, you have all the first editions of Gumilev. I never read him; he's not in print. Ooh, that's terrific:

> In the hour when over the new world
> God bent his face, then
> the sun was stopped with a word,
> a word that destroyed cities.

"Mayakovsky echoes it somehow: 'I know the power of words, I know the tocsin of words.' It's particularly strong at the end: 'And the trains crawl up to lick poetry's calloused hands. . . .' The Gumilev gets worse toward the end. Too pretty. Of course, Blok has a lot of bad poems, too. 'So pierce my heart, yesterday's angel, with your sharp French heel'—that's just tawdry trash. *The Scythians* isn't a Russian poem at all. We're neither Scythians nor Asians; we're something else. But *Free Thoughts, Retributions, The Twelve*—now they're something! Akhmatova doesn't have any bad poems. But I still like Tsvetayeva better. Everything vibrates like a high-voltage tower. I managed to borrow her one-volume collection for three days, and I didn't sleep for three nights. I copied it on my typewriter. My father bought me the typewriter with his bonus from the factory. 'Maybe you'll really become somebody,' he said."

"And will you?" Seryozha asked carefully.

"I don't know," Krivtsov said, suddenly turning deathly white. "I'm very old already, sixteen."

Then, choking, he muttered tightly, "Would you like me to recite my poems to you? Just don't tell anyone."

"All right, I won't," Seryozha promised.

Krivtsov came down from the ladder, stood with his back to the window so that his face was in darkness, and announced, as a challenge, "I warn you—my poems are still very bad and not free of outside influences. But I will write better. Our generation must have its say."

And he started reciting in a steely, completely transformed voice, while fiercely slashing the air with his hand to keep time:

> Under Leningrad's wet bridges
> where the lanterns tremble in the cold,
> the Neva flows lazily between
> as it had in the year '16.
>
> But imbued with memory, like gunpowder,
> and so much like an arsenal of bombs
> is the author of '17: Petersburg,
> its head filled with shrieking.
>
> When a worker walks along the street,
> and the ice crackles underfoot,
> then '17 roars in his memory
> like a scream hidden inside his coat.
>
> And the cold glint of his bayonet eye
> suddenly shoots from beneath his cap,
> and once more arises the feeling of class
> ignorant of its own greatness.
>
> Amid all the jokes and drinking
> and satiety which sucks us in,
> I believe in your screaming, Petersburg,
> I believe in you, working class.
>
> And I walk past drunken Finns
> and past someone's satiety, until
> I stand and silently take out of my pockets
> two fists filled with memories.

The light of distant campfires hasn't been extinguished
The Smolny's windows have only to glimmer at me:
and suddenly the Red Guards' armband
will spurt like blood on my sleeve. . . .

Krivtsov froze. His hands were trembling slightly. His gaze, which had passed through Seryozha and gone out beyond the confines of the room, was slowly returning. The boyish voice had almost returned, too.

"Well, Lachugin? You don't have to say anything, I know it all myself. I'll read you another one. It's called, rather ironically, 'Family Portrait.' But I love my family, Lachugin, remember that."

My father goes to the
factory year after year.
In his best tie,
in his best jacket,
he hangs on a nail
on the honor board.

And year after year
my mother goes out to the store.
But for Mother's tiredness
and Mother's boredom
there still is no pity in the world
and no honor board.

"How nice," said Auntie Klanya, who had been listening, clasping her hands. "At first you scared me a bit—an old woman—but this one was good. You remembered your mother, understood that the poor woman gets tired."

"She's not poor," Krivtsov replied huffily. "She never complains about anything. Listen, Lachugin, could you lend me some books for a while? I'll type them for myself. Don't be afraid, I don't lose books. I respect books more than people. Though I detest some books just like lowlifes."

Auntie Klanya invited Krivtsov to stay to supper. He tried to beg off but finally sat down.

"No caviar," he said curtly. "I don't want to get used to it. But the potatoes—with pleasure."

Leaving with the Gumilev, carefully wrapped in a copy of *Leningradskaya Pravda*, he looked back and said, not exactly with envy, or with cynicism, but as a sort of warning, just in case, "You live well, Lachugin!"

Some time after Seryozha visited the Krivtsovs. The four of them lived in a basement room of a communal apartment.

"We've been waiting and waiting for an apartment, but we still don't have one." Kostya's mother sighed, explaining and rocking her year-old son. "But it's all right, our turn is soon. So don't think badly of us. There's no shame in being cramped. . . . Kostya's books crowd us a bit. But he needs them. He's a writer, you know."

"Mama, I'm not a writer yet," Kostya burst out.

"If you write, then you're a writer." Kostya's father laughed, putting vodka on the table for himself. For the boys he poured cherry liqueur from a large bottle filled with dark, swollen fruit. Kostya's mother brought out homemade aspic and pickles and proudly took a small can of black caviar from the cupboard.

"Look what I have. I was saving it for a holiday, but our guest makes this a holiday."

It was impossible not to eat the caviar.

The Krivtsovs' room, despite stains on the ceiling from the inevitable dampness, was nevertheless clean and homey; everywhere there were white lace curtains and embroidered covers for the cushions. In the corner, set off by a screen, stood Kostya's desk, piled high with manuscripts. On the desk were a Moskva typewriter and large earmuffs made out of bicycle headlights stuffed with styrofoam.

"I wear them when I'm working," Kostya explained. "So that outside noises don't disrupt my inner rhythm."

Kostya really did have a lot of books, but most of them he hadn't bought but typed from rare editions, neatly binding them himself.

"You typed the whole novel *The Master and Margarita*!" Seryozha exclaimed. "How much time did it take?"

"Much less than it took Bulgakov to write it," Kostya joked. "What else could I do? I couldn't get the book. I don't have pull. And a book like that should always be around. So I typed it. By the way, it's very beneficial. You really come to sense the author's style, the course of his thoughts; you feel every word. I managed to get Maya-kovsky and Yesenin. But I had to retype Pasternak's one-volume collection. And then I understood with my own fingers that his early poems are denser, more complex; the later ones are more transparent but diluted. He gained something, but he lost something, too.

"And you know who I borrowed the Bulgakov, the Pasternak, the Tsvetayeva, and the Akhmatova from? From Alla. Her shish kebab papa buys up all the rare books, but he doesn't read them, naturally. There's a new breed of people now: They acquire books like furniture, as a status symbol. I recently saw some foreigner pile out of a Be-ryozhka store* with ten copies of Akhmatova under his arm. Some college girls were walking by, and they just gaped. The foreigner just laughed, handed one of them a book, and caressed her cheek—in a fatherly way. Anna Andreyevna has lived to see her books given to Russian girls as gifts from foreigners. We have a book famine in our country, that's the problem."

"Well, it's a good thing it's only books," his father said. "Thank God you haven't seen the other kind, as we did."

"What's so good about it?" Kostya exploded. "Which do you think is more important—the spirit or the flesh?"

"The spirit, of course," his father said to soothe him. "But don't forget about the flesh either. Have some more meat—it's good with garlic. I was in Moscow for a conference of high-ranking workers. They put me in the Hotel Ukraine. I was standing in the lobby, wearing my military and labor medals—for the occasion. And I see this amazing kiosk. It's selling black caviar and red, and canned crab, and vodka with a screw cap. With this one," he said, tapping the bottle on the table with his finger, "you pull off the seal, and that's it, you can't put it back. You have to drink it all up, whether you want to or not. But on that one, you unscrew the cap, drink a bit, and then screw it back on—all very cultured. And besides that, this fairy-tale kiosk has fur hats and colored silk scarves, and wool sweaters, and those

*Beryozhka stores are stores exclusively for foreigners; they accept only hard currency.

—what do you call 'em?—those stockings that go up to the waist."

"Pantyhose! Oh, you kill me." His wife burst out laughing.

"Yes, that's what I was saying, pantyhose." Kostya's father continued this seemingly happy story. "So I go up to the salesgirl and say, 'Please pick out a sweater for my wife, and a scarf, and about ten pairs of pantyhose, if you please, also a fur hat for a sixteen-year-old boy, and I'll pick out the vodka myself.' And she glares at me with these huge eyes, and her eyelids are painted blue, like they belong to somebody just dredged up out of the river, and she says to me in an iron voice, 'No, this is for hard currency, not for Soviet citizens.' She says this as though she was born under swaying palms in Rio de Janeiro. But no powder in the world could hide her Russian pug nose. So I went over to the other kiosk, and everything is different there: the magic, fairy-tale tablecloth is gone, and there's no caviar, no crabs, no fur hats, no pantyhose, and no vodka at all, not even with the regular caps. Instead, there's clip-on ties swirling on a carousel, combs in putrid, disgusting colors, funereal sateen underwear. . . .

"When my comrade and I looked into the restaurant, we're met by a sign: FOR FOREIGN DELEGATIONS ONLY. So we bought some vodka in a store, and some sausage, and had a good dinner in our room. The room was beautiful: mahogany furniture, velvet drapes, a painting on the wall, and even a TV. But I never felt too comfortable in that room. Our basement ceiling is lower, of course, but on the other hand, we own it. And my factory—I walk through there like I own it. We make ships, and every time we launch another ship, you feel like you're going out into the world yourself. You young people are facing a bigger world now. You gab in English, write poetry. But keep thinking in Russian, not in borrowed terms."

Seryozha began spending time at the Krivtsov house, and once Kostya's father obtained special permission to take the boys to the shipyard. Seryozha had encountered workers before—mostly at beer stands, slowly sprinkling salt on the edges of their mugs and cleaning dried fish over newspapers. The only ones he'd seen on the job were street repair crews, women with crowbars at streetcar switches, young female house painters on scaffolds in front of building walls, and the plumber, Uncle Misha, whom everyone called Uncle Threesha, because he never left without a three-ruble bill, even if the work only took a minute. He spent every evening, no matter what the weather, lying on the sidewalk. The next morning, muttering incomprehensibly to himself, he would struggle ostentatiously over someone's toilet bowl, dropping his tools into it, in order to get some cash for a drink to soothe his hangover.

At the shipyard Seryozha saw, for the first time, workers whose faces were transformed by that intelligent, fierce concentration imparted only by a sense of doing important work. It was the same expression Kostya's face had when he wrote poetry in class. Here Kostya's father was transformed, too. Waving his arm around the shop and shouting over the noise, he looked like a giant to Seryozha. It was impossible to imagine him fitting into the tiny cellar room or that the odious salesgirl could have refused to take his Soviet rubles.

Kostya's phrase "You live well, Lachugin," continued to echo in Seryozha's head. So one day he asked Vladimir Vikentievich, "Father, are we rich?"

Vladimir Vikentievich's spoon froze in midair, and he choked on a meatball. Looking attentively at his son, as if for the first time, he asked, "Who told you that?"

"It doesn't matter. . . . Then we are rich?"

"You can see we're not poor." Vladimir Vikentievich hedged, unable to answer directly. "Yes, of course, we do live better than many. But both your mother and I work, and everything we have was earned by our own labor, honest labor."

"How much do you make, Father?"

"Why do you ask me that? I make around seven hundred rubles a month, and your mother makes three hundred," Vladimir Vikentievich replied irritably. "But we didn't always live that way. The first time I saw a pineapple in a store window, right before the war, I bought it with my last ruble as a present for your mother, and we didn't know how to eat it. During the blockade, when I returned from the front, your mother made me pancakes out of potato peelings— that's all she had. And you throw the potatoes from your soup behind the cupboard."

"I don't do that anymore, Father," Seryozha said. "But it's your fault I did it in the first place."

"You mean, it's my fault that I want you to have a better life than we did?"

"No, that's not it. It's just you forgot to tell me how people live with a lot less money, huddling in a crowded basement room."

"Ah, that's it! You visited some basement, and now you're feeling guilty, filled with ideas of equality and brotherhood? I grew up in a basement like that, Seryozha. It can't happen all at once. Apartments cost less here than anywhere else in the world, but there just aren't enough of them. We shouldn't artificially make living conditions worse for those who live well; instead, we have to raise the standard of living for those who live poorly. Ultimately we'll close the gap to a minimum, but some difference will always exist—total equality is impossible, Seryozha. How can you make things equal for a hopeless idiot and a genius?"

"But if a hopeless idiot comes from a family that's well-off, then he'll have many privileges from childhood."

"He must have the dignity not to take advantage of that," his father replied curtly. "You have to create your own life, not live off your mother and father."

"Tell me, Papa," Seryozha said softly but firmly. "You say that before the war you saw a pineapple in a store window and bought it. Now there are almost never any pineapples in the stores, but we have them all the time. The meat in the stores is frozen, but ours is always fresh. It's impossible for most people to get sturgeon, smoked fish, or caviar, but they're always on our table. Why do you use pull if you hate it so much?"

Vladimir Vikentievich rose and went to his study. He sat and smoked for a long time, even though his doctor had strictly forbidden it.

Am I just avoiding Seryozha's questions by giving him banal lectures? How can I explain it all to him? And to myself? He's spoiled, that kid. No, he's asking because he's not spoiled, thank God. Do I want him to be different —cynical and smug? That was my worst fear. So why am I afraid now that he's not cynical? Have I changed? No, I'm the same, just a bit tired of thinking. But if you're tired of thinking, then aren't you already different?

That evening Irina Apollinarievna returned late after a recital by her pupils at the conservatory. Vladimir Vikentievich slipped the full ashtray under his bed just in time.

"Irina, I have a request to make: Don't get our groceries where you usually do anymore."

"Why, Volodya? I'm very busy, and it's so convenient—everything's prepared and packed. Besides, a lot of things you can't get just like that."

"So we don't need them," Vladimir Vikentievich said. "We lived half our lives without them, and we'll manage again somehow."

"Have you been smoking again?" Irina Apollinarievna said, fishing out the ashtray from under the bed and wagging her finger good-naturedly at her husband. "I know what's going on. Seryozha's been making you feel guilty, of course. There, you see—and you were worried about him. Neither of his grandfathers would be ashamed of him."

At breakfast Vladimir Vikentievich was stern.

"Listen, Seryozha. From now on you're in charge of the grocery shopping. You'll get an allowance. It's too hard for Auntie Klanya to stand in lines now, and your mother and I are too busy."

Seryozha tried to be a good provider, and one day, laughing slyly, he pulled out, by its green tail, a real pineapple from his shopping bag.

"Papa, do you see what this is? Something as strange happened to me as happened to you before the war. I was walking down the most ordinary street, past the most ordinary store, and suddenly in the store window—I could hardly believe it—there was a pineapple. Show me how to eat it, Father. I've already forgotten."

At the English school Seryozha attended, an "elite" group developed. Its members, who kept to themselves with an exaggerated aloofness, were children of important scholars and other influential citizens: the deputy of the Orient Restaurant; the goods manager of the second-hand commission store; the head engineer of the automobile repair shop; the manager of the food gastronome. Frequently these kids were brought to school in company cars, and it wasn't unusual to see an elderly chauffeur running after some fifteen-year-old boy, shouting, "Igor Ignatyevich, you've forgotten your briefcase, sir!" Although Seryozha took the streetcar to school, he was accepted in this clique because everyone knew his father had a company car anyway. He was the "son of Academician Lachugin"—that had a good ring to it. Krivtsov had no such credentials, and therefore, he wasn't accepted. Also, Seryozha was the best English student in the whole school, and the clique had one inexorable rule: to speak English among themselves not only in school but also everywhere else. They all wore only Levi's (never stooping to Polish or Yugoslav jeans) and wore Seiko, Rolex, or Omega watches; all had their hair cut by the same barber, George, an Armenian repatriate from Iran; all smoked only Kents or Marlboros; and all had stereo cassette players. The leader of the clique was Igor Ignatyevich Seleznyov, a boy with a handsome, slightly cruel face. He liked to stare intently at people he spoke with, making them feel uncomfortable. Igor didn't in the least resemble his father, the director of one of Leningrad's biggest factories. He sometimes appeared at school—an elderly, harried man with a simple Russian face, who was perpetually confused by the complications of not only production schedules but also family life. Neither his massive gold cuff links nor the checked tweed jackets with center vents that his wife picked out remotely suited him.

Igor, laughing with condescension at his father, said (naturally in English), "Well, what can you do with him! He is such an incorrigible old square! He spent his whole youth dressing like a peasant. Now my mother's trying to turn him into a fashion model, but she's not getting very far."

At the Seleznyov house, miniature turbines and books on turbines stood on the desk and shelves, and photographs of turbines in various stages of construction hung on the walls of his father's study. In Seleznyov junior's room, on the other hand, an entire wall was taken up by a collage of pictures of Ringo Starr, Elvis Presley, Muhammad Ali, and Phil Esposito.

"I don't look upon diplomacy as my goal in life, but merely as the key to open the world with," Igor Seleznyov often said.

Naturally Seryozha also wanted to find his own key to unlock the world. He also dreamed of distant lands: following Huckleberry Finn's route down the Mississippi; touching the walls of Notre-Dame in Paris; climbing a coconut palm somewhere in Africa; walking through the Prado. But unlike Igor Seleznyov, his idea of opening the world did not simply boil down to the concept of "abroad." Seryozha could discover an enormous world just in his grandfather's library. Every street, every window of his own country presented a new world: the old woman asking the clerk to weigh not a kilo, not a half kilo, but one single apple. The college girl in the subway car, pressed in on all sides by passengers —swaying to the rhythm as it bumps along the tracks, she still continues to read Gabriel García Márquez's *One Hundred Years of Solitude*. The gray-haired man on the boulevard bench noiselessly weeping in broad daylight, the black loop under the collar of his raincoat sticking up weirdly. The snow-white bride, looking like a spray of wild cherry blossoms, riding in a car with a pink celluloid cherub affixed to the hood. A line of people extending almost the entire length of Liteiny Boulevard, waiting in the pouring rain, their heads covered with umbrellas or soaked newspapers—a subscription for a new edition of Dostoyevsky had been announced. The fresh-looking Red Fleet sailors—squeaky clean, they look with embarrassment at the mysterious naked beauties of Gauguin in the Hermitage. The building super sweeping red maple leaves from the sidewalk, suddenly picking up a leaf and carefully smoothing it out with her hand, as though she were seeing it for the first time. A husband and wife on the street, triumphantly carrying a mirror, the reflection of the clouds swimming in it like swans. A wave of scent from someone's perfume; a goldfish in a glass jar in the hands of a boy; the air, composed of thousands of breaths, one of which is yours. All these were Seryozha's daily discovery of the world.

A child of the city, he didn't know the country; the closest he got was vacationing at a dacha. When his tenth-grade class was sent to the countryside to harvest potatoes, Seryozha discovered a completely new world, where there were no refrigerators, bathtubs, gas stoves, toasters, sausage, or oranges. For the first time he learned what Russia really was. For the first time he slept in a hut and saw a Russian stove. For the first time he touched the living Russian soil.

Igor Seleznyov, on the other hand, touched no Russian soil. He dug out the potatoes in rubber kitchen gloves his mother had sent him. He called the villagers plebes, and in their presence he continued to speak English with his pals, in order to keep a proper distance. "The Englishmen," as the villagers called them, dug potatoes badly, leaving a lot of tubers in the ground. When the class attended village dances, Igor Seleznyov brought along a Japanese cassette player and condescended to teach the local girls how to dance to rock 'n' roll. Unexpectedly the girls caught on very quickly and soon outdanced the "Englishmen." Sometimes they sang their native *chastushki* ditties accompanied by the accordion, improvising and mocking the city slickers on the spot. One of them—a black-eyed singer named Tonya —was especially good at it. Holding her scarf with her fingertips, boldly using her eyes and her whole body to dance to the staccato beat, she once tossed out a ditty:

> The Englishmen from Leningrad
> to our kolkhoz paid a visit
> and they got a whiff at last
> of our village shi-it.

"Now that's a poem!" Krivtsov laughed. "Good for you, Tonya! You hit it right on the nose. You've performed a great service to society—one just waiting to be done."

"I'll remember this insult, Krivtsov!" Seleznyov warned in English.

"You'll make a terrific diplomat, Seleznyov." Krivtsov laughed. "How can you represent a people you despise?"

"I don't believe in the gray masses; I believe only in strong individuals" came the reply.

"The strong personality rising above the masses? It's not a new theory, Seleznyov. Of course, you don't promulgate it at Komsomol meetings, where you only give reports that will help you get ahead. Even this trip to harvest potatoes will look good on your record; that's why you deign to dig around in the soil, even if it is with gloves. But you're suffering from megalomania, Seleznyov. It's a fashionable disease, often mistaken for spiritual resolve, but I suggest you get treatment."

Seeing that the two city boys were about to come to blows, Tonya came between them. "Just don't fight! When we've got all the potatoes picked, then you can fight." And turning to Seleznov, she flashed a guilty smile. "Please don't be insulted by my song. I didn't intend to be mean."

"Don't be silly," Seleznyov replied, feigning boredom. "You have a beautiful voice and marvelous gift for improvisation. . . . I've had my eye on you a long time. There's something Renoiresque about a girl like you."

"What?" Tonya asked, bewildered.

"Ivan Renuaresky is a contemporary Soviet artist, laureate of many prizes and, I think, even an academician. His specialty is portraits of award-winning kolkhoz girls," Seleznyov explained without batting an eye.

The rank and file of the clique cracked up, covering their mouths. Tonya looked around without comprehension. She sensed that they were laughing at her and blushed hopelessly.

Seleznyov commented in English, "She's not bad-looking, especially when she blushes. She reeks slightly of onion, but with those natural pink cheeks of hers she probably makes a tasty borshch. Actually I wouldn't mind at all tasting that borshch."

"Are you saying something bad about me?" Tonya asked, even more confused.

"On the contrary," Seleznyov replied calmly. "I was telling my friend Seryozha how much I liked you."

"Don't believe him, Tonya," Seryozha burst out. "He's saying vulgar things."

"My friend is jealous, Tonya." Seleznyov laughed. "Whom do you believe more—me or him? Come on, look me in the eye." He took Tonya by the shoulders and, pulling her closer, gazed into her moist black eyes with his practiced, imperious stare.

"I don't know," said Tonya, lowering her eyes, and tearing away from Seleznyov's grip, she ran out into the darkness.

He turned to Seryozha. "I don't think we should ruin our friendship over this little girl; she's just a short episode in my life, and I'll never see her again. But you and I are from the same circle, and we could be of use to each other later on, in the future that belongs to us. I advise you not to quarrel with me!" he said in English.

One night Seleznyov returned very late to the hut where they were billeted and, lying down next to Seryozha on the floor, said with his usual feigned boredom, "It was hard work—she was a virgin."

Seryozha grabbed Seleznyov, lifting him from the floor, and slammed a fist into him, shouting, "You bastard!"

The other boys jumped up from their blankets and lit the lamp. The old woman with whom they were staying looked down from her plank bed. "Lord Jesus! They're fighting! And city boys at that."

Seleznyov, swaying slightly, stood in front of Seryozha in his undershirt and underpants, his muscles bulging. "Notice I haven't touched him even though I could squash him like a bug. And why did he hit me? Let him tell you. He's got nothing to say."

Once more Seryozha hauled back and punched Seleznyov in the jaw. Immediately he was jumped from all sides, his arms twisted behind his back. The affair ended with Seryozha's being reprimanded by the Komsomol "for hooliganism during the potato harvest campaign."

Once Seryozha's school was visited by a group of American high school students. The principal was very worried; the whole affair had to go perfectly. As it turned out, the American students behaved rather casually, but the tall man from the State Department accompanying them displayed the same strained, anxious politeness as the principal, who had nevertheless dressed for the occasion in a rather playful pantsuit.

Of course, it's no accident that she's attached to the Russian kids, thought the man from the State Department about the principal. *Of course, it's no accident that he's attached to the American kids,* thought the principal about the man from the State Department, and in a strange way this distrust imparted to them a special bond. They both were worried about the same thing: that nothing happen.

Seleznyov gave the welcoming speech. The Americans raised their eyebrows at what they later described as his "Oxford pronunciation." Seleznyov expressed, without grammatical errors, their solidarity with the American students who were fighting for peace in Vietnam and against racism in America. He finished his speech with a quote from Lincoln. At the words *Vietnam* and *racism* the man from the State Department grew so tense that his Adam's apple bit into his starched collar, but at the Lincoln quote he gave a sigh of relief, as though he and Lincoln worked in the same office.

Then one of the Americans—a boy with red hair that looked like a puff of copper wire—took the floor. He wore dirty basketball sneakers and a T-shirt with a picture of Che Guevara, and he spoke Russian rather well, even though he lacked perfect Moscow Art Theater pronunciation.

"I'm from Tucson. . . . Near our city grow large, very beautiful cactuses. Some of them stand embracing each other with branches like arms. It looks like love. The cactuses don't rustle, but they creak in a strong wind. That creaking is their song. We also have mountains. They are copper red, like the faces of Indians. We also have a cold, swift river, and trout frolic in it. But I have never seen a trout that wants to eat a cactus or a cactus that wants to eat a trout. Only people destroy the trout and the cactuses and the mountains and the river and themselves. I wanted to study ecology after school because I love nature. But then I thought: It hasn't occurred to anyone yet to put man on the endangered species list. Now I want to work on the ecology of man. My father's hand is buried in Vietnam. He works in a motel coffee shop in Tucson. It's not easy making sandwiches with one hand, but he learned. Recently he and some other veterans went to New York and got inside the Statue of Liberty. They barricaded themselves from the police for several days, to say to all America, 'It's time to end the war.' I carried sandwiches to them, which I made with my two hands. And it wasn't politics; it was the ecology of man. Otherwise there won't be anything left: not our Statue of Liberty; not your Kremlin; not our cactus; not your birch tree. Do we need a new Hitler for us, Americans and Russians, to understand each other as well as we did on the Elbe River? The Elbe is a small river, but for me it's bigger than the Mississippi. . . . That's all."

A barbed, hoarse laugh was heard, and there was nothing childlike about it, even though it belonged to an American boy of sixteen or so in a black leather jacket with innumerable zippers. He didn't even think of standing when he spoke. "All that is sentimental bullshit. The struggle for survival is just human instinct. Man has been fighting for survival since prehistoric times, and he always will. Only strong people and strong nations survive. War is the same game, only with bigger weapons. No matter how many pretty words we say about peace, there will be wars as long as there are people. But don't think that I'm an American imperialist. I don't have any desire to fight. . . . I'm more interested in motorcycles. And one thing I know is that our motorcycles are better than yours."

The principal tensed up. Was the meeting turning into a failure? The man from the State Department squinted. No, even the radicals were better than this kid.

Krivtsov leaped to his feet, disheveled, intense as though tightly coiled. "I'm afraid of people who think sentimentality is something shameful. Dostoyevsky wrote that all the best ideals of humanity aren't worth the tears of an innocently tortured child. And he also said, 'Everyone is guilty of everything.' Telling yourself that war is inevitable is a cowardly avoidance of personal responsibility. Go right ahead and be interested in motorcycles, but don't gloat that yours are better than ours. Nothing breeds mutual distrust like gloating. If a Russian poet gloats because some American poet has bad lines, will that make the Russian write good poetry?"

"Good for you!" shouted the red-haired leader, and stamped his feet on the floor, making both the principal and the man from the State Department wince.

A dark-haired American with biblical eyes stood up.

"About sentimentality . . . At our school we studied Chekhov's story 'Vanka Zhukov, a Country Boy.' Even though it's not about war, it terrified me. Remember how the boy begs his grandfather to come help him: 'Dear Grandpa, come,' and then writes on the envelope, 'To the village, to Grandpa,' and thinks that's address enough? I think that in every country there are more good people than bad. But they don't know one another's addresses; they don't know how to shout to one another over the heads of the bad people. Many adults are also Vanka Zhukovs. Most important is to feel one another."

The principal spoke. "I'm pleased you know our classics. Of course, the story of Vanka Zhukov is the distant past of our country."

The man from the State Department made a note to himself: "Chekhov's short story about Ivan Zhukov—read next weekend."

The dark-haired fellow with the biblical eyes pulled out a six-stringed guitar from a canvas case. "And now I'll finish what I didn't say with a song."

> We shall overcome,
> We shall overcome,
> We shall overcome someday.

CHAPTER · 11

We shall overcome, Seryozha Lachugin thought, remembering that Leningrad night. Now he was in the Siberian taiga, separated by such vast distances from his childhood. *In Russian you can't say that in the first-person singular, "I will overcome,"* thought Seryozha. *The grammar resists it. Perhaps you simply can't overcome by yourself. Only everyone together.* He laughed bitterly. *But everyone can't ever be together. How can I be together with people like Igor Seleznyov?* He thought about the millions of people who had lived, had died, and were buried on the planet. Probably the earth was entirely built on their unrealized hopes and silenced hearts, right down to its molten center.

Seryozha didn't want to be known as "the son of Academician Lachugin," so after high school he went to Moscow and entered the geological institute. He lived on a stipend, trading Auntie Klanya's repasts for the dining hall's potluck soups and Bulgarian canned stuffed cabbage reheated on a hot plate in the dorm. Krivtsov didn't pass the entrance exams to the Literary Institute, and he went to work in his father's shipyard. Seleznyov entered the Institute of International Relations in Moscow. Once, walking past the Lira Café, Seryozha saw him loudly speaking English with his date and leading her past a line of meek people who had taken them for foreigners.

During his first field expedition in Kazakhstan, Seryozha learned to gouge the earth with a pick, to dig pancake-flat samples out of rock with a hammer, and to split a matchstick into three pieces with a razor. The cook assigned to the expedition was a kind two-hundred-pound creature, who glowed with pleasure while he was eating or even when feeding others. One of his duties was to fill a wooden barrel with water from the river; this involved hauling it several kilometers each way on an old cart. This water was used by the cook to make soup and cereal and also by the geologists, who drank it, washed in it, and laundered their shirts in it.

Every day the geologists left at sunrise and returned at dusk. But one day the sun beat down so mercilessly that they decided to return a bit earlier. Their backs were bowed down by the weight of the packs, filled with samples; their flasks were empty, and their lips parched. Barely dragging their feet, they had only one desire: to get back and dig into the barrel with the iron scoop, to quench their thirst with long, delicious drafts. Suddenly, in the distance, from behind the hill, came a strange joyful, wordless song. The geologists looked at one another and quickened their pace. Coming around the hill, they saw the mangy mare dragging the cart and barrel up from the river. But no one seemed to be driving the mare. Where was the song coming from? And suddenly they saw a pair of underpants hanging on the wagon and the cook's head sticking out from the barrel. In the ninety-degree heat the naked cook sat in the cool water, splashing like a child and enjoying life. The experience was so delightful that he broke into joyful, guttural song. The geologists did not exchange a word. With grim concentration they ran for the barrel. The cook shut his eyes in horror. The geologists dragged him out of the barrel in all his naked splendor. They didn't beat him. They just shook him and kept asking, "Have you been doing this all along, you bastard, or only today?"

"Only today! Only today!" the cook swore, his teeth chattering in fear.

They released him, and he pulled on his underpants, sobbing. The geologists looked at the water, torn between their thirst and revulsion. The river was a long way off, and they had no strength left to go for more water. Finally, Kolomeitsev, the head of the expedition, said, "All right, it's still water."

And he dipped his flask in the barrel and drank. Seryozha drank, too.

Seryozha loved to sing when he was alone. He didn't have a good ear, nor was he blessed with a particularly fine voice, but he couldn't control himself, so he sang. The path to the excavations led through tall, umbrellalike trees, and Seryozha always tried to leave before the others, so he could be alone and sing. Sometimes he sang the words, sometimes not, but he was happy, no matter what, when he could blend his own voice with the chirr of the crickets and the limitless blue expanse overhead. One evening, while the geologists were eating, a horse appeared in front of the fire from out of the twilight. On its broad, bare back sat a young woman, brandishing a willow-branch riding crop. She looked no less imposing than her impetuously snorting horse.

"Which one of you sings in the morning?" she asked as if challenging them all.

The geologists looked around.

"Why, do you like it?"

"I like it," she replied, in the same tone of voice.

"Lachugin is our singer." The geologists laughed and pushed forward Seryozha, who was so embarrassed he didn't know where to look.

"You, then?" she asked, gently prodding him with the willow switch.

"Well, I guess so," Seryozha replied reluctantly, expecting her to laugh at him.

"Do you remember the words?" She looked at him inquisitively, pressing the sides of the nervous horse with her tan, bare knees.

"I remember them." Seryozha turned bright red.

"Come to my place. I'm not far—at the apiary. I'll feed you; I can see you're all losing weight on this camping grub. You'll sing. And then I'll copy down the words."

The geologists roared with laughter. The collector Sitechkin, who kept a perfect part in his hair even on an expedition, laughed the loudest. "Oh, my God! Write down the words! This is hilarious! Oh, I can't stand it! Help me!"

The beekeeper leaned over and started whipping Sitechkin with her willow crop, so that he had to cover his part with his hands. The others got a few licks, too.

"You're a bunch of foulmouthed swine! And you're supposed to be geologists. Get up with me, my friend. Come be my guest, and we'll sing songs. It's a special day for me today."

"If it's so special, maybe you'll want to do more than sing?" Sitechkin couldn't resist and got another lashing.

"Behave yourself, Sitechkin," Kolomeitsev said harshly. "And you, Seryozha, go on. You have my permission." He smiled slightly without abandoning his formal demeanor. "I hope you appreciate how extraordinary this invitation is."

Seryozha clambered up onto the horse behind the beekeeper. She dug her heels into its reddish sides, and they rode off into the night, which was gradually pouring its twinkling stars onto the world.

"Don't be embarrassed, hold on tighter," the beekeeper called back to Seryozha as she fearlessly urged the horse on through the twilight; apparently this territory was familiar to both of them. The apiary was located about five kilometers from the geologists' camp, perched on a mountain slope, where, unexpectedly, an island of wheat swayed in the steppe. The geologists had never gone this way, and they knew nothing about the existence of the apiary, let alone why this fiercely independent beekeeper lived there alone or how she knew to gallop and protect herself from men's jokes, even if it took a willow-branch whip.

The beekeeper led Seryozha into a sparkling clean hut and sat him at a table, which she instantly covered with a white tablecloth. In a flash, a feast materialized: plates, knives, and forks; a steaming pot with baked potatoes; honeycombs oozing honey; two large metal ladles; and, finally, a bucket filled with a golden, foamy liquid.

"What's that?" Seryozha asked, bewildered, as the beekeeper dipped the ladle into the bucket.

"Mead. Don't worry, it doesn't give you a headache," she said, sitting down opposite him. Clinking her ladle against Seryozha's, she extended her other hand across the table.

"I'm Grunya. And you?"

"Seryozha."

Seryozha, trying not to embarrass himself, did everything Grunya did: He drained the cup of its honey-scented liquid and bit into the scalding potatoes and then the honeycomb.

"It's a special day for me today," Grunya repeated mysteriously, filling the ladles again, and her eyes glimmered with gold, as though the mead had imparted its color to them.

"Why?" Seryozha asked, made bold by his second ladleful.

"Special, that's all. Don't ask anything else. I'm not asking you anything, am I?"

After the third ladle Seryozha's head was still clear, but when he tried to move, he couldn't. It felt as though the mead had insinuated itself into every cell of his body. He was astonished by the strange sensation of being simultaneously light and heavy. And Grunya's eyes glowed a deeper and deeper gold. She looked at Seryozha benevolently, all the while refilling their ladles. Then she propped her chin on two strong, red fists and said soothingly, "And now sing, Seryozhenka."

Seryozha took another gulp of mead for courage and, raising his eyes to the ceiling so as not to be embarrassed, sang, "We shall overcome . . ."

For some reason he had wanted to sing that song. The song came even more easily than it did on the path, and his voice felt unusually powerful. But when he looked down, he saw that Grunya's face was distorted by you wouldn't call it fear but horror.

"You're not the one," said Grunya. "You're not the one. . . ."

"I am," Seryozha said. "I always sing on the path."

"No, it's not you," Grunya said, shaking her head. "I made a mistake. I meant the one who's always singing about a corridor."

"A corridor?" Seryozha was stunned. "I don't sing anything like that."

"The song doesn't matter. Your voice isn't the same."

And then Seryozha remembered that in the mornings, when Sitechkin combed his part in the pocket mirror on the tent peg, he usually sang in a velvety baritone, "Toreador, bravely you go."

"It's not a corridor; it's a toreador," Seryozha, now chilled, said in a crestfallen voice.

"That's it! 'In the corridor . . . surely you go.' And the voice, it's a real voice, not like yours. You shout instead of sing, but he sings. Who is he?"

"Sitechkin," Seryozha muttered. "The one you lashed with your switch."

Suddenly tears welled up in his eyes, smarting from the insult that he shouted instead of sang, and he cried. He was ashamed. He wanted to get up and run, but his legs wouldn't obey. Suddenly calloused, gentle hands caressed his face, wiping away the tears.

"Oh, I hurt your feelings. . . . You're like a child, just like a child. Why did God give that fat-faced foulmouth a voice and not you?" Grunya's mouth froze. "I'm sure you have a good voice, too. Maybe, even better . . . But your voice hasn't been coaxed out from your insides."

"What do you mean, 'not coaxed out'?" Seryozha said, still sobbing slightly.

"It sticks in your throat. You don't let it out. You should sing with your chest. And why sing foreign songs? Don't we have enough good Russian songs?"

"Maybe I have a terrible voice, but it's a good song," Seryozha said. "It's sung by American progressive students."

"What kind?" Grunya asked. "You mean, Negroes?"

"Why Negroes? There are progressive whites, too."

"And what's the song about?"

"The refrain is 'We shall overcome, We shall overcome, We shall overcome someday.'"

"Ah. I didn't understand. Now I do. Sing it in English. But softly."

Seryozha sang.

And suddenly a miracle occurred: Grunya immediately repeated the melody, without the words, in an unusually beautiful, full, open voice. She lifted it higher and higher, making it grow stronger, expanding it beyond the confines of the hut. Now it was no longer clear what kind of song it was—American or Russian.

"Would you like me to sing another one?" Grunya asked. "This is my mother's mowing song."

And Grunya sang:

> Once amowing, off her lashes
> Three tears tumbled down
> One sat on the scythe and asked:
> "Take me into town."

Once amowing, next what happened,
the second tear it said:
"I'll stay in the village where
your father's with the dead."

And the third one hopped and skipped and jumped
along the unmown hay;
'twasn't crying, 'twasn't crying,
but laughing all the way. . . .

"Why do you say it's your mother's song?" Seryozha asked.

"She made it up. She liked making up songs."

"She wrote them herself?"

"No, how could she write! She couldn't read or write. She made them up. In her head."

"Is she alive?"

"I told you: Don't ask me anything. It's a special day for me. Why don't I teach you how to sing?"

"I won't be able to," Seryozha said glumly.

"What do you mean, you can't? That fatface can sing, and you can't? Let's go sit on the porch. The porch will help."

Realizing how difficult it was for Seryozha to stand up, she lifted him up as if he were a feather, set him on his feet, and led him out to the porch. They sat on the steps, and from all sides the night whispered.

"Do you hear that?" Grunya asked.

"Yes."

"Let me put my scarf around your shoulders. Don't be so afraid, I won't bite. . . . Listen to the night breathe! You try to sing the way the night is breathing. Look at the stars—they seem to pull out your voice. But don't shout; start softly. Breathe with your voice, so that it comes up from deep inside."

"What will we sing?"

"Whatever you want. How about your foreign song?"

"Could we sing your mother's song?"

"You liked it? All right. Don't come in right away, follow me. And don't look at me; look at the stars."

And Grunya began:

Once amowing, off her lashes

Very gently her hand touched Seryozha's shoulder under the
scarf. Seryozha looked at the stars, as Grunya told him, and followed
along:

Three tears tumbled down

The stars really did seem to pull out his voice, and it flowed
together with Grunya's voice as well as the gurgling, rustling, and
shivering of nature around them. Seryozha didn't even notice when
the song ended; it felt as though he were still singing even though he
was silent.

"Well, you see how it turned out?" Grunya said. "It's because
your soul is pure."

"How do you know?"

"You can see it right away," Grunya said. "Let's sing something
else. I like singing with you. I'm glad I whipped that fatface."

And they stayed what seemed like forever on the porch, singing
songs, many of which Seryozha had never heard before. Then Grunya
led him inside by the hand and put him to bed like a child, this time
bringing him a ladle of water. His teeth chattered happily with disbe-
lief on its frosty edge as she undressed next to him, repeating once more
in the dark the mysterious phrase: "It's a special day for me today."

Early in the morning, when the horse's hooves dipped into the
low-lying ground fog, Grunya brought him back to the tents. She
kissed Seryozha roughly and said with abrupt concern, "I hope they
don't ruin you." Then, lashing her horse with the willow switch, she
disappeared. Seryozha managed to slip into his sleeping bag so that no
one noticed, and only fifteen minutes later Kolomeitsev energetically
called, "Let's go! Get up, everybody."

Sitechkin spent the next hour giggling and poking Seryozha in
the ribs with curiosity, but Kolomeitsev's disdainful gaze stopped him.
Later that day, when the geologists returned from the field, the cook

took Seryozha aside with an especially meaningful look and showed him a birch-bark basket. The basket held several jugs filled to the brim with light, sparkling honey.

"A good woman," the cook said. "She left these to thank you for the songs."

After dinner Seryozha headed in the direction of the apiary, trying to disappear unnoticed, but before he had lost sight of the campfire, Kolomeitsev's hand fell on his shoulder. "Don't weaken, Lachugin. Adventures are adventures, but work is work. We have a long trip ahead of us tomorrow."

Seryozha came back from the field three days later. When he arrived at the apiary, the hives were gone. The windows and doors were boarded up. The geologists soon ate all the honey.

Kolomeitsev was Seryozha's idol. He had the hard elegance of a gentleman-adventurer: He never pried into another's soul, and he never allowed people into his. He wholly subordinated himself to his work and permitted himself a little relaxation only when others would not notice; he permitted others to relax only with his consent. Otherwise, he felt, everything would fall apart. On an expedition he never displayed even a trace of familiarity, and he discouraged camaraderie among his subordinates. In private some of the other geologists dubbed his manner enlightened despotism. But no one could accuse Kolomeitsev of putting himself in a special, privileged position above the others. He retained only one privilege: deciding everything himself.

He went on the hardest trips, displayed greater courage than anyone in difficult moments, and never appeared to worry. This was certainly preferable to expeditions on which the leaders tried to pander to their subordinates or asked in a quavering voice at general meetings, "What should we do now?" or fell to shouting, which resulted only in disrespect. Even as a child Seryozha had realized that certain people have a pathological fear of deciding any issue at all. Kolomeitsev was never afraid to decide; it seemed he was created for decisions. Seryozha, who considered his own worst fault to be spinelessness, a tendency toward sentimental indecision, wanted to be just like that.

Seryozha had an anti-hero, too. His name was Nakhabkin, and

he worked as a supply clerk at the expedition's base camp in a small mining town. Seryozha was sometimes sent there to get tools and food, and he was forced to avail himself of Nakhabkin's slimy hospitality. Nakhabkin was about fifty. He had a large, bald head with tiny, mocking eyes, which seemed to seek out something vile in people. It was set on a short but sturdy body, like a mushroom. Seryozha was stunned by Nakhabkin's first question at the warehouse, posed while handing him food. "Do you steal?"

"No," Seryozha said warily.

"You're lying. Everybody steals," Nakhabkin exclaimed gleefully and laughed. "And do you practice the five-fingered exercise?"

"What?"

"Don't pretend not to understand," Nakhabkin said, his eyes drilling into him.

Seryozha turned red, unable to find the right words, and muttered, "No."

"You're lying. Everyone does it at your age. You're blushing. Don't be embarrassed, it's no big deal. Of course, it has its good points —you don't have to walk anyone home." Nakhabkin giggled.

"Stop that disgusting talk," Seryozha said sharply.

"It's not disgusting," Nakhabkin soothed. "It's just part of life— nothing to be ashamed of. Don't get mad, I just wanted to see what you knew. You, my friend, watch out for tender words, not dirty ones. Tender words confuse you; they sap your vitality. Dirty words, even if they go a little overboard, toughen you up. It's scary to go out on the street when you're a nice guy: The slightest nastiness will scare you, but if you're crude, even tenderness won't scare you—and it won't be able to fool you. Did your parents beat you when you were a kid?"

"No," Seryozha replied against his will.

"I can see that, because you don't like crudeness. You should appreciate Nakhabkin, you should. My grandma beat me when I was a kid. You know how? She'd wrap me in a wet sheet, so that there wouldn't be any marks on my body, and then hit me with a freshly cut log. But that log beat life into Nakhabkin." The supply clerk proudly lifted the rusty nut, which he wore on his index finger.

Nakhabkin invited Seryozha to his house and expounded further on the themes of how people were basically rotten, that love and friendship and so on were invented by writers who, in their personal lives, were rotten like everyone else. And it came out in passing that Nakhabkin himself did some writing, and he even recited excerpts from a poem, written in a fat accounts book in the Onegin meter. Seryozha remembered only:

> She was brought up
> not by the emigrant Folbalage,
> not in a noble pension,
> but in a Bolshevik orphanage.

And also:

> Him and his suitcase, brothers two,
> Crossed Arbat Square straight through.

Nakhabkin had a common-law wife, who worked as a dishwasher in the tea shop—a homely woman who meekly hid her eyes from people. He used her as an object of constant humiliation. When he came home from work, she always washed his feet. Nakhabkin especially loved performing this ritual when someone else was there. In his own opinion, it elevated him, and he humiliated the rest of humanity in the person of that woman. Once, when Seryozha was there, he ordered her to bring the basin. He lowered his feet into it, moving his hairy toes in the hot water, and grunted with pleasure, all the while sipping his favorite drink—alcohol mixed with strong tea (punchie, he called it tenderly), and blathering on. "You think that society is based on love, my friend? Well, look here. I sleep with her, but she disgusts me. She hates me, but she sleeps with me and washes my feet, and she needs me to give her some place to live. Society is held together not by love but by mutual hatred. That's how it is, pal."

Seryozha looked at the woman. She continued kneeling at Nakhabkin's feet. Seryozha noticed how a few of her tears slipped into the dirty water next to the blissfully soaking toes. *While amowing, from her lashes three tears tumbled down.* Nakhabkin inspired a complicated reaction in Seryozha: disgust mixed with curiosity. Seryozha had heard more than once that there was no such thing as an absolutely evil person or an absolutely good person. They said that Nakhabkin didn't steal even though he was a supply clerk. They noted this with surprise and respect. Even Igor Seleznyov also had one quality which was enviable—physical daring. Once, during the spring thaw, he crossed a river, leaping from ice floe to ice floe. Seryozha envied him then but didn't dare follow. Sitechkin? What good qualities did he have? He had to have at least one. . . . It was hard to find; he really was repulsive. Actually he did have a good quality: diligence. He was always given the dirtiest tasks, and he performed them assiduously. *But what good is honesty, physical courage, or diligence, if people are cynics?* thought Seryozha. *"What's the point of trying to exonerate them, to prove that they are not "absolutely bad"?*

Once Nakhabkin took Seryozha with him into town to pick up the wages for the workmen. The driver was a taciturn fellow with a solid row of metal teeth and tattooed arms.

"Watch out for him. He's served time," Nakhabkin whispered before they set off. "We're getting a large sum of money. I have something in here," he said, patting his pocket. "But you still keep an eye on this guy."

Nakhabkin spent a long time at the bank, counting the money. He stuffed it into his worn leather briefcase, and the three of them got into the truck's cab. Ahead of them lay two hundred kilometers of roadless desert. As they drove, the sun glinted off the salty, dead lakes. Steppe eagles, sitting on telegraph poles, majestically acknowledged them by their heads, which were tiny compared to their wings. Halfway there, Nakhabkin started talking.

"Think how interesting life is," he said to the driver. "You must know I have a lot of money in the briefcase, and I'll bet you'd like to get your hands on it. But you also know that I have a revolver and that you won't be able to get away even if you kill me. You've had plenty of experience in your life, haven't you? And you could kill a man, couldn't you? . . . You would, right?"

The driver stopped short, and Seryozha hit his head against the windshield. In a flash he saw that the driver had seized the gun and was pointing it at Nakhabkin's stomach.

"Get out, you louse!" the driver said. "Toads hop out of your mouth instead of words. This cab stinks like a gutter. And leave the money."

The driver yanked the briefcase out of Nakhabkin's trembling hands, shoved Nakhabkin out of the cab, and stepped on the gas.

"You know what he thinks now? That I'll run off with the money. He measures everyone in the world by his own standards. Give people like that their way, and they'd dirty up the whole world. We'd all be knee-deep in shit."

Seryozha looked back. In the middle of the empty steppe, Nakhabkin ran after them, shouting something and vainly waving his arms.

"He'll survive," the driver said, gritting his teeth. "They've got nine lives."

"Why does he think all people are thieves?" Seryozha asked. "Does he himself steal?"

The driver laughed. "No, he's too much of a coward to steal. In his head he steals. And then before he goes to sleep at night, he groans about not having done it for real. That's why he thinks everyone's a thief."

"But there are real thieves, too," Seryozha said carefully.

"There used to be, but they all left," the driver said curtly. "Real thieves are like dinosaurs now—extinct. Petty thievery did them in. For petty thieves money is just optional. They want to steal a person's soul—and that's a lot worse than bumping someone off."

When they were about ninety kilometers from the mining town, the truck stopped.

"Water's boiled out," the driver said grimly, jumping away in the nick of time from the column of steam issuing from the radiator. He announced, "Here's the plan. You stay here and guard the truck; I'll go for help. I'll take the money because you never know who might come along here. There are lots of dangerous types in the steppe. Wait for me."

The driver took the money out of the briefcase, stuck the packets into all his pockets, and headed off, wrapping his head in a dirty handkerchief to protect himself from the unbearable, burning sun. A little way off he turned and said, "Don't worry about the money. I don't even steal mentally."

Seryozha was left alone without water or food in the middle of the steppe. The sun rose and set twice. Seryozha wandered in the vicinity of the scorching truck, sucking the sour juice of the tough cactus tubers. He became delirious. Thousands of giggling Nakhabkins appeared on the horizon; their feet were washed by thousands of quiet and uncomplaining women. But Seryozha knew that the driver would return. On the third night, when he lay in the cab too weak to move, he was struck in the face by two blinding white beams. Black figures surrounded the truck. The door opened, and a pair of tattooed arms embraced Seryozha.

"He's alive! Alive!"

And Nakhabkin really did have nine lives, reappearing soon thereafter on the horizon at the expedition base.

CHAPTER · 12

Kesha, the mechanic, sat on a promontory washed by the violent current of the river. Kesha stared at the sky. There was nothing extraordinary in that; there are lots of reasons for looking at the sky. Most people do it simply when they think about the weather. But Kesha looked at the sky and saw his thoughts whirling around there, grand and marvelous, totally independent of any weather. He thought how lucky he was to have been born. If he hadn't, he would never have met Kalya, the cook, and would never have learned how wonderful it was to be in love—even if you're not loved back. Kalya stood next to him on the boulder, her knee-high boots splashed with foam, her vest charred by the campfire. She was trying to catch *khairuzy*. She and Kesha both were twenty years old. On that afternoon Kesha's pleasant duties included untangling the innumerable tangles that Kalya invariably created on the reel. Now once again she came over and pulled Kesha's eyes from the sky. Kesha had whortleberry, infantlike eyes, which enveloped Kalya with the sheer joy of unconditional adoration.

What beautiful eyes he has, Kalya thought. *If only he didn't have that hump.* She was ashamed of herself and joked brusquely. "Take it, take the reel! What are you staring at? What a parasite!"

And she said the word *parasite* so gently that Kesha's heart leaped.

"Kalya, look at the sky!" he said ecstatically.

"It's the same as always." Kalya shrugged.

"No, it's unusual today. And look at the sun!" Kesha tore off his shirt and waved it at the sun.

Everyone on the expedition loved Kesha, for he was one of those rare people who truly delighted in life, despite his congenital misfortune. Kesha grew sullen only when they approached settled areas, when he would try to remain by the boat. For a long time Kalya didn't understand why he did this. But once, when they went down together to Shelaputinki for supplies, two boys danced around Kesha and chanted, "Humpback horsey!" Kesha pulled his head into his shoulders, and she understood. But here, in the taiga, there were no strangers, and when it was hot, he could even take off his shirt without embarrassment.

People are like that, thought Kalya. *Maybe he's just a blessed idiot. No, he's not; he's smart. But how can he be smart? He's too kind, and all kind people are stupid because they don't see the evil around them. Maybe it shouldn't be seen—evil. At least you don't have to rub your nose in it, like some. But sometimes I can't help it. When they paw me with their filthy hands, it makes me want to cry. Everything seems filthy then. And I don't like swearing or other crude behavior. Kesha would never behave that way. Well, maybe he's kind because life has tricked him. If he didn't have that hump, he'd be like all those other filthy men. . . . No, he wouldn't. He has a pure soul, and that's not located in his hump. God, they say that you still exist. If you do, you should give all the bad people humps. But why poor Kesha?*

Just then Kesha spread his arms to the sun, turning his back to her, and Kalya saw two defenseless birthmarks on his pale hump. She looked away and shoved the reel at Kesha. "Come on, come on, get going."

"Oh, boy, what a huge tangle." Kesha laughed joyfully. He removed the spool, shook it, and, performing magic with his small, feminine fingers, made everything fall into place. Kalya could never have managed by herself.

"Do you know, Kalya, it feels as though I've lived forever," Kesha said suddenly.

"What do you mean, 'forever'?" Kalya didn't understand. *No, he is a blessed idiot,* she thought.

"Forever, like the sun, the sky, the earth." Kesha's golden, loose forelock bounced. "It couldn't be any other way. You see, a small hill's even been added to me." And for once a sad smile crossed his face. But it was gone instantly, and the glow in his eyes returned.

I should marry him. I'll never find a better husband, Kalya thought sadly. *What a bitch I am.* She cast the line out again, this time without tangling it. But nothing bit.

"Let me try" came Kolomeitsev's confident voice from behind Kalya. He had suddenly emerged from the taiga with a group of geologists and workmen. Now he cast twice and pulled out two sparkling *khairuzy* one after another.

"Don't push your luck," said the fat and usually good-natured Burshtein. Raising his mosquito net, he revealed an unexpectedly grim, almost angry face. The others turned out to have similar expressions.

"Why not?" Kolomeitsev laughed, casting the line, which pulled taut like a string, immediately.

"A pike!" Kesha shouted gleefully. "Play it out, play it!"

The warning spool clattered. Kolomeitsev gave the pike some line, only to pull it in closer. Trying to free itself, it leaped out of the water several times, but the hook apparently was firmly set. Its white wake came ever closer to the shore.

"Shoot," Kolomeitsev called sharply. "It'll get away."

Geologist Vyazemskaya instantly pulled the shotgun from her shoulder, placed the sight to her thick horn-rim glasses, and shot. Vyazemskaya and her shotgun were never separated, which no one would have guessed from the way she squinted to take aim, not to mention her carefully applied blue eye shadow.

The pike flew up over the water one last time and rapidly turned crimson. Then its lifeless body was dragged onshore behind the float.

"What a beauty!" Sitechkin said, fussing around the prize. "I'll be right back. I want to get the camera."

"You know I can't stand everybody snapping pictures on an expedition, Sitechkin." Kolomeitsev frowned.

Then he turned to Kesha and said, trying to sound casual, "Has Lachugin come back yet?"

Now Kolomeitsev's face was grim, too. The prevailing blackness of mood was no accident. The previous year a research team had come across quartz veins with a high cassiterite content. Cassiterite, a dark gray to black mineral that sparkled like diamond, contained tin. Back in Moscow these early samples were analyzed, suggesting that the site showed promise of containing a major deposit. But now the mineral seemed to have disappeared. They dug up innumerable samples, finding it only accidentally. It would tease them and vanish again. Kolomeitsev personally believed in this deposit, but it seemed he was going to be proved wrong. None of the other geologists on the expedition thought it existed anymore, and there were times when Kolomeitsev himself even had doubts. But he forced himself to believe, equating that belief with belief in himself. And you must believe in yourself; otherwise you were nothing—that was Kolomeitsev's conviction. He now sought the cassiterite with his pride instead of his intellect. So despite the negative results of the field assays, Kolomeitsev ordered Lachugin to take samples to Irkutsk for a decisive determination. This was the reason he waited for Seryozha so impatiently.

Kolomeitsev looked with distrust and condescension on those of Seryozha's generation; they were born after the war and never had to worry about losing their bread ration cards. He laughingly called them children of détente and thought that they didn't have enough guts to withstand a war, if it came. Neither did they have enough faith in themselves or in anything greater. True to his tendency to categorize, he divided them up into "parrots" (those who were nauseatingly susceptible to anything foreign—from rock 'n' roll to rags), "sparrows" (those who unassumingly chirped in the native manure), "woodpeckers" (those who were capable only of repeating back what they were taught), and "turkeys" (those who preened in public from an early age). But Seryozha Lachugin didn't fit into any of Kolomeitsev's categories.

Not bothering to take off his boots, Kolomeitsev stretched out on top of his sleeping bag by the tent. He thought about Seryozha with envy, which was rare for him. *A pure person. He'll never do anything to be ashamed of.* Kolomeitsev immediately repressed his envy. *Maybe he's just a sissy. Like Prince Myshkin.* Out loud he said, "Naturally you like Prince Myshkin, Boris Abramovich?"

"More than Stirlitz, at least," Burshtein replied reluctantly, oiling his parched boots.

"Myshkin is wishy-washy," said Sitechkin as he worked on his part before a shard of mirror. He had caught the chief's intonation and was trying to curry favor.

Kolomeitsev grimaced at the unsubtle support. He liked teasing the clumsy, shy Burshtein, but he felt this was his personal privilege as an old friend. No Sitechkins should involve themselves. Kolomeitsev loved Burshtein in his way. Burshtein never volunteered an opinion, but when asked, it always turned out he had one. Therefore, many preferred not to ask. But Kolomeitsev asked. It was an old game. Kolomeitsev derived special pleasure that this man, whose thoughts were not at all like his own, worked under his direction and executed his commands. It was boring to subordinate toadies; subordinating a thinking man wasn't easy, but it was a real pleasure.

"In every Russian there is a little bit of each of Dostoyevsky's characters," said Kolomeitsev, smoking. "Each of us somewhere has a little Nastasya Filipovna, and Rogozhin, and Raskolnikov, and Captain Lebyadkin, and Smerdyakov, and Stavrogin, and Petenka Verkhovensky, and Myshkin. . . . The only question is which one predominates. I killed the Myshkin in me, Boris Abramovich. He was in my way."

"Whom did you spare?" Burshtein asked.

"I hope none of them. I killed them all."

"And you don't regret it?"

"Not a bit. And if one of them does remain, it's a weak spot. Dostoyevsky never created a single full-fledged hero. They all have a crack, a fatal flaw. A collapse of will. The sick hero. Probably it's because of his own epilepsy."

"Or maybe it's because he looked so deep into man that he became sick," Burshtein said slowly. "Why are you afraid of Dostoyevsky? I think it's because you haven't killed all his heroes inside you—that's why you're afraid. And what did Prince Myshkin do to you that you have to keep returning to him like Raskolnikov to the scene of the crime?"

"Myshkin is fleshless, boneless. History is made by people with flesh, bones, and willpower. Myshkin is essentially a variation on Oblomov. All that naïve wringing of hands and sermons on loving mankind are useless because they're simply hiding laziness or fear of action." Kolomeitsev turned the radio dial, tuning in a squeaky, breathless voice: "Under the sun of the ideas of Mao Zedong our people . . ." He cursed and turned it off. "In the prison camps Myshkin would have been a goner. And what would he do here on an expedition? Can you picture Myshkin, Boris Abramovich, riddled with mosquito bites, hauling a backpack filled with rocks bouncing against his fragile back and making it bleed?"

"I can. He could have taken it. And his sermons would have done us some good. Preaching is also an action," Burshtein replied softly but with conviction. Having turned the radio back on, he managed to locate Rachmaninoff's Second Piano Concerto, and sighing with relief, he said, "If it were up to me, I would create a new profession: the person who makes you ashamed."

"And I would appoint a person whom people are afraid of. A person with a strong will, a man of action," Kolomeitsev said, turning the Rachmaninoff down a bit.

"Shame and fear are two completely different things," Burshtein said, shaking his head. "Shame teaches you to think, and fear keeps you from thinking."

"Nevertheless, a strong hand is needed, or everything will fall apart." And foreseeing the reply, Kolomeitsev added immediately, "Strong but reasonable, of course. Do you know why millions of people sit glued to their TV sets at night and the streets are emptied when there's a new episode about Stirlitz? Because everyone really wants action."

"I think the explanation is a little more complicated. The viewers identify with Stirlitz, and that tickles their egos. A pleasant aberration. Some think vaguely: *I also hate my job, I also have to hide my true thoughts, but in my heart I'm still a man and I do good as much as I can, even though it's sometimes dangerous.*"

Rachmaninoff was replaced by the breezy voice of a sports commentator. "The puck is in the goal of the Czech All-Stars . . . our team . . ." Now Burshtein himself turned off the radio, which was immediately turned back on by Sitechkin.

* * *

In the next tent Yulya Sergeyevna Vyazemskaya, mineralogist and mother of a family, wept uncontrollably, her cheek leaning on the open shotgun which she used so well. Kalya, the cook, comforted her, stroking her rough, straight hair, which had pine needles stuck in it, in addition to the noticeable strands of gray. Kalya didn't ask what had happened but merely comforted her as women always have: "It'll pass. . . . It'll be all right." When Kalya ran out of the tent, thinking that the fish chowder was boiling over on the fire, she found Kesha removing the scum from the kettle with a pine stick. Naturally she said nothing to him, even though she had just had an amazing revelation: Yulya Sergeyevna could cry just like Kalya herself.

Vyazemskaya had been in love with Kolomeitsev for twenty years, although no one knew it—not even, she thought, Kolomeitsev himself. It had all begun at a May First student party when she was a freshman, and he, a graduate student. Then he had seemed significantly older than he really was—perhaps because of his faded army uniform, which still had slight traces of the epaulets. They danced in the dormitory to a hoarse Victrola playing "Rio Rita," a prewar song. On the table stood a bowl painted with Chinese birds, holding devil's punch, a mixture of the cheapest fruit wine, vodka, cider, and beer. They drank by scooping their teacups right into the basin, and it wasn't long before the photographs of Ladynina, Marc Bernes, and Marika Rokk on the wall woozily swayed and multiplied. Food consisted of the cheapest available canned items, which filled all the stores at the time: crab and cod liver. Someone knocked over a can, splashing oil on Yulya's crepe de chine dress, the only fashionable thing she owned, and Kolomeitsev tried to wipe it off with his handkerchief, only making the stain worse. Then they danced again, and he took her head in both his hands, forcing her to look directly into eyes, which were filled with his overpowering will. Stepping on her Wedgies with his tarpaulin boots, he led Yulya through the fox-trotting crowd into the hall. There, on the torn wallpaper, hung the telephone, surrounded by a motley collection of messages written in pencil. He pushed her head back against the telephone and tried to open her lips with his. She was afraid he wouldn't know how to kiss. Tearing himself away from her primly shut lips, Kolomeitsev took her back to the dance floor again, this time pressing her so close that she felt the buckle of his army belt. Then he slowly danced her down the hall to the landing, carried her down to the entryway, which reeked of cats, and out into the dark courtyard. Golden squares of festively lit windows surrounded them. He laid her down in the damp sand of the children's playground and took her imperiously and crudely before she had time to think. Most of all, it hurt her back because in the sand there was a metal toy, left behind by the children.

The next day on the volleyball court, when she scraped her knee saving a dead ball, Kolomeitsev looked at her as though nothing had happened and slapped her back in approval. "You're one of us, Yulya." His hand struck her lower back, which still ached from the metal toy. Yulya understood. It was his way of telling her nothing had happened.

She acquiesced and accepted his terms. She became "one of us." She attended his wedding to a pale, colorless girl whose father was a top-secret aviation constructor. Unlike his daughter, he was an irrepressible merrymaker, stuffed with an explosive lust for life. Dancing the Gypsy with Yulya, he made the mahogany furniture shake so hard that the glass shelves in one of the cupboards collapsed upon each other, reducing the Czech crystal and Saxon porcelain figures to rubble. (This was the first noncommunal apartment Yulya had ever been in.) And then, hugging Yulya and gazing at her with delight, he shouted out to Kolomeitsev so that the entire party heard, "This is the girl you should have married, not my plain Jane!" This caused a certain embarrassment, which was overcome at first by forced and then by genuine laughter. Even two men who had not been introduced to anyone exchanged a dull-witted look and finally laughed; they wore matching raincoats and suits and had matching faces, and they ate and drank standing up, never having removed their rubber boots or hats in the foyer.

Kolomeitsev and his wife soon after attended Yulya's wedding to a taciturn and sad-faced dentist, Dodik. He had pulled out her wisdom tooth—the first ever of his practice—and the great mutual suffering led, three days later, cheek still swollen, to the registry office. The wedding took place in the student dining room, where the unadorned plastic tables were pushed together, and loaded with platters of red-beet-and-potato salad and steaming hot dogs. Directly in front of the newlyweds was placed the *pièce de résistance,* an astonishing miracle of culinary art: a wedding cake, baked by female geology students in the shape of a tooth.

"May I have the first piece of the bride's tooth?" shouted Kolomeitsev from the far end of the table. Yulya cut it herself and served him. *But nothing had happened.* She gradually got used to Dodik, who had appeared at her side so unexpectedly; she even came to love him for his gentleness, his courtesy, and because he never tried to pry into her heart, even though he may have sensed something lived on there despite her will.

Yulya went on many expeditions with Kolomeitsev and observed his "field romances"; usually, according to his iron rule, they were brief and went unnoticed, except by her. There was never a hint of what had once happened between them—Kolomeitsev knew how to turn off his memory when he didn't need it—and they even addressed each other formally. Yulya Sergeyevna noticed that with the years Kolomeitsev was growing hardened. A certain harshness had always been part of his personality, but in his youth it had seemed to be part of his ecstatic hunger for life, and now it was sometimes frighteningly grim.

He was used to taking women easily, and he left them easily, too. He wanted to take life the way he took a woman. He already thought that he had. He pulled life to him compulsively, but it always slipped away again. He called it back angrily, but it no longer heard. Yet life was the only woman Kolomeitsev really loved. His pride wouldn't permit him to understand it had turned from him, but he felt it instinctively, like an animal, and tried to hold on, no matter the cost. More than anything else, Kolomeitsev feared looking like a failure, especially in his own eyes. The fear of failure turned out to be his worst failing. He was constantly imposing his will in order to overcome, and without noticing it himself, he overcame the best in himself. And his best was: courage; disdain for hypocrisy; dedication to his profession; a quick mind. Seryozha Lachugin liked him so much because of these qualities, and so did the son of Yulya Sergeyevna, now twenty years old and also a geology student. Yulya was continually astonished that her son physically resembled Kolomeitsev, although it was impossible he was the father. She read somewhere that this could happen when a woman constantly thinks about a man, even if he's dead.

This day, for the first time in twenty years, Yulya Sergeyevna broke down. While they were mapping the excavation, looking for any tiny sign of cassiterite, Kolomeitsev suddenly blocked out the sun and leaped down. Unwitting, they found themselves face-to-face inside a narrow rectangle hacked out of the earth. The sun, as though avenging itself against Kolomeitsev for having dared to block it, now ruthlessly splashed his face with light as he caught his balance, and Yulya Sergeyevna saw with horror how haggard and harried he was. He seemed old to her for the first time. Before, she thought that only she was getting old and that Kolomeitsev would remain eternally young, the graduate student in that dark courtyard garden. She was suddenly seized with such emotion that while not touching or kissing Kolomeitsev, she allowed herself to gaze at him in a manner that violated the twenty-year-old agreement pretending *nothing had happened*. Kolomeitsev shaded his eyes with his hand and looked straight at Vyazemskaya.

"You really shouldn't use eye makeup. It doesn't suit you." He cruelly punished her with these few words.

Kolomeitsev's face, now in shadow, no longer seemed defenseless the way it had in the full sun. The shade hid his wrinkles, his vulnerability, leaving only roughhewn, arrogant features. Yulya Sergeyevna reeled back to the pit's wall, striking a sharp rock with the small of her back, which had always secretly ached from the metal toy.

Later she wept not for herself but for Kolomeitsev, hiding his face from the sun. In the pit he had resembled a fierce lone wolf, unthinking, unable to understand how miserable it was.

In a third tent the senior excavator, Ivan Ivanovich Zagranichny, whose last name means "from abroad" in Russian, but who had never been abroad, began a conversation about cats. The impetus had come from one of the workmen who had casually used the word *cat*. "We keep digging, and for what? It's like trying to catch a cat by the tail."

And so the topic of "cat" hung in the air, above the exhaustion and the longing for a good, stiff drink, above the aches and blisters and bruises—its mysterious tea-leaf pupils glinting, its sharp claws hiding in soft, stealthy paws, while it ingratiatingly twitched its tail to gain your trust and purred with dubious sincerity.

Ivan Ivanovich Zagranichny's pitted face, which was almost as tiny as a fist, and especially his murky eyes quickly became animated with burning interest. "When I worked at the helicopter base, we had a cat in the dining room."

If someone had said *blini*, they would have had a conversation about *blini*—what was the most delicious way to serve them: with butter, or buttermilk, or sour cream, with salted fish, or jam—and there might have been someone who could recall eating *blini* with caviar. But that would have been an old man. Then they'd begin boasting about who could eat the most *blini* at one time, and finally particular incidents with *blini* would be recalled: how somebody, having stuffed himself with *blini*, gave up the ghost; how someone, who'd had one too many, put a *blin* on his head instead of a cap. *Blini* would definitely lead to women—how can you avoid that before bedtime! Someone, perhaps, would tell how he kissed a girl through a *blin*. "Big deal—kissing!" someone else would say with a feeling of immense superiority. "I'll tell you guys something a lot more exciting than that." And he would wink, promising great things to the delighted giggles of all assembled. But now the topic was "cat," and all thoughts turned to cats.

"So this dining-room cat of ours was incredibly arrogant," Ivan Ivanovich Zagranichny continued. "The pilots had spoiled him. They let him hang around the table, and he got so obnoxious there was no stopping him. Sometimes we'd be sitting there eating, and he'd jump over your shoulder onto the table, grab a meat patty, and take off. Once the big bosses were in from Irkutsk, and our kitchen ladies really wanted to show off. They made special chicken cutlets with chicken liver inside and a bone sticking out from each cutlet and wrapped in paper. And the paper was fancy, too—with little curlicues. The biggest boss proposed a toast to the air fleet, but out of nowhere our cat hopped up on the table and grabbed the cutlet right out from under his nose. The little bastard grabbed it right by its little bone, as though he had been brought up in some aristocratic family! And the boss frowns and says, 'What kind of place is this, a dining room or a zoo?' In other words, the cat had decayed morally and turned into a parasite. So the pilots flew him out and gave him to the geological camp as a present, but they sent the present back on the very next run. 'He won't let people eat . . . tears food out of our mouths,' they said. 'And he caterwauls all night. He misses you.'

"We began to think: What do we do with this cat? We couldn't kill him; after all, it was a living creature. Should we put him in a cage? Who'd ever heard of keeping a cat in a cage? People'd laugh at us! So we tried something sneaky. We made the cat a little parachute, tied it under his belly, and dropped him from a helicopter about a hundred versts from base into the middle of the taiga. We were afraid he'd grab onto the helicopter's tail in order to stay with us. But the pilot circled, made sure the parachute had opened, and watched the cat, legs dangling, come in for a landing. At last we could eat without looking over our shoulders. But I forgot to tell you, the cat was a beauty. One of our native cats, a Siberian. Your hand just disappeared in his fur. People loved to pet him, and he really knew how to purr and rub up against your leg so you'd forgive him almost anything. . . . So we started remembering our little friend. Something was missing. One night we were sitting at dinner, poking at our cutlets with our forks. They had no taste without the furry threat hanging over them. Boy, were we suffering pangs of conscience! What had happened to our parachutist cat? Did he get hurt landing? Did he manage to unhook the parachute, or was he stuck in some bush? Did he die of hunger—there are no special cutlets in the taiga? Did some bear tear him to pieces, even though, we thought, who likes cat meat? A whole week had passed.

"Suddenly there he was, in person—*splat*—on our table, as though he'd fallen through the ceiling. Scraggly, skinny, with the parachute belts still under his belly, and he grabbed my cutlet. . . . We were so glad to see that cat! From that day on, whenever we were at the table, the cat had his own plate with his own personal cutlet. The cat was happy, and we were happy. He'd proved his feline rights. People should learn a lesson from him!"

Everyone laughed sympathetically. But the cat theme cried out for further development. A rough voice came from the back of the tent. "That cat may have been something, but he fought only for himself. I have a brother in Irkutsk, and he had the real king of cats. Not only didn't he steal from the table, he put food on it. Probably because he was a Siamese. That's the way it is over there in Siam. People are dropping from hunger, so the cats come to their aid.

"My brother lives in Irkutsk right across the street from a grocery store. But when I say 'grocery store,' it's only because that's what the sign says. It's stocked with vodka and other liquor, but as for meat or sausages, you might say it's an emporium of empty shelves. Housewives check it out from time to time, because occasionally they do throw some food out. But my brother's cat is no idiot. He figured out that there was no point in hanging around the store. But there were enticing aromas emanating from the service entrance. He got in, unnoticed, between the legs of the manager's friends, who used the service entrance. And—behold!—there were stacks of food cartons. Our Siamese shows up at home with a small package for my brother between his teeth. My brother opened it and couldn't believe his eyes: smoked salmon! He gave the cat his share and didn't let his conscience deprive him of eating the rest. Whose loss was it anyway? And so it went on. My brother started to find out how many friends he had. Even I started visiting him more frequently. He always had various types of sausage on his table: 'tea sausage,' 'connoisseur's sausage,' and once even 'filet sausage.' Sometimes there was ham, pink and beautifully sliced, like they have abroad. The cat perched on the refrigerator, watching the visitors and blinking—like the merchant patron of the arts, Savva Morozov, urging his guests to help themselves.

"Now, on the street between the grocery store and my brother's house, there was an arch. It had been put up way before the revolution. The cat had adopted it for its feline needs. Nobody could catch him as he ran over it with a package in his mouth.

"One day the president of some country or other was visiting Irkutsk. I don't remember whether he wanted to admire Lake Baikal or taste our salmon, but in any case it's not important. The shacks that would have been along the president's route were razed in the blink of an eye. The old women who lived in them lit candles to him in church. Thanks to him, they were getting new apartments! You could see them wandering about in their new kitchens, sniffing the gas ranges the way they would a nosegay.

"Under the arch over the street they erected a scaffold for painters and painted WELCOME TO OUR CITY! on the arch in our language and in the foreign one. They lined up the populace, who had been given the day off, to applaud the president. Our Siberians are hospitable, especially when they get a day off to boot. But my brother's cat was indifferent to the solemnity of the occasion and went shopping as usual. On the return trip he was crossing the arch again, package in mouth, when he slipped on the wet paint. Just at that moment the president's car was passing, and suddenly—pow!—something heavy and extremely bloody landed on the windshield, obliterating all visibility. The driver panicked and threw on the brakes. The police blew their whistles frantically. The president cowered in a corner of the car, protecting his face with his arms—all foreign presidents are afraid of terrorism. But it was only my brother's cat, and when he slipped, he dropped a package of chopped meat on the president's car. The president waited, but there didn't seem to be any shooting. He took his arms away from his face, saw the meat on the windshield and the cat on the arch, and smiled in relief. Supposedly he said to the people with him, 'I've heard a lot about Russian hospitality, but I never expected this!' "

Everyone laughed.

"Well, I'll tell you about Ruslan and Ludmila," another voice said, from the depths of the tent.

Ivan Ivanovich Zagranichny grunted with a boss's arrogance. "You think we haven't read our Lermontov? Don't get sidetracked from cats."

"Ruslan and Ludmila, for your information, Ivan Ivanovich, is a cake."

"What do you mean, 'a cake'?" Zagranichny was taken aback.

"It's a kind of cake. They make it in Leningrad."

"And what does it have to do with cats?"

"You'll see. . . . Just be patient, Ivan Ivanovich. . . . I was awarded a trip once. 'Where would you like to go?' I said, 'New York.' They were shocked. 'Why is that?' I said to them, 'We have to study our enemies.' They scratched their heads. 'We'll put your name on the waiting list.' They offered me Truskavets, Kislovodsk, but I'm healthy, I don't need to take the waters. 'Give me Leningrad,' I say. 'At least I'll study our former enemies.' 'Who's that?' they ask anxiously. I explain, 'The tsars.' They calmed down. Gave me the trip. First I traveled around with a group, but then I went on my own way—they went too fast. It's better to be outraged by the life-style of sovereigns at a slower pace. The remains are beautiful. I wanted to sit on the furniture, at least touch the past with my ass, but there were ropes everywhere. I stormed all the palaces until only Pavlovsk was left. I took the commuter train, carrying a bottle of port wine with me. I sat there and sipped on it, preparing myself for the imminent cultural experience. Opposite me sat a little old lady, looking noble, museum-like. And next to her was a cake, wrapped and tied—called a Ruslan and Ludmila. The old lady was giving me dirty looks but pretending not to notice my wine. Then a noisy crowd got on, carrying packages and bottles. Longhairs—you couldn't tell the girls from the boys. They flopped down next to me. They didn't swear, but they turned on their tape recorders, and the music coming out of them was worse than any swear words. The old lady was so outraged she even shut her eyes. Soon this group got off; my ears were still ringing. The old lady opened her eyes, sighed, and tugged my sleeve. I could hardly believe my eyes: They had switched their own box for the cake! The box was almost the same, but instead of 'Ruslan and Ludmila' on it, it said 'Fruit and Berry.' The old lady started to cry.

" 'Please, lady,' I say. 'They probably did it by mistake.'

" 'Some mistake!' says a woman sitting in the next seat. 'Just try to get a Ruslan and Ludmila cake. Those wretched hippies know about shortages, too. Those kids! No respect for their elders. That's what long hair leads to.'

" 'Calm down, lady,' I say. 'At least you still have a cake. You won't come visiting empty-handed.'

"And the old lady says through her tears, 'I wasn't going to visit anyone. I was on my way to bury Vasya.'

"I say, 'Accept my condolences. Was Vasya your husband or your son?'

"And the old lady says, 'Vasya was my cat. I had him for eighteen years.'

"I practically choked. 'Then what was the Ruslan and Ludmila for—the cat's funeral?'

" 'I was carrying poor dead Vasya in the box. I wanted to put his body to rest somewhere in the country, near birch trees.'

"When I heard this, I went wild. On the one hand, my hair almost stood on end. On the other hand, it was kind of funny: I imagined those kids dropping by someone's house with the Ruslan and Ludmila cake, putting the present on the table, and untying the twine."

Ivan Ivanovich Zagranichny frowned; he had a feeling that he'd heard this story somewhere else. It seemed to be something perilously close to an old chestnut. But even Ivan Ivanovich's own cat with a parachute belt was a composite, if the truth be known: a little of his own; a little from others. There is a peculiarity of the taiga camp story: Even the storytellers themselves don't know exactly where the truth ends and invention begins. But since everybody wants to believe it happened that way, and happened to him personally, let him, as long as it's funny. It makes things easier in the taiga, where laughter is a faithful comrade. That's why Ivan Ivanovich did not express his reservations about the cake story.

Someone else started to tell the story of how a cat landed in a washing machine, but Kalya interrupted from the tent's entrance. "Hey, come on, the chowder's getting cold."

From all three tents they gathered around the campfire. Nothing unites people like a campfire.

Seryozha Lachugin saw it in the distance as he rounded a bend of the river, which the path was following. He smiled and thought: *Everything is all right when there's a fire.* He walked faster, even though it was dark underfoot, and only the moon, diving in and out of the clouds, fitfully lit the path. The campfire disappeared from view and then reappeared, already much larger and aromatic through the enormous trees. With every step, the outlines of people sitting around it grew more distinct, and finally, the orange glow began molding faces out of the thick darkness. Just as he reached them,

Seryozha stopped for a second, still unnoticed, and knocked on a pine tree.

"May I come in?"

They didn't hug or kiss him or bombard him with questions. They simply made room for him, and Kalya poured some fish soup. While Seryozha gulped down his steaming bowl, they all watched him, unable to eat themselves—the answer Seryozha brought was that important. The one exception was Kolomeitsev, who seemed to have little interest in it. Seryozha tried to talk a few times, but Kolomeitsev casually motioned with his hand, as if to calm him. *Now that's will-power,* Seryozha thought with awe. *If I were him, I wouldn't be able to wait. I'd ask.*

Finally, Kolomeitsev said in a languid, even bored voice, which he used only when he was agitated, "Well, ambassador, let's go get some fresh air," as though they were sitting in an office filled with nosy people, rather than around a campfire under the open sky.

Durshtein snorted and shrugged. Vyazemskaya didn't even look up. Sitechkin, with loyal canine eyes, also rose to "get some fresh air," but the chief stopped him in his tracks with an icy stare. Kolomeitsev used his pocket flashlight to lead Seryozha to the riverbank, where they sat down on a log. He slowly lit up his pipe and, only after several slow drags, asked, "Well?" He could hold back no longer, and the word tore out hoarsely, tensely. Seryozha took the envelope out of his Aeroflot bag. Kolomeitsev ripped it open, unfolded the paper, and shone his flashlight onto the text. The letter, bearing an official stamp and the familiar impressive signature, was brief: "In accordance with the laboratory results, further exploration does not seem worthwhile. Finish up your work. Turn over your people to the Upper Sayan group. The samples they sent in are promising." Kolomeitsev folded the page in two once more and stuck it into the map case hanging from his belt.

"Did you read the letter?" he asked, not looking at Seryozha.

"No, Viktor Petrovich," Seryozha replied. "But I know what's in it."

"You don't know a thing," Kolomeitsev said. "Understand?"

"Understood," replied Seryozha, submitting, as usual, to the most unexpected decisions of this man who had greater knowledge than anyone else.

"Letters from the authorities have to be read like poetry," Kolomeitsev joked. "The most important part is between the lines. They're afraid of responsibility at the main office, and so they put it all on my shoulders. If we succeed, they'll take credit along with us. If we don't, they can duck responsibility with a piece of paper. Office psychology. But we're on the front lines, Seryozha."

Kolomeitsev returned to the dying fire, sporting one of his broadest smiles. His face betrayed not even a shadow of doubt.

"My congratulations. I quote: 'The samples are promising.'"

Seryozha was amazed by the chief's composure and his readiness to assume risk so courageously. Burshtein raised his eyebrows in surprise. Vyazemskaya didn't move. Sitechkin looked around with a victorious air, as if to say, "What did I tell you!," and even stood up. Kolomeitsev did not give them a chance to recover but took out a worn map from his case and unfolded it on his lap.

"We must push on. We can't let that cassiterite get away."

"And how are we going to stop it?" Ivan Ivanovich Zagranichny shook his head. "It's as slippery as an eel. We've excavated everywhere."

"Not everywhere," Kolomeitsev said curtly, pointing at the map. "We have to go down the river to here and excavate on the left bank. All the accompanying ores are there—granite pigmatites, hydrothermal veins. The cassiterite has got to be there; there's nowhere else for it to go. Kesha, get the boats ready for morning. Do we have enough fuel?"

"We have fuel," Kesha replied with a note of hesitation that obviously caused him embarrassment. He scraped his spoon against his empty bowl. "But the water's pretty low. And there are two sets of rapids, one after another. Maybe we should wait for rain, when there'll be more water."

"Oh, Kesha, that's not like you." Kolomeitsev tossed a charred log back into the fire. Then, knowing how to get Kesha where he was most vulnerable, he said to Kalya, "And how about you, Kalya? Are you afraid, too? Will our oatmeal get wet?"

"Why should I be afraid! If it gets wet, it'll dry out," Kalya said, shrugging. But she immediately came to Kesha's defense. "Kesha doesn't like to rush into things."

But Kesha kept scraping his spoon and staring at the empty bowl, which was sprinkled with ashes from the fire. "The water's too low."

Burshtein cleared his throat. "Maybe we could call in a helicopter for the move?"

"Why not an ocean liner? Or a Boeing? With a bar on board?" Kolomeitsev was angry. "We're geologists, not a travel agency."

"Right," Sitechkin agreed, pulling himself up and glaring triumphantly at Burshtein.

Vyazemskaya still remained silent.

"And what does the working class think?" Kolomeitsev asked, turning to Ivan Ivanovich.

"If it's necessary, then . . ." Ivan Ivanovich Zagranichny grumbled reluctantly, and as he signaled the three other workmen to go back to the tent with him, it was clear that they'd be getting up early tomorrow. Kalya collected everyone's bowls and went down to the river to wash up. Kesha wandered after her, morose, as though it were his fault the water was low.

"Kalya, what's an ocean liner?" Kesha asked.

"You bumpkin," Kalya replied haughtily. "A huge ship, that's what!"

"But that wouldn't fit into the Oka River. What's a Boeing?"

"The same thing. Just like it." Kalya tried to stop the questions.

"And a bar?"

"A little learning is a dangerous thing. Why don't you dry the bowls?"

"Forgive me, Boris Abramovich," Kolomeitsev said, speaking more softly and leading Burshtein away from the fire. Kolomeitsev didn't like others to witness his apologies. "I didn't mean to insult you. But you must admit, calling for a helicopter when we can get there by boat is humiliating. Life is humiliating enough without making it more so."

"I didn't take it as an insult," Burshtein said, lowering his eyes. "Kesha grew up on this river, and he knows it better than we do. He's no coward. And I'm no travel agent, as you so blithely put it. But this risk is pointless."

"What do you mean?"

"Because I don't believe there's a deposit there," Burshtein said finally, looking up and sighing with relief, as if freed of a great burden.

"May I ask you one question, Boris Abramovich?" Kolomeitsev asked casually, as though he had been expecting this confession for days.

"Of course," Burshtein replied, not taking his eyes off Kolomeitsev's face, trying to catch a glimpse of something resembling doubt.

"What do you think faith is?" Kolomeitsev said, driving back Burshtein's gaze.

"Believing what you know," Burshtein replied.

"No, faith is believing what you don't know," Kolomeitsev said. "You can never know enough; that's why people cling to faith. Of course, some faith comes from pity, but another kind comes from inner strength. You'll never win any game if you don't believe in what you're doing. You have to play a game to the end, even if the cards aren't going your way. When your fingertips are charged with faith, the good cards will leap into your hands. We've put too much into finding that cassiterite to allow ourselves the luxury of not believing in it."

"But you're not playing with cards; you're playing with human lives," Burshtein muttered. "And I'm not saying you're taking risks only with others. You're playing with yourself, too. Don't lose yourself."

"You mean you're giving up?" Kolomeitsev asked harshly.

"I didn't say that." Burshtein frowned. "I don't think I've ever let you down."

"I know, Boris Abramovich," Kolomeitsev said, nodding. "You may not believe me, but you never let me down. That's a lot right there. But—forgive me—you lack one quality: fanaticism. And without it you can't achieve anything in this world. I'm not talking about morbid fanaticism or hysterics, but active, healthy fanaticism. All social revolutions, all scientific and technological revolutions were created by possessed fanatics, not people overwhelmed with doubts. I know it's impossible not to have any doubts. But some people get so accustomed to the smell of shit that they can't smell the future. Do you think I'm so stupid I don't have any doubts at all? But I don't allow myself to be weak. I know that cassiterite is around here somewhere, and we'll find it if we keep digging. Don't you realize that instinct is stronger than reason?"

"It's fanatics who drive people to doubt even the most noble souls!" Burshtein wasn't giving up. "By the way, I don't think you're a fanatic."

"What am I then? A cynic?" Kolomeitsev demanded.

"No, you're not a cynic. You're simply confused. And you're afraid of that, so you want to look like a fanatic—even to yourself," Burshtein said.

Kolomeitsev suddenly looked as if someone had wounded him; his unshaved cheeks stood out sharply in the light of the dying fire, and something in his eyes recoiled with exhaustion. Burshtein felt sorry for him. No matter how much they disagreed, Burshtein never lost his affection for Kolomeitsev. Once Kolomeitsev had saved his life on the Vitim River, when an enormous oar struck a boulder and knocked Burshtein off the roof of the boat. Kolomeitsev had dived into a whirlpool to save his friend.

"Let's talk about fanaticism some other time," said Burshtein. "And as for the cassiterite, I'll be happier than anybody if you find it. You've always been lucky anyway." Burshtein knew this was something he liked to hear. The irritation on Kolomeitsev's face was replaced immediately by an almost childlike smile.

Sitechkin, meanwhile, noticed that the official envelope had fallen from Kolomeitsev's map case, which had been left by the fire. Sitechkin knew it was not nice to read other people's mail. But he also knew it wasn't unprofitable. He looked around. Convinced that no one was looking, he pulled the letter out of its envelope, hastily glanced through it, and then replaced it.

The truth was that while Sitechkin slavishly fawned upon Kolomeitsev, he did not, in reality, like him much.

As a child Eduard Sitechkin lived in a tall, beautifully appointed apartment building, but he lived in the basement. His mother worked as the elevator operator, and his father as the janitor. In the evenings his parents sat around and gossiped about the famous tenants. "Yesterday the cosmonaut dragged himself in at one in the morning," his mother announced. "I was already snoozing on the couch, and the bell doesn't work, so our highly decorated hero began banging on the door with his fist. He doesn't care if he wakes up a working person. Go ahead and bang, I thought, and I didn't move, pretending not to hear. You're the boss in space, but I'm the boss in the lobby. And what do you think he did, that shameless man? He opened the window in the propaganda room and climbed in, popping off all his buttons. 'What kind of outrage is this?' he says. 'Why don't you open the door?' 'You should be considerate,' I say. 'You should come home on time and respect the workers on duty. And you, a cosmonaut, go out and get drunk at night. I'll write a letter about this to your Cosmonauts' Union, and you won't get a medal for it.' Well, he got really mad then. 'I'm not out getting drunk; I just got back from training.' Hah! He thinks I'll believe anything. We know what kind of training sessions. . . . And they photograph him for the papers. They should photograph him climbing in the window, like a tomcat."

"You're right, they've got no respect for the working class," the janitor agreed, nodding sadly. "The singer Svetozarova called me in. The one who used to live with the accordion player—now she's screwing around with her chauffeur. 'You've got to help me,' she says. 'I was washing out my stockings in the sink, and my ring came off and went down the drain.' So I open up the pipe, and there's the ring, stuck in the slime. The people's artist was overjoyed; she puts on her ring and laughs. 'So even clogged-up plumbing has its advantages!' She was reproaching me. And then she rummages around in her wallet and gives me a fiver. A fiver for a diamond ring! It probably cost three thousand. . . . And she's a laureate of state prizes!"

It's hardly surprising that Eduard Sitechkin had contempt for most people. If even the most famous of them—the ones on TV—were like that, then what were the rest like! His father often described the furniture, rugs, and lamps in those celebrities' apartments, and Edik was eaten up with envy: Why did they have all that when he had so little? How could he make his way up there, to the upper floors? Probably he had to become educated, an intellectual. His name already sounded intellectual; his parents had apparently called him Eduard with foresight. Edik began studying the manners of those who lived on the upper floors.

He had no special talents and flunked out in both physics and mathematics. So he got into geology—by accident. A geology professor who lived in the building once got stuck in the elevator for five hours. When they finally got him out, it seemed he hadn't been able to control himself. Edik's mother was about to raise a stink, so to speak, but she realized she could use the professor's embarrassment to her advantage. "This will remain just between us," she said, "I won't make a fuss, and you, Professor, help my dimwit son find a place, at least in the geology department." The professor, overwhelmed by the ridiculous situation, got him a spot.

Once Sitechkin's father told him a parable: "When I was working in the construction battalion, our sergeant could barely read and write, but he loved wielding power. He couldn't stand insubordination. He lined us up, the new recruits, and said, 'Your first task is clearing this whole quadrant; then pick up your aluminium spoons and eat your soup.' One recruit says with a smile, 'Excuse me, sir, but it's aluminum.' The sergeant looks at him like a snake looks at a rabbit. 'Fall out.' He fell out. 'Who are you?' 'I'm a philologist, Comrade Sergeant.' 'So then, philologist, see that pine?' 'I see it.' 'You'll uproot it yourself; no one will help! And only then—take up your spoon. Your aluminium spoon.' After everyone had eaten lunch and dinner, that intellectual was still struggling with the pine tree. Finally, he reports to the sergeant, covered with dirt, barely able to stand up but with enlightenment visible in his eyes. 'May I report, Comrade Sergeant? The pine tree is uprooted, as ordered.'

" 'By the roots?' the sergeant asked suspiciously. 'By the roots,' the intellectual replied. 'And what was under the roots?' the sergeant asks. The intellectual thought a bit and replied, 'A spoon, Comrade Sergeant.'

" 'What kind?' the sergeant asked sarcastically. 'Aluminium, Comrade Sergeant,' the intellectual said with a sigh. So you, Edik, don't try to be independent—it's useless. They'll eat you alive. And the sergeants are more important than the generals because they're always around." This parable fell deeply into Sitechkin's soul.

Actually Sitechkin envied Kolomeitsev. Kolomeitsev inspired respect, if not exactly love. People took him into account. No one took Eduard Sitechkin into account. He was despised by everyone, even those to whom he sucked up most blatantly, including Kolomeitsev himself.

Having read the letter from the directorate and appraised the situation, Sitechkin realized that this was his moment. Those in power had to notice a young specialist who did not follow his chief in disobeying their orders. Kolomeitsev was going to get in a lot of trouble. Why go down with him? But what if Kolomeitsev actually found the cassiterite?

Sitechkin vacillated. No, even if Kolomeitsev were successful, they wouldn't forgive disobedience. They'd thank him for the cassiterite and find some other blot on his record. And they wouldn't forget Sitechkin. People like Sitechkin always came in handy.

Sitechkin made his decision.

When Kolomeitsev and Burshtein returned and bent their heads over the fire, Sitechkin tossed out his challenge in an artificially loud voice. "Viktor Petrovich, what does the letter say really? Why are you hiding it?"

Kolomeitsev couldn't even imagine that Sitechkin's slimy, fawning voice was capable of such a brazen, imperious demand. There wasn't a trace of his former toadying; before Kolomeitsev stood an enemy who had unexpectedly straightened his servile back. Even Sitechkin's eyes were different. Before, they had scurried about, begging, showing rapture, agreeing. Now they were frozen and staring, full of obnoxious superiority. Lachugin shuddered and understood at once: Sitechkin knew. Burshtein studied Sitechkin with astonishment —as if he were a genie who had finally released himself from a bottle. Vyazemskaya glanced at him without a trace of surprise and, with quiet scorn, said, "That letter is addressed to the chief of the unit, not to you, Sitechkin. You don't know enough as a geologist to question your superior."

"How do you know what I know!" Sitechkin screamed. "Do you think that I'm a nothing? You'll see! I have a right to know what's in that letter."

"You already know what's in it," Kolomeitsev said slowly, suddenly feeling a deathly fatigue and revulsion. "You took it out of my map case."

"I didn't take it! It fell out," Sitechkin squealed. "You're insulting me!"

"Here it is." Kolomeitsev handed the letter to Burshtein. "I didn't want to show it to you. Forgive me . . . I can't obey. I ask you to trust me as geologists and as my friends."

Burshtein didn't take the letter, pushing Kolomeitsev's hand away. "I guessed what it said. It's all right. We'll keep on looking."

"I'll report this. As a young specialist I protest," Sitechkin yelled breathlessly.

"You were never young, Sitechkin," Vyazemskaya said.

"And you're no geologist," Burshtein added.

"Seryozha." Sitechkin appealed to Lachugin. "You're a witness to these insults."

"I'm no witness of yours," Seryozha said firmly.

"This is a conspiracy against me. It's some sort of Mafia here. You'll all be punished! All of you—" Sitechkin was hysterical.

"*Will be arrested?*" Burshtein interrupted. "Is that what you're going to say? Strange you didn't blurt it out sooner."

Kolomeitsev, so recently shattered by Sitechkin's blow, suddenly pulled himself together. He felt younger and happy to be angry again. It struck him that he wasn't alone at all. Something more than his personal will was involved.

"Go away, Sitechkin. For good!" he ordered.

"You'll be sorry!" Sitechkin ran into the tent and came out, dragging his sleeping bag. "I'm leaving in the morning. I'll go straight to the directorate!"

Burshtein put his hand on Kolomeitsev's shoulder. "I have a suggestion. We should split up. We haven't excavated everything here. For instance, this break." And he pointed to the map. "Vyazemskaya,

Lachugin, and the workmen should stay and finish up this work. You and I will take the boat. We'll excavate ourselves. If we find the cassiterite, everyone will join us."

"I'd rather go with you," Vyazemskaya said intransigently.

"Me, too," said Seryozha.

"Me, too," said Ivan Ivanovich Zagranichny, unexpectedly appearing out of the darkness. "My mates can manage here without me. And my hack will come in handy. What is that ass screaming about?"

"I give the orders," Kolomeitsev said, once again filled with determination. "The proposal to separate is accepted. All the workers stay here. Vyazemskaya is in charge. Lachugin . . ." The silent entreaty of Seryozha's eyes made him stop. "I think that Yulya Sergeyevna can manage alone with the documentation. We'll take two boats. In the first—myself, Burshtein, and Ivan Ivanovich. In the second, Kesha, Seryozha, the instruments, and food. We have to find the cassiterite before we're forcibly dragged away from this area. Any questions?"

There were no questions.

CHAPTER · 13

The scintillatingly silver Boeing traveling between Seattle and Honolulu lowered the landing gear from its belly over the scattered emerald islands and began to descend so abruptly that the tiny elderly lady in a straw hat with artificial flowers superstitiously clasped the small St. Christopher medal on her breast—it was her first time flying. On her lap bounced a wicker basket with a lid, which she had refused to check with her luggage or let be put in the closet up front, despite the polite suggestions of the Pan American stewardesses, who now moved with balletic grace along the aisle. The stewardesses did not know that under the basket's lid lay nothing more than five dozen eggs, each individually wrapped in a Kleenex. Of course, the eggs truly were magnificent. Unlike city eggs, these were large and, more important, devoid of that suspicious incubator whiteness; instead, there were pieces of straw and manure sticking to them. The lady lived on a small chicken farm near Seattle, and she was bringing the eggs to her son. He was a young rock singer, and he had invited her to his first big-time concert in Honolulu. The eggs were good for his voice.

To her disappointment, her son didn't meet her at the airport. In his stead there ran up a hirsute, lanky fellow, wearing a T-shirt stenciled with a picture of her son and the other members of his group, which was called The Tails. He introduced himself as the manager, and his hairy hands, which were peeling from sunburn, reached for the basket to help her. Looking at his dirty suede shorts, which exposed indecently furry, peeling legs, and trying in vain to guess what kind of eyes were hidden behind the mirrored lenses of his glasses, the lady instinctively clutched her basket. It fell open, and most of the eggs fell out onto the marble mosaic floor of the airport, turning into a yellow-white mush. The manager remained calm, as if he had spent his whole life at airports, meeting ladies carrying farm-fresh eggs on Boeings. He slipped a dollar to the Hawaiian porter who appeared out of nowhere and, with a praiseworthy respect for nature's bounty, picked up the few eggs that had been miraculously spared. He placed them back in the basket, which he now carried himself, and then went to baggage claim for the old-fashioned suitcase wrapped with straps just in case. Finally, he deposited the little lady into a black limousine, sun-baked on the outside and deliciously cold inside, in which sat three other ladies. They had arrived by different flights at approximately the same time, all to attend their sons' concert. The ladies introduced themselves with reserved politeness and cautious joy en route. One was the mother of many children, the wife of an automobile factory worker from Detroit; the second worked as a dishwasher at a Holiday Inn near Nashville and said nothing about her son's father; and the third was the widow of a miner from Arizona. They had in common red, rough hands which betrayed the harshness of their lives, so removed from the leisured existence of those who come to Honolulu to ride surfboards or sip rum punch from a pineapple half, served at the beach by bronze Hawaiian waiters in bathing suits. They were visiting Hawaii for the first time, thanks to the tickets sent by their sons. The famous resort city flashed by at an amazing clip on the other side of the limousine's windows—an artificial paradise that scraped the sky, erected to replace the indigenous, natural paradise. The ladies even spotted colorful ads with pictures of their sons.

The manager suddenly slapped himself on the forehead and ordered the chauffeur to stop. He ran to the trunk and got four necklaces of multicolored Hawaiian leis, which he put around the necks of the mothers, who began examining them and giggling like girls. The manager, sitting next to the driver, watched in the rearview mirror the simple, glowing faces of these tired women, spirited away by the magic of Pan Am to the best possible holiday: a meeting with their sons. His own mother's face floated before him; she was a cashier in Woolworth's in Salt Lake City—a city of Mormons, where they didn't drink liquor, but they did have the best ice cream in the world—and the manager thought what a bastard he was for not having seen his mother in so many years. The manager suppressed his sentimentality. The Tails were his baby, his ticket to success. He had created the group at a festival of school bands two years before and proceeded to lock them up in a cheaply rented, abandoned beach house in California, to prepare a musical program, running the rockers through their paces like young dogs till they were ready to pounce on the public at any minute and grab it by the throat. Borrowing money from everyone he knew and a few he didn't, he invested in a preliminary promotion campaign to spread the word through payola. Then he quietly began putting his boys on radio and TV, trying to keep a low profile, leaving the listeners hungry for more. Finally, he released their first single record.

His tactics worked. The single was a hit. But he hadn't made back his investment. Several companies approached him with an album offer, but he bided his time. He decided he had to put on a supershow, in the style of the Beatles, to guarantee that their first LP would go gold. But where? Madison Square Garden was too expensive. Besides, New York was a city glutted with celebrities, and The Tails' single had sold mostly in the provinces. So the manager chose the fifteen-thousand-seat Sports Palace in Honolulu. He wasn't counting on the tourists—their shorts usually revealed legs that were arthritic and varicose-veined. The manager was betting on Hawaii's young people, who couldn't afford to listen to the famous entertainers in the fabulously expensive nightclubs and cabarets—the children of the barmen, waiters, and doormen of the clubs, of the ice cream vendors, hairdressers, manicurists, masseuses, and prostitutes. In the veins of these kids the island blood pulsed, confused, bizarrely mixed with the American, Anglo-Saxon infusion. They were on edge; they wanted something, but only one fate awaited them: to be the same bartenders, doormen, and ice cream vendors as their parents. The octopus of service jobs dragged them in with its tentacles and swallowed them inexorably. But still they struggled irrationally, still hoping. The sun-roasted tourists, sitting at pontoon tables floating on an artificial lake and listening to a harpist strumming in a swaying gigantic shell, did not notice the faces of the native boys and girls, pressed against the filigree fence. But sometimes the adolescents' eyes glinted with island hatred for these invaders, whose genes had intermixed with theirs. The manager sensed this with professional acuity, and he knew his rock group had what these kids wanted: not protest but a longing for protest. The manager carefully studied how many records The Tails had sold in Hawaii—a lot, but nothing overwhelming. He started a special campaign in the papers, gave his boys a special commission: to write a song about Hawaii, not a treacly tourist song but one that a native Hawaiian might have written. Again the strategy worked; after being played on the local stations, the single sold out in Hawaii. A left-wing student newspaper spread the rumor that The Tails were for Hawaiian independence. With paid employees the manager organized fan clubs in the schools. Buttons appeared saying, "The Tail is our symbol." The atmosphere was charged. It was time to turn them loose on the public. SRO was guaranteed. The crowds that couldn't get tickets assailed the Sports Palace, ripping buttons from their idols' clothes, tearing the zippers off jeans, smashing electric guitars to bits, overturning police cars. When one of the boys mentioned he wanted to invite his mother to the concert, the manager immediately transformed this filial affection into a publicity stunt and invited all four moms. The public liked idols from so-called ordinary families.

After the four provincial ladies had left their luggage in their rooms at the Hilton and taken quick showers, combed their hair, and powdered their faces, the manager led them into the banquet room, crowded with reporters. The sons rushed to their mothers, embracing them in a most sincere manner, but at the same time turning to the cameras with their newly developed instincts. The mothers blinked at the flashes, bewildered, and involuntarily pressed closer to their sons.

"Did you ever think that your son would become a rock singer?" the mother from Seattle was asked.

"No," she replied, only now getting a good look at her black-haired son with biblical eyes and being taken aback by his patched jeans: Didn't he have enough money to dress better for such an important moment? She was also amazed that he was wearing such high heels —he wasn't short—and that his thin neck was encircled with beads more suitable for women, and that there was a red spot on his forehead, the kind Indian women wear.

"What would you like to see your son doing?" the reporters pestered.

"I don't know. I'd like to see him happy," the mother from Seattle replied.

They liked the answer. That's the simple way America should answer in the person of a mother from Seattle.

The mother from Detroit was asked about Watergate. She wasn't embarrassed and said firmly, "I don't believe that our president could be dishonest."

Part of the gathering greeted this statement with applause, part with condescending smiles.

The mother from Nashville was cautious. "Who knows?"

The mother from Arizona was more direct. "There are so many crooks around I wouldn't be surprised by anything."

The mother from Seattle said that she didn't understand a thing about it and looked guiltily at her son—had she let him down? Her son nodded comfortingly.

The supershow began before it began. The Hawaiian teenagers took the palace by storm, knocking down ticket takers and policemen. Inside, it was impossible to tell who had tickets and who didn't and who was sitting in whose seat.

Passions were building. Tambourines jangled, drums banged, and horns blared deafeningly. The manager barely squeezed the four mothers into the added-on row, and they peered around fearfully at the overheated, bubbling magma that made up their sons' fans. The lights went out, eliciting an exultant howl from the crowd that had been kept waiting a bit too long. Over the thousands of heads, spotlights exploded in purple, illuminating a gigantic screen above the stage. The screen was alive with strange designs and shapes, intermingled with documentary scenes of soldiers falling in Vietnam, holding their spilling intestines with trembling hands, then a close-up of a woman's nipple with tiny hairs sticking out around it, a thundering stampede of bison across the prairie, then a bare foot wriggling its dirty toes through a hole in a sneaker.

"What is this?" the mother from Seattle asked in horror, wondering where her son was.

The idols appeared onstage, waving their guitars. And the whole fifteen-thousand-throated audience screamed as one. The youth with biblical eyes came up to the microphone and tried to say something; apparently he was trying to announce their first song. However, the hysteria did not subside but continued to increase, drowning out his words. The youth's face, projected overhead on the screen, was at first happy but then confused. He started singing anyway, but nothing could be heard—the crowd's roar covered everything. The mothers didn't understand. Why didn't the crowd want to listen to their boys; why were all these people going mad and shouting as though they had come to their own concert? The mothers wanted to hear what their sons were singing, after all, that's why they were here, but it was impossible.

At first the band tried to silence the crowd, to force it to be quiet. They shouted into the microphones, and the mothers saw their sons' frustration at the crowd's ecstatic indifference. But soon the boys were running around the stage with their soundless electric guitars, convulsively moving their soundlessly singing mouths; they were swept up, shaking their hair, as though infected by the senseless hullabaloo, becoming part of it. What else could they do? Their eyes, mercilessly magnified on the screen, were frenzied, dull, maddened by the crowd's screaming and their own indifference. The mothers wept, pushed from all sides by shoulders and hands. They wept because everything that was happening was an insult to their sons. If they had shown the manager's face on the screen, then everyone would have seen that he was almost in tears, too. He had overplayed it; he had unleashed the crowd's hysteria, and he couldn't control it now. The manager realized that he had won, but at the same time he had lost something, too. He cared for The Tails and knew how nervous they had been before the concert, preparing several truly wonderful songs with words as important as the music. All that seemed absurd now; the crowd needed only the opportunity to scream, to let loose, to unfetter itself artificially from the rut of everyday life, to pretend to be free with open throats.

Afterward there was a party at the estate of the local pineapple king, a tiny, clever Hawaiian with a baked-apple face who had worked his way up from being a porter. He smiled so sweetly it seemed that his wrinkles were sprinkled with invisible sugar. There was no alcohol because the host had arranged this party not so much for The Tails as for his four young daughters, their fans. He knew that his daughters belonged to the school club Virginity—only to The Tails! and that's why he hired agents from a local detective agency to circulate as waiters with trays of nonalcoholic drinks through the well-kept gardens. The girls were, respectively, thirteen, fourteen, fifteen, and sixteen and had apple faces that were not yet baked. With their numerous girl friends they crowded around their idols. Their mother, half Chinese, half Japanese, a kind creature crammed into a bursting corset, poured jasmine tea into porcelain teacups from the Napoleonic Era for the four mothers. According to rumor, she once had been the owner of a brothel for sailors.

The manager had sneaked in a bottle of whiskey under his shirt and hidden it behind the tank of the toilet. The Tails, bored to tears, made occasional forays there for a drink or a snort of cocaine. When at last the "party" was over and the limousines carried the victors back to the Hilton, the mother from Seattle, who was boldest, looked up at her son. "Maybe we could take a little walk?"

The other mothers joined them with their sons, and they walked along the beach in pairs, softly. It was very late, and when they sat down on the beach, the pure breeze from the ocean seemed to blow away the sweaty stink of the concert's roaring crowd. The black-haired fellow with biblical eyes picked up his guitar and started to sing the song that had opened the concert. The song, it turned out, was about his mother, about her farm near Seattle, about the roosters outside his window, whose cries made the stars fall into the raw fresh herbs of the field. Then the others joined him; they now sang the songs of their soundless concert. Now no one kept the mothers from hearing their sons. The black-haired boy with biblical eyes recalled another time when he had felt this good: that white night in Leningrad, when the streetlamps slowly tipped back as the drawbridges raised, and a Russian boy read his poetry, chopping the air with his hands.

CHAPTER · 14

The leader of the literary club at the shipyard sucked on an almost dissolved tablet of antacid, while his enormous belly, which seemed to start just under his chin, spilled over onto the plush red tablecloth of the Red Corner room. On top of that comfortable expanse he clasped his short, plump hands, which were covered with red hairs, and twiddled his thumbs; he was listening or, rather, half listening, to the poems gushing forth from the novice writers. Actually this appearance of inattention was misleading: His weird, lobeless ears, popping out practically from his fleshy cheeks, were like a sonar that would instantly awake to fish out the slightest hint of a good line from the verbiage. An albino fitter was reading, as if he were hurling down a sledgehammer, menacingly raising his white eyebrows on the word *they,* which included all those who "feast, chatter, dipping their hands in blood."

> Let the villain bankers gloat
> The time for truth will out.
> Fly, dove of peace, fly, through any kind of weather—
> I wish you neither tar nor feather!

Next an old but spry cashier, who resembled a sly little fox, continued the international theme, moving his nose along a manuscript contained in a folder:

> In my dream a skyscraper, it grew.
> Suddenly it was a coffin, I knew.
> But I thought automatically:
> Why is it standing vertically?

Then the canteen waitress read or, rather, sang, poignantly rolling her eyes and suffocating the group with the cheap scent of Red Moscow. Under the table her elephantine legs clasped a zippered bag stamped "USSR," suspiciously fattened after a day at work.

Oh, Russia, nurturer of my song!
Here I am waiting, young and fair,
From out of my depths I long to pour
Everything you poured into there. . . .

We're all nuts, the leader of the literary circle thought sadly. *There's something abnormal about writing in damned columns with rhymes. We should all be put away!* Russia was crawling with literary clubs. Literary clubs at Pioneer Palaces, at Societies of Old Bolsheviks, at bakeries, at atomic centers, at breweries and criminal departments, institutes and penal colonies for minors. It was funny yet somehow touching. The leader realized that this indiscriminate versifying was somehow futile, but at the same time he felt that people's thirst for confession should be supported, even in rhyme. If a person's feelings and thoughts were kept locked inside, behind a rusty bolt, the person himself would eventually rust. The literary clubs might not produce a multitude of great poets, but they would create great readers, without whom there could be no literature. The leader ruthlessly scolded his beginners for lack of culture, for imitation, and for thematic and stylistic timidity. But he could not have lived a day without those anemic girls assiduously trying to capture Akhmatova's chasms with their eyes, without broad-hipped women howling in voices as loud as the trumpets of Jericho, without nervously twitching "pale youths with burning eyes," who had Yesenin whirling about underneath their Beatle haircuts. He loved them all, and on the chance of finding even the most meager talent, he continually exposed his balding head to the deafening Niagara of self-defeating hopelessness. After the canteen waitress, self-defeating hopelessness appeared before him in the shape of the director's secretary, wearing a tight denim skirt with embroidered flowers. She beat time to her compositions by tapping her Japanese wooden slippers, which opened to reveal her tense red heels.

You left, squashing my heart with your heel,
You're out of reach, regardless of how I feel. . . .

A severe case. The leader sighed, noting, however, the attractive
tightness of her skirt and thinking about how nice it would be to spend
time with the author under different circumstances.

The leader had himself begun writing poetry at the Leningrad
front, holding a neatly licked pencil in his stiff, half-frozen fingers.
When he was eighteen, he drove trucks carrying matériel and food
along the ice of Lake Ladoga. Frightened, cold, and hungry, he
couldn't have pictured himself, potbellied and suffering from high
blood pressure, dragging an equally potbellied briefcase with a gilt
fastener from publisher to publisher. It contained not only manuscripts
—his own and others'—but also cellophane-wrapped packets, neatly
labeled: "12 o'clock"; "2 o'clock"; "4 o'clock"; "6 o'clock." This was
his strictly prescribed diet: boiled beets; raw carrots; a piece of boiled
beef; a chunk of cheese. The leader was a sociable man, and he couldn't
resist the opportunity to sit at a table in the Writers' Club or the Orient
Restaurant or even in a *pelmeni* bar. He didn't drink cognac or vodka,
only dry wine, which was conducive to prolonged, rather than lightning-fast, spiritual rapport. Taking out hors d'oeuvres from the bowels
of his briefcase, he would look at his watch and follow the schedule.
But sometimes he fell off the wagon, gobbling down all the time-
allotted food at once and then morosely telling the waiter, "An order
of ham," adding, "Lean." The waiters knew him well and brought the
fattiest portions. Then he ordered a shashlik, then another, then a third,
and it all disappeared like buns into the mouth of Gogol's Patsyuk. He
then would triumphantly waggle his finger at unseen enemies and
recite Pasternak's lines:

Bohemian friends, we do not tolerate sobriety.
We announce war on the dependable piece.

These food binges would end with the return of the prodigal son
to the Institute of Nutrition, where he would lose about thirty pounds
in a month, only to start heroically all over again. He had several suits

in different sizes for his different physical stages. In answer to his doctors' rebukes, he merely spread his hands in resignation. "You cannot live in society and be free of society."

The leader had a beautiful wife, whom he ruled with an iron hand. As he traveled through the jungles of gastronomy, he telephoned home to make sure she was there. He didn't like people telling him she was beautiful; his eyebrows shot up as if to say, 'It's my business whether she's beautiful or not.' However, he couldn't stand staying home, and the line "I was happy in my family heaven, every evening until seven" could have been written about him.

The leader felt that a poet's life had to be red-blooded, even though that sometimes led to hypertension. But that had to do with the life of his body. The life of his soul was completely different. The casing of jolly-fat-man-with-reddish-mustache hid a harsh, ruthless professional. Though he dreamed of hams and slabs of bacon, he couldn't stand any fat in poetry. In order to determine whether someone was a real poet, he didn't even need to read the poetry; he merely glanced at a few lines. The word order told him everything. That's why it was enough for him to listen with half an ear.

One day the senior member of the literary association—a hulking but shy welder with a drooping black mustache, which made him look like a repentant Mexican bandit—introduced the new lathe operator from the assembly unit, Kostya Krivstov. Krivstov began to read. Suddenly the oily eyes of an imbibing cat quivered on the leader's face with the rapacity of a connoisseur. His ears stood straight up and did something rare: They began listening intently. The leader immediately caught in Krivtsov's voice the special ring that exists in a true poet's voice. . . . "The verb of time—the metals' chime!" Krivtsov's gray eyes seemed to have simultaneously widened and narrowed, concentrating somewhere above the table. The poems were solid, sharp. The words were firmly bound together. Naked nerve endings projected from the lines. Ruthless toward himself, compassionate toward others. The poems carried a challenge to spiritual laziness and satiety. This challenge made the leader wary, even though part of him liked it. He had a cautious attitude toward social initiatives, feeling that in the long run they broke up into droplets against the moss-covered cliff of human psychology. And droplets dry up or they're sucked up by the sand, so everything remains the same. He often imagined reformers as climbers, who wanted to topple those on top, for no other reason than to sit in their still-warm seats and suppress even newer reformers. Therefore, he manifested initiative only in his personal life, and then carefully.

"Some parts are successful," the albino fitter said glumly when Krivtsov was finished. "But it's wrongheaded, somehow."

The cashier babbled, "You're always finding fault with something, young man; nothing suits you. If you had shared our lot, 'eating soup with hazel eyes . . .' You probably don't even know what that is?"

"I do," Krivtsov said. "From literature. 'Soup from Vobla.' The twenties."

"It doesn't sing," the canteen waitress said. "It's a lot of screaming. There's plenty of screaming around as it is."

"I suggest you write on more eternal themes." The secretary sighed with superiority but also with some sympathy.

The repentant Mexican bandit exploded. "The hell with your eternal themes! This guy's stuff is to the point. . . . He writes well. Better than all of us. Don't listen, Krivtsov, keep up what you're doing."

The leader pulled apart the hands covering his belly and tapped the carafe with its stopper in order to stem the flood of passions more effectively. "It flows. Powerfully. But there's also a lot of rubbish." And he quoted some of the bad lines from memory.

What an ear, Krivtsov thought in awe. *You can't fool him. And I thought they'd slip by.* The leader went on. "You have a dangerous mania, Krivtsov. You want to solve all the world's problems in every poem. One thought trips over the next. You have to be more economical. Everything's at top speed. But poetry is a marathon. Will you have strength left to go the distance?"

"He will." The repentant Mexican bandit nodded confidently.

"Everyone is swimming in vagueness nowadays," the leader continued, paying him no attention. "That's boring. You can't tell who's writing the poetry or what they want. With you it's just the opposite. You've gotten trapped by your attempts to be concrete; you're overdoing it. . . . You want to redo everything immediately. . . . It doesn't happen that way. Even Mayakovsky stumbled there. Philosophers have racked their brains trying to save humanity. But new problems just replace the old ones. Or perhaps the old ones just seem new. And now you think you can change the whole world? You think it'll give in so easily? It'll change you first. To get revenge. You want to turn chaos into harmony. Impossible. Harmony is created on top of chaos, but not out of it."

"What about Blok's line 'But you, artist, have firm faith in beginnings and in ends'?" Krivtsov demanded in a huff.

The leader liked his impetuousness, his unsettling, wolf-cub gaze. Hoping against hope, he thought again, *Yes, I think he is a poet,* and then clasped his fingers once more over his belly and began twiddling his thumbs.

"Blok also said in the same place, 'But the world is beautiful, as usual.' 'As usual,' note. Don't get hung up on perfecting the world. Concentrate on perfecting poetry."

"Why does one exclude the other?" Krivtsov insisted.

"Who said it did?" The leader's left eyebrow arched upward artistically. "But perfecting begins with oneself, not others. Poetry has plenty of professional reformers who suffer for pay over oppressed peoples but never learn how to shape a rhyme. I was in Africa recently with a man like that, on a so-called specialized guided tour. A most vile little man, though once upon a time he had some poetic ability. The only good thing about him was that he was extraordinarily arrogant. On a trip abroad that's better than being a coward. But there are limits to arrogance. Near a rubber plantation we came upon a lake where young African maidens were bathing. They ran out of the water, naked, with lilies in their teeth, and surrounded us, their child-like eyes sparkling, babbling, smiling. Our reformer also smiled, friendship and peace in his eyes. Meanwhile, he was mouthing the most disgusting filth about these girls, who fortunately didn't understand. Later he published his foreign cycle, imbued with lofty internationalism but held together with snot and exclamation points. . . . Of course, there was an ape who seemed to get revenge for that cycle. Our author was holding a half-peeled banana in his hand and teasing the ape at one of the local zoos, extending the banana through the cage, then pulling it away. The ape, no fool, spit in his face. That episode did not appear in the cycle."

"Are poets really like that?" the albino fitter asked in amazement.

The leader smiled. "Poets, no. But professional reformers, yes."

"But Yesenin behaved like a hooligan sometimes," the cashier added insidiously. "And he even admitted it."

The leader grew angry. "What terrible things did Yesenin do, really? Turned over a dozen tables, punched a dozen faces, and—who knows?—all dozen faces may have deserved it. If he was guilty of anything, he repented and punished himself. He punished himself too harshly, undeservedly. Some people will never overturn a table or punch anyone's face—quiet, modest people—but they'll betray you in a moment, ruin you. And no one calls them hooligans. Of course, you can write bad poetry and be a good person. But you can't write good poetry and be a bad person."

"My opinion exactly," the director's secretary said, looking at everyone with great dignity, as if the last phrase had been meant for her.

Making his way in literary circles, Krivtsov experienced things that left him horrified. The poetry editor of one journal was also a well-known lyricist. He had the face of a coyote, sniffing at the wind. As he weighted down Krivtsov's manuscript with a pack of Marlboros, he casually said, "It needs a locomotive."

"What do you mean, 'locomotive'?" Krivtsov was amazed.

"Some ideological stanza that will pull the rest along behind it. Something about the KamAz automobile factory or virgin soils. Don't pretend to be naïve."

"I don't specialize in engine building," Krivtsov said darkly, pulling his manuscript out from under the Marlboros. He was shocked that a person who called himself a poet could say such words to him.

Once Krivtsov ended up at one of those so-called literary apartments. They were expecting the arrival of a salon poet, widely known in narrow circles. Excited ladies set out demitasse cups around a homemade napoleon, alongside which lay a gleaming silver server. The poet arrived about an hour and a half late, accompanied by two correspondents—one Swedish, one American. Contrary to all expectations, he looked rather well fed and animated. For starters he drank straight from the touchingly lone bottle of cognac standing on the table and chased it with water from a vase of flowers. Then, waving the cake server and spilling crumbs into his Shakespearean beard, he launched into an exposé of Soviet literature instead of reciting poetry. Mayakovsky he called a toady, Gorky senile, and every living writer a *podonok,* or scum.

The Swedish correspondent wanted to know the meaning of the Russian word *podonok,* and it was translated graciously by his American colleague, who apparently was quite familiar with the word. The Swede wrote it down in his notebook. The host, an old lawyer renowned for his collection of rare books and engravings, interjected tactfully, "You see, Mayakovsky is not among my favorite poets; however, Pasternak valued him. . . ."

"And who's Pasternak? He buckled under, too." The salon poet took another gulp from the bottle, which he had never put down.

The Swedish correspondent nervously looked up at him. The American reporter grimaced.

But the guest was off and running. "All Russian poetry to this day is nothing but ass kissing and toadying. After all, even Nekrasov confessed, 'I haven't sold my lyre, but there were times I would have.' They all sold out a little. But we're starting a new account."

"Excuse me, just a minute," the host said, turning pale. "Of course, Nekrasov made certain mistakes. But then, what do you think of Pushkin?"

The salon poet laughed, taking another drink. The words came pouring out of him. "Well, who wrote, 'Inspiration isn't for sale, but a manuscript can be sold'? Who came running, tail between his legs, to gendarme chief Benckendorff—and incidentally, it's not even clear what for? Who begged the tsar for a gentleman of the chamber uniform and wrote to him, 'No, I'm no sycophant when I compose flowing praise for the tsar'? Some national genius."

The Swedish and American reporters shrugged apologetically,

rose from their chairs, and closed their notebooks. The monologue had clearly exceeded the boundaries of their journalistic expectations.

"Get out of my house!" the old lawyer shouted in a quavering, cracking voice. "You're no poet! To talk like that about Pushkin!"

But the guest persisted. "All your famous Russian culture is only gilding for a slave's chains. An obsession with patriotism. Sobbing into the ragged hems of illiterate women . . . Kowtowing before an imaginary 'people.' " The salon poet went on. "The fear of democracy . . . Absence of spiritual freedom . . . The intelligentsia's stinking dirty linen . . . Only the West . . . And it's full of fairy tales about the mysterious Russian soul. . . ."

The American grabbed the silver server and the unfinished bottle away from the overwrought guest and, with a powerful, athletic shove, sent him flying toward the door. "Shut up!"

The Swedish correspondent shook his head. *"Podonok."*

But there were other literati Krivtsov came across who held that salvation lay only in "Russianness" and who claimed, moreover, that they alone had a monopoly on Russianness. Krivtsov had gone to one of their so-called literary houses and was struck by how the decor contrasted with the other apartment. Everywhere, even in the hall, hung ancient icons, sleigh bells, and spinners brought from various villages. Beneath a Hungarian lamp on the Czech parquet, as a symbol of Russian Orthodoxy, stood a church bell. The conversation was fueled by flavored vodka, poured from a crystal decanter of Catherine's reign and bearing the initials of the revered Grigori Potemkin. The host, a nostalgic essayist who wrote about trampled traditions, sported a long, bushy beard in the style of the Old Believers. He was telling everyone that for a time he had been posted abroad, on a secret mission, about which he had obscurely hinted in a lyrical digression in one of his essays—"the heady aroma of risk." Apparently his cover was blown, and he saw the light, realizing his holy mission to return and "save Russia."

Alternating with the icons, as though by accident, were souvenirs of more recent history: photographs of Skobelev on a white horse, Nicholas II reviewing the St. George cavaliers, Lavr Georgyevich

Kornilov, and also Roosevelt, Churchill, and Stalin at Yalta. Accompanying himself on the guitar, the essayist liked to sing such songs as "Soar, falcons, like eagles," "Prince Oleg is preparing to avenge himself on the foolish Khazars," and many other bravura songs. The refrain "For the Tsar, the homeland, and the faith . . . we'll cry a loud 'Hurrah'!" sounded particularly inspired, even possessing a contemporary ring, the kind against which the essayist railed so heatedly in his articles on the "foolish Khazars" of the theater. He also liked to propose toasts to "the Russian officer corps," proffering a glass of vodka at shoulder level and demonstrating an excellent military bearing, which was at odds with his Old Believer beard. The beard looked glued on anyway, as perhaps it had been during his "heady odor" period.

The essayist wanted to be mysterious, but it didn't always work; his smugness gave him away. For instance, in telling Krivtsov the story of how he obtained an icon of Nicholas the Miracle Worker, he bragged about his own shrewdness and showed himself in a very unflattering light. This was the story: He came across the icon in the Vologda region, in a dilapidated wooden house, inhabited by a solitary old woman. She refused to sell the icon—it was a sin. And a house wasn't a house without an icon. So the essayist bought the house for a mere three hundred rubles—including the icon, of course. Confident the icon would remain in her great-grandfather's house, the old woman moved to Sakhalin, to be with her granddaughter, an officer's wife. The essayist removed the icon and sold the house for a thousand to a Moscow landscape artist. So Nicholas the Miracle Worker created seven hundred rubles.

Several poets attended the essayist-ideologue, helping themselves to flavored vodka and reading poems about Holy Russia. The poems, while completely devoid of the purity of Yesenin, strung together grandiloquent words, allegedly derived from folklore, and always returned to the same dark hatred of "foolish Khazars"—violators, defilers, Christ sellers, and modernists. Fixing his honeyed eyes on Krivtsov as a new recruit, the essayist maintained Russian art of the twenties was the bacchanalia of modernism, a violation of tradition. The thirties, it turned out, were a renaissance. And now everything in the arts was supposedly in the clutches of "Them." According to the essayist, "it is time to save ourselves and to save Russia, time to rally." But Krivtsov did not want to "rally" with people like him, instead of Pushkin and Mayakovsky. . . .

The leader of Krivtsov's own literary circle was often thought to be sneaky, a grumbler, too critical of others. Actually he was a fat, simplehearted child. Beneath his contrived skepticism dwelt the same spontaneity that he admired in Krivtsov. One meeting of the literary circle had somehow adjourned to the nearest *pelmeni* bar. There, flushed with port wine and waving a bluish, undercooked *pelmen* on a bent fork, the leader lectured to Krivtsov. "Don't take up the literary life. Just take up life. Don't try to follow the herd. No matter how much they huddle together, impotent poeple will never give birth to anything. Don't take any advice, not even mine. I'm glad you're not morose—I'm sick of young, old men. You don't seem to suffer the cheerfulness of fools either. . . ."

Krivtsov walked the leader home, and he talked and talked, as if he wanted to help Krivtsov avoid all the pitfalls that he hadn't.

Suddenly a woman screamed. They were in a narrow alley, and in the dirty yellow light of the streetlamp they saw a middle-aged woman wearing ragged slippers and a gauze scarf over her hair rollers. She was being beaten sluggishly and without mercy by a short drunken man in a T-shirt and pajama pants as he tried to free himself from her desperately clutching hands. Krivtsov ran toward them, but the leader grabbed his sleeve.

"Don't get involved, Krivtsov."

Krivtsov tore away and pulled the man off the woman and threw him against the building wall. The man was so drunk that when his back hit the wall, he slid down the rotten laths sticking out of the broken plaster and collapsed onto the sidewalk, breaking off a piece of drainpipe in the process. The woman set up an even louder howl and rushed to his aid with extraordinary tenderness.

"Police! They're beating my husband! Damned hooligans!"

Somehow having propped up the remains of her husband against the wall, she attacked Krivtsov, grabbing the broken piece of drainpipe and swinging it fiercely, like a cudgel. Krivtsov had no time to get out of her way, and the blow landed directly on his head. Everything spun: the lamppost; the stupidly grinning man in pajama pants; the woman's angry and frightened eyes; the bristling rollers. Pain, shame, and embarrassment shot through his mind. Barely managing to remain upright by holding onto a lamppost, he felt his head and looked at his hand: It was covered with blood.

"Vasya, I think I killed him," the woman gasped. The anger disappeared from her eyes, and pity appeared in its place. After yanking the half-finished bottle of vodka from Vasya's unmoving hands, she poured it over Krivtsov's head. Then she made a bandage out of her gauze scarf.

"Forgive me, buddy, forgive me. I'm sorry. This was a family affair, and then you came along. Just don't report me to the police. Do you need money for a taxi?"

She quickly dragged Vasya into the dark belly of the courtyard entrance. Krivtsov was coming around. He couldn't stop himself from crying.

"She really let you have it," the leader said, poking the piece of drainpipe with his toe. "A nasty chunk of iron. Shall we go to the emergency room?"

Krivtsov shook his head, looking away.

"That's what you get for trying to save the world," the leader grumbled. "Put some iodine on your head when you get home. Do you have iodine at home? We can stop at my place."

Krivtsov, reeling, turned to go home. The leader looked at his thin, shaking back. Then he disappeared around the corner.

He'll make it as a poet, thought the leader with concern and tenderness. *It's all right, they beat me, too.* He sighed and shifted his briefcase from one hand to the other.

CHAPTER · 15

I gor Seleznyov was repelled by the faces of passengers in public transportation. Especially in the morning, when people were traveling to work, and in the evening, when they were coming home.

A bunch of losers, he thought, his gaze moving across the tired faces of his fellow countrymen with the cold detachment of an alien observer from another planet. *Every day is like another, shuttling back and forth, like cattle between yoke and stall. . . . There, let's take you, sitting opposite me—Mr. Harried Office Worker, frayed bottoms of long underwear sticking out from your trouser cuffs. What's that on your puffy knees? Ah, an attaché case, made in Hungary, with an engraved plaque reading: "To dear Ilya Ivanovich on his fiftieth birthday from his grateful co-workers." You carry that with such an important air, as if it held bundles of Swiss francs. But I can see through the crack where you couldn't force it shut, and there's a jar of yogurt dripping out onto the metro floor. With the experienced eye of a radiologist, I also see a ring of Poltava sausage next to it and a few processed cheeses. And that's the important contents of your attaché. That's what you've managed to achieve. . . . And you, Miss Saleswoman in a haberdashery, or perhaps you're an accounting clerk for a factory manufacturing metal tips for shoelaces. There you stand, clutching the metal handrail with your fat fingers, your nails flashing golden flecks of color painted on at some creepy suburban beauty salon! Do you think nobody knows about the plotting and conniving and wheeling and dealing it took to get everything you've got on: your monstrous bluish wig with gray tinges, bought at a cheap Hong Kong store by a sailor on a freighter; your white nylon blouse, created with chemicals by the Japanese out of larch shavings from Yakutsk; your bilious cucumber green bra peeking through relentlessly; and your red plastic shoes with a fake cork sole, made by Armenian peasants who refused to give in to the leather shortage? What really gives you away is the toy Gillette razor blade made in Sukhumi, dangling with a cross—for some reason a*

Catholic one—on a chain that's too orange to be real gold; and your cellophane bag from Winston, which reveals to the naked eye nothing but a pack of Bulgarian Opal cigarettes and the familiar yogurt and processed cheese. How you long to escape from your ninety-ruble-a-month salary and the communal kitchen stinking of fried fish! But that painfully obvious darn on your left stocking is your white flag to reality.

For you, passengers of public transportation, Saturdays are spent in required volunteer work, cleaning up the city and planting shrubbery. Sundays mean mass mushroom-picking excursions in the woods, littered with empty cans, or writing "Vasya + Katya = Love" with your skis on a snowbank, in the same forest in winter. Devourers of frozen meat. Swallowers of cheap port wine. Purchaser of hideous black sateen undershorts and clip-on ties. Watchers of the "Blue Light" variety show and "Well, Just Wait, You Rabbit" cartoons on TV . . . You're too weak to pull yourselves out of the swamp of your lives.

This, or something like it, was how Igor Seleznyov thought in his college student days. He couldn't even imagine that he wouldn't make it. He didn't mean make it out to the West, like some. He wanted to make it inside. Entry into international circles was merely a means of being your own boss at home. Besides, a Mercedes on Ordynka Square is much more impressive than one on the Champs-Élysées— where there are plenty of Mercedeses. No one will be amazed if you stroll along in American clothes on Broadway. Swedish Tandberg speakers sound even better on Kutuzovsky Prospekt.

Seleznyov liked the special foreign atmosphere that reigned in the lobbies of hotels like the National, Metropole, and Intourist—for instance, the smell of perfume and cigars that would never reach the riders on the metro. Sometimes Igor Seleznyov fancied it was this particular smell that enabled foreigners to be so confident that they, not the natives, seemed to be the masters of this country. He wanted to go abroad so he could return, surrounded by the same smell, which would create an invisible wall between him and the little gray people. For this he was prepared to do anything; the amorality of getting privileges by any means did not scare him. Igor Seleznyov felt he had a right to them. Igor Seleznyov never stopped to think whether he was good or bad. He put "strong" above "good." The strong, in his opinion, had the right to be anything they wanted. That's why he wasn't too upset if someone called him a bastard. But once he heard that from his own father.

Seleznyov rarely spoke to his father except in the presence of his mother. She doted upon her son and always stood up for him, never suspecting that he despised her for being so overbearing. She saw him as the embodiment of the male ideal, so unlike her husband, who was simple, unpolished, incapable of learning it wasn't desirable for a plant director to socialize with the one-armed janitor—a certain Vasutkin, who had been a buddy since the army. She detested Vasutkin, if for no other reason than he was a constant reminder that her husband hadn't always been a director.

No matter how she tried, clothes never seemed to fit Seleznyov senior. Everything had to be altered, and this was no small problem because it was almost impossible to drag her husband to the tailor's. But everything fitted Seleznyov junior like a glove. Seleznyov senior still hadn't lost the horrible habit of smoking Belomorkanals. Seleznyov junior smoked only American cigarettes. Seleznyov senior couldn't learn a single sentence from an English phrase book. Seleznyov junior spoke English brilliantly and French passably. Seleznyov senior didn't play sports. Seleznyov junior played tennis, snow and water skied, figure skated, and studied karate. Seleznyov senior kept rereading the same book—*War and Peace.* Seleznyov junior read Henry Miller's *Tropic of Cancer* in the original. With her son Mrs. Seleznyov avenged her husband's peasant background.

The night before he was to leave for Moscow to take the college entrance exams, Seleznyov junior lay in bed, reading a biography of Churchill. His father came in, wearing silk pajamas, painted with palms and monkeys, which he secretly hated, and simple black slippers with felt soles, which he hung on to despite his wife's many attempts to replace them with Dutch clogs, which made as much noise as tanks.

Seleznyov senior smelled of vodka now, having downed a glass in Vasutkin's janitor digs after work. He tripped over a dumbbell, and after sweeping the records off the couch to clear a space, he sat down, dropping his heavy, freckled arms so that his hands almost touched the Peruvian llama rug.

"Your mother made me call the rector in Moscow, to speak on your behalf. I knew him at the front. We were in the same unit—Vasutkin, he, and I. . . . I called, even though I thought it was disgusting. I've become a coward. I'm afraid of scenes with your mother."

"I'm not responsible for my mother's lunatic ambition," Seleznyov junior replied, marking his place in the Churchill biography. "I can get accepted without your help. Or the powerful influence emanating from the janitor's basement."

"Yes, they'll probably accept you," Seleznyov senior said, studying his son. "Gold medal . . . Wonderful record. Everything's in order with your father, too. An active public worker. They say you make brilliant speeches on the international situation, exposing capitalism. . . . Oxford pronunciation . . . You know how to make people like you when you need to. But you haven't managed to make me like you. Me, your own father."

"I haven't tried," Seleznyov junior said with a shrug. "Father and son . . . the eternal problem. There's a lot I don't like about you either."

"Well . . . I didn't come here to lecture you; it's too late for that. I have a special request—a milestone in our relationship. You're flying to Moscow tomorrow; could you take something with you?"

"What?" Seleznyov junior grimaced with annoyance.

Seleznyov senior got up, went to his room, slippers slapping, and returned, carrying something that made Seleznyov junior shudder with revulsion. Seleznyov senior had brought a leather and chrome arm with dangling, unfastened straps. He was carrying it like a familiar and friendly object, as if the arm were alive and warm.

"This is Vasutkin's prosthesis. . . . Something's wrong with its hinges. It digs in. But basically the prosthesis is wonderful," Seleznyov senior muttered, engrossed in the mechanism of the leather and chrome arm and not noticing the disgust on his son's face. "Vasutkin and I tried everything, but we never figured out what's wrong. It might be a trifle —some screw that needs tightening or loosening. It's a tricky thing. The Leningrad prostheticians refused to repair it. 'Bring it back to Moscow,' they said, 'to the manufacturer—they'll either fix it or replace it.' So take it with you; drop it off at the factory; I'll give you the receipt and the address. It won't take long. And then give ten rubles to a conductor, he'll get the prosthesis to Leningrad, and you'll call me and tell me the train and car number, and I'll meet the train."

While Seleznyov senior was muttering all this, Seleznyov junior was picturing monstrously humiliating scenes: at the airport checking his suitcase and babbling something about hand luggage, while turning colors; holding the clumsily wrapped package, tied with string, and proceeding to the control point, where the guard calmly tears open the package and the black glove sticks out menacingly. Surprised and curious glances, giggles, jokes—it's all so humiliating, so unworthy of him, Igor Seleznyov, flying into his brilliant future, stuck for some reason with somebody's leather and chrome arm. And visiting the factory, standing in line with invalids reeking of beer and smoked fish; the pathetic unwrapping of the prosthesis, handing over the receipt to the obnoxious clerk with fake rubies in her meaty earlobes; and then begging the Red Arrow conductor to take the package to Leningrad.

"I don't understand what Vasutkin's prosthesis has to do with me," Seleznyov junior said with a shudder. "Why do I have to take care of it?"

"What it has to do with you?" Seleznyov senior repeated slowly. "How about just this, that without men like Vasutkin you wouldn't exist? Nor your gold medal, nor your English, nor your tennis ... I knew you'd refuse. I still hoped secretly, but it didn't work. It's not a problem of fathers and sons, as you say. It's not a question of generations. You think you belong to a different class."

"And what class is that, in your opinion?" Seleznyov junior smirked.

"The most disgusting one—the class of careerists."

"Well, you've had a pretty good career yourself, compared to, say, Vasutkin." Seleznyov junior laughed.

"I wasn't doing it for a career; I was doing it for a living. And not for myself, but for others," Seleznyov senior responded angrily.

"Well, for yourself a little, too," Seleznyov junior cracked.

"I made a bad life for myself. Bad. And I didn't do what I wanted for others either." Seleznyov senior suddenly slumped over, feeling an incredible weariness, which had collected over so many years of lack of sleep, making deadlines, meetings, telephone calls.

"Well, if you didn't manage to make your life what you want, what can you teach me?" Seleznyov junior asked cruelly.

"No father can teach his son to be a genius. It can't be taught. But if the father isn't a bastard, he can at least make sure his son isn't one. I didn't. I failed. Being occupied is no excuse. The main occupation of adults should be children."

"What basis have you for considering me a bastard?"

"You're worse than a bastard with a past. You're a bastard with a future."

"Are you afraid that radiant future you're building will belong to bastards?"

"No. Thank God, not everyone in your generation is like you. There are some wonderful fellows in your school. . . . But people like you are frightening."

"What's so frightening about me?"

"What's frightening is that someone like you was born under socialism. I don't know capitalism well, but I've been to a few places. Careerism isn't considered shameful there. On the contrary, careerism is condoned, promoted, elevated to the status of a good deed. I read Ford's book *My Life.* His main purpose in life was his career and nothing else. But we live under socialism. Socialism, at least ideally, places morality above career."

"Ideally . . . What about reality?"

"Reality has many faces. One of them is yours. Our careerists are more hypocritical than capitalist ones. In order to pursue a career, you have to appear moral. If you're asked on an exam why you want to enter the institute, naturally you're not going to say, 'To make my career.' An American, for example, wouldn't be embarrassed to say that. But you'll give it a moral underpinning. You'll denounce the right things. You'll call Churchill a sworn enemy. You'll quote Litvinov or Maysky appropriately. Yet between them and you lies a moral abyss. They had ideals. But you're not stupid. You know having ideals isn't profitable. It implies fighting for them. But you also understand that it's profitable to pretend. You know the rules of the game. Will you really be promoted to a position where you'll speak for the people whom you despise, for Vasutkin, whose prosthesis clashes with your elegance?

"You're a potential bureaucrat. But of course, the new, improved type . . . In the old days the bureaucrats were different, more primitive. I hated those dullards in gabardine raincoats and velour hats, sticking their noses into production they knew nothing about. When I was promoted and shoved headfirst into the paper work swamp, I was afraid. What if I became like them? I don't think I have, but I'm still afraid. But now with technology, bureaucracy has modernized itself, too. It's not as provincial as it used to be. It's gotten some education. It's better dressed. More cynical . . . I wish you misfortune. Great misfortune. So that it knocks you down on your face in the dirt, which you don't know and don't want to know. Perhaps you'll understand something then."

What have I come to? thought Seleznyov senior. *I'm wishing my own son misfortune. Is that the only teacher? I'm shouting at him, accusing him. A shouting teacher is no good. I have to find other arguments besides shouting and accusation. But what?*

The door slammed behind Seleznyov senior so hard that a picture of Ringo Starr hanging over it fell down. Seleznyov junior, crawling on the floor, started looking in the thick forest of the Peruvian llama rug for the tack and found it by pricking himself on it. He suddenly froze, experiencing a rare sensation of loneliness and fear. It had happened also in early spring last year, when his class went on an excursion to Kaluga. Seleznyov had found himself ignored even by his entourage. The schoolchildren stood on the riverbank, faces skyward, in front of an enormous real rocket. Its sleek white body strained to escape its red supports into the blue, beckoning infinity, which was shot through with wisps of clouds. Suddenly they heard a crackling, which quietly crescendoed, as though a secret engine were awakening in the rocket. The students froze, expecting a miracle to occur and the rocket to take off.

But it was an acoustical illusion. The crackling and rumbling came from below, from the river. The students ran, sinking in the grainy, crumbling snow, and stopped before the astonishing sight of cracks suffusing a solid chunk of ice. This wasn't the spectacular ice movement of one floe piling up on top of another, but the ice was breaking up before their eyes, and a forgotten ski pole suddenly ended up with its pointy metal tip on one floe and its handle with the leather loop on another. It seemed to connect the two floes over the black expanse of the ever-increasing crack. Just before, Seleznyov junior was wondering whether he should take a year or so in space and decided that he would. But the opportunity to prove his courage in space was a long way off, so now, tossing his jacket to a friend, he jumped into the ice, as if someone had dared him, even though no one had. He surged forward, gleefully listening to the desperate pleas of his class-mates calling after him, "Come back, Igor! Come back!"

The ice attached to the bank was still solid, and Seleznyov junior walked on it carefully but confidently. He was the center of attention once more. But as he got farther out, the ice underfoot began to get mushy. Before his eyes there lay nothing but patches of water. The ice was coming to life, a life that depended on the whim of the spring water. At first the cracks were easy enough to step over, but then he had to start jumping. Jumping was scary because it was impossible to guess whether or not the next piece of ice would hold him. After one jump Seleznyov slipped. His shoe sliced over the crumbling edge and filled up with water; he managed to hold on and began crawling, breaking his fingernails on the ice.

Looking back, he saw tiny black figures waving their arms, and looming over them, the rocket, distant, but still enormous, spring sunshine glittering off its sides. The humiliating realization that his audience saw him crawling brought Seleznyov to his feet. Retreat was impossible not only because they were watching but because the last floe was now separated from the one he was now on by a wide expanse of black water, swirling with white foam. Seleznyov managed to grab the ski pole, which was floating by, and testing the ice with it, he headed for the other shore. But the pole deceived him, and jumping onto a spot he thought was solid, he sank waist-deep and barely scrambled out. The ice floes were taking on speed and bumping into one another, breaking up into very small pieces, too small to step on.

Gathering up all the strength of his athletic body, Seleznyov started running, leaping from chunk to chunk. When he made it to the solid ice of the opposite shore, he didn't stop running, not until he fell into the snow. He dug deep into it, and felt the slightly thawed clay, to confirm it really was land. . . . He was shivering uncontrollably, tormented by the thought that what he had done was pointless after all. He wasn't saving anyone; he just wanted to attract attention, to stand out at any cost, to inspire delight and horror.

And now that same sense of his own emptiness, his aloneness and fear, but without the redemptive smears of dirt, arose in Seleznyov after the door had slammed behind his father. But there were no observers to help him to his feet. Seleznyov junior was leader of his group because he never bowed to anyone, respected anyone, loved anyone. But he had a secret which he meticulously hid, even from himself. The secret was that while despising the mother who had nurtured him, Seleznyov loved his father madly, unnaturally, with deeply hidden jealousy of his father's faith in what he, his son, did not believe. And he couldn't forgive him for that.

After leaving his son's room, Seleznyov senior held Vasutkin's leather and chrome arm close, looking around for a place to put it. His eyes searched the bronze door handles, the Yugoslavian velvet couches, the Indian bamboo bar, the Swedish lamps with the ever-changing colors. The closets were stuffed with clothes that represented a course on international fashion. There was no place for Vasutkin's arm. Seleznyov senior did not go to the bedroom, whence came his wife's gentle snore. He huddled on the couch in his study, still clutching Vasutkin's arm as if afraid it would be taken away from him and thrown out of this apartment that was so alien to him.

CHAPTER · 16

The next morning Kesha didn't need to wake up because he hadn't gotten to sleep in the first place. The insult of being called a coward tormented him. More important, he couldn't stop thinking about the river they had to face. Kesha knew it well. But what does that mean? Sometimes you think you know a person well, and suddenly . . . On his last expedition Kesha shared a tent with one volunteer who had come to Siberia from far away and had hoped "to make some money" there for a new house. Dozens of times he'd shown Kesha the color photograph of his fiancée—the future mistress of that house, who was then working as a salesclerk in a village store. Her mighty breasts surged menacingly out from the shiny picture like a battleship's guns. Breasts aside, the volunteer looked so much like his fiancée that it was uncanny: They had the same round, porcelain faces; the same rosy blush that looked painted on; the same thick wrestler's necks; the same protruding blue eyes; the same flawless rows of teeth; the same flat, pancakelike ears. He was hardworking, sober, respectful, taciturn—although he knew how to enjoy the conversation of others —and he never swore. But he ate by himself, apart from the others, and that is not considered good form on expeditions. He claimed to have an ulcer. Filling a mug with boiling water, he would sprinkle in his own tea, then pull something out of his backpack and chew on it. Everyone joked about it; he really didn't look as if he had an ulcer, but there are plenty of people who invent ailments for themselves. On the last night of the expedition they decided to throw together a communal feast, as was the custom. Because they wanted to find out what he had been eating and also because they were out of general provisions, they fiddled with the straps and opened his backpack. They gasped: There were three slabs of bacon, stuffed with garlic. No one's ever treated ulcers with garlicky bacon. Since the owner was picking cedar cones (for souvenirs, as he put it), they requisitioned—in the most humane manner—only two of his three chunks and cut them up into slices, which were as pink as their owner's cheeks. He returned after dark, when the feast was in full swing, staggering under the weight of his bagful of "souvenirs." Seeing the cut-up bacon, he began to quiver, and his face flooded with blood, as if someone had stuffed cherries in through his pancake ears. Raising the stick he'd been using to beat down the pine cones, he struck full force at the hands of a workman reaching for the last of the bacon. The man's fingers were mangled for life, it turned out. Of course, the bacon lover wasn't allowed to get away with it; they tied him up and forced him to eat the third piece of bacon, and if he tried to stop, they beat him. What a monster he turned out to be—and they thought they knew him.

That's the way it was with the taiga river. You thought you knew it, but it had a dark soul. It would cuddle up to you, pretending to be gentle, and then smash you so hard that your scattered bones would never be found.

Kesha tossed in his sleeping bag, mentally traversing the entire river to the accompaniment of Ivan Ivanovich Zagranichny's snoring —at first a one-nostril melodic whistle which sounded like a teapot, then switching to a civil defense siren with two nostrils. Twice the imaginary journey resulted in the boats capsizing, and twice people died. Once again Kesha marshaled his imagination to put the remains back together and return the boats to the starting point. Once again he led them forward, trying to outsmart the river, to maneuver among the slippery boulders exposed by low water. It was something like a boat slalom; his head spun from the turns. But even on the third trip Kesha didn't manage to swerve in time, and for the third time he saw Yulya Sergeyevna's head striking the rocks so hard that the surrounding water turned crimson. Why Yulya Sergeyevna? She wasn't even going with them; Kolomeitsev had ordered her to stay. Damn it all! . . . Kesha tried to make himself sleep, but it didn't work. Writhing in his sleeping bag, he went down the river unsuccessfully again and again, and each time Yulya Sergeyevna died.

But in real life you could die only once and it's impossible to return to the starting point for a second chance. In real life you couldn't rebuild a boat from splinters or put dead people back together out of bones. Kesha was not afraid for himself. He loved life, of course, but he didn't consider himself very important. He didn't read much—not because he didn't want to but because he had no time. He felt that the truly valuable people were those who had obtained wisdom by reading many books. When people like that died, the wisdom perished with them, and then the rest of humanity grew more ignorant and was the worse for it. Kalya, though, hadn't read as many books as Yulya Sergeyevna, but the earth would seem empty if she disappeared. And Ivan Ivanovich Zagranichny—he wasn't as well educated as Burshtein or Kolomeitsev, but perhaps he only seemed simple; no one knew if still waters bubbled through his hairy nostrils as he snored. And humanity would be impoverished if there were one Ivan Ivanovich Zagranichny less, even though this loss wouldn't be mourned with funeral music on the radio.

Oh, Viktor Petrovich, Viktor Petrovich, Kesha thought bitterly about Kolomeitsev. *You're a smart man. Fearless. It's a good thing you're not afraid for yourself, of course. But that you don't fear for others— that's bad.*

But Kesha knew that Kolomeitsev's decision was irreversible, and he began mentally going over the river again; maybe he'd manage to get through.

The tent flap opened a crack, and he heard a barely audible whisper: "Kesh, hey, Kesh."

Kesha had never heard Kalya whisper before; her loud, rather hoarse voice was one of her salient characteristics. And suddenly here she was, whispering. The hoarseness was still present, but it had modulated to a chestier, softer sound. Kesha convulsively climbed out of his sleeping bag and, shivering, stuck his bare feet into his freezing rubber boots. Kesha had wanted for so long to hear that whisper he was afraid he'd imagined it.

But it wasn't the night, imitating Kalya's voice; it was Kalya herself. She stood near the tent, a quilted cotton jacket flung over her shoulders. Like Kesha, she was wearing rubber boots on her bare feet.

As Kesha climbed out of the tent, he looked up at Kalya, and it seemed as if the big, cold pale blue moon were sitting right on her shoulder. When he stood up, the moon was far away, above the black tips of the pines; someone had frightened it away.

"Why aren't you asleep?" Kalya asked in her chesty whisper, even though they were now far enough away from the tent so they wouldn't wake anyone up.

"I'm not sleepy," Kesha replied, trembling from the novel thrill of whispering with Kalya. "And how did you know I wasn't sleeping?"

"I knew, that's all. Take my jacket, or you'll catch cold after being in the sleeping bag," Kalya said.

"Don't be silly, I'm not cold," Kesha said, blushing in the dark.

"Let's go down to the river and sit awhile," Kalya suggested. When they sat down next to each other on a log, she put the edge of her jacket, warmed from her body, over Kesha. Now her whisper blended with the noise of the river. "There's enough jacket for both of us. Don't get embarrassed, like some teenaged girl. You'll never get ahead being so shy, Kesha. I notice you're even too embarrassed to eat; you turn your face away from the fire when you eat. As if you're doing something shameful."

Kesha felt strange and confused when he found himself beneath the same jacket with Kalya. For the first time in his life he felt a warm female body touching his—its heaving softness, the taut ribs, and the living curve of the hip. And it wasn't any woman's body; it was Kalya's, and that made Kesha even more flustered and awkward. He was mortified by the thought that his hump was lifting the jacket too much, pulling it off Kalya's shoulders. He surreptitiously tried to shift his back so the jacket would cover more of Kalya than him.

Kalya took his hand, and he felt with his palm the whole life of her palm—all the cuts, rough spots, and blisters.

"Kesh, why don't you ever tell me about your life?"

"There's nothing to tell," Kesha said defensively, gradually freeing his hand.

"Well, I'm interested," Kalya said, softly but firmly apprehending his escaping hand. "Why are you the way you are. Were you born this way?"

"Oh, you're talking about that." Kesha grew glum and pulled his hand away. "They say when my mother was carrying me, my father got drunk and kicked her in the stomach. She miscarried me. I've been like this since childhood, with a hump."

"No, I'm not talking about that at all. You silly fool. Why are you even thinking about that? You don't have a hump, none!" Kalya slipped her hand under the jacket and ran it along Kesha's back, caressing it. "I can feel with my hand—there's nothing there. You've imagined your hump. . . . Understand? I was asking why you're so good."

"I'm not any good," Kesha said, shaking his head. "I'm so ignorant."

Kalya suddenly grabbed the hand he was hiding and kissed it quickly but firmly, as if to imprint it with her chapped lips.

"Do you think those who know a lot are always good? You're already good because you don't know you are. Your soul isn't stained with any foul deeds or even your thoughts. A child's soul. I never had one. I was thrown straight into adulthood. There are a lot of bastards, Kesha. . . . And they think they're good people. There are men who are good to their friends but just bastards to women. They don't even count women as people."

"Not everyone is like that, Kalya." Kesha shuddered at her directness.

"They're the only kind I know. Maybe I don't deserve any better," Kalya said curtly. "Do you want to know how many men I've had in my life?"

"Why?" Kesha said, bewildered.

But Kalya wouldn't be stopped. "No, you listen. . . . I never had any girl friends. You may be my only girl friend, Kesh. Don't get insulted. I'm not turning you into a woman. I'm putting you above all those other men—a whole eight of them! At my age—twenty. That's what they call moral decay at the meetings. . . . And I'm not some . . . God knows what. You see, what happened to me. I was looking for an easy spot. Fool. But I only came across hard, rocky ones."

"Kalya, Kalya, don't say bad things about yourself," Kesha begged.

But Kalya was lashing herself with her words. "The first one was my stepfather. Right in the cellar, on top of the rotten potatoes I was picking over, and I wasn't even sixteen. The second was a lieutenant on leave from the Kuril Islands. He told me pretty stories about volcanoes. He strutted like a rooster and promised to marry me and show me the volcanoes. But after he left, not even a postcard. My grandmother poked out the child with a knitting needle. He used a green cologne—chypre, it's called. Whenever I smell that scent, I feel like throwing up. The third was a helicopter pilot. This one really did want to marry me. He liked that I was hardworking, soft-spoken. He even liked the fact I was uneducated. He wanted a maid, not a wife. He was a brave pilot, but even a louse can be brave. He lived for money. . . . speculated in pelts. With his helicopter he'd buy them up cheap at fur farms and then sell them at three times the price in Irkutsk. All his glorious bravery boiled down to one lousy, earthly dream: to buy a house on the Black Sea and take in boarders, and I would cook for them and wash their sheets. He didn't want children; he was too cheap. And if a man doesn't want children from a woman, does he really love her? The fourth—"

"Kalya. What are you doing to me, Kalya?" Kesha wept at the spitefulness of the monologue.

"Listen, my little girl friend, listen. . . . The fourth—"

"Don't, Kalya, don't. . . . Take pity on yourself."

"I won't pity myself. But you I will. So you see what I'm like; the only thing I haven't laid down under is a locomotive. Let me tell you about just two others. One was my own fault. A student, a young boy, not spoiled yet, sort of like our Lachugin. No, it's not him, so don't get upset. . . . I pitied him for the pimples on his forehead. And did he need pity, without love? You see how badly it turned out: I was ruined, so I began to ruin others. It would have been better for him just to suffer with his pimples and wait for real love. I wanted to do something good for him and he knew it, and he hated me for it probably. And I hated myself. You can't do that out of pity.

"And the other. The other, well, listen to this, my little girl friend . . . is Viktor Petrovich—yes, Kolomeitsev. To be honest, I had a crush on him at first. He isn't like the others; he's smart and strong. But that's like the pilot's bravery; they don't make up a good soul. Of course, he's not like that pilot; he doesn't give a damn about money. I respected him for that. But what scares me a little is that . . . he doesn't seem to give a damn about people, especially women. He broke Yulya Sergeyevna a long time ago! She told me about it once, crying; she lost control. With me it happened only one time with him. Right by the excavation. And you know, he held me with only one arm; he never let go of his hammer with the other. And right afterward he said, while my heart was pounding like a hammer, 'If you squeal about this, I'll kick you out of the expedition.' Strength is more important than kindness for him. He likes to make people obey him. And with women that's all it is for him—a method of subjugation."

"Why, Kalya? Why are you beating me?" Kesha sobbed, covering his face with his small, girlish hands.

"I'm not, Kesha. I'm beating myself. For good reason. So you'll never care for me, who's such a bitch. Don't bring grief into your life. I'm not worthy of you, Kesha, that's the point. . . . Someone will love you. . . . But now you won't be able to love me. That's what I want."

And Kalya, adjusting the jacket, which had slipped off Kesha's hump, snuggled even closer to him and began crying, too. But Kesha stopped. Seeing Kalya helpless for the first time immediately made him stronger.

"Yes, I will," Kesha said. "I'll always love you, Kalya. You said I invented my hump. And you've invented your own hump, too, Kalya. You don't have one. You think I've never seen bad people, is that it? But they don't make the world go 'round, Kalya."

Kalya wept into Kesha's lap, choking through her tears. "Kesha, just don't die tomorrow. Don't ever die, Kesha."

"I won't die," Kesha replied. "I can't die now, Kalya."

"Come with me if I don't disgust you," Kalya said.

"Don't," Kesha said, resisting. "You just feel sorry for me. And you said yourself you can't do it out of pity."

"There's nothing to feel sorry for," Kalya said. "I think I love you. But I don't know what it is, Kesha. Don't go away on the boat tomorrow. . . . I'm afraid of losing you."

"Don't be afraid," Kesha breathed. "I'll be back."

They didn't even notice when it began to get light. White, steamy mist, dimly lit by the still-invisible sun, lay across the river they would soon be on. Suddenly Kesha's hump smarted from someone's gaze, which seemed to penetrate the jacket under which he and Kalya lay. Kesha looked around and saw Eduard Sitechkin wearing his backpack. Sitechkin flashed a nasty smile, filled with the joy of knowing someone's secret—something funny—which might come in handy someday. Kalya rose up and attacked like a she-bear on her hind legs, defending Kesha as though he were her cub. Sitechkin smirked and shrugged, feigning indifference, and then disappeared into the taiga. *Our local Quasimodo and Esmeralda,* he joked to himself, and he immediately pictured how he would also describe this picturesque scene to the authorities, ending with the woeful conclusion: "As you see, the unit has been completely corrupted."

Eduard Sitechkin, having abandoned his comrades, walked energetically toward his bright future.

Kalya started a fire going and made breakfast. Kesha puttered about with the motor, looking up at the smoke from time to time and smiling so shyly it looked as if he thought the entire world could see his expression.

Kolomeitsev and Burshtein were shaving by taking turns looking into the single round mirror, which hung on a pine branch. They laughed when they bumped into each other; the arguments of the night before had vanished. Seryozha Lachugin packed his gear, surreptitiously glancing at Kolomeitsev with awe and admiration. The anticipation of danger had wiped a dozen years off Kolomeitsev's face, and little pinpricks of light danced in his eyes. Yulya Sergeyevna Vyazemskaya saw that the tired, hunted wolf of a man had turned back into the carefree, handsome youth who long, long ago had danced her out into the hall and pressed her up against the telephone.

Kalya's breakfast of bird cherry salad and soup with meat and dried potatoes was eaten quickly and enthusiastically. Kalya joyfully noticed that for the first time Kesha didn't turn away from the others when he ate; he wasn't embarrassed.

Only Yulya Sergeyevna didn't touch her food. She was chain-smoking. Her customary blue eye shadow was missing. She rose and went to her tent. As everyone went down to the river, Vyazemskaya unexpectedly appeared on the bank and tossed her backpack into the boat with determination. Her shotgun hung over her shoulder.

Ivan Ivanovich Zagranichny, sitting at the motor, looked up quizzically at Kolomeitsev. Kolomeitsev's eyes narrowed angrily, even though he automatically continued to smile. "Yulya Sergeyevna, didn't you understand my order to stay?"

"I did. But the workmen can manage here without me. You'll need me more," Vyazemskaya replied, placing her shotgun in the boat. She didn't look into Kolomeitsev's eyes, and he realized this was no time to give her orders.

"There'll be a slight overload," Ivan Ivanovich Zagranichny said, scratching the back of his head.

Kesha bobbed up in front of Vyazemskaya and clutched her sleeve. "Yulya Sergeyevna, dear . . . don't . . . don't go with us. For God's sake, don't go."

The interference of a subordinate to help resolve a problem displeased Kolomeitsev. He stopped smiling. "Why are you panicking, Kesha? Mind your own business."

Kesha ran to him, his eyes rolling in despair, and he babbled, humiliated but persistent, "Viktor Petrovich, don't let her. She can't."

"Why can't she?" Kolomeitsev frowned.

"I know that she can't. . . . I had a dream."

"Cut out the superstition, Kesha. Start the engine. Yulya Sergeyevna is coming with us." Kolomeitsev silenced him, and turning up his rubber boots, he waded out into the water, pulling the boat with him. Then he deftly swung up over the side and helped clumsy Burshtein get in next to Vyazemskaya. Ivan Ivanovich Zagranichny angrily spit, not at the water but into his own hands, and pulled the rope so hard that the motor started the first time. But Kesha couldn't start his motor; his hands burned on the rope, and he kept muttering, now to Lachugin, "She shouldn't come, Seryozha, she shouldn't . . ."

Suddenly Kalya ran waist-deep into the water, pulled Kesha toward her, and kissed his damp curls, without shame.

"Well, well, ha, our quiet little Kesha," Ivan Ivanovich Zagranichny said in amazement, and opened up the throttle.

For some reason, Kolomeitsev found that kiss distasteful, but he suppressed the sensation, as he did his hostility toward Yulya Sergeyevna, who had once again violated the rules of the game. Any feeling extraneous to the immediate goal had to be ignored now.

Kesha's motor started right after Kalya had kissed him so unexpectedly, and the second boat raced after the first. Kalya stood waist-deep in the water at the very beginning of the motor's foamy wake, and just as the boat disappeared around the bend, she quickly and nervously blessed it.

CHAPTER · 17

The river was not dangerous at first, but everyone knew what lay ahead. Such torturous moments are met differently by different people: Some are silent, while some want to talk about things completely removed from the danger at hand. Ivan Ivanovich Zagranichny wanted to talk. So when the engine warmed up, switching from its initial screeching and wheezing to an even chug, which allowed them to hear one another, Ivan Ivanovich tossed out his conversational bait. "Incidentally, I *have* been abroad, Viktor Petrovich."

"No, really?" Kolomeitsev feigned amazement, calmly peering at the river.

"Yes, I have. . . . And without filling out any of those forms . . . So that my surname, even though everyone laughs, is actually appropriate," Ivan Ivanovich said, laughing softly.

"Where did you manage to go without filling out forms, Ivan Ivanovich?" Burshtein asked, squinting.

"To three countries. During the war. In a tank . . . And I made some interesting comparisons." Ivan Ivanovich spoke and pretended to be through.

"Well, and what are they?" Kolomeitsev asked, never taking his eyes from the river.

"That there's more order there."

"God save us from order like Dachau or Auschwitz," Burshtein said with a bitter laugh.

"Why are you nagging, Boris Abramovich? Order established at gunpoint is disgusting, of course. I'm not talking about that. I'm talking about national character. . . . Our system is supposed to be founded on organization, but the Russian character is the most disorganized imaginable. That's why we waste so much. We've even come up with a proverb to justify it: 'You can't chop wood without letting chips fly.' But I'd like to add that you can't grow a forest out of chips. The wealth of our natural resources has spoiled us a little. We have so much; that's why we don't cherish every twig, like the Europeans or the Japanese. By the way, speaking of the Japanese, I used to work floating logs down the Lena River to sell to the Japanese. At first we used to strip the bark so that our Soviet wood would look better over there in Japan. Then a Japanese representative arrived and complained, politely. 'Prease, good comlades, don't stlip the balk.' The bosses suspected some political, ulterior motive: 'What strategic object does the bark serve?' 'The stlategic object is to chemicarry tlansfolm Soviet balk into nyron blouses, and your young radies, good comlades, will stand in rine for them.' Now there's our silliness. Why do we still have lines? Because we're poor? Ludicrous, as that Japanese representative would say. No country is richer than ours. But take a look into our railroad stations: They're mobbed, people sleeping there, piled up on one another. As though everyone's carrying out an emergency evacuation, except everybody's going in opposite directions at the same time. An epidemic of place changing. And why? You know where I had to go to get an outboard motor? To Moscow. Residency permits—that's the end result of our disorganization. If the permits were done away with now, Moscow would balloon up into five times the size of New York. But a country forms a single body, and all the veins and sinews are connected. What kind of body would it be if the head swelled up like a cabbage and the legs became as skinny as matches? When will we get organized like normal people?"

"Don't worry, we managed with industrialization. We got organized. And we won the war. We got organized." Kolomeitsev's voice grew harsher. Of course, you're right about a lot, Ivan Ivanovich. . . . But no nation is without its faults, just like people."

"Who's arguing?" Ivan Ivanovich Zagranichny said, seemingly placated but really just waiting to continue. "So what are we supposed to do, wait for the next war to get organized?"

"Touché, you got me right where it hurts." Kolomeitsev laughed. "But you have to know how to live in peacetime as if there were a war. War is the naked essence of life—survival of the fittest."

"Stop, stop, stop. . . . I can't go along with that, Viktor Petrovich," Ivan Ivanovich Zagranichny said, shaking his head and adjusting the motor. "How can you feel nostalgic for war when the last one killed twenty million people? Our war was so bloody that peacetime should in no way resemble it. In war, order comes from orders, even though orders don't always help. But I don't want order like that —not for myself and not for others. Order must come from within, from the conscience; it shouldn't be dictated. Of course, you can't get too soft; excessive cruelty must be punished cruelly."

"It's a complicated problem: how just it is to punish cruelty with cruelty—can you determine the rules of revenge yourself?" Burshtein mused, scooping up some water in a cup over the side. "That might cause justice to grow so severe that it stops being justice. But then war can present such unexpected situations that you have to make instantaneous decisions, depending not on your conscience but on instinct. Do you know, Ivan Ivanovich, during the war I was an adjutant? To a general. He commanded a cavalry corps—"

"You can ride a horse, Boris Abramovich?" Ivan Ivanovich Zagranichny asked dubiously.

"I can," Burshtein said with a smile. "My knowledge of German got me into the cavalry. I learned to ride."

"He rides well," Kolomeitsev added merrily. "He and I rode all over the mountains of Altai. He'd pick up samples without getting out of the saddle, with his teeth, like in the circus."

"Now here is the story," Burshtein continued. "Once in Belorussia we found ourselves hemmed in on all sides by swamp and low hills, and on top of the hills were Germans. Our horses had not been fed; the men were hungry, our supplies running out; communications were out. The Germans began dropping leaflets from planes and telling us to surrender over loudspeakers. Their propaganda was clever: 'Who among you doesn't have a grudge against the Soviets? Is there even one person who hasn't had a relative arrested? Why are you still defending all that? Ruining your lives?' Our middle-aged general called a meeting of the commanding staff and said, 'It's true, every one of us has his grudges. But they're making one mistake: Our grudges are not against the homeland, nor can we have any. Even if some things were wrong at home, their fascist injustice is a hundred times worse than ours because even its roots are loathsome. And we'll pull it out by the roots. We've got to break out.' 'How can we break out,' the chief of staff asked, 'when the entire distance between our men and the Germans is littered with demoralized, defeated units?' 'We'll try to rouse them,' the general said. 'And if we don't?' the chief of staff asked.

"That night the general and I went on horseback to the campfires close in front of our corps. We ourselves didn't light fires at night— why help the Germans kill us? But these men did, illuminating not only themselves but our men, too. I could tell that the general's temper was boiling, but when we saw the men sitting around those fires, his anger disappeared. They were covered with stubble, bloated from hunger, deaf from the bombing; they sat or lay right in the mud; their eyes had that dull stare of the hopeless. The general rode from fire to fire, explaining gently that tomorrow morning at five hundred hours they had to move when they saw the flare. They didn't seem to hear him; no one even stirred. So the general tried getting tough. 'Do you hear me, you motherfuckers, or not?' At exactly oh-five-hundred, when our flare shot up, not one of them moved. The general gave orders to open machine-gun fire over their heads. They still didn't move. The general's face went gray, but he didn't carry out his threat to open fire on them. There was no other way. Our horses and tanks had to break out by rolling over them. Some came to their senses and joined us, and those who didn't get up died. But what could we do? Kill only two or three hundred people or add another four thousand to them?"

"The general had no choice," Kolomeitsev said. "Cowards don't deserve pity. . . . Ivan Ivanovich, I think your engine's only working on one cylinder."

"Not at all." Ivan Ivanovich took offense. "You're going deaf, Viktor Petrovich."

"They weren't cowards," Burshtein said, correcting Kolomeitsev harshly. "They were dazed. . . . But some of them woke up and were saved."

"How many survived?" Ivan Ivanovich Zagranichny asked.

"About fifteen hundred . . . We waded across the river under bombing and artillery fire. The men died silently, but the horses screamed—I can still hear their death cries. Then we dismounted and walked, sneaking through the silence. After all the bombing, the stillness collapsed on top of us, suffocated us. A young lieutenant, probably my age, couldn't stand it and began to look like one of the hopeless. Shell-shocked, he pawed at his holster, pulled out his gun, and raised it to his temple with a shaking hand. The people who saw him froze, but no one tried to grab his hand; they knew it was too late. Then, suddenly, another person began to follow suit and started unbuckling his own holster. A chain reaction of suicides might have started; there would have been general hysteria. It wasn't that we'd run out of courage; we had just run out of strength. But the young lieutenant didn't have time to shoot himself. Another shot rang out, and the lieutenant fell forward onto the dried branches. The general had shot him. Then he ordered in a whisper, 'Don't stop. . . . Forward.' Immediately that other person's confused hands started closing his holster. We went on. We met up with our troops. The general was immediately arrested on orders from Supreme Headquarters. They gave it to him for everything at once: that he allowed his troops to become surrounded, and that he led the cavalry over the infantry, and that he shot the lieutenant. They say that Marshal Zhukov saved him, defended him to Stalin. So the general reached Germany, just like you, Ivan Ivanovich. . . . Yulya Sergeyevna, let me have your cigarettes. I did quit, but—"

"Be careful, Boris Abramovich, you're sitting by the gasoline canister," Ivan Ivanovich Zagranichny warned, tossing a slicker over it. "Did you meet that general of yours after the war at all?"

"Once . . . I read his memoirs, but they contained nothing remotely resembling what I remember. Only descriptions of military operations, but not the reality of war. And the language wasn't his either; it was official jargon. Of course, they did say, 'As told to so-and-so.' Now if it had been told to Hemingway, it would have been another thing. It would have been a great book. . . . But I'll tell you how I met the general after the war. About three years ago I was walking along Pokrovsky Boulevard, past the benches where the pensioners play chess, and suddenly I saw the back of a head that looked familiar. A military head, even though it was under a straw hat with a black band. The bumps on the head were characteristic—they seemed to breathe; each had a life of its own. This head belonged to an old civilian man, strong, even though he carried a walking stick. He was watching someone else's game, kibitzing, interfering, irritating the others, who smiled at him condescendingly. And no one knew he was one of the great unknown heroes who actually won the war. His name, of course, is famous, and his memoirs, too. But who he really was, the way I know him, no one else knows. He didn't recognize me. I had changed more than he had since the war, but I reminded him: 'Your adjutant, Comrade General . . . Borka, the cavalryman from Birobidzhan.' "

"Are you from Birobidzhan, Boris Abramovich?" Ivan Ivanovich Zagranichny asked in surprise.

"Not at all, I'm from Sretenka Street in Moscow. . . . That was a joke the general used to make about me. 'Well, how are the oats in Birobidzhan?' he asked gleefully, even though his eyes had faded. He dragged me to his house, which was nearby. He lived completely alone. He sat me down under a steel saber and, like a true bachelor, offered me vodkas flavored with dill and garlic. The first toast stunned me: 'Well, let's drink to our cavalry, which will decide the fate of the next war if, God forbid, there is one!' Well, thought I, this general I used to idolize has gotten senile. He is very old. 'What do you mean, Comrade General?' I asked. And he replied, 'What will the result of the next war be? Nothing but ruins. No technology will remain, no —what do you call it?—electronics. . . . So who'll traverse the ruins? The cavalry!' He laughed, realizing that the joke was rather horrific, and then grew serious and thoughtful. 'Eh, Borka, Borka, cavalryman from Birobidzhan . . . Even though I'm a peasant from the boondocks, I'm a professional soldier—I began waving a saber over people's heads when I was eighteen. I fought generals and became one myself. But I never came to love war. . . . Do you remember the time we broke out, Borka? Remember how I had to send the cavalry over our men? And remember how I let that lieutenant boy have it? It's almost thirty years, and I still suffer over it. . . . Tell me, Borka, was I right or wrong?' I replied, 'If you'd acted otherwise, other people would have died, and more of them. You would be suffering anyway.' " Burshtein stopped talking, immersed in memories of the war and his private war.

"Yulya Sergeyevna, give me that shotgun! There are ducks ahead . . . on the water," Kolomeitsev exclaimed.

"But that's a mother with babies. They can't even fly yet." Ivan Ivanovich subdued him and then sighed. "But war is such a damned thing. . . . It forces good people to make horrible decisions, no matter how you look at it. There's nothing beautiful about it at all. I don't even like children playing at war. May it die, once and for all, the bitch. Now weren't you in Vietnam, Yulya Sergeyevna?"

"Yes," Vyazemskaya replied reluctantly.

"Well, what was it like? Like in the newspapers or not?" Ivan Ivanovich Zagranichny demanded.

"I read about the other war, World War Two, in the newspapers," Vyazemskaya replied. "And it was different from what they said. Even more horrible. It was the same in Vietnam. I caught the tail end of the big war—in Zlatoust. I worked at a lathe in a shell factory as a child. They accepted only boys at the factory, but I begged them. You weren't the only ones who won the war; we children did, too. Later, when I played volleyball at the institute, they praised me, saying I hit like a man. 'What's so good about a woman hitting like a man?' you might ask. But when I was in Vietnam, I couldn't ignore the horrors, the way the men did, and I hated myself. I'd always considered myself a man, and suddenly it turned out I was a woman."

"Tell us about it, Yulya Sergeyevna," Ivan Ivanovich Zagranichny prompted gently. "That's the theme of the day—war reminiscences. If we don't tell, then who'll learn the truth about us?"

"Well, whatever else you say, you can't complain about the underdevelopment of oral history in this group," Kolomeitsev grumbled. "But actions speak louder than words—well, my friends, what do you think, will we find the cassiterite? We must."

"But what will action lead to if you don't look back at where you've been?" Ivan Ivanovich Zagranichny rebuked him gently. "Viktor Petrovich, don't worry about our actions. Conversation won't spoil them. When a man shoves his memories deep inside, they can tear him apart. . . . So what happened to you in Vietnam, Yulya Sergeyevna?"

"The driver on our expedition—a Vietnamese boy, about twenty years old—was named Nguyen. A pure soul, like our Kesha, he smiled even when he was sad. And his smile was marvelous. It reminded me of Gagarin's smile. Actually he resembled Gagarin a bit—maybe a Gagarin painted by a Vietnamese artist. Once we were working in a rather dangerous zone with some Vietnamese geologists. By the way, we were looking for cassiterite, too, Viktor Petrovich. I could see that Nguyen wanted to tell me something, but he was embarrassed and didn't dare. Finally, I got it out of him. He told me, in very funny Russian and mostly with his hands, his fiancée lived in a nearby village, and he hadn't seen her in a year. So I said, 'Go visit her, Nguyen.' He shook his head no, but his eyes betrayed him. I could tell he was afraid of his Vietnamese boss, so I got into the car with him and drove off —supposedly on geological business. Nguyen began to sing, he was so happy. While we drove, they began shooting over us. But Nguyen barely noticed, just kept on singing. We parked by a wooden well. Bombs and artillery shells had flattened the village; only the well had miraculously survived. There was a wooden trough next to the well, where several women were doing their laundry. A shell would howl past or a bomb would explode nearby, and they didn't even look up. Where do they live? I thought, and looking around, I saw dozens of children's eyes staring at me from underground, through log camouflage blinds. It was just like in Nekrasov, but a more horrible, Vietnamese version—the sky had become such an enemy that they were forced underground. Nguyen talked with the old women, smiled apologetically at me, and then quickly ran off to find his bride. Suddenly there was a tremendous roar, and a black fountain of earth flew up. I was thrown on the ground by the jolt. Spitting mud and leaves from my mouth, I got up and saw Nguyen's body on the ground, his head with its slanting eyes rolled toward me. . . . But the Vietnamese women went on washing and wringing their clothes, as if nothing had happened. They were tired of noticing death. And then for the first time in my life I experienced real horror, not for myself but at what man can do to such a beautiful smile, by cutting it off from its body. I howled in a voice I didn't know I had—thrashing on the ground like an epileptic. When I got hold of myself, I saw the old Vietnamese women, their hands still wet from the laundry, placing the body and smile on a bamboo stretcher and taking it away silently. Behind them, also silent, was a young girl who resembled Nguyen enough to be his sister, probably his fiancée. Like a lunatic, I got in the car, started the engine, and drove off, not knowing where. In the bushes near the road I saw an antiaircraft gun camouflaged by branches. I stopped the car, went over to it, and pushed the Vietnamese soldiers aside. I wanted to shoot at the sky, even though I didn't know how to shoot. The tiny Vietnamese soldiers grabbed me, shouting something and signaling that it wasn't allowed. . . . That's why I don't like to see children playing war either, Ivan Ivanovich." And Yulya Sergeyevna lit another cigarette.

"Children imitate heroes by instinct. . . . Without heroism life would be nothing but existence," Kolomeitsev noted.

"Real heroism is a response, not an action that's initiated," Yulya Sergeyevna said. "By the way, don't denigrate existence. For a long time now, just existing demands heroics."

"This tendency to denigrate heroism infuriates me," Kolomeitsev said, huffily.

Ivan Ivanovich Zagranichny swore. "And now, Viktor Petrovich, one cylinder really is out. . . . Oh, I see, the spark plug is loose. That can be fixed." And he continued. "But we don't worry enough about something else: Will we let down our children? We will if they find they can't believe us or if they believe us and we're lying. Don't you worry that the young generation doesn't know about heroes, Viktor Petrovich? Just take a look at Lachugin. He's a wonderful boy and, incidentally, responsible. He adores you, Viktor Petrovich; forgive me, he even adores you too much."

"Oh, stop exaggerating, Ivan Ivanovich," Kolomeitsev said not without a little satisfaction. "It's just that Lachugin has a need for authority, unlike certain representatives of our great working class and our intelligentsia. I've probably been a bit too easy on you, my dear opinionated subordinates."

"I know it's a real chore for you, Viktor Petrovich, to lead us ideologically unsound sinners, but it's your burden. Actually it's not so easy for us to follow you either." Ivan Ivanovich Zagranichny laughed.

"You're the one who was ranting a few minutes ago about order, organization. Well, how can you have organization without leaders?" Kolomeitsev goaded.

"This gas is watered down," Ivan Ivanovich concluded aloud, listening to the outboard motor. "Those bastards . . ."

Burshtein continued. "War may let you determine many things about a person, but not all of them. I know people who weren't afraid to risk their lives in war, who were fearless when it came to bullets. But in peacetime they grovel before so-called powerful people, always afraid they'll endanger their careers. But what's a step on the ladder of success or even the whole ladder compared to your life, which is really all you've got! I thought about it for a long time and came to this conclusion: In war sometimes it's easier to be brave. Of course, it's terrifying to face gunfire, but next to you there are others marching toward those same bullets. Besides, you don't have a choice; you're following orders. But in peacetime you're alone, there's no support from somebody else's courage, no one's giving you orders, and you can be punished instead of rewarded for displaying courage."

"It's true, Boris Abramovich," Kolomeitsev said. "That's why I'm for real heroic courage in peacetime."

"Well, there's no shortage of heroic courage around here yet. . . . You're leaning against the gas line, Viktor Petrovich," Ivan Ivanovich Zagranichny said. "If needs be, we'll defend our homeland. But if everyone spends all his time getting ready to defend the home-land in war, who'll defend it in peacetime? From lackeys? And fast talkers? And cowards? Not to mention our own disorganization?"

"From Eduard Sitechkin," Burshtein added, and everyone laughed.

And suddenly Kolomeitsev felt a strange stinging in his eyes. Tears? He was astonished. *Damn it, you're getting old, Kolomeitsev, but is crying really necessary?*

Summoning his willpower, he blinked them back and sneaked a look at the others; no one seemed to have noticed. He sneered at himself. *I can even put armor over my eyes. Why not cry, Kolomeitsev? Because suddenly you know what people these are in the boat with you, how unique they are, how irreplaceable this conversation with them is. You love these people, Kolomeitsev, even though you don't want to love them. You force yourself to believe that love is a weakness. Ivan Ivanovich . . . Burshtein . . . Yulya Sergeyevna . . . Why are you inventing risk for these people, who have risked their lives so many times before? And there, in the other boat, Kesha, Seryozha Lachugin . . . They're just starting life. . . . Cassiterite? What is it compared to human lives?*

But it was too late to stop the boats now.

"I received two . . . two serious wounds, and three minor ones, and a concussion," Kolomeitsev said, suddenly contributing his recollections. "But one wound was special. Even though you can hardly call it a wound. My pal Kostya Shmelyov and I were dropped into the Belorussian forests to make contact with the partisans. Shmelyov had done parachuting for fun before the war, and he wasn't afraid of jumping. When the plane door opened, he let me go first and gave me a sympathetic pat on the rear. I'd only made two training jumps, and to tell the truth, I was shaking. But I pulled myself together and jumped. I landed normally, but Kostya, with all his experience, got skewered on a branch; it went right through him. He died on the tree; when I took him down, he was already dead. Kostya had suffered but didn't make any noise—he was afraid to reveal our position. I wrapped him in the two parachutes, buried him, and went on alone. A day later I met a shepherd—a boy of twelve or so. By coincidence his name was Kostya, too. His face was covered with freckles. He said he could take me to the partisans. We were walking through the woods, Kostya in front with two mangy cows, me in back. We came to a road, and Kostya went out on it first, while I hid in the bushes and waited. Kostya stood there awhile and was just turning to signal me to come out, but suddenly he stopped. From the other side of the road Germans came out of the bushes, with branches on their helmets, about twenty of them, and two *Polizei*—that is, Russians who worked for the Germans as police. They were waiting to ambush partisans. They surrounded Kostya and started questioning him. This was all taking place about twenty meters from me; I could see and hear everything clearly. 'Where are the partisans?' a *Polizei* asked. 'I don't know, sir,' Kostya said, shaking his head. 'I take care of my cows and don't know anything.' 'Which village are you from?' the other *Polizei* asks. 'From Eremichi,' Kostya replied. 'From Eremichi and you don't know anything?' The first *Polizei* laughed. 'That's a hornet's nest of partisans.' At the sound of the name Eremichi, the *Oberleutnant* smiled. He made a sign to the *Polizei,* and they tore off Kostya's shirt. The *Oberleutnant* took the cigarette from his lips, which were as thin as worms, and pressed it to the boy's chest. Kostya screamed, cried, and tried to wrench himself away, but the *Polizei* held him tight. And the *Oberleutnant* moved the cigarette along his chest, touching here and there. Finally, he ground it out right on his skin and lit another and began caressing the boy with the new one, particularly around the nipples, the son of a bitch. And Kostya kept shouting, 'I don't know anything, nothing.' My finger was on the trigger of my gun, but what could I do against two dozen Germans? But I felt the cigarette burning right through me. The *Polizei* began torturing the boy from all sides and roaring with laughter. Kostya passed out from the pain. They let him go, and he fell to the ground. One of his cows came over and started licking his wounds. The *Oberleutnant* pulled out his Walther, placed it tenderly in the cow's ear, and shot. It fell next to Kostya. Then the *Oberleutnant* pointed at Kostya for one of the *Polizei* to come finish off. The child's bare feet jerked in the dust of the road, and that was it. . . . When I reached the partisans, I took off my shirt and started to wash in the stream. One of them asked me, 'What happened to you? How did that happen?' I looked. My whole chest was covered with cigarette burns, even though no one had tortured me. A doctor later told me that this kind of thing sometimes happens, though it's rare."

"If we always felt for others like that, we'd soon be in our own graves," Ivan Ivanovich Zagranichny said. "But skin gets thicker, it does. We learn to live with our own burns and with those of others."

Suddenly he jumped. "There it is—Wild One!" he shouted, and pulling his cap down on his head, he tied the earflaps under his chin.

About five hundred meters ahead the river's silvery back was roiling with white foam and smashing against black boulders.

CHAPTER · 18

"**S**eryozha, do you ever feel as though you've lived forever?" Kesha asked, steering the boat into the middle of the river so as to follow exactly in the first boat's wake.

Seryozha didn't have to ask him to repeat it; he understood.

"Sometimes it does, Kesha. I'll be standing in some unfamiliar city or an unfamiliar street, and suddenly I imagine I've been there before. In some other life. But what my name was and who I was then, I can't remember."

"Do you ever see yourself in places you've never been? Seeing what you've never seen?" Kesha kept pressing, managing simultaneously to watch the river, the outboard motor, and Seryozha's eyes.

"Well, I don't," Seryozha admitted honestly. "No, wait. . . . When I listen to music, I do."

"What do you see?"

"Different things. Flowing lava . . . The ocean. Strange gigantic plants . . . Enormous birds. Something like the beginning of the world. And I fly above it. They say some people fly in their dreams. I fly when I listen to music." Seryozha sighed and squinted, as if the Siberian expanses around him had become a gigantic conservatory, filled with magnificent echoes.

"I fly, too," Kesha said, "but without music. It's true, something whispers and echoes inside me, like this river. But it's not real music; it's my own. I don't even play the accordion. And not only do I fly, Seryozha, but sometimes I crawl, as though I hadn't grown arms or legs yet and there were scales on me, and I rub and rub against the grass, trying to get rid of the scales. And sometimes I swim and breathe through gills, and I see gardens and cities underwater. And suddenly I grow into a tree, with branches instead of arms, and I rustle to the other trees, and they understand me, but I don't understand them.

Sometimes I'm a mossy boulder in the middle of the river. Sometimes I'm a drop of dew on a blade of grass, and when the sun evaporates me, I rise up to the sky and stick to the edge of a cloud. And then I fall back to earth as a raindrop, trying to find the same blade of grass I came from, and I can't find it. There are millions of blades of grass."

"Kesha, have you ever written letters to anyone?"

"Yes. But not very often—I'm embarrassed about making mistakes. I never finished seventh grade, Seryozha. I wanted to join the police, but they wouldn't take me. You have to have at least a tenth-grade diploma. . . . Well, maybe because of my hump, too—but they didn't say so."

"The police? Why the police?" Seryozha was astonished.

"I like people. Sometimes I feel sorry for them, but I still like them. And only people who like people should join the police. I've noticed that people who run up against bad policemen can lose faith in everything. I'd also like to be the director of a children's home. I'd even like to be a janitor there or a stoker. They didn't take me either. They said the children would tease me to death. But that's not true. Maybe at first they would, but then they'd stop. They'd find out I loved them, and they would have loved me, too. I don't have a hump at all, Seryozha. Kalya told me that. And if she says so, it's true."

Tears welled in Kesha's eyes, and he turned away.

"Don't cry, Kesha," Seryozha asked. "Kalya was telling the truth."

"I'm not crying. It's the wind," Kesha replied. "Actually I do cry, sometimes. Kalya says I'm her girl friend. Tell me, do you think Kalya can fall in love with me?"

"I saw the way she kissed you," Seryozha said. "You don't kiss a girl friend like that."

"I'd like for Kalya and me to have children," Kesha drawled dreamily. "I want them to be educated. I feel many things, Seryozha, but I know so little. You were talking about the beginnings of the earth. When did it begin? Wasn't it always there?"

"I don't think it was," Seryozha said without conviction. "In any case that's what we were taught."

"But if we feel we were alive before, maybe the earth had another life, too? Before it became the earth?"

"Maybe, Kesha."

"Seryozha, can you draw?"

"Yes, but badly."

"But you have drawn. Now before an artist paints a picture, what does he need, Seryozha?"

"What do you mean? Canvas, paints . . ."

"No, that's not what I mean. What's in his head before he draws the picture?"

"I guess the mental image of the picture, the preconception of it."

"And the earth is also like a picture. More than all the rest of paintings put together. That means it had an artist, too. That means that before the earth there was the thought of the earth. But whose thought was it, Seryozha?"

"Probably nature's, Kesha."

"Maybe God's?" And Kesha's whortleberry eyes stared at Seryozha with an unsettling inquisitiveness. "Look, a stag!"

As the boat rounded a bend, a stag appeared, crossing the river, right in front of the bow. A butterfly sat on its velvety horns. When the stag saw Kesha and Seryozha, a very human terror flickered in his eyes. He desperately paddled his legs until he reached the opposite shore and then rushed into the bushes. Looking back for just an instant, he seemed surprised no one was shooting at him.

"He's afraid!" Kesha said. "And he should be. But he belongs to nature, and so do we."

"I think that people call nature God because they can't explain it completely," Seryozha said.

"But maybe people are calling God nature?"

"Well, what's the difference what you call what? Lots of people call things one name or another simply out of ignorance. Kesha, you say you don't know much. But I'm convinced that even the greatest scholars know very little. No one knows everything."

"No one?" Kesha was saddened. "That means there's no one to

turn to, to ask advice from. Yet some people look like they're the ones who definitely know it all."

"They're the ones who know the least, Kesha. They're just pretending."

"Actually, Seryozha, I have a question that's been bothering me for a long time." Kesha grew embarrassed. "If man came from the apes, then why didn't all the apes turn into people?"

"You see, Kesha, there is this theory. It's not proved, of course. A scientist told it to me." Seryozha began carefully.

"Don't be afraid, talk." Kesha moved closer to him, rocking the boat. "Sometimes unproved things are the truest of all."

"I don't know if this theory is true or not. But it interests me. It has nothing to do with geology, but without geology you can't understand it. Maybe I'll take it up more seriously sometime."

"Don't tease me—what is it?" Kesha begged.

"In short, once upon a time the magnetic equilibrium of the earth was destroyed. And then some of the weaker apes underwent mutation . . ." Seryozha began.

"What's that?" Kesha began to sweat.

"A pathological change. Well, some kind of abnormal development. These apes lost their hair; physically they became ill-adapted, helpless. But the instinct for survival made them smarter. Their brains began developing. They began walking on their hind legs. They learned to make fire by rubbing two sticks together. They stopped being apes; they became humans. But the other apes remained apes. That's the theory, Kesha."

"Then we really do come from apes?" Kesha sighed in disappointment. "I remember being a bird, and a fish, and a tree, but a monkey . . . never."

"There are other theories," Seryozha said, consoling him. "There's a theory that we descended from aliens of another planet. There's also a theory that the earth is the creation of the highest intelligence of the universe. That's what Tsiolkovsky thought. . . ."

"The man who invented the rocket?" Kesha asked, overjoyed at having recognized the name.

"The first one to send a rocket into space." Seryozha corrected him gently. "But very few people know that he was a great philosopher."

"What?" Kesha asked dispiritedly.

"A philosopher. A man who has his own thoughts," Seryozha clarified. "His own system of thought."

"But everyone has his own thoughts. Even fools. Little thoughts, but they're their own."

"Fools only think their thoughts are their own. They're factory-made."

"So what is this highest intelligence?" Kesha asked.

"Tsiolkovsky didn't define that precisely. He left it for us to guess. He figured that everything in the universe is born of this intelligence, everything is interconnected. I came across some pamphlets Tsiolkovsky printed in Kaluga, and they were fascinating. You know, Kesha, Tsiolkovsky would have understood your feeling that you've always existed. According to Tsiolkovsky, nothing disappears; things are merely transformed into another configuration of atoms. You know what an atom is, right?"

"Who doesn't know that, since the atom bomb?" Kesha was offended. "Atoms are just tiny pieces of our body. But does our soul have atoms?" Kesha demanded. "Where does it go, the soul, when the body dies?"

"I don't know. See how little I know. But probably if the body doesn't really die, then the soul doesn't die either," Seryozha said, and smiled gently at Kesha. Never in his wildest dreams did he imagine that someday he would be discussing all this on a wild Siberian river, in a boat that reeked of tar, wet tarpaulin, and fish.

"And I have one more question," the indefatigable Kesha said. "Where does time go?"

"It turns into memory," Seryozha said after a brief pause.

"Nobody's memory is big enough to hold all the time that's passed."

"Memory is probably transmitted in the genes."

"In what?"

"It means it stays in the blood. For instance, why are you so kind?"

"I'm not kind. Sometimes I'd like to get hold of Chapayev's machine gun, especially for snakes like Sitechkin," Kesha said, and in his whortleberry eyes there gleamed something that didn't resemble kindness at all.

"You say that because you don't have a machine gun in your hands. Anyway, perhaps you're so kind because once a long time ago some distant ancestor of yours was walking through the primordial forest without a weapon and found himself facing a mammoth or maybe a she-bear, which could easily have torn him to shreds. . . . And the animal took pity on him, didn't touch him, circled him, and carried off her cub in her teeth. And your ancestor was so amazed by the kindness of nature, as embodied in that she-bear, that he became kinder himself. And through the centuries that passed down to you in your blood. . . . I think there's some kind of memory like that."

"And what if that bear had mutilated my ancestor?" Kesha asked doubtfully. "What then, would I be evil?"

"You might. Of course, I'm not sure. But I think that in any case the suffering, insults, and humiliation our ancestors experienced are bound to have some effect on us; they remain somewhere in our blood. There's even an expression: the blood of slaves. Chekhov said you had to squeeze it out of yourself, drop by drop."

"Then what we are depends only on our ancestors and we have nothing to do with it?" Kesha frowned. "If that's true, slaves would come only from slaves, the wise only from the wise, and fools only from fools. But I've seen smart fathers with such stupid sons you wouldn't believe it, and some stupid fathers have sons so smart they could have been sired by a gust of wind. My father was a hard drinker, but I don't touch a drop—I'm afraid I'll turn out like him. And then you tell me about those cheans." Kesha looked into the gas tank. "It's time to add some more. Hand me the canister."

"Genes," Seryozha corrected. "They do contain some form of memory. And there's another kind of memory—the common memory of mankind. Folklore, history, literature, art . . . I saw Surikov's painting *The Boyarynya Morozova* many times on postcards and in reproductions, even though I never really noticed it. But the first time

I saw it in the Tretyakov Gallery, I was stunned. It was almost as if the boy in the fur hat and sheepskin jacket running behind the cart were me. I thought if he turned his head, the face would be mine."

"Who is Boyarynya Morozova?" Kesha asked, again feeling glum because of his ignorance.

"She was a religious dissenter, a Raskolnik. She's blessing herself with two fingers as they take her away in chains," Seryozha replied.

"Raskolnik, I know. Blessing yourself with two fingers, I know. We had a lot of them in Siberia. But why don't I know that painting, that *boyarynya*?" Kesha sighed in despair. "If that's the memory of mankind, then it looks like I got left out. When was I supposed to have time to learn things when my father died from drinking and left me with this hump! ... At thirteen I was the man of the family, with eight kids. All my memory went into feeding them, dressing them, getting them shoes. That's why I never finished school. I even got Tsiolkovsky all wrong. I thought he invented the rocket and that was all. What do I know about Ivan the Terrible? Only that he was terrible. Or Napoleon? That he set fire to Moscow and then went back home, and nothing else. That's my real hump, my ignorance, and even Kalya can't convince me I don't have it. No, I'll do anything, but my children won't be without that memory!"

"You yourself still have time to learn." Seryozha consoled him. "You're only twenty."

"That's right!" Kesha was astonished by this discovery and then suddenly grew anxious again. "But that's four whole years. I'll have to stop working. And who'll bring up my brothers and sisters? I send them my whole salary. And if I ... if I ... get married? Then what?

"Are you a weakling, Kesha?" Seryozha needled him.

"No, I'm strong. Kalya doesn't even know yet how strong I am. I've worn you out with my dumb questions, as if you were a visiting lecturer. ... Get some sleep, Seryozha. You've just come back from a long trip, and now you're on the road again. Turn over on your side and sleep. There. I'll cover you from the spray with the tarp. It's awhile to the rapids. I'll wake you. They'll wake you. You'll hear it a verst away. They're noisy, those rapids."

Seryozha dozed; he really was tired. Kesha concentrated on the river, which was carrying the boat onward. He could still find a channel that was deep enough—sometimes in the middle, sometimes closer to the shore—but he noticed exposed sandbars and that islands had emerged even in the deeper water. He muttered, "The water's gone down. If only it were higher. Where can more water come from?"

CHAPTER · 19

van Kuzmich Belomestynkh got up later than usual, and when he
came out into the yard, it was already flooded with early-morning
light. He saw the note on the nail—Thanks for the hospitality. S.
Lachugin"—and remembered the young geologist approvingly. *Re-*
spectful. Not like some. He even knows how to write a nice note. Inside
the house the infant cried and then was still, probably soothed by
Ksiuta's breast. Ivan Kuzmich felt more hopeful about life. After all,
what was a house without children underfoot?

But the berry commissioner could not appreciate the promise of
the bright new dawn. He awoke to a dull throbbing pain below his
stomach. *Overdid it last night, I guess. Damned essence,* thought Tikhon
Tikhonovich, shifting positions, trying to ease the pain. He was no
stranger to the many faces of liquor and its morning-after effects, but
this hangover was something frighteningly different. A new, stabbing
pain appeared and grew more frequent, as a red-hot pressure girdled
the area below his waist. He bit his lip until it bled, to keep from crying
out and frightening the child. He wanted to get up, but it was impossible; the pain made him recoil and fold up into himself. He writhed
along the floor, barely making it to the threshold, and from there he
slid down the porch steps, holding his stomach and moaning. Frightened by the sight of a man rolling in the dust, Charlie whimpered and
hid in his doghouse. Old man Belomestynkh rushed to lift him up, but
Tikhon Tikhonovich wouldn't let him; he pushed him away, gritting
his teeth. Ivan Kuzmich even made the sign of the cross. He thought
a demon had possessed the berry commissioner; his eyes didn't even
look human; they bulged out of their sockets so. He ran to get the old
mushroomer and Grisha, the driver.

"Oh, the hour of my death has come. Oh, Lord, what have I done
to deserve such torment?" Tikhon Tikhonovich gasped, unable to

sit, or stand, or lie down; whichever way he turned, it still hurt.

"Your 'pendix, is it?" asked Grisha, perplexed and terrified.

"Taken out long ago," Tikhon Tikhonovich whispered.

"A stone then." The little old mushroomer shook his head compassionately.

"What stone!" Tikhon Tikhonovich rasped, grimacing as the unbearable burning sensation continued.

"In your kidney. One of my Japanese friends had one just like it. We brewed horsetail tea to help him pass it. I held it right in my hand—it was tiny, like a grain of sand, but with jagged edges. Afterward my friend tied it up in a bag and wore it to ward off other stones."

"How do you get it, the stone?" Tikhon Tikhonovich snarled as the pain flung him from one side to the other.

"Who knows? All kinds of garbage settles little by little and then forms a stone."

"You can also use tree ears to help it pass," Ivan Kuzmich recalled. "I have a whole jar left. They've gone a little bad, but . . ."

"Let's not have any witch doctoring here," Grisha announced with determination. "What if it's an ulcer instead of a stone? We've got to get him to a hospital."

They put Tikhon Tikhonovich in the cab of the truck, and Grisha drove him back to Zima as fast as possible. But unable to sit or lie, Tikhon Tikhonovich moaned and groaned and suffered so much that he begged to be put in the back of the truck, where he continued to howl—but at least the roar of the engine drowned it out. There was no one to feel embarrassed in front of, since only the omnipresent taiga could hear. It was so bad that Tikhon Tikhonovich even thought about God, something he did only at life's worst moments. What prayers wouldn't Tikhon Tikhonovich mutter, what promises, feasible or unfeasible, wouldn't he give, if only God would stop the pain? It was so bad that for a second he sank his teeth into the top of the pickup's side, and a bump in the road almost knocked them out.

Grisha dragged him into the admitting room shortly after dark. A woman was on duty—a doctor of forty-five or so with a tight bun of black hair, touched with gray, and eyes so green they were the color of malachite. Despite his agony, Tikhon Tikhonovich noticed, with the eye of a practiced ladies' man, her strong, elegant legs, one of which had a large brown mole that was repellent yet attractive. Her face, remarkable for its high cheekbones, was still very beautiful, but her expression was severe and devoid of any compassion or anxiety; it merely showed workmanlike concentration. *The mistress of copper mountain*, Grisha called her to himself, his eyes riveted to the birthmark, from which several bristly hairs protruded.

"Lie down!" the doctor ordered imperiously, without even asking Tikhon Tikhonovich what his complaint was. His hands clutched his lower abdomen, immediately indicating to her the location of the pain.

"Will you lie down! You're behaving like a child!" she said, pressing down on Tikhon Tikhonovich's shoulders. Pulling his hands, she unfastened his belt and quickly started palpating the abdomen, ruthlessly digging her fingers into his body.

"Don't tense up. . . . Breathe deeply."

Staring in fear at the doctor and expecting the worst possible diagnosis, Tikhon Tikhonovich suddenly thought he recognized this woman. *Where do I know her from?* The berry commissioner racked his brains, but the pain in his belly overwhelmed his concentration.

"What's the matter with me, Doctor?" Tikhon Tikhonovich moaned, twitching at the touch of her fingers. "An ulcer?"

The doctor smiled with the corners of her well-defined dark lips. "No, it's not an ulcer."

"Is it cholera?" Tikhon Tikhonovich asked, rising on his elbows and stuttering at the thought of this new, terrible threat.

Her malachite eyes, once again reminding him of someone, icily glided over him. "Don't fill your head with such thoughts, or you'll really get it."

"That 'pendicitis—what do you call it?—can you get it a second time?" Tikhon Tikhonovich went on, refusing to give up and groaning while he thought: *I know those green eyes, I know them.*

"No, you can't," the doctor said curtly. "Tell me, how are things with your prostate?"

"What is that?" Tikhon Tikhonovich was bewildered.

"Good—you don't know. But I have to check it. Your friend should turn around. Zoya, the glove! And you turn on your side. There. Bring your knees up to your stomach. Now, hold on!"

Tikhon Tikhonovich howled—this time from both pain and shame that a woman could do that to him.

Grisha couldn't resist peeking over his shoulder, and even he squirmed.

"Your prostate is a little clogged, but there's nothing terrible going on there. . . . It's not causing the pain," the doctor concluded. "Sit up." She struck Tikhon Tikhonovich's back lightly below the waist. "Does that hurt?"

"Uh-huh," replied the berry commissioner, writhing.

"Now, lie on your back. Let's feel that abdomen once more. Aha, is it most painful right there? It looks like a kidney stone. Or sand."

"Sand?" Tikhon Tikhonovich was really afraid. "Sand is pouring out of me?"

"That's the trouble. If it did pour out, you'd feel better." The doctor joked without a smile. "We'll do an X ray tomorrow. At any rate, it's definitely kidney colic. Zoya, give him an injection of baralgin right away."

The enormous, masculine nurse, who had arms like a blacksmith's and bizarrely manicured carrot-colored nails, whispered into the doctor's ear. But her basso voice did not escape the acute hearing of a patient anxious to hear about his illness.

"I reserved the baralgin for Yuri Serafimovich. . . . The last six ampuls."

"Who's Yuri Serafimovich?" The doctor frowned.

"What do you mean, who? The deputy head of the shoe store. Remember, he got you those Italian boots."

The doctor blushed deeply and frowned so severely that her eyebrows met over her nose.

"Zoya, we're not running a medical pawnbrokerage here—trading medication for boots. This man is in pain. Give him the injection. And use a thin needle."

I've seen those eyebrows, I know I have, thought Tikhon Tikhonovich, submissively offering his arm and shutting his eyes like a martyr.

After the shot he felt better; the pain in his abdomen receded, leaving only a sensation of heaviness. He grew more bold, curious. "Doctor, I have the feeling I know you from somewhere."

"I don't know you," the doctor said. "Incidentally, I've got to admit you. You'll have to remain here."

But no sooner had she dipped her pen in the inkwell than the door opened and a puny blond policeman entered, dragging a lanky drunk with a bleeding head.

"Where do I put him?" the policeman gasped, barely able to stand under the weight of the lifeless body crumpled on top of him. The lifeless body was snoring, however.

"We'll admit you tomorrow," the doctor told Tikhon Tikhonovich. "The nurse will take you to the ward."

The doctor gently but firmly helped the berry commissioner up from the cot, and then she and Grisha, holding their noses against the horrible, raw brandy fumes, helped the policeman drag his snoring burden to the examination table.

"Found him on Komsomol Dawns Street," the perspiring policeman reported. "He was lying in the nettles. As for his head, either somebody hit him, or he fell down. It's payday today."

But Tikhon Tikhonovich remained, leaning against the lintel and straining to recognize her by staring at the doctor's malachite eyes. The doctor shoved ammonia-soaked cotton up the drunkard's nose, which provoked a deafening sneeze. He opened his cloudy, senseless eyes, then shut them again and snored even louder.

"A hard head," the doctor said, washing out the wound. "Either he fell on a brick, or someone patted him on the head with one. You see, Comrade Policeman, little pieces of brick are on the cotton. Luckily the wound isn't deep. Zoya, a tetanus injection. Comrade Policeman, would you like a bit of alcohol? It helps when you're tired."

"Well, I am on duty." The policeman hemmed.

"It's all right, I'm on duty, too," the doctor said, smiling and pouring alcohol into two beakers. "I'm dog-tired today, too. Only one real patient. But I saw thirty-four victims of payday. . . . Would you like a little water in it?"

"Generally I don't dilute it," said the policeman, even more embarrassed.

"Neither do I," the doctor said, and drained the glass with a lightning-fast, masculine gesture.

"To your health!" said Grisha, enchanted by the doctor.

"Get out of here," the doctor said severely, and then noticed the berry commissioner. "And you, with your cholera, get to the ward immediately. What are you staring at me for? You've never seen a woman drink alcohol? It doesn't matter now, you can't tell the women from the men. If I don't have a drink myself, the smell of that drunk's breath will make me sick."

"Has green eyes been here long?" Tikhon Tikhonovich asked the nurse, struggling into the shrunken hospital pajamas, which had been washed too many times.

The nurse confided in a deep voice, fluffing up the scrawny pillow by smashing it with her powerful hands, "She's new. Some of the doctors here were replaced. They were on the take. And who can blame them when their salaries are so low? But this one is honest. Yuri Serafimovich brought her boots as a present for his catheter, and she gave him money. 'They're beautiful boots,' she said, 'but they've got a hard life ahead of them.' One woman carted in a turkey for her, but she hurt her feelings. 'I accept only peacocks,' she said. She's not human, somehow. The only human thing about her is that she drinks. Of course, she's good at her work."

"Where's she from?" Tikhon Tikhonovich asked.

"She's one of ours, Siberian, from near the Lena somewhere. . . . But she's private, I can't find out a thing."

"What's her name?" The berry commissioner kept prying.

"Zalogina, Darya Sevastyanovna." The nurse began to fuss with her instrument. "Well, I'm off. Here's a jar. In the morning give me a specimen. . . . What's the matter? Does it hurt again?"

"No, no," muttered Tikhon Tikhonovich, whose face was contorted almost beyond recognition. "Just sleepy."

"Well, that's fine. I'll just put the jar under your bed."

Tikhon Tikhonovich pulled the itchy wool blanket up to his chin and then over his head, even though no one could see how upset he was in the darkness. His face was turning to putty; in fact, it was on the verge of dissolving completely in a puddle of tears as he realized whom the woman doctor resembled—Dasha Zalogin from Teteryovka, the girl from whose breasts he had nibbled bird cherries, on Crooked Hill, forty-three years ago. The same malachite eyes; the same thick black brows; the same sharp cheekbones under taut, bronzed skin. But that Dasha was some twenty-five years younger than this one, there had been no gray in her hair, and she never drank.

Tikhon Tikhonovich figured in his head only to discover that this doctor could indeed have been their daughter, even though her patronymic wasn't right. As he grew less and less able to avoid the inevitable conclusion, Tikhon Tikhonovich burned with shame and horror because he would never have met his only daughter, would not have even guessed she existed had it not been for the kidney stone. *Maybe it's only a coincidence?* He was too much a coward to give up all hope. *The patronymic is wrong.*

Tikhon Tikhonovich tossed off the blanket, put on the worn slippers, and stealthily crept down the stairs. The door to the admitting room was ajar. The drunkard with the head wound had been replaced by a weeping middle-aged woman with an enormous purple-yellow contusion under her eye. The green-eyed doctor was applying a compress and angrily scolding. "What the hell do you need to live with a husband like that for if he disfigures you every payday? I live alone, and sometimes I suffer, but at least when I'm done suffering, no one else torments me. What's wrong with you, don't you respect yourself?"

"He doesn't beat me because he's mad at me but because he's miserable himself. His life didn't work out. He's an invalid; he works as a miner. It kills him that I make more working as a cashier in a steam bath. But when he's sober, he's kind," cried the woman.

"Well, pretend to leave him. Scare him. Maybe he'll come to his senses. Do you want the key to my room? You can spend two or three nights there. Don't tell him where you are," Zalogin suggested.

"No," the woman said, shaking her head. "The fool can't even feed himself. He once cooked eggs for an hour to soft-boil them. He's like a child, helpless. I'd better go. Don't put green iodine on it—last time it had healed completely, but I couldn't get the green stain off. You've been so kind. Come to the steam bath, and I'll let you in free."

The woman left, and Zalogin was alone. She poured a bit of alcohol into a beaker and gulped it down again.

And suddenly Tikhon Tikhonovich felt the unfamiliar pain of a father and shuddered. *She's drinking . . . alone. My little girl.*

"Who's there?" Zalogin heard the door creak.

Tikhon Tikhonovich came in from the dark corridor, squinting in the bright light.

"Why aren't you asleep?" Zalogin asked. "Do you have some pain?"

"Daughter," Tikhon Tikhonovich exclaimed. "Daughter."

"I don't like being called that," Zalogin said with a frown. "Call me Darya Sevastyanovna. Didn't the baralgin help? Here, I'll give you some cystinal."

She took a sugar cube, put a few drops of brown liquid on it, and held it up to Tikhon Tikhonovich's face.

"Open your mouth, don't be afraid. Just don't swallow it. Put it under your tongue."

Tikhon Tikhonovich obediently put the cystinal under his tongue.

"By the way, since you're here, I'll register you," Zalogin said, opening the logbook.

"Surname, Tugikh," the berry commissioner mumbled, with the undissolved sugar cube still under his tongue. "Tikhon Tikhonovich Tugikh." He stared at the doctor's face with fear and hope: Did she know?

The doctor bent over the book and showed no sign of recognition.

"Year of birth?" Zalogin asked dispassionately.

"Nineteen ten," the berry commissioner replied, depressed in the face of his salvation. "Doctor, what was your mother's name?"

"Same as mine—Darya Sevastyanovna. But why do you ask?"

"Is she alive?" The berry commissioner pressed on, without explanation.

"She died in childbirth. Doesn't it seem to you that you're overstepping the bounds of the doctor-patient relationship?" Zalogin asked harshly.

"Your father, then, was Sevastyan, since you're Sevastyanovna?" Tikhon Tikhonovich babbled.

"I didn't have a father," the doctor barked. "My grandfather gave me my patronymic; he was Sevastyan Prokofich. Why are you haranguing me, sir? You weren't so curious when you had your attack. Are you in the travel commission of the regional committee? Did I guess right? They're mostly pensioners there. Are you going to offer me a trip to America for removing your kidney stone? Or at least to Trinidad and Tobago? Perhaps some sort of medical exchange would be nice—to compare Siberian and tropical conditions. I could tell them about the medicinal properties of bird cherries, which we use when there's no medicine. And they could tell me about the medicinal properties of pineapples. Have you ever tried a pineapple?"

"Only canned," Tikhon Tikhonovich muttered.

"I've never even had canned," Zalogin said with derision. "By the way, maybe that's what caused your kidney trouble. All right now. Off to bed with you. If you do have a stone, we'll get rid of it—I promise you. Sleep well. Don't forget about my unhealthy interest in Trinidad and Tobago."

Tikhon Tikhonovich, reeling, tried to make his way up the stairs before he sat down on a step in the dark, covered his face with his hands, and wept. The kidney stone didn't bother him, but everything else did. The words of the mushroomer came back to him: "All kinds of garbage settles little by little and forms a stone." And when he cried until he could cry no more, he began thinking nonsense: where to get a pineapple for Dr. Zalogin.

CHAPTER · 20

Two pine cone collectors were industriously at work in the taiga. One was a scrawny old man in ragged old clothes, with an impossibly filthy cap shoved down to his nose. His green tarpaulin overalls were blackened with campfire singes; his beard was a tangle of bits of *makhorka* tobacco and cedar nut shells. His teeth, however, were as white as birchwood. The old man found the cedars, gathered the cones they knocked down, and put them into his patched bag. The other man was a Buryat, not yet old, but close to it, even though he was still in good shape and sturdy, in a crooked sort of way. But his teeth, unlike his partner's, had let him down badly. The Buryat struck the cedar trees with a long hammer-headed pole. The cedars shook, groaning hollowly and reluctantly shedding a sprinkling of cones onto the grass. The echo of the blows reverberated upward and nudged the clouds hanging in the top branches. Sitechkin heard that sound and headed toward it.

"God help you," Sitechkin said, lowering his backpack onto a fallen branch.

The Buryat stopped hammering in midair and set the pole down against a cedar. His eyes were wary. The old man's eyes, hidden in the shadow of the cap, could not be seen; however, he tossed out a clever retort. "God comes to your aid when the sun shines shade."

"Here's some more cones," Sitechkin said, bending over and tossing a few cones into the half-filled sack. The old man laughed from under his cap, took Sitechkin's cones out of the bag, and threw them into the bushes.

"Those cones are fallen, not knocked down; even the squirrels pass 'em with frowns. Their nuts are few, just laughing at you."

Realizing the old man spoke in rhymed couplets, Sitechkin grew rather nervous.

"Well, how's the cone harvest?" Sitechkin said with a smile, trying to be as ingratiating and pleasant as possible.

"Slim pickings in this wood; the picking here just ain't no good. And those are no cones for sturdy tooth bones." The old man shook his head. "The planes squirt poison on the taiga, to kill the bark eater, like a spider. But the poison just kills the trees—how's that for nature-loving, please? They used to cull the sick spots, and not destroy entire lots. But now it's one fell swoop; just cover all the trees with goop. They kill the healthy with the sick; the cedar wood is vanishing quick. They've even declared war on the birch, putting acre after acre to the torch."

"Why is that?" Sitechkin asked indifferently.

"They say it doesn't sell. . . . But I say to them, what the hell! Beauty was never for sale before; it's nature's gift to rich and poor. What is Russia without birches? Like a kolkhoz without workers."

The Buryat sprang to the birch's defense, too, but not in rhyme. "Cedar likes birch, really does. Without the birch there'll be no cedar."

Sitechkin was getting bored, and he changed the topic. "You, grampa, are you in a kolkhoz or retired?"

"My kolkhoz of old is the Siberian cold. . . . And I'm a February, a hobo, and a fibber merry," the old man replied incomprehensibly, pulling his cap even lower onto his nose.

"What does *February* mean?" Sitechkin asked.

"It's a Siberian word, means 'wanderer,' or haven't you heard? In the February Revolution they freed all the tramps—what a solution. They didn't settle anywhere; they wandered here, they wandered there. Of the Febs, I may be the last, though my screwing days have not yet passed."

The Buryat laughed and wagged his finger at the old man. "Oh, I don't believe it! I don't!"

"Believe it or not, I'm still pretty hot. An old man takes his time, he's slow, that's why the women love it so. But a woman's house and steady hand are something that a Feb can't stand. One tried to marry me; it was the death of her, you see."

"What do you mean?" Sitechkin asked with a strained smile.

The old man pulled a piece of newspaper from behind his ear, rolled it up, sprinkling some juicy yellow *makhorka* into it, and exhaled some new rhymes with the acrid smoke.

"I usually leave a woman at dawn, but this one claimed me for her own. Breakfast was garlicky pork on the first morning; I ate and fell back into bed without any warning. Pickled salmon I ate on the second day; I was much too full to get away. The third morning, an enormous goose; but I whispered, 'February, get loose!' As soon as she went to the cellar for more, I put my boots on and went for the door. But she heard me and ran as I slipped on the goose fat; well, I wasn't about to stay and take any of that. I found an old iron and whacked her a bit, but obviously her head was soft where it hit. I didn't want to kill her, I swear. I turned myself in, all fair and square. They gave me ten years, shipped me off in a cart; filled with cabbage heads, it was hard from the start. They made me weave, what a bore, but I escaped with some criminals, left behind dirty chores! I was just about sixty then, but my wandering soul felt younger by ten. These criminals had hidden a nugget of gold, which to a crooked dentist we sold. In Yalta we really painted the town, until our funds went considerably down. We got drunk, and a glove store did rob, but they caught us; the trial made my head throb. The store manager was a man whose fate was to live high on the hog in a socialist state. Instead of two hundred knit gloves, light as a feather, he said we stole two thousand pairs of good leather. As I told the court, 'A February I may be, but who's got the higher socialist morals? Me!' "

"And then what happened, were you released, or did you escape again?" Sitechkin asked in a subdued tone, instinctively moving away from this bizarre, rhyming old man, who might really be a killer and thief.

The old man, seeing Sitechkin's eyes, tried to reassure him, but without much success. "They paroled me because I'd gotten so old, but even now my life's pretty bold."

"Well, I've got to be going," Sitechkin said, as he quickly hoisted the backpack up onto his shoulders. His thoughts were jangling: *This guy is crazy. Or a killer. Or maybe both.*

"Just a minute." The old man moved toward him gently. "Get it all off your chest. What thoughts you're hiding, what you know best! The taiga's the place for a good talk; don't be afraid, don't go for a walk! There's no one more honest, no one more true, than a former thief, I'm telling you. . . ."

Sitechkin backed away from the old man and, barely preserving his dignity, disappeared into the bushes. The Buryat, holding his stomach, rolled with laughter. "Oh, was he scared! He was really scared!"

"A coward, it's sad, like a cone that's gone bad," the old man decided. "What's scary about me? I'm dead practically."

"All that stuff you made up!" The Buryat choked with laughter. "I'm going to tell your old woman, and she'll hide all the irons. Oh, she will! So you won't kill her."

"Was it lies? Was it true? I'll never tell a person like you." The old man frowned. "Let's pick up pine cones by the tank and put the money in the bank."

When he found himself a decent distance away, Eduard Sitechkin slowed to a calmer pace. *The devil only knows what kinds of suspicious characters you come across in this goddamn taiga!*

Sitechkin was afraid of the taiga. He didn't trust people, and he didn't trust nature. But the bear cub, picking up the curious scent of man through the trees, still knew nothing but trust. When it jumped out of the bushes and rushed Sitechkin with the most harmless of intentions—to play—Sitechkin became so alarmed that he grabbed his rifle and shot point-blank. The double stream of shot ripped through the cub. Squealing in pain, it rolled on the grass, trying to stop the blood from coursing out of itself. Sitechkin feverishly reloaded and shot once again. But the gun was old and misfired; the bolt exploded, blinding Sitechkin, and the gun flew out of his hands. Reeling, he pressed his hands to his eyes. When he took them away, he saw the hazy outline of a she-bear on her hind legs, ready to avenge her cub. Sitechkin bolted for the river, shimmering through the trees. Branches lashed his face, twigs caught in his clothes, and the she-bear roared a split second behind. Sitechkin ran onto the bank and miraculously spotted a rowboat. It was empty except for two sacks, with cedar cones peeking through their holes. The bow was on the gravel; the stern bobbed in the water. Sitechkin gathered all his strength and pushed the boat into the water. He jumped in and shoved the oarlocks into their holes, but the she-bear followed him into the water. She reared up again, and pulled the boat toward her. The last thing Sitechkin saw was her enormous paw flung up over his head and her enraged maternal eyes. . . .

The river tore the boat away from the bear and carried it along the current. She watched it until it disappeared around the bend. Only then did she leave the water.

CHAPTER · 21

Rapids are caused by fast water flowing over submerged or partially submerged rocks. Deep water covers them; low water reveals them. The larger the rocks, the fiercer the water. It's a good idea to take the time before your approach, if possible, to chart a route mentally down through the boulders: where to turn right, where left, how to avoid the white foam—a sure sign of a treacherously submerged rock. Among the white-capped turns it's best to take the dark channel of current. But if that channel doesn't exist, and there's nothing but foam all around, the frenzied water will hurl your boat out of control and smash it against the rocks, which loom one behind another, like a diabolical chess pattern. Sometimes the bank slopes, and you can drag your boat around on dry land, by putting logs under the bottom. But sometimes there're only sheer cliffs, to which a lone pine occasionally clings, resembling a suicide poised to leap into the water but eternally frozen in horror at the water's wild thrashing.

That's exactly what the two rapids—Wild One and Raven—were like. And Kesha and Ivan Ivanovich knew they were dangerous in high water, when you could slip over some of the boulders, scraping your bottom. But in low water your only hope was to play hide-and-seek!

Wild One was an honest antagonist; at low water its boulders stuck out frankly, like stumps. Raven, so named because of the black sheen of the surrounding cliffs, was sneakier. Smaller rocks, only slightly darkened on top by the rushing current, hid treacherously behind the backs of larger boulders. And Raven was located at a bend in the river; part was hidden around the bend and invisible at the beginning. Also, it was impossible to stop after Wild One and take a breather, to get ready for Raven, since one set immediately followed the other, and the force of the current didn't permit one to pull over to the shore. There really was no shore, only a stone wall of funereal color. Boats that smashed up on Wild One were never tossed out by the river before Raven because there was nowhere to toss them; the pieces were sucked into Raven, where they were finished off against the rocks.

That churning stretch of the river harbored many memories in its depths, and if the river could write a book about itself, it would be about human hopes smashed against rocks. Long, long ago the ruins of Buryat dugouts, explorers' rowboats, merchants' longboats, and prospectors' canoes decayed along the river's banks. The shards intermingled with one another and the bones of the dead, turned into soil, from which rose the red speckled lilies, flaming like votive lights, offered in memory of the dead.

Now people use the river for recreation, and lacking any historical memory, they didn't understand that you can't joke with the taiga. Here and there on the sandbars you saw smashed rafts, which had been flimsily hammered together by city hands. The logs of one such raft, snagged in the trees near the bank, were freshly cut, and Kesha heard music drifting from it. Kesha turned off the engine and moored next to the raft. A Sony radio, washed gently by water coming up through the cracks between the logs, lay on its side near a pair of plastic sunglasses; it was all that was left of some tourists who had decided to have some fun in Siberia. The voice of Muslim Magomayev came from inside the radio: "The discarded heart lay in the snow . . ." Kesha took the radio, turning off Magomayev, so as not to awaken Seryozha, and pulled the sunglasses out of a crack. Then he pushed off and started the outboard motor, to catch up with the first boat.

Just as Kesha had predicted, Seryozha woke up on his own; the approaching roar of Wild One could be heard more than a verst away. Suddenly the river became blindingly beautiful; it looked as if a flock of thousands of white gulls were sitting on the water, beating their noisy wings against the air. Just over the water hung a luscious broad rainbow, shimmering in the mist of the spray breaking against the rocks. The first boat was about a hundred meters ahead of the second, and Kesha and Seryozha saw it dive through the rainbow and disappear into the smoke screen of mist. Unable to see what was happening to their comrades, they felt as if the hidden boulders ahead were magnetically drawing them on.

"Lift out the motor!" Seryozha shouted, trying to be heard above the ever-increasing noise of water rushing over rocks.

But Kesha either didn't hear or pretended not to. Staying as still as a lump, he merely decelerated and tried to distinguish at least one smooth path in the cloud of spray underneath the rainbow. "Just a little more . . . a little more," Kesha muttered to the motor, as if it were a live creature trembling under his hand. "Keep it up . . . keep it up, my dear."

And only when the boat was right inside the rapids' open jaws, dripping foamy saliva from the boulders that sat as solidly as molars, did Kesha use the full weight of his small body to lift out the engine. Then he picked up a paddle in both hands.

Now the boat, deprived of its own power, was at the mercy of the river. But the outboard motor, saved at the last second, managed to express its gratitude to Kesha for his trust and kindness; the direction of the boat prevented it from spinning helplessly in the whirlpools and instead carried it between the first two boulders. However, right after that narrow passage a third boulder reared in front of the bow. Seryozha thrust his pole into the river bottom as hard as he could, but it stuck and was torn out of his hands. The push helped anyway, and the boat swerved in time, scraping its side against the boulder as it passed.

"Good for you, Leningrad!" Kesha shouted, so soaked from the spray that he resembled a tiny, desperate water sprite.

Kesha paddled furiously to avoid the next boulder, but all he accomplished was to change a direct hit to a glancing blow. Kesha was thrown to the bottom of the boat, which listed to the left, scooping up water. Seryozha, however, fell heavily on the opposite side and righted the boat. *He figured out what to do!* thought Kesha joyfully, trying to get up, but a new blow threw him against the gas tank. The river toyed with the boat, tossing it from boulder to boulder. Kesha struck his head against the outboard motor so hard that he saw stars; Seryozha was thrown on top of the anchor, the sharp end of which went through his padded jacket—luckily only scratching him. Barely extricating himself, he began rowing with the butt of his Berdan rifle, useless against the mighty power of the river.

The river roared its outrage, as though the boat were a painful splinter lodged deep in its powerful, rippling muscles. Between two boulders, Kesha spotted Burshtein's cap, tossing in the foamy water, but there was no time to get upset—he had to use his oar to fight off the water carrying them to the next boulder. When they cleared it, Kesha found himself kneeling with the splintered oar in his hands, stunned by the realization that there were no more boulders ahead; they had passed through Wild One. Half-blinded by the glare of the water, he desperately looked ahead and saw the first boat with four figures in it.

"They made it!" Kesha yelled. "They made it, son of a gun!" And he waved the splintered oar at the first boat.

Someone waved back with a still-not-lost hat. But there was no time for joy. The sheer cliffs moved closer together, blocking the sun. The boiling silver of the water turned to boiling lead. The cliffs' color also changed—from gray to black with a bluish sheen, like a raven's wing. And ahead, half-hidden around the bend, hemmed in by the cliffs, Raven churned in anticipation, and the current, accelerating as the riverbed narrowed, inexorably whisked both boats toward it.

Maybe I should start the motor? Kesha's thoughts raced. *Risk it with the motor? Pull toward the side; it's deeper there. We'll only have boulders on one side. Of course, we might hit the cliff, that's no better. But at least there's a dark strip near the shore, almost a border. Current . . . But so narrow. Will we fit through it? Will the engine even start; it must be waterlogged. Well, I'll try it. . . . Who knows? Maybe you'll save us, my dear golden, diamond engine.*

Kesha plunked the outboard motor in the water, and it began sputtering and sneezing immediately, as if conspiring with Kesha.

"What's Kesha doing, what's he doing?" Ivan Ivanovich muttered with disapproval as he heard the engine behind him. "We'll lose the engine in a flash."

"Maybe we should start our engine, too?" Kolomeitsev suggested, spitting out a piece of tooth which had been knocked loose when his chin hit the side of the boat. "That tooth was no good. . . . Eaten through, rotten. But I would never have had it pulled otherwise. I'm deathly afraid of dentists."

"Don't stick your nose in my motor, Viktor Petrovich," Ivan Ivanovich Zagranichny growled. "You won't find stores around here with engines or spare parts."

"All right, I won't," Kolomeitsev agreed. "Stick to the shore; it's deeper there."

"I know that; I'm no idiot," Ivan Ivanovich said, puffing as he rowed.

But the current was stronger than the oars, and they were pulled to the middle. Burshtein, and Kolomeitsev, and Yulya Sergeyevna tried punting to help, but the boat refused to go to the side.

"It won't go, the bitch. . . ." Ivan Ivanovich Zagranichny, already soaked, was now wet with sweat, too.

Kolomeitsev yanked out his seat and began rowing with that. The boat straightened a bit and started moving at an angle. Nevertheless, it couldn't reach the dark side channel. Circling an enormous boulder higher than the boat's side, Ivan Ivanovich saw another one, gleaming with a black, oily sheen through the lace of the foam.

"Hold on!" he yelled, and immediately a terrible blow racked the bow. The boat shuddered and cracked; splinters showered right into the passengers' eyes. It seemed that the boat was about to disintegrate. But it was an old Siberian hand, and it held together as half its bottom crawled up the black, iridescent back of the boulder. The dark border of deeper water was very close, but a whirlpool dragged the boat along the boulder's back toward the other boulders. The bottom continued to crack, and fountains gushed through the cracks.

Ivan Ivanovich and Kolomeitsev climbed up on the boulder and, slipping on its lacquered surface, lost their balance in the current. They pushed the boat, trying to move it in the direction of the dark flow. Burshtein used his bending, vibrating pole, but it kept slipping, unable to find a point of support. The boat continued to crawl away from the dark flow.

Suddenly the second boat was next to them, miraculously squeezed into the channel between the sheer cliffs and boulders. Kesha stood on the bow, twirling the rope with the anchor. Ivan Ivanovich and Kilomeitsev immediately understood and jumped back into the boat.

When the boats were abreast, Kesha tossed the rope and anchor, while emitting an animallike scream out of nowhere. The anchor pierced the very edge of the gunwale, and the rope stretched taut, pulling it right through. The boat jerked and half turned, crawling along the boulder in the direction of the shore. It ended up in the dark flow, towed by Kesha's boat, which was now in front. "Well, my sweet little rope, my nylon beauty, hold on," Kesha muttered, and thought: *Should I lift the engine out or not?* Who knew what was beyond the bend? . . . Everything would be fine if the channel continued to follow the shoreline beyond the bend. A cliff overhanging the water blocked visibility.

Suddenly Kesha saw the foamy, round contour of a boulder. He leaped over to the engine, trying to pull it out, but it was too late. A tremendous blow caused the entire hull to shatter, and the motor whined in farewell, tearing out its bolts as it plunged into the water. The boat was thrown away from the boulder right into the cliff. Ivan Ivanovich's boat raced past, and the only thing Burshtein had time to do was to push Kesha's boat into a crevice between two rocks near the cliff. It wedged there, creaking and disintegrating, but at least not moving. The towline stretched taut and broke, and Seryozha and Kesha looked up just in time to see the other boat overturn and ram into the cliff. Yulya Sergeyevna's head struck the rocks, just as Kesha had dreamed the night before.

Then the current managed to catch Kesha's boat, knocking it out of the space between the two rocks and hurling it into the cliff, smashing it to pieces. . . .

Kesha was awakened by an unfamiliar voice: "President Allende, after a provocative demonstration of so-called housewives, instigated by right-wing circles, announced that the government of Chile, maintaining faith in its people and armed forces, will continue to follow the path of freedom and independence."

Kesha opened his eyes and found himself lying in a hollow in the cliff so tiny that his feet dangled in the cold, rushing water. Next to him, hugging his knees, sat Seryozha, and between them was the Japanese radio, miraculously saved once more. Seryozha was not wearing his shirt; its remains were wrapped around Kesha's dully aching head. Kesha touched it and looked at his hand; it was covered with blood.

"Where are the others?" Kesha asked.

Seryozha didn't respond. His eyes were empty, without expression, resigned to this hollow, to the water swirling around them, to the hopelessly vertical cliffs.

"Where are the others?" Kesha shouted this time, frightened by Seryozha's silence.

Seryozha finally heard but continued to stare straight ahead. "They're dead. They're all dead. . . . And we'll die, too."

"Now you're not being much of a hero, Leningrad," Kesha said, animated by Seryozha's despair. "And you were doing so well. All right, we'll show you how to be a Siberian. Who told you they're dead? Radio Moscow? They capsized—I saw that. I've capsized around twenty times, and here I am, still alive, and I have no intention of dying yet. I'll dance at your wedding, Seryozha, and you at mine. We've got to get out of here."

"I already looked," Seryozha said. "You can't get out of here."

"Two heads are better than one," Kesha said, wincing with pain as he got up and leaned out of the hollow to look upward.

The black cliff rose almost vertically, without outcrops. Kesha caught sight of a crooked pine tree growing about five meters above the hollow and then another a bit higher. But how do you reach the first tree? Kesha's brain functioned calmly, like his metal comrade that had died in the line of duty—the outboard motor. He pulled Seryozha's geological hammer out of his belt and handed it to him.

"Well, Leningrad, enough napping. Get to work. Climb up on my shoulders. Start digging out steps."

Seryozha looked at the hammer dubiously and then at the cliff.

"But hammer gently," Kesha warned. "And don't drop the hammer in the water. Make a little hole, and then widen it. . . . And don't hammer across the grain; go with it. The rock will give in by itself."

Seryozha climbed up on Kesha's shoulders, lurching above the wild white foam below, and began hammering at the cliff, not desperately but in a focused way. Every blow seemed to bring back a little more of his life, which had been slipping away. Life apparently was nothing more than consciousness. Suddenly Seryozha froze.

"Well, what's wrong?" Kesha shouted impatiently. "Did you fall asleep?"

Seryozha climbed down clumsily and handed him a flat piece of stone, which looked as if it had been specially hewn to be an ore sample. It contained a crystal that sparkled like a black diamond.

"See that!"

"See what? It's a rock. The whole cliff is like that here," Kesha grumbled.

"No, look at the fresh break," Seryozha insisted, holding the rock in the sun so that it began sparkling and shining. "That crystal, it's cassiterite, Kesha! The real thing. Kolomeitsev was right."

Kesha took the rock and held it up.

"So that's what it's like." Suddenly angry, he shoved the rock back at Seryozha and said, "Damn it to hell, that stupid cassiterite! People come first. Metals, even precious ones, come after people, Seryozha. Come on, get back on my shoulders. We have two steps already? Hammer some more, as far as you can reach."

"It's ready," Seryozha said at last, and jumped down from his shoulders.

"Take off your belt," Kesha said. "And your pants." And he began undressing himself.

When a makeshift rope was assembled out of two belts and two pairs of trousers, Kesha tied one end around the piece of cassiterite and climbed up on Seryozha's shoulders. Holding the top step with his feminine hands, he pulled up his feet onto the bottom one, freeing Seryozha's shoulders.

"Wish I had a third hand," Kesha muttered through his teeth, and gripping the top step with his left hand, he threw the rope up with his right. His aim was good. The "rope" sailed over the pine tree, and Kesha lowered the other end, a trouser leg with the cassiterite tied to it. Using the doubled "rope," Kesha climbed up the cliff, leaning back and pushing his wet sneakers into the stone. When he reached the pine, he took a deep breath and laughed.

"Hey, Leningrad! You see, your cassiterite was of some use, after all."

Kesha tossed the rope down to Seryozha and tied his end to the tree to counterbalance it. The pine creaked but held up. Soon Seryozha was next to him.

"See that other tree way up there. Go to it, Leningrad, the same plan." Kesha suddenly realized: "You left the Japanese radio."

The radio in the hollow continued its commentary on international events.

CHAPTER · 22

Salvador Allende watched the demonstration through the blinds of the presidential palace, La Moneda. This was the second of its kind: a crowd of women walking around the square past the windows, banging empty pots and shouting, *"¡Algo comer! ¡Algo comer!"*

The president scrutinized their faces. They were the wives not of workers or peasants but of vegetable sellers, grocers, and butchers, the merchants who had themselves hidden food products. No exhaustion was noticeable on these women's smooth faces. Allende recognized the wife of the deputy editor of the newspaper *El Mercurio*. He laughed bitterly at her sleek hands, which had never known a kitchen knife, and the housewifely oilcloth apron she had donned especially for the demonstration. Once she had studied at the same school as Hortensia, his wife. She bumped into Hortensia recently in a flower store and pulled her aside, asking sympathetically, in the name of their old friendship, "Tell me, is it true?" "Is what true?" Hortensia asked dryly. "Well, that everything's not good with Salvador's head? They say he's terribly overworked. . . . I think he should retire. . . . He himself is, of course, an honest man, but he's been confused by the Communists," she rattled on acidly. "And is it true that he brought galoshes from Moscow and wears them?" "Yes," Hortensia replied. "And he also brought back a Siberian fur hat with a shortwave radio sewn into the lining—instructions from the Kremlin go straight to his head. That's why things aren't good with his head. Why don't you suggest that as a topic for an article to your husband!"

But Allende saw poorer women in the ranks of the demonstrators, too: wives of clerks; secretaries; telephone operators; salesgirls. Some carried children in their arms. The children waved spoons, probably thinking they were at a party. Their mothers were convinced that all the trouble emanated from him, the president, when he was actually doing everything he could for them. But he couldn't do everything.

"Maybe we could pose a bit more?" came an ingratiating voice from behind the president.

Allende sighed deeply. He had forgotten that a European artist was in his office. They said he was European because no one knew precisely what his nationality was. According to rumors, he had several passports. The only additional information known about him was that he had a bank account in the principality of Liechtenstein. After politicking for a month through various committees, which included artful appearances at official visits, and bombarding them with catalogues of his exhibits and writing letters in which he stated he had come to Chile only to paint the president, the artist finally pushed his way into Allende's office with canvas and palette "for just an hour." "You go on and work," the artist said. "Don't even pay any attention to me." But the artist had forced him to don tails instead of his usual checked flannel jacket and made him stick on the presidential ribbon as well.

The president looked at the artist. He didn't like the way he was dressed: shoes with very high, almost feminine heels—a parody of Greek buskins—and a traveling salesman's Dacron suit with a lascivious shimmer. He didn't like the artist's face—vague, epicene, with darting, businesslike eyes, an underdeveloped, pointed nose, and a feminine, receding chin that wasn't helped by the attempt to lengthen it with a spadelike beard. The president didn't like the artist's manner of turning around after every few strokes to praise the Patagonian folk embroidery hanging on the office wall.

"Take it," Allende said, wearily covering his eyes.

The artist, scattering his thanks, pulled the hanging from the wall with the practiced fingers of a magician and rolled it up into a tube.

"A few more strokes, and that's all. There, it's done. I understand how busy you are, and that's why I painted the portrait in just—" The artist pulled back his white cuff, bound with a tasteless gold cuff link depicting an Oriental dragon, and looked at his Rolex. "I painted Gina

Lollobrigida in fifty-two minutes, and I took only forty-four for you. Would you like to look?"

Allende yanked the presidential ribbon from his throat where it was choking him and took off the tailcoat. He went over to the portrait, which the artist was manipulating as if it were a mirror to find the most flattering light. A total stranger looked back at the president, smugly gazing into the inspirational distance. The blueness of the presidential ribbon cleverly echoed the cloudless azure sky overhead. Behind his shoulders with theatrical majesty were mountains that were supposed to represent the Cordilleras. The artist turned the portrait every which way, and for a second the August sun splashed a powerful ray through the closed blinds onto the canvas, washing away the portrait with its radiance.

Allende immediately felt better, seeing his false double disappear, but the magician's hands turned the portrait again and fooled the sun, and the pompous figure of his double, so distasteful to the president, was fatally resurrected. Allende thought drearily: *What if this illusionist never leaves my office and, by painting my Doppelgänger every day, never allows me to work?*

"I have to touch up the background some more," the artist said cheerfully. "But I think I've captured you."

Allende almost added, "By the throat," but he controlled himself. Trying to make the artist evaporate, he muttered, "I'm very grateful. Flattered."

To which there came an immediate, repulsively sticky reply: "No, I'm grateful to you."

Allende looked about in quiet desperation. "Is there something you like in my office? For instance, this?" He hastily took a small marble bust of Socrates from his desk, where it was weighing down papers marked "Secret"; apparently the great Greek was the only remnant of the previous president.

The artist shoved Socrates into his pocket, as though he were afraid it would be taken back, so that only the philosopher's marble curls protruded. He picked up the Patagonian embroidery with one hand and took the portrait from the easel with the other.

"I don't trust anyone to hold my fresh canvases. Once they almost smeared the king of Sweden." Elaborately bidding farewell, he backed out, opening the door with his feminine heel. At last only his head peeked through the crack in the door. "Could someone help with the easel and paints?"

"Of course, of course," Allende assured him, in an obviously strained voice before he kindly, but firmly, shut the door, almost catching his guest's head.

Then he sat at the desk and pushed a button. His assistant came in—a sweet, modest man who looked rather undistinctive, except for his jacket, which bulged under his arms with two revolvers.

Allende pointed out the remaining tools of the European illusionist's artistry. "Take that stuff away. Soon, if possible." Noticing the swollen armpits, he frowned. "I've told you to stop wearing those things. You look like a Hollywood detective."

The assistant listened to the reprimand without even blinking. He removed the easel and paints and then reappeared, his armpits still bulging.

"An American correspondent is waiting for you."

"Screw all these artists and correspondents," roared the president, something he did very rarely.

"But you set up this appointment yourself," the assistant reminded him gently. "The interview will be signed, so there won't be any distortions."

"But he may add his own commentary. Even good meat can be served with a stinking sauce," grumbled Allende. "All right, invite him in."

The American turned out to be a young, large fellow, wearing a tweed jacket with leather elbow patches. The American's dusty hiking boots made a refreshing contrast with the artist's high heels.

The correspondent noticed that the president was out of sorts, so without wasting time, he placed a cassette player on the edge of the desk and opened his notebook.

"How do you feel about the aphorism that 'Power corrupts and absolute power corrupts absolutely'?"

"There is bitter truth in it," Allende said. "In any case, examples to the contrary are few, but they do exist. Except in the case of absolute power. Absolute power is merely a humiliating distrust of others."

"Do you feel that politics is the oldest profession?" the correspondent asked.

"If that's true, it's frightening. There's nothing more unnatural than politics as a profession. Nature created men to be plowers, fishermen, carpenters, and scientists, so that they could delve deeper into nature's mysteries. Even poets, so that they could hear and re-create the music of nature. But even a divinely gifted poet like Pablo Neruda can't dispense with politics. Why? Because politics, the vile art of dividing people, has to be transformed into the art of uniting people. Only politics by honest, good people can make politics disappear altogether."

Allende went over to the window and pulled back the blind to look at the demonstration continuing outside.

"Politics is the result of human weakness. A thinking person does not need to be led; he will never use his freedom to take away the freedom of others. Some people are like that, but not many. There are others who'll immediately translate their freedom into lack of freedom for others, into violence and exploitation. Of course, there aren't many of them either; they're simply better organized than the thinking people. The majority of people make up the unconscious or semiconscious masses, who don't understand how to use their freedom. They are easily fooled."

The correspondent looked sadly at his questions in the notebook; this kind of Latin American monologue was all too familiar by now. *Does he really believe all this, or is he just playing a game?* flashed through his mind, and because he couldn't ask the president that question directly, he asked himself, *But what do I think?* He didn't get an answer from himself either.

"No one likes the police," the president continued feverishly, "but try to imagine the world without it—think what would go on! For now, unfortunately, government is still a necessity. But it depends what kind of government! A terrible government becomes a coercive rather than a creative force. And those who merely control others inexorably begin to degenerate. Even the possibility of exploitation should disappear. How can this be accomplished? Through anarchy? It will merely frighten the man on the street, and riding on his trembling shoulders like a white horse, fascism will arrive. Government should be truly of the people. But this is a goal not for tomorrow but for the day after. Today we must convince people who have lost faith in the very idea of power that power must and can be of the people!" The president's eyeglasses reflected the sunset breaking through the blinds.

The correspondent watched Allende with pity and envy. *No, he really seems to believe what he says. In that case, he's the last of the Mohicans in politics. Doesn't Allende understand that he's doomed?* Just yesterday, in a bar, a fellow American, a very drunken executive from ITT, whispered to him, "You'd better hurry your interview. If you're lucky, it'll be his last one. Which will make it pretty important. Do you know who's against him? Pinochet. That snake in the grass. But his sting is lethal. A bastard, of course, but who's decent these days? But not a word about this!"

The correspondent liked what Allende was saying. He shouldn't have liked it, but he did. He didn't want a man like that to be doomed. *What if I mention Pinochet? But this office must be completely bugged. If they can bump off General Schneider, why couldn't they arrange a car accident for an American journalist? They'll blame it on "red terrorists."* . . . *I think I'm turning into a coward. Have I been bought, too? Not with an obvious bribe, but with a position, a by-line, a so-called career? Was it really me who used to march in antiwar demonstrations?*

When the correspondent left, the president noticed a piece of paper from the American's notebook had been left on the edge of the desk. There was one word printed in block letters: "Pinochet." The president crumpled the paper and set fire to it in the copper ashtray given to him by the miners of Antofagasta. *This must be a provocation,* Allende thought, watching the letters burn, black on gold. *The left is also provoking me, trying to make me start arresting the generals. They want to ruin my relations with the army, so it will turn against national government.* . . . *I can't give in to that.*

The president recalled how General Pinochet had taken his arm after yesterday's meeting and said confidentially, "You need to rest.

You look tired. You can sleep peacefully—the army is behind you." Pinochet's fingertips felt as cold as steel. *I'm becoming paranoid.* The president frowned. *A mediocrity like Pinochet conspire against me? He's too stupid, too much of a coward for that. . . . Nerves, it's my damn nerves. . . . Yesterday someone from the Ministry of Internal Affairs put a report on my desk about the rumors of my mental illness. I felt he was mocking me as he watched me read it. But I looked up, and there was nothing on his face but loyal concern. Paranoia again. . . . I have to take hold of myself. But how do I take hold of the situation? It wriggles like a fish, slipping away, disappearing. Why did Neruda come back from Paris, where he loves it so much? "I'm an antirat," he said. I didn't get it then, but now I do. It's simple. Rats desert a sinking ship, and Pablo has returned to the ship. But is the ship sinking? It creaks, it's full of holes, but it still floats. It'll reach the port. If I don't get there, too, it doesn't matter. Neruda's joke was a warning. Poets may not be a nation's brain, but they are its heart, its intuition. Jiménez once said that Pablo Neruda was the world's best bad poet, referring to Pablo's verbosity. But after Jiménez spent some time in Latin America, he changed his opinion of Neruda: "Neruda seems to want to fill the vast wordless expanses of Latin America and unite them with his poetry." Now that's accurate. . . . Twenty countries that speak one and the same language will unite someday. But how can you find a common spiritual language for so many different people when we can't even find one for as small a country as Chile? I'm being urged to make arrests. But once arrests begin, they'll snowball, turning into an avalanche that sweeps away the guilty and the innocent. Cruelty, even when called for by circumstances, turns justice into injustice. But if justice gets too flabby, cruelty replaces it, squashes it. You unwittingly create just as many victims. How do you find that mean—where justice isn't so cruel as to become its opposite and at the same time is still able to defend itself?*

This was what President Allende was asking himself, while a crowd of women, banging on empty pots, made a scene under the windows of La Moneda.

It was the middle of August 1973.

On September 11 Pinochet gave the order to bombard the presidential palace.

CHAPTER · 23

Kesha and Seryozha broke all their nails on the jagged cliff in order to reach the top of the mountain, where they collapsed facedown. Far below, the Raven lay. Like a watery cemetery, its gloomy boulders rose like tombstones, surrounded by white rings of foam which looked like ice from such a height. The wind whistled so shrilly between the cliffs that the water's noise was obliterated; one could hardly tell the river was moving.

"Look, there's something dark over there," Kesha said, grabbing Seryozha. "Over there, right by the water . . ."

"It's probably a snag," Seryozha said, exhausted.

But pursuing that tiny hope, they started descending in a place where the slope was gentler, tearing their hands on the sparsely growing bushes. Soon the white rings whirled around the boulders, and they could hear the river's roar once more, but the black spot remained a mystery.

"A man," Seryozha said, straining his vision.

"No, two," Kesha said.

At last their feet sank deep into sand, and they ran toward the black spot.

Lying on the shore, thoroughly soaked, were Vyazemskaya and Kolomeitsev, holding each other tightly. They were dead, but no— their boots stood by their bare feet, and their socks were spread out on the gravel. The dead don't dry their socks; Vyazemskaya and Kolomeitsev slept, so soundly it was hard to awaken them. When her eyes opened, Vyazemskaya immediately pulled back the arm that was embracing Kolomeitsev. Kolomeitsev rose up on his elbows with difficulty, shaking his head, forcing himself to consciousness. Finally, the blurred contours in front of him took the shapes of Kesha and

Seryozha. A weak semblance of joy appeared in his eyes, and then he stared straight ahead in a stupor.

"Where's Ivan Ivanovich? Where's Burshtein?" Kesha asked, shaking him by the shoulder.

Kolomeitsev made a tremendous effort to lift the dead weight of his heavy arm and pointed to a clump of hawthorn. Kesha and Seryozha ran there.

Clothing was hanging on the bushes, and on the other side, hopping up and down, naked, was Burshtein, lashing himself with branches, trying to fend off the gnats. The first thing he asked was "Do you have any matches?"

Kesha pulled a box of matches wrapped in a balloon and tied with a string from inside his shirt, and in an instant there was a stream of smudgy smoke to drive away the bugs. On a rotting log nearby, plastered with gnats but not paying any attention to them, sat another naked man, who was trying to separate the waterlogged pages of a black oilcloth-covered notebook; it was Ivan Ivanovich Zagranichny. He looked up at Kesha and Seryozha with distracted eyes and once again lowered them to his notebook, trying to make out the hopelessly blurred letters it contained.

"They're done for," he muttered.

"Who's done for?" Seryozha demanded, fearing that Ivan Ivanovich had lost his mind. "We're all here; we're all alive."

"My thoughts are gone," Ivan Ivanovich said dully. "Thoughts about life. The water ate them up. I was planning to send this notebook . . ."

"Where?" Seryozha asked in amazement, never once having imagined that Ivan Ivanovich wrote down his thoughts.

"There." Ivan Ivanovich vaguely nodded somewhere up. "They might have come in handy. . . ."

"Please let me see!" Seryozha asked.

Ivan Ivanovich reluctantly handed him the notebook. "You won't be able to understand anything anyway."

The writing really was almost completely washed away. Seryozha could make out only fragments of phrases and words. On the first page under the oilcloth cover, the title, printed in large capital letters, had survived:

"I. I. Zagranichny. THOUGHTS ON ORDER AND DISORDER." But what followed was confusion, washed out.

"in -- saw the slog-- 'Glory to Sov--- Pioneers!' Why sh---- they have glo-- they haven't done anyth--- yet. Instead -- slog--s they should hang prover-s -- more sense -- them."

"Don't ta-- about other countries, your own is "

"If all interbureau----ic paper wo-- is cut -- half, there'll b-enoug- -aper for -ll the goo- books."

"It easier to choose th- bett-r of tw- good-. No need to tal- abou-the lousy."

"No one can mana-- to b- a docto-, geolo----, carpen-er, cosmon---, smith barbe- cobbler laundere-, tailor, janito-. Why can the government manage? We have to help the government relax a bit. . . ."

"Can't unlearn vodka drinking, you have to teach how to dri--."

"Whoever doesn't answ-- let---- from workers should have ----- mailboxes removed -- no letters will reach them at a--."

" et -irectors of shoe and clothing factories wear only their own ---duction."

"Newspapers must be checked electronically for repetit---. If there is --- the print-- ma--ine should stop and not go until they pic- a differe-- word."

"Wage war on speculation no- wi-- courts but with sur-lus."

"Give me the notebook." Ivan Ivanovich suddenly became annoyed. He pulled it from Seryozha's hands and tossed it into the bonfire. Ivan Ivanovich Zagranichny's thoughts didn't want to burn; they twisted and hissed, but gradually they were devoured by the flames, shriveling and turning to ashes.

Everyone changed into dry clothing and ate some canned food that had fortunately survived. It was time to go, but Kolomeitsev gave no orders and merely sat silent. His expression was distant, as if he still wandered in the dream from which Kesha and Seryozha had awakened him. He hadn't said a single word, and only his lips, swollen with insect bites, moved soundlessly, and his eyes were fixed on a spot invisible to the others. Kolomeitsev imagined that the people sitting with him around the fire were merely ghosts—that actually they had all died and it was his fault. Finally, he began to believe they were alive, but this didn't make him feel less guilty. He also recalled the girl with the yellow-flecked eyes, who had asked him in the haystack, smelling of the storm, "Will you remember me?" And then her again, dropping nails from the torn paper sack onto the dust in front of his jeep and muttering, "Your shirt, you forgot your shirt." And one after another his guilts surfaced. Some had resulted in death; some had not, but no thanks to him. They surfaced like the invisible burns he had gotten in the Belorussian forest.

Everyone around the fire exchanged worried looks, understanding Kolomeitsev was going through something, but no one dared talk to him. Seryozha was the first to find the courage. He handed Kolomeitsev the black, sparkling stone. "Viktor Petrovich, do you see?"

Kolomeitsev picked up the rock, his hand visibly sagging under its negligible weight. He slowly turned it, showing no sign of recognition.

"It's cassiterite, Viktor Petrovich, cassiterite!" Seryozha almost shouted, choking on his words.

Kolomeitsev opened his fingers and the rock fell softly into the sand.

"Yes," he said inaudibly, unsticking his lips with difficulty. He tried to smile, without success.

"What's this?" Vyazemskaya called out, suddenly leaping up and pointing at the river. "Look!"

Just offshore a battered boat rocked. On its listing bow stood a patched sack, which dropped cedar nuts into the water with every smack of the waves. Clutching the sack with one hand, a man with a bloody head lay motionless in the boat. The other hand dragged in the water, which indifferently splayed and then sucked up its lifeless fingers.

Ivan Ivanovich and Kesha accomplished the difficult task of retrieving the body from the boat, and they lowered it onto the sand.

"A bear put its paw on him. They don't attack without provocation. This one really connected, however," Ivan Ivanovich said.

Silently they dug a grave with pieces of the oars and lowered the body into it. They covered it with soil, trying not to look at the disfigured face of the dead man.

And suddenly Kolomeitsev stopped them—his first conscious gesture since he came to. Reeling, he stood next to the grave, then straightened abruptly and looked at everyone. "I know you are not supposed to speak ill of the dead. But you can't avoid the truth. He was a bad man. Something made him that way. Maybe we're responsible for that 'something.' He knew we didn't like him. Our dislike made him worse. Too bad he died. Now he can't be helped. We're to blame for that."

And Kolomeitsev made a second gesture, ordering them to fill in the grave.

Ivan Ivanovich and Kesha dragged stones to form a mound on top.

"It's time to go," Kolomeitsev said. "Seryozha, put out the fire. . . ."

P R O L O G U E

My biography unwilling consists of
life's trifles and my works. . . .

K. Tsiolkovsky

Varvara Evgrafovna Tsiolkovskaya was walking through the Kaluga marketplace along the blood fair—the butchers' stalls. Purple-stamped carcasses hung from hooks, leaking dark, heavy drops onto the counters, which were arrayed with porcelain suckling pigs, clean-plucked amber ducks, shiny pebbles of kidneys, brown, lacquered slabs of liver, pale pink brains with patterns of fine veins. The meat row had its own music: the crunch of cleavers; squealing cries. Varvara Evgrafovna did not often listen to this music, and she was afraid to get too close to the counters, so as not to be attacked, grabbed, or have something foisted on her. The Tsiolkovskys ate meat at home only on Sundays, and the rest of the week they managed from the garden and their canned and pickled goods.

An overdressed bourgeois Kaluga housewife carried a beheaded goose by its yellow feet. Its neck still reflexively twisted. She nudged an equally overdressed friend carrying her own goose. "Lookie there. Lady Tsiolkovsky shows up. What a miracle!"

Her friend giggled. "They say they get by on nettle and sorrel soups. I've heard that they even eat dandelions. And Tsiolkovskaya picks nettles with gloves on. Gloves up to her elbow, evening gloves —a nettle aristocrat."

The first wife mused suspiciously. "But her hubby has to be hauling in quite a bit in the diocese school. What do they do with the money?"

Her friend giggled even harder. "He spends it on the stars. No one will publish his books, so he prints them himself."

And they both laughed, making the beheaded geese dance in their hands.

Varvara Evgrafovna approached the butcher meekly. "I'd like a piece of veal."

The butcher self-importantly stroked his beard, which separated into two parts.

"What kind of veal, madam? For soup or for something else? I have fillet, too—it's very good for British beefsteak."

Varvara Evgrafovna hastily stopped him. "Soup."

The butcher sounded slightly less obliging but still respectful. "May I offer you this piece? . . . With a marrow bone. Like sugar."

He deftly weighed it. "It comes to three pounds and a little over."

Varvara Evgrafovna muttered, "How about this piece—the smaller one? . . . I need about a pound and a half."

The butcher, unperturbed, changed the pieces on the scale's hook. "Why not? You should have said so in the first place, madam. But this is more than a pound and half. It's almost two."

Varvara Evgrafovna felt the eyes of the two women on her and blushed painfully, but she held her ground. "Cut some off, please."

The butcher put the meat on the block with a sigh and then stopped his cleaver. "Oh, it's all right. We'll come to terms, madam."

The owners of the two geese, who had watched this scene with amusement, immediately changed their expressions when Tsiolkov-skaya turned to them.

"Hello, Varvara Evgrafovna! We haven't seen you in a long time!"

"Hello," Varvara Evgrafovna said reluctantly, trying to pass between the two geese.

"You've disappeared lately." The first woman sympathetically advanced on her.

The second babbled compassionately, "Your dear one has worn you out, he has. . . . Just skin and bones you are. Nothing to hold on to. And a woman's flavor is in the meat." She smugly slapped her ample hips.

The first bent toward Varvara Evgrafovna confidentially. "I look at you, Varvara, and I wonder: How do you put up with your husband? He's a horrible person."

Varvara Evgrafovna suddenly smiled. "He is horrible. . . . And so am I." And there was something so eerie about her rather Asian cheekbones, covered with yellowish skin, and her small dark eyes that the women stepped back to let her through.

"What an idiot," the first one said, recovering from her fright. "She really is horrible. She hypnotizes you with those eyes, the old hag. They say they perform evil deeds at their house. Her husband buys up tin spoons and turns them to gold. Eccentric blessed fool . . ."

"He's no blessed fool if he turns tin to gold," the second woman said, shaking her head. "How are you going to cook your goose—with apples or with cabbage?"

"Neither." The first housewife laughed with satisfaction. "I'll take the little devil and stuff him with rice and prunes—the works."

At that moment Konstantin Eduardovich was at the winery, respectfully accompanied by its owner—the merchant Semiradov. Semiradov bore no resemblance to the nineteenth-century merchant, so well described by Ostrovsky. His father was such a merchant, but he had passed away about five years earlier. God spare you a death like that—he choked on a leg of lamb during meatless Shrovetide. He left his son an enormous inheritance. Young Semiradov didn't sport blacked boots, a long caftan, or beard; he didn't have his hair cut "in parentheses" or use burdock oil on it. On the contrary, he wore a Parisian plaid three-piece suit, patent-leather boots with gaiters on top, and a silk tie with a large ruby pin. His red hair was curled in Moscow by Georges on Kuznetsky Prospekt, and it peeked out from under his soft London hat, its dent cleverly placed. Semiradov spoke both French and English (both, of course, with a Nizhny Novgorod accent), and he had a sturgeon factory in Astrakhan, a flour mill in Tver, several steam baths and drinking houses in Saratov, and was planning an automobile venture with Belgian partners. He collected Impressionist paintings and held séances. His winery was something of a family heirloom; his father had started it when he was a shoe salesman, with the dowry he had received by marrying the boss's daughter. Semiradov junior, whose two daughters studied with Tsiolkovsky at the diocese school, in contrast with all the other merchants of Kaluga, did not laugh at Konstantin Eduardovich but visited him in his workshops, ran his hands over his dirigibles, and slowly learned about his work.

Semiradov was very interested in dirigibles. He had to ship his sturgeon to Paris from Astrakhan by a tortuous route—partly by water, partly by rail—and constantly changing the ice. But a dirigible stuffed with sturgeon, their powerful tails splashing in enormous tanks filled with their native Volga water, bringing them straight to the Champs-Élysées by air—this was something to be reckoned with. Semiradov viewed the Russian nobility with scorn and superiority; they had been reeking for a long time now, like a bad sturgeon, and no matter how often they changed the ice around themselves, it didn't help. In Semiradov's opinion, the future lay in the union of money and science, and he was far more interested in getting to know new inventions than counts and princes.

"And this, Eduardovich, is what you could call my poison section —port wine. I don't drink it, and I don't recommend it. The fastest route to gastritis, if not an ulcer. Literally everything goes into it, including almost ground-up soles from old boots. . . ."

"Then why do you produce it?" Tsiolkovsky grimaced.

Semiradov laughed and spread his hands in resignation. "The people like it. . . . On the top of our tongues, Eduardovich, are special taste buds. But what kind of education have they received? You know yourself. Those buds are so burned by vodka they cannot appreciate fine, dry wine. It simply seems sour. And who wants sour wine when your life is sour? A life like that needs to be drowned in vodka or sweetened with cheap port wine."

Tsiolkovsky stopped in amazement. On the wall above an enormous oak cask, in which workmen stirred a suspicious smoking brew with poles wrapped in rags, hung a large icon.

"That's my innovation," Semiradov said with a smile. "God is like my senior foreman: He doesn't drink, and He watches the drunks. And you know, it helps. They're drinking less on the job now."

"Do you . . . believe in God?" Tsiolkovsky's eyes gleamed behind his glasses.

Semiradov laughed and lowered his voice so that his workmen couldn't overhear. "God, as you see, is working for me. And I never fully trust those who work for me."

"I wouldn't want to work for you," Tsiolkovsky said, shaking his head.

"You have been, for a long time; you just haven't known it." Semiradov laughed. "How will you realize your inventions without people like me? Progress is a genius with a customer. Without a customer even the greatest ideas of genius will perish, like unknown soldiers in the trenches of the brain's furrows."

"You speak colorfully," Tsiolkovsky said with appreciation. "But things won't always be that way."

"Yes, they will," Semiradov said in a tone of certainty as he flung open the doors to the next room for Tsiolkovsky. "And this is my pride and joy, Konstantin Eduardovich. My liqueur and infusion department. No poisons here. All natural . . . galingale, St.-John's-wort, mountain ash—just as good as the ones from Shustov's winery! Birch buds, currant leaves, pepper, rose petals. The Chinese use snakes, too, but I hope we won't go that far. And here are the liqueurs—strawberry, raspberry, black currant, cranberry, bilberry, cherry, apple, cornelian cherry. . . . Here's one made with the fruit of the feijoa. Imported from Sukhima. Would you like to try it? It'll make you lick your fingers."

"I'm sorry, I don't drink." Tsiolkovsky declined politely.

"Forgive me, I forgot. What would happen to me if everyone was a teetotaler like you? Bankruptcy." And Semiradov happily knocked off both crystal glasses with the sparkling emerald liqueur from the Sukhima fruit.

"Do you know, one day all people will stop drinking?" Tsiolkovsky noted.

Semiradov wagged his finger at him gently, as at a child. "Now don't scare me. Russia, at least, is in no danger of that. . . . The Russian cannot live without two things: vodka and the tsar. If he overturns the tsar, he'll regret it later."

"As far as I have seen, many in Russia live without a tsar in their head and manage quite well," Tsiolkovsky said with a smile. "And I think our own tsar has no tsar in his head—he's got a weak brain. He botched the war with the Japanese, and now, judging by everything, he's planning to fight the Germans. War is the most meaningless activity on earth, and to use your language, unprofitable."

"You're wrong there, Eduardovich," Semiradov countered in a lively tone. "If war weren't profitable, believe me, no one would ever start fighting."

"But there is, after all, moral profit, too. Does it exist in war?" Tsiolkovsky muttered.

"Of course," Semiradov exclaimed, unruffled. "When there's no war, everyone blames his problems on the Jews. People get fired up and wave their bludgeons around in a pogrom—and a burden's lifted from a man's heart. But gradually it comes to his mind: Pogroms don't make life any better. Then whom can they bludgeon? The tsar. And the tsar's no fool; in order to deflect the blows from himself, he serves up a new enemy, who is to blame for everything—Jap or German. And in Japan and Germany the authorities are also inventing enemies—but they call them Russian. There you are, Eduardovich, a direct coincidence of moral and material profit. The mechanics are simple."

"Vile mechanics," Tsiolkovsky said with a frown.

"And man isn't vile?" Semiradov laughed. "People like you are exceptions. If everyone were like you, then we wouldn't need authorities, or the army or the police either. Everyone complains about the police, but everyone needs them. At least they protect you from robbery."

"The very existence of the police is robbery," Tsiolkovsky said, trying to unhook a bronze winged lion from his cape, which had caught on the corner of one of the wine cases stacked to the ceiling. "If only because so much money is spent on the police that could be used for hospitals, schools, libraries."

"I agree," Semiradov quickly said, deftly freeing the bronze lion. "The police are robbery; the army is robbery; the bureaucracy is robbery . . . I know that very well since I'm a robber myself. But who made up this system of government? The people themselves, afraid of their own unmanageability. . . ."

They went out into the yard, where men in leather aprons were loading cases of bottles onto a cart. One of the men, not seeing Semiradov, took a bottle of port wine out of the box, pushed in the cork with his strong finger, and started guzzling. Semiradov crept up behind him, and grabbed him by the ear so that he howled in pain. "Take a look at this *Alcohomo sapiens,* Eduardovich!"

Having said good-bye to Semiradov and politely refusing his carriage, Tsiolkovsky went home along a ravine on the outskirts of town, jabbing his umbrella stick into the roots that stuck out onto the path.

It was quiet in the ravine, and Tsiolkovsky's muttering blended with the rustling of the autumn leaves. Suddenly, blocking his way, a three-button accordion opened to its full width with a groan. The accordion was in the hands of the local hero, his brazen olive black eyes befogged by one of Semiradov's products. A wild lock of hair burst out onto his forehead from the broken patent leather visor of his cap. His snappy Russian shirt, embroidered with cornflowers around its off-center opening, was tied at the waist with a strap. The toes of his boots were muddy, but the shins shone like mirrors. Next to him appeared two of his pals standing watch, servilely following every move of their leader's eyes. One of the thugs reached into the top of his boot and pulled out a cobbler's knife, which he pushed into Tsiolkovsky's beard. The other, guffawing, felt his pockets with exaggerated gentleness.

"Your watch, Your Lordship."

"Here," Tsiolkovsky said, and took his watch out of his vest pocket. "Pavel Boure. Never repaired. Shall I show you how to wind it?"

Already holding the watch, the thug gaped at such politeness and, stunned, looked to the leader for guidance. Remorse and recognition mingled in the leader's foggy gaze. "That's no lordship. . . . It's the Bird."

That was Tsiolkovsky's mocking epithet in Kaluga.

The leader signaled with his eyes, and the thug returned the watch apologetically to Tsiolkovsky's vest pocket, and the knife disappeared inside the boot. The leader laughed with condescension. "Well, Bird, when will we fly off to the stars? Hasn't anyone broken your wings yet?"

His pals giggled.

"They're strong," Tsiolkovsky replied. "And we will fly to the stars. We definitely will."

All three grabbed their stomachs and rolled on the ground, laughing.

"Ah, you phony Stenka Razins* . . . You drown your souls, like the Persian princess, in vodka. You can't even steal properly." Tsiolkovsky sighed.

The leader grew angry. "No, Bird, don't pick on us. We drink out of sorrow."

"Sorrow should make you think, not drink. You think I'm not one of you because I don't lie around in a ditch. I'd be better off if you had stolen my watch, now you're stealing my time."

"Watch it, Bird," the leader rumbled, and responding to the change in his tone, the thug reached for the knife again, only to be stopped by a look from the leader.

"I'm not afraid to die," Tsiolkovsky said with annoyance. "But I'm afraid you'll die an idiot. And people should live forever."

"What?" the leader said, not understanding.

"Forever!" Tsiolkovsky shouted. "That way people who start out stupid might get wiser."

Tsiolkovsky unexpected grabbed the leader by his accordion, which caused it to emit weird noises. He shook him by the lapels, trying to explain, even though it was almost pointless but perhaps still not hopeless.

"For so many people there is nothing but a lousy, good-for-nothing life, a dirty grave pit, and the end. And what's the result?" Tsiolkovsky asked feverishly, forgetting to whom he was talking. "Mutual misunderstanding, wars, impotence in the struggle with na-

*Stenka Razin was a cossack brigand and folk hero who lived during the reign of Catherine the Great.

ture, hard labor, disease, a short, martyred life, eternal fear of eternal disappearance . . ."

The leader, frightened, tried to free himself from this madman's hands, which were surprisingly strong. "What's the matter, Bird, what's the matter with you?"

But Tsiolkovsky would not release the firm grip and shook him. "Death is only an illusion created by human intelligence, blockhead. Every creature must think and live as if it will achieve everything sooner or later. People can achieve immortality if we all think about it together as the most important thing."

The thugs tried to pull their leader away from Tsiolkovsky, but it wasn't easy, and he continued even more fiercely. "When all people become immortal, the earth will be too small for them. That's what the stars are for—understand? And for the stars, we need rockets."

The leader finally extricated himself and tried to catch his breath. "I get it, I get it."

And Tsiolkovsky went down the ravine, again lost in thought and muttering, "Oh, no. Man will not stop in his development. His mind has long been hinting to him of his moral imperfection. Intelligence without will is nothing, and so is will without intelligence."

The leader adjusted his shirt and looked over at his pals—had they seen him in a weak moment?—but they lowered their eyes deviously. One of them put his finger to his temple and twirled it—that Bird wasn't playing with a full deck.

The leader looked angry, and the thug's finger instantly fell from his temple. The leader, reestablishing his dignity, patronizingly called after Tsiolkovsky, "Hey, Bird! Do you need some kerosene for your rockets? We can arrange it."

But Tsiolkovsky didn't hear him.

The leader watched the figure in the black cap melt into the bottom of the ravine and mused aloud. "My mother told me a dream of hers. She had died, and in the other world she was still washing floors, cooking, doing the laundry, the mending. It scared her. What does she need immortality for, my ma! Ah, Bird!" And chasing away the depressing thought that spoiled his merrymaking, he once again brought his forelock close to the accordion and tore apart its colorful bellows.

In the meantime, Konstantin Eduardovich had no idea that his every move that day was observed by two invisible creatures, a young married couple. He was called Y-Y, and she was I-I. They were invisible because they were two radiant atoms, much smaller than even the dust motes that danced about in the rays of the sun passing through the branches of the autumnal Kaluga trees. In the Galaxy of Immortality, where they dwelled, scientists had long ago resolved the problem of transforming their inhabitants into a radiant condition. The scientists figured out that death is the result of the disintegration of combinations of atoms and that those very same atoms will go on to become part of trees, mountains, and even living creatures. But each atom lacked an individual memory; it couldn't think or appreciate the joys of immortality, as it moved from one form of matter to another. So after many long centuries of careful experiments, the galaxy dwellers transformed themselves into a radiant state, giving every atom independent thought, feelings, characters, and the ability to reproduce. The galaxians struggled for a long time to resurrect their ancestors, whose atoms had scattered. They learned to communicate with the atoms of trees, flowers, grass, earth, and clouds and awakened their memories, thereby learning much of their history. The Galaxy of Immortality was not run by anyone; there was no government, no bureaucracy, no army, no police; everything was coordinated by the consciousness of the tiny fellow citizens, who were elected for a single term of one year to the Council of the Conscience, which consisted of the galaxians themselves as well as representatives from the animal world, trees, mountains, and clouds. Most professions disappeared. Teachers were no longer needed because children were born with a memory of the entire accumulation of history and culture. Doctors were no longer needed because no one was sick. Food was no longer needed because it was enough for the galaxians to subsist on solar energy. Transportation was no longer needed because the galaxians could move about freely merely by using their will—not only within their galaxy but beyond its borders. Houses were no longer needed because the atmosphere itself became a house.

Freed of the necessity of earning a living, they developed harmoniously and simultaneously evolved into scholars, poets, musicians, and artists. There was no need to publish poetry because at the moment of its creation a poem flowed from the poet to everyone else. Music sounded without musical instruments, filling the galaxy with its echoes. Paintings swayed in the air without any nails. The galaxians didn't talk; they only thought, and one's thoughts immediately passed to one's interlocutor, or rather, intercogitator. Y-Y and I-I, as you already know, were a young married couple—young, of course, by galactic standards. They were celebrating their honeycentury.

"We're offering you a trip to earth," said the tree whose turn it was to be chairman of the Council. "We hope that it will brighten your honeycentury. But at the same time this will be, as some earthlings would call it, a business trip. Earthlings are on an extremely low level of development not only in science but in consciousness.

"The idea of immortality is embryonic in Christianity but is more poetic than realistic. The Russian philosopher Fedorov is closer to the reality of immortality, even though his propositions have weak scientific foundation. But one of his students, now living in Kaluga, a teacher of mathematics and physics named Tsiolkovsky, has reached incredible conclusions. In particular, he was the first to express the idea of the possibility of humanity's transformation to a radiant state. Setting himself the question 'If extraterrestrial civilizations much more highly developed than ours do exist, then why don't they enter into contact with us?' he answered it this way: 'But we don't try to enter into contact with ants when we see an anthill.' The reply is rather crude, and I don't think that many earthlings will like it. What tsar or prime minister or even storekeeper will want to consider himself an ant? Though there's nothing insulting in it—according to our data, ants are much more rational than people. We don't think that an artificial acceleration of their development through external intervention will be fruitful. If we reveal the full horror of their life to earthlings, they may become so horrified that they will lose their energy and plunge into pessimism. Your mission, dear Y-Y and I-I, is to observe one day in the life of the worthy representative of humanity from Kaluga and report to us upon your return whether or not he is the way our reports have it. If it is so, then the fate of mankind is far from hopeless."

Y-Y and I-I concentrated their transporting energy and found themselves in the city of Kaluga.

He thinks as if he were already transformed to a radiant state long ago, thought Y-Y.

A personal example is important, I-I thought in reply. *The inhabitants of our galaxy were once similar to earthlings in many of their faults. But individual galaxians appeared who had stepped beyond the thinking of their contemporaries. They weren't understood; they were mocked. Some of them were even executed or put in those . . . what were they called?*

Insane asylums, Y-Y prompted mentally.

Thank God we have nothing like that now nor can we ever have. Someday it will be like that on earth.

Konstantin Eduardovich, going uphill, stopped and caught his breath. *There you have it, shortness of breath. What the hell is immortality for if we're going to be immortal old men?*

When Tsiolkovsky reached home, Varvara Evgrafovna was cooking dinner. Her high-cheekboned face was dark with heavy thoughts, and she looked up at her husband with barely disguised hostility. She felt that way more and more frequently of late, even though she hated herself for having such unworthy feelings about a man she loved.

"Kostya, why does everyone tell me that I'm unhappy?" she asked, slicing onions and damning the stupid onion tears.

"Who is 'everyone'?" Tsiolkovsky asked harshly. Then he softened, picked up a knife, and started helping her, weeping with the same onion tears. "This is a strong onion. Are you happy?"

Varvara Evgrafovna avoided a direct answer. "I don't have time to think about it, Kostya. . . . Are you?"

Tsiolkovsky avoided an answer, too. "It's good that you don't have time. I don't have time to think about it either."

Varvara Evgrafovna threw the onion into the frying pan, and it hissed and twisted in the bubbles of sunflower oil.

"I wish we could travel somewhere. We could always borrow the money. I'm going to die without ever seeing Paris. Are we always going to be stuck here in this miserable Kaluga?" Varvara Evgrafovna burst out angrily and immediately despised herself, for she had never even dreamed about visiting Paris.

"When 'everyone' goes to Paris, so will we," Tsiolkovsky replied calmly. "You know, everyone alive should be happy, but that happiness is difficult for man to understand."

"And how!" Varvara Evgrafovna laughed, throwing the meat into the pan.

Tsiolkovsky retreated into his mind and continued cutting the onion she no longer needed. "Life is based on injustice. Not only a happy life is good, Varya, but just the thought of happiness is good."

"It makes things worse," Varvara Evgrafovna replied dryly, taking away his kitchen knife. "Why did you chop up so many onions?"

Tsiolkovsky was very far away from her by now.

"If, in the course of your entire happy life, you suffered for just one second, you can't consider the whole life a failure. And we can't consider the life of earth a failure because earth is still in its infancy, still in its first second of unhappiness. Earth will be happy yet, Varya."

"When? When we're no longer here?" Varvara Evgrafovna asked, taking hold of the frying pan.

"But we should exist forever," Tsiolkovsky thought aloud.

His thoughts crowded one another. *Maybe it's too soon to realize Einstein's formula? If it's premature, then forget it: You can't explode people's heads. The world would turn into hell. There wouldn't be a stone left on stone, let alone people. But slowing down the rocket—that means stopping exploration of space, slowing down the movement toward immortality. Progress is impossible without risk. But here humanity is risking everything.*

People will be immortal, Y-Y thought. *Maybe in a different way from us, but they will. And why does everyone have to be like everyone else? Then it will be boring in the universe.*

This man is immortal even now, I-I thought back. *It only seems that people like him die.*

Y-Y and I-I pressed tenderly close to each other, and their contact instantly gave birth to a third tiny sparkle—their child, who already knew more than they did. Y-Y and I-I picked up the newborn galaxian and rushed off with him to their distant homeland.

Tsiolkovsky thought: *The only thing that could end war forever is changing the human psyche. Those who fly up above earth and see her in all her beauty and fragility will undergo a psychological change. At first only individuals, but then hundreds, then millions. It will be a different civilization, a different humanity. They will reevaluate the earth's beauty, the taste of each of her berries.*

And he smiled and thought: And probably one of them will remember the line "Along the midnight sky an angel flew."